The Judas Apocalypse

THE JUDAS APOCALYPSE

DAN MCNEIL

To Susan:
Here it is. Hope you like it.
Dan McNeil

PUBLISH PRESS

I Publish Press
P.O. Box 20036, Newcastle, Ontario. Canada L1B 1M3
(416) 619-5261
http://www.ipublishpress.ca
http://www.ipublishpress.com

Cover art and design: artbrowse.com, © I Publish Press
Author photograph: Janice Mark
Set in Life BT

08 09 10 11 12 5 4 3 2 1

ISBN 978-0-9809160-2-7

For Stinder ... for your unconditional friendship and for always looking over my shoulder, no matter where you are.

Author's Note

On March 10, 1204, Pope Innocent III called for a Crusade against Count Raymond VI of Toulouse and the heretical Cathars who flourished in his territories. The Cathars held beliefs that set them apart from the dominant Catholic faith. In the Church's eyes, their religion, which comprised dualist and Gnostic elements, and their unorthodoxy in social matters, including a disapproval of marriage and procreation, required the sect's extermination.

Rumors abounded that the Cathars of southern France had in their possession a magnificent treasure which had been looted from Rome by the Visigoths in the fifth century. This treasure was supposedly the fortune of riches discovered in Solomon's Temple when Rome sacked Jerusalem in AD 70 during the First Jewish Revolt.

For ten months between 1243 and 1244, Montségur, the principal stronghold of the Cathars, an impenetrable fortress situated atop a rocky crag in the Pyrenees, was besieged by ten thousand French knights and men-at-arms under the command of Hugues des Arcis, the Seneschal of Carcassonne. According to testimony later given to the Inquisition, after the capture of the eastern barbican of Montségur in January of 1244, two Cathars were sent out of the fortress, past the encamped army and into the night, carrying something of immense value to the sect. In March, following a two-week truce, the besieged garrison surrendered and 200 Cathar *perfecti* gave themselves up to be burned to death in a huge bonfire at the foot of the mountain. That very night, as the remains of their brethren smoldered, four *perfecti* escaped with the help of the garrison's commander, Pierre-Roger de

Mirepoix. It was said this was done so the "Church of the heretics might not lose its treasure." No trace of the treasure of the Cathars was ever found.

Although *The Judas Apocalypse* is a work of fiction, some of the people and institutions actually existed and some of the events really took place: Otto Rahn, the Ahnenerbe, the siege at Montségur, and the story of the curious wealth of Bérenger Saunière. They have been used, however, in a fictional context, and historical fact is freely blended with fiction. The intent of this story is to entertain, and it should not be seen as a commentary on the truth or reality of either Christian doctrine or history.

Judea
AD 33

IT WAS THE MOST beautiful stone she had ever seen. The sunlight bounced off the facets in a multitude of colors. She bent over to pick it up, marveling at its polish. It was as big as her hand, and heavy, but not too heavy for a little girl like herself. She ran her thumb over the stone, over the dulled edges. The little girl would spend all day in the hot sun, looking and collecting small rocks and stones like this one, but this was the best yet. She couldn't wait to show her mother.

As she watched the blue and purple light sparkle, she became aware of a low rumble in the distance. She looked up into the sky but she could see no clouds. It couldn't be a storm, she thought. She looked around but saw no one and nothing out of the ordinary. The sound seemed to grow louder and that's when she realized where it was coming from. Quickly she stood up and headed back towards the city.

When she got to the city walls, she saw that people had lined up along the road and were chanting and yelling. Why is everyone so upset? she wondered. She could feel the anger and the fear all around her as she dodged between the legs of the crowd, looking for her mother.

It was then that she saw him.

His face was covered in blood and welts, his mouth half open in a mute groan. His legs were buckling under the weight of the beam of olive wood on his shoulders. Without warning, rocks and stones began to rain down on him in a shower of hate.

The little girl gripped her stone tightly and she felt, for a brief moment, as if she too were about to hurl her beautiful stone at him. She felt like she was out of her body, slowly losing her free will.

No control.

She felt herself raising her hand to cast the stone as though powerless to stop it. She didn't want to throw her beautiful stone, but felt that she had to.

It was then that he stumbled. The little girl, suddenly shaken clear for the moment, watched as he turned to look at her. As their eyes met, he managed a small smile. It seemed to her that she had seen him before.

It looked like the teacher, but it was so hard to tell now.

The teacher had been to her house before, with the others. He had talked many times with her parents, about things she didn't really understand, but there was something about the way he spoke, the sound of his voice, his manner that made her feel warm inside. She had always been happy to see him.

She was upset when she realized she was about to throw her stone at him so she lowered her hand. Unexpectedly, a rock flew out of the crowd and struck him full in the cheek. Horrified, she watched as blood began to seep from the jagged wound. One of the soldiers accompanying him on his torturous trek kicked him in the side and told him to get up. Someone from the crowd was then hauled out to help him. Slowly and painfully, he raised himself to his knees. The girl was watching quietly the horrible events playing out in front of her when she felt a hand on her shoulder. She looked up, and saw that it was her mother. She dropped her beautiful stone and grasped her mother's robe tightly, resolving never to let it go.

She was wiping the tears from her face on her mother's mantle when she became aware of two voices beside her. She only noticed them because they were different from the cacophony that swirled around her. Turning, she saw two men talking in very hushed tones. She strained to hear what they were saying but they were being carefully guarded, and the crowd's noise was now rising to a fever pitch. It occurred to her that she had seen them before. After a few moments, she remembered. They had been with the teacher. They were friends of the teacher.

The taller of the two handed the other a satchel, leaned in, and whispered something and the shorter man nodded in agreement. They moved away from the crowd, and she watched them for a few minutes as they headed off in the direction of the place that scared her so much. The place where the bodies rotted as they remained nailed to the crosses. It was called the Hill of Skulls.

The little girl turned from the men to again watch the procession. She unexpectedly felt emptiness in her hand and then she realized that she had lost her beautiful stone. Panicked, she dropped to her knees and her eyes darted between the multitudes of sandaled feet. Abruptly, the crowd shifted and she suddenly saw it, lying on the street just in front of her. Lunging forward, she snatched it before someone kicked it away. Moving back against a wall, she held it close, waiting for the crowd to thin out.

It really was a beautiful stone.

At the Hill of Skulls, Maryam had already arrived. She had gone on ahead and waited for the procession that was just now filing past her. The guards half carried, half dragged the tortured victim until they reached the spot where he would eventually be crucified. They dropped him unceremoniously to the ground next to the olive-wood cross. She watched as he was laid on the cross and his arms were lashed to the beam. The morning sun blinded him and then he coughed, spitting up a small amount of blood. Lifting his head slightly he saw Maryam and he smiled weakly. One of the Roman guards looked down at the battered victim. He turned to the other guard.

"Look — he smiles," he smirked.

"Not for long," replied the other as he steadied the spike against the condemned man's wrist and raised his hammer.

The nail ripped through his wrist, smashing tendon and bone, spraying blood across his face. He gritted his teeth, and although he had resolved not to make any noise, a small whimper escaped nonetheless. His fingers curled involuntarily into a fist. Maryam put her hand to her mouth in horror and looked away. She fell to her knees and let out a small cry. One of the soldiers looked at her with contempt as he moved to the other arm. He again raised his hammer, momentarily blocking out the sun. As he looked down at the prisoner, the soldier paused. For a moment, he thought that he might have seen this man before, but it was hard to tell, since his face was a mask of bruises and blood. Slowly, he lowered the hammer. He now remembered where he had seen him. He looked like the Jewish preacher who had caused the riot at the Temple. Was that why he was here? he wondered. For upsetting some fellow Jews? That certainly was not a Roman issue. It did not even warrant a death sentence.

The other soldier, seeing his partner's hesitation, called to him. "Finish it. We have two more yet," he said.

From a distance, the two friends of the teacher watched the scene unfold. The taller one sat on the ground and sighed. He wiped his brow and looked up at the smaller individual. He noticed how tightly the shorter man held on to the satchel, seeing his knuckles had drained of blood and had turned white as marble. The bigger man finally spoke after a long silence.

"Kipha, be calm and sit," he said and tapped the ground. Kipha continued to stare at the stomach-churning scene in front of them.

"Do you not feel repulsed by this, Yakob? Do you not feel sickened by this?" He looked at Yakob. "I don't think

I can stand for this much longer. I know he agreed to do this, but — "

Yakob cut him off.

"Kipha," he commanded in a low voice. "I need you to be strong. If this is to work, you need to be strong."

Kipha turned back to the crucifixion, and his grip on the satchel loosened slightly. Yakob tapped the ground again. "Kipha..."

Kipha continued to stand but finally turned to look at Yakob. He breathed out heavily and sat down. He handed the bag to Yakob, and began to weep silently.

Maryam was on her knees, her eyes focused on the ground, when she heard a noise behind her. Turning, she saw that it was the little girl. She had followed everyone to the hill. The soldiers, still occupied with the other criminals didn't notice her making her way towards the cross. Kipha began to rise, but Yakob held his arm. He shook his head and Kipha sat back down.

The girl was now next to Maryam, who turned sadly to her. Clutching her stone, the little girl continued forward, edging closer to him. She could see his hands curled in pain and the wet blood on his wrists and his forehead. She stood over his prostrate form. He looked up at her and smiled weakly. He was totally unrecognizable to her now. As the tears began to well up in her eyes again and she began to sob, he shushed her quietly.

"It's ... all right, child," he whispered. A small amount of blood trickled out of the corner of his mouth. The girl knelt down and delicately touched his forehead. Sweat and blood from the thorns that encircled his head mingled together on her fingers. She wiped away her tears with the back of her hand and felt the desire to give this poor man something. As she moved to his right side, the fingers of his hand spasmed slightly.

She took her beautiful stone and gently pressed it into his palm. Although the nail in his wrist constricted his hand movement, he managed to slowly close his fingers over the gift. She backed away and wiped her eyes just as the guards finished with the last criminal.

It was almost time.

Without looking at Yakob and Kipha, the little girl ran from the scene as the guards began to raise the crosses. She put her hands over her ears and began to run faster as the cries of pain split the air.

The bodies were yanked forward, gravity pulling the mens' arms downward, tugging at the nails in their wrists. In an effort to ease the pain on their arms and chests, they pushed upwards, shooting paroxysms of pain into their nailed ankles and feet. The deliberate, painful death of crucifixion had begun.

Kipha turned away and although Yakob was saddened, he unexpectedly smiled faintly as he shielded his eyes from the sun. He then glanced down at the satchel by his feet.

In a matter of hours it will be sundown.

In a matter of hours, it would be time to act.

Rennes-Le-Château, France
January 17, 1917

Abbé Rivière hurried along the snow covered road, his cassock flapping in the wind. The cold air stabbed at his cheek bones but he hardly noticed it. His eyes watered slightly. As he wiped them, he thought about the task at hand.

He had never given absolution to a priest before.

And this was not to be just any priest. The curé of Rennes-le-Château was a tough, insolent, and undisciplined minor legend in the area. Bérenger Saunière had been the parish priest since 1885 and had done much to improve the church over the years; he was much beloved by his parishioners. In the beginning, his career had been very promising but he had angered the prefect and had been sent to Narbonne. The villagers made such a clamor however, that he was immediately sent back. "Donnez nous Saunière!" was heard daily until the prefect gave in. Saunière reveled in his glory.

It would not be the first time his lack of discipline or his impertinent attitude would get him into trouble.

In spite of what his superiors thought of him, Saunière had put his heart and soul into the parish. He had done, on his own, renovations to the chapel, built a tower in memory of Mary Magdalene, and constructed a beautiful rectory, all paid for by himself, and all on a priest's salary.

And that was the mystery.

There were many stories floating around about the parish priest of Rennes-le-Château, and it was hard to discern the truth from the fiction. Some said he had found a fabulous treasure. Others said, more mundanely, that he was guilty of simony, selling masses and using the money to fund his pet projects. This accusation in particular angered Father Rivière. The young abbé couldn't believe that Saunière would stoop so low, yet, even if he had, how did it explain the vastness of the priest's wealth? A franc here and there for a mass in a deceased relative's name wouldn't come close to the kind of money that Saunière was rumored to have.

Just how had Saunière pulled it off?

Curiouser and curiouser, as Alice would say in Wonderland.

Whatever the truth, Father Rivière was resolute in his duty. Bérenger Saunière was a fellow priest, and a good and trusted mentor. The younger priest would perform the last rites for his dying friend.

Saunière's maid, Marie Denarnaud, had sent for Rivière immediately when the stroke had occurred, as it was important that last rites be administered as quickly as possible. The wind whipped up, so he pulled his lapels closer together. Rivière picked up his pace slightly as he checked his watch. He hoped to reach Saunière's home within the hour, before darkness fell.

Marie Denarnaud paused to grab a kerosene lamp as she hurried to answer the door. She smiled gratefully at the sight of the young priest brushing the snow from his shoulders. He handed her his snowflake-covered hat as he stood in the doorway waiting to be invited inside.

"Please come in Father," she said quietly. "Thank you for coming so quickly."

When Father Rivière took her hand gently in his own cold hands, she gasped slightly.

"How is he doing?" he asked with concern.

Marie breathed in deeply. "He's resting well, now. But ... I don't think he will last much longer." She looked like she hadn't slept in days.

She sat down at the table and absent-mindedly played with the salt and pepper shakers. Her mind was obviously elsewhere.

"Would you like some tea, Father?" she finally asked. Father Rivière smiled and nodded. As Marie got up and went to the stove, Father Rivière watched her as he sat down.

The years had certainly taken their toll on her. He remembered seeing her for the first time years ago when she was a vibrant, beautiful young woman. She had taken the job as Saunière's maid twenty-five years before, and had served him ever since. It was obvious to anyone that she was completely devoted to the older abbé. It was also clear to many that although they were employer and employee, there was much more to the relationship than met the eye. There was sixteen years' difference between them and this was the cause of some gossip throughout the parish. In the town it was whispered that Marie was "the priest's Madonna." What was true, however, was that Saunière was well acquainted with the Denarnaud family, and had known Marie from an early age. It was only natural that she would one day come to work for him.

Marie poured the boiling water into the teapot and brought a cup over to the priest. As it steeped, she began to say something, but then changed her mind.

What is she hiding? Rivière wondered. He decided to press her.

"Marie?"

She looked up.

"Is there anything wrong? Is there anything you wish to tell me?" Rivière reached out to pat her hand. "I am a priest, you know," he smiled. "You can tell me anything. Cross my heart," he said with a grin.

Marie continued to look away from the priest. Leaning in, he said soothingly, "It will be between us ... just you and me ... oh, and God, of course ... "

Marie looked at the young priest. He saw her eyes moisten.

"Father ... I'm afraid," she said.

Rivière nodded. "It's all right, Marie. Everyone feels afraid at times like these. Father Saunière — "

She cut in. "I don't mean about Father Saunière." she began. "I'm talking about the ... the ... "

"Rumors?" Rivière offered.

Marie looked blankly at Father Rivière. She slowly, almost imperceptibly began to shake her head.

"Marie — "

Suddenly there was a small noise from the bedroom. They both stood up and made for the door. As Rivière became accustomed to the low light in the bedroom, he was shocked by the appearance of his former mentor.

Saunière was propped up on the bed. He was extremely pale and looked much older than his sixty-seven years. The stroke had paralyzed his right side. Saunière turned his head slightly and coughed as Rivière hurried to his side. The younger man put a handkerchief up to the dying priest's mouth. Saunière opened his eyes slowly and looked at Rivière. For a moment, it seemed as if the older priest didn't recognize the younger one.

Then he smiled faintly.

"Bonjour, Abbé ... ," he said weakly, out of the left side of his mouth. Rivière smiled back and softly brushed the hair off of Saunière's forehead. "Bonjour, Father Saunière," he replied. "Would you like some water?" The older priest barely nodded. Rivière reached for the pitcher of water sitting by a package of cigarette papers on the bedside table. The younger priest looked grimly at the papers, convinced, though never quite sure, that somehow smoking may have played a part in the older man's stroke. How many times had he tried to get him to stop? He poured a glass of the cool water and held it up to the older man's lips. Saunière swallowed slowly, the water dripping slightly down the right side of his face. Rivière leaned in with a handkerchief to wipe away the dampness at the corner of his mouth. When Saunière had had enough, he lay back against his pillow and sighed. Rivière put the glass down and pulled up a chair to the bed.

"Would you like to rest a bit, Father?" he inquired.

Saunière remained silent for a few minutes. He was thinking how he would love to have a cigarette. It was a pleasure he had picked up while he was in Paris during that particular time when he was the darling of high society. The only trouble was that he could never roll the cursed things himself, and he wasn't about to ask the younger priest to do it, not unless he wanted another lecture from Rivière about what the young man considered a thoroughly disgusting habit. Would it kill him to have a cigarette? He was dying anyway.

God certainly did work in mysterious ways, didn't he?

If he hadn't found it, how would things have turned out?

"No, I think we'd better get down to business," he finally said in a soft voice. "I'm not sure how much time I have left." Rivière nodded quietly.

"It's funny," Saunière continued. "When I was younger, I always thought that when my time came, I would go quickly. I would be received into God's arms ..." A look of consternation crossed his face. "I should have known ...," he mumbled. He turned away as Rivière tried to comfort him.

"Be thankful that He saw fit to give you time for absolution, Father. He must love you very, very much."

Saunière saw snippets of his life flash through his mind. He thought of his arrival at this little parish and how he had tried to change things for the better, his discovery of the Church's secret and how his life had changed from that moment. The sudden wealth, the accusations, his fall from grace — and for what? To die a lingering, pathetic death in this broken shell of a body?

Yes, he thought sarcastically, He must really love me. Saunière turned to face the young priest. "Father Rivière, I am ready to confess my sins."

When he finally came out of Saunière's room, Father Rivière sat at the kitchen table for a long time. Marie offered him more tea, but he didn't notice her. He sat, unblinking and shaking, his thoughts pounding in his brain until he heaved a huge sigh.

"Father, are you all right?' Marie asked. She put her hand on his shoulder. In a sudden outburst, he violently shook it off. Rivière leaped from the chair and began to pace quickly.

"No!" he shouted, "No, I am not all right. I'm not all right at all. Marie, how did this ... how could this ... I mean, my God, Marie!" Rivière wrung his hands in frustration. He kicked the chair into the table, upsetting the teapot and causing it to fall to the tiles where it smashed to pieces and sent the hot liquid across the floor. Marie ran to get a cloth.

Rivière grabbed at his head and immediately dropped to his hands and knees. "I'm sorry, Marie," he said, taking the cloth from her hand and wiping up the tea, "I didn't mean to upset you."

Marie knelt beside the overwrought priest. "I understand, Father ... I thought that ... well, you know."

Rivière continued to mop up the tea. He stopped for a second and rubbed his eyes and then he turned to her. For a moment the two just looked at each other. "Yes, Marie, I *do* know now ... and I ... I don't know what to do. All I know is that I can't ... help him," he said finally.

Marie took the cloth from Rivière. He looked helpless. Tears welled up in Marie's eyes. "Poor Father Saunière … ," she wept. She looked at Father Rivière with imploring eyes. "Is there nothing you can do for him?"

Rivière turned to her. In a low voice he said, "Marie … what he confessed to me … "

He slowly stood up.

"I … I cannot do it. I cannot give Father Saunière absolution. I won't. Marie … I am afraid there will be no Kingdom of Heaven for his soul."

Rivière put on his hat and then headed for the door. Above the lintel, he noticed a crucifix. Impulsively, he reached up and pulled it forcefully from the wall in a cascade of plaster and splinters. Dropping it to the floor, he stalked out into the cold, snowy night without turning around or saying goodbye.

The wind picked up, masking the mournful sobs of Marie Denarnaud.

PART ONE

1

August 2, 1944

THE CUMULUS CLOUDS PARTIALLY obscured the new moon and sent slivers of light which reflected off the wake of the U-boat as it sliced through the water. Running silently just inches below the surface, it headed south, towards the coast of France. Only a few hours away from its destination, the lone occupant in the guest quarters moved quietly about, trying to keep the noise to a minimum.

Archeologist Dr. Gerhard Denninger flicked the switch on the small lamp over his table. He sat down and put his hands on his thighs. Slowly he rubbed them back and forth, drying the perspiration that had moistened his palms with a continual dampness, plaguing him since his departure from Bremerhaven. Breathing out slowly and quietly, he looked long and hard at the tube on the table in front of him and thought about what was inside.

He couldn't recall another time when he had been this excited. He picked up the tube, and once he had removed the contents, he slowly and carefully unrolled it. It was a withered, yellow piece of parchment, adorned with carefully inscribed letters in a large, box-like pattern. He held it under the gentle light of the lamp, and although it looked very fragile, it seemed to be very robust. As his eyes scanned it, he felt a slight shiver spiraling down his spine.

"Beautiful," he marveled, "just beautiful."

His wrinkled fingers hovered over the letters on the parchment. It gave the archeologist a chill just to look at it. He couldn't believe it was in his hands again after five years.

Five long years. It felt like a lifetime.

He took his glasses off and rubbed his eyes.

How long had it been since he'd slept?

He got up, stretched and moved about the cramped cabin, letting the blood flow through his stiff legs. Both his knees ached and he felt a slight twinge in his back. I'm getting too old for this, he thought tiredly. He poured some water into a basin on the little table and slowly dipped his hands into it. Bringing a handful of the cool liquid up to his face, he watched in the mirror as it cascaded down his sixty-year-old face. He looked at the reflection of his large, round head and noticed that he was indeed losing even more hair than he had previously thought. The remaining gray, almost white, wisps seemed so thin. He remembered a time when his thick black hair was his best feature. It wasn't really his rapidly balding pate that captured his attention so much as it was the preponderance of lines that had, in the last couple of years, seemed to capture his once youthful face and refused to let it go. He sighed.

Why couldn't this have happened when I was so much younger? he thought mournfully.

As he stared at the document, he knew that this was likely to be the defining moment of his career. As an archeologist, he was aware that, while many legends are based on factual events, they are also stories that have been passed down orally, often unreliably, such as those of the Lost Inca City of Gold, King Solomon's Mines, Camelot and others. Many had searched for these things and places, yet they continued to elude the historians and treasure hunters alike.

The one legend that had haunted Denninger for most of his life was the story of the Cathar treasure. As a younger man, he had been captivated by the idea that the Cathars, a doomed Christian sect, had somehow secreted away a vast treasure just before they were burned at the stake as heretics. He had studied the story for decades and was fairly convinced that it was real, though he had no proof that it actually existed. He had no tangible evidence, other than stories that, at the very most, alluded to it rather than definitely established it to be genuine. For the last seven hundred years it had been searched for, but no one had ever found it.

This was Denninger's Holy Grail.

Eight years ago, he had found himself working for Heinrich Himmler's *Ahnenerbe*. The Ahnenerbe, also known as the Heritage Bureau, was devoted to the cultural history of, and proving the superiority of, the Ayran race. The Bureau also dedicated itself in part to archeological missions with the aim of finding religious artifacts for Adolf Hitler, a known religious-relic fanatic. Hitler and Himmler believed that artifacts like the Spear of Longinus (the spear that had pierced the side of Christ at the crucifixion) or pieces of the True Cross (said to hold magical qualities) would ensure the triumph of the German Army. Of course the holy grail of all religious finds would be the Holy Grail itself, and the Ahnenerbe spent much time and money looking for this wondrous object without success.

It was interesting work, to be sure, but there was a price to pay. As a member of the Ahnenerbe, one had to be part of the SS and, although Denninger may have been a member of the SS because it was required, he was certainly no Nazi by choice. He was never one for politics. His passion was history and archeology. Politics, quite frankly, was a useless distraction.

He was also Jewish, and being Jewish in Nazi Germany was a dangerous thing. Denninger never talked about his life or his background, and this had led to the perception that he was an eccentric loner. In truth, he would rather have it that way because it was certainly safer.

One of Denninger's major assignments had been to find a copy of *Germania* by the Roman historian Tacitus.

In the early 1930s, a surviving copy, known as the *Aesinas Codex*, had been discovered in Italy but Italian leader Benito Mussolini had refused to part with such a historical treasure, much to the annoyance of Adolf Hitler. For the next three years, Denninger and his group had looked for another copy, but without much success. Not that Denninger had been trying very hard, though.

Germania was one of the cornerstones of the Nazi idealization of the Germanic race adhered to by maniacs like Hitler and Himmler. The myth of an untainted race that embodied the Aryan ideal of blond hair, blue eyes, and a propensity for making war, was nothing short of pure rubbish as far as Denninger was concerned. As a man of science and as a Jew, he found ideas such as these repugnant. And deadly.

He recalled the horror as he saw his fellow countrymen's shops and homes destroyed during Kristallnacht, the Night of the Broken Glass, a nationwide attack against the Jewish population on November 9, 1938 that foreshadowed the terrible events that were to unfold a few years later.

Denninger had sworn that as long as he was with the Ahnenerbe, he would use its resources to further his own research and his own agenda. Five years later, sitting in a U-boat on his way to France, it seemed he was finally reaping the rewards.

He sat on his bunk and began rummaging through his pack. He soon found what he had been looking for. He pulled out a worn, leather-bound diary that had obviously seen better days, and began to turn the pages, slowly at first, looking at, rather than reading the fluid French writing. He remembered the day when he had first seen the diary. When he had read it the first time, he hadn't been able to see how its contents, about a French priest who became suspiciously wealthy seventy years ago, would have any bearing on a centuries-old document.

But Otto had known.

Denninger thought about the strange fellow who had given him the diary and about how that particular moment had changed his life. He reflected back to that day in 1939 when the rash young researcher had burst into his office. Although Denninger hadn't met him before, he had certainly heard of him. Otto Rahn was a lot of things: brilliant, liberal, a bit of an oddball—and dangerous. He was not what most of his co-workers would describe as Heritage Bureau material, not by a long shot, but since he had been brought aboard by Heinrich Himmler's "Rasputin," the occultist (and former mental patient) Karl-Maria Wiligut, Rahn had to be tolerated. Rahn's theories had rankled those in charge, and had put him on a secret blacklist. He had been told a number of times that he was on thin ice but he hadn't cared.

He had just returned from the area of Carcassonne in France and he was on to something ... huge. The only problem was that he couldn't do it all himself and he knew it. He would have to find someone else, a kindred spirit, so to speak. It would have to be someone who was an expert in the history of the Cathars and the Languedoc area of France; someone who had the same basic disregard for the politics of the Bureau and, most importantly to him, someone who could keep a secret.

March 10, 1939

Denninger was going over some papers in his office when Otto Rahn made his grand entrance. He burst through the door like a hundred-meter sprinter.

"You are Gerhard Denninger, yes?"

Rahn was out of breath. Denninger never liked to be disturbed, and stared at Rahn with a look of annoyance. The wheezing man standing in front of him was a slim, nervous type of about thirty years old. His suit was tailor-made and stylish for the day; the pleats were so sharp that they looked like they could draw blood. His sandy hair was slicked back, making his large forehead appear even larger, and Denninger noticed that not one hair follicle was out of place in spite of his harried manner. Placing his palms on Denninger's desk he leaned forward.

"My name is Otto Rahn. I am a researcher here and I think I may," he whispered confidentially, "have found the Cathar treasure."

The Cathar treasure.

It was certainly a novel first impression.

Rahn's own interest in the Cathars had been fired up by the medieval story of *Parzival* by Wolfram von Eschenbach. Rahn was convinced that the tale held clues to the resting place of the Holy Grail, and this had led him to spend three months in Southern France. He had explored the ruins of the fortress of Montségur, and the region surrounding Rennes-le-Château. He was utterly convinced that the Holy Grail was somewhere in the area, but it somehow eluded him. On his return to Berlin, he had heard of Denninger's interest in the Cathars and that had prompted him to seek out the archeologist.

Rahn placed a book on his desk.

"Have you read this?" he asked, pointing to the volume.

Denninger blinked. "What do you mean, you think you have found the Cathar treasure?" he asked incredulously.

Rahn grinned and wagged his finger. "Ah, not yet, not yet. You haven't answered my question."

Denninger took his glasses off and blinked. "You burst into my office, and tell me this fantastic...thing, and you want to know *what*? Are you crazy?"

Rahn continued to look at Denninger without speaking. He had a grin that reminded Denninger of the Cheshire Cat in *Alice in Wonderland*. It made Denninger feel as if Rahn was sizing him up (for what he wasn't exactly sure), and he didn't like it either. The older man began to squirm uncomfortably in his seat.

"Will you stop staring at me, please." he ordered.

Rahn kept grinning at him. "Answer my question and maybe I will."

Denninger breathed out slowly and looked at the book that Rahn had dropped on his desk. He turned it around so he could see the title and the author.

"I have read this, as a matter of fact. It's a little wordy, if I remember," he said. *Lucifer's Court* was well-known to the student of Catharism and it was written by Otto Rahn. Denninger had actually read it three times.

Rahn pulled up a chair and put his feet on Denninger's desk.

"Mr.Rahn, please ... get your feet off of my desk."

"They are so stupid here," he vented, ignoring the request. "What is with this Aryan nonsense anyway? Do they have you working on this shit too?"

Denninger just leveled a stone-like stare at the interloper.

Rahn continued with his rant. "It's ludicrous. It's beneath me, and quite frankly, I'm not going to waste my time with it. They can all go fuck themselves!"

Denninger sputtered as he jumped up out of his chair to swiftly shut the door. "Are you insane? Do you have a death wish?" he hissed at Rahn.

"Did you know that Himmler believes he is the reincarnation of King Arthur?" said Rahn. "He has a castle in Wewelsburg complete with round table and chairs for twelve knights — imagine, Camelot right in the middle of Germany!"

Denninger rubbed his head vigorously and said, "Will you please keep it down. You will get us both sent to Dachau if you do not stop, and I'm too old to spend the rest of my life at a concentration camp."

"Dachau," he said disgustedly, "I just got back from there. On assignment. It seems they are less than thrilled with my attitude," he remarked. Leaning in, he said, "Listen, I'm here to let you in on something..." He leaned back and mouthed the word "*big*" as he pulled out a package of cigarettes.

Denninger grimaced. "Yes, I know, the Cathar treasure. Please don't smoke in here," he ordered as he returned to his seat.

Rahn turned his head to follow Denninger. He shrugged and put the cigarettes away. "You think I'm joking?"

Denninger leveled his gaze at the grinning researcher. "Actually, I think you're a lunatic."

Rahn put his feet down and got up. He ran one hand slowly through his hair and aimed his Cheshire Cat grin at Denninger. "You know, before my unfortunate sojourn in Dachau, I was in Carcasonne for a few weeks. You know where that is, I'm sure."

"Of course," Denninger said indignantly.

"Of course," Rahn repeated. "Ah ... the land of my beloved Cathars. Springtime in Paris *is* quite lovely but Carcassonne in the summer, and Rennes-le-Château ... well, I don't have to tell you, it's an absolute ..." He smiled devilishly as he drew out the word "treasure." Rahn then rubbed his hands together.

"I will be plain," he continued, and then, leaning in, said in a low voice, "I need to speak to you, but I don't want to do it here. I frequent a little place around the corner from here — Carlotta's. You know, the one where all the degenerates like myself hang out."

Denninger closed his eyes and shook his head. "No, I *don't* know. I've never heard of such a place."

Rahn's eyebrows narrowed and he rubbed his cheek with the crook of his index finger suggestively. He certainly had a way of making Denninger uncomfortable.

"Oh, very well. I'll leave you directions, then. I'll be there tomorrow night at seven thirty. It's quite a place, you know. They have a variety of acts for...um, shall we say, *all* tastes? They have this midget performer there who can...." Rahn then pantomimed a crude attempt at autofellatio using his hand on the back of his head, pushing it down towards the vicinity of his lap.

"You know what I'm saying?" he said, winking.

Denninger looked positively horrified as Rahn chuckled at the older man's obvious discomfort.

"Relax, Gerhard. You really should lighten up," he smirked. "Tomorrow, Maria Del Guardia, the jazz singer, is performing — all the way from New York. Teddy Stauffer's swing band is playing as well. It will be a *gas*, as they say in the vernacular. If you do decide to come, however, make sure you use the back door."

"Why?"

"The Gestapo, it seems, are not fans of the swing, I'm afraid; which is perfectly fine as I am not much of a fan of the Gestapo either. Anyone visiting such places are... dissuaded, shall we say, from going, so ... we go in the back way," he winked.

He paused for a moment and then smiled. "In the back way ... ," he chuckled.

Denninger winced uncomfortably. There was a rumor around the Ahnenerbe that Otto Rahn was homosexual. It was a rumor that Rahn himself did little to squelch, probably because it caused much consternation at the bureau. Anything, it seemed, that made his superiors uncomfortable, Rahn thrived upon.

He was also not surprised that Rahn would patronize such a disreputable establishment; however, it certainly would make an ideal place for a private conversation, and although Rahn made the older man somewhat disconcerted, there was something charismatic about the man that made Denninger want to talk to him again. What if the lunatic was really on to something after all?

As Rahn turned to leave, he passed by a framed picture of Himmler. He stopped for a second and decided that it needed straightening. In the process, the picture fell to the floor with a startling crash. Glass and splintered wood mixed together in a symphony of destruction. Rahn turned to Denninger with his hand coyly over his mouth. "Oh, I am sorry, Gerhard. I'll replace it, of course," he said with a look of mock sorrow. Suddenly he brightened. "I have a picture of a chimpanzee that looks remarkably like our friend Heinrich here," he said, motioning to the mess on the floor. "I hope you don't mind that he is picking his nose, though — just like Heinrich, I imagine, when he sits in his castle. I am sure no one will notice the difference anyway." As he went through the door, he turned, smiled his Cheshire Cat smile, and gave a little wave. And much like the cat in Lewis Carroll's story, Otto Rahn's grin stayed with Denninger for quite a while, even after he was gone.

2

THE NEXT NIGHT, DENNINGER found himself standing in the back alley of Carlotta's, waiting his turn to utter the password that Rahn had provided him in order to get into what he was certain was a modern-day equivalent of Sodom and Gomorrah.

What the hell am I doing here? he thought.

He pulled his collar up close to his face, hoping no one would see him, though he was fairly sure that anyone who knew him wouldn't be caught dead anywhere near this place anyway. Still, he thought, better safe than sorry.

As he approached the door, he was suddenly seized with an urge to leave, but Rahn's tantalizing hints the previous day about the Cathar treasure kept him from bolting.

The Cathar treasure.

God damn it, thought Denninger. He hated to admit it, but he was hooked.

The sound of American jazz music filled the air as he tried to acclimatize himself to the smoky, dimly lit bar. While it was cool outside, inside it was an oxygen-sucking hot box. A trickle of sweat immediately began its descent down the middle of his back. He removed his hat and handed it to the cloakroom girl, who then gave him a ticket and thanked him in a low, raspy voice. As Denninger's eyes began to focus, he realized that the beautiful young thing behind the counter had an Adam's apple and a five o'clock shadow, obscured by copious amounts of cosmetic powder.

The bar was hopping, as they said in the lingo, and Denninger felt hopelessly out of his element, surrounded as he was by the spectacle known as the swing kids. What had started in Hamburg as a fad had blossomed into a full-blown movement that had overtaken the local youth like wildfire. Some likened it to a disease. Zoot-suited boys, wearing fedoras and hairstyles right out of the American cinema, mingled with purple-lipped girls in expensive dresses smoking cigarettes through long cigarette holders. The Nazi party was aghast at what they perceived as Jewish and American influence over the youth of Germany, and did everything they could to curtail the surging phenomenon.

The dance floor was crammed with dancers, making it virtually impossible to move. One dancer, he noticed, openly mocked the German national greeting by extending his arm in a typical *Sieg Heil* salute but he augmented it with two fingers splayed out like a vee, a sign of English defiance that went all the way back to the Hundred Years War. The vee sign was, of course, a serious breach of German law, but to the swing kids, defiance of the status quo was what it was all about. Fuck the National Socialist Party, fuck Adolf Hitler, and basically just fuck everyone and anyone you can.

Denninger tried to hide his face and hurriedly make his way through the crowd. In his haste, he wound up bumping into one sartorially resplendent swing kid. "Excuse me," said Denninger, but as he attempted to pass, he felt his progress impeded. He looked down to see the ornate handle of an umbrella sticking out like a curved erection between his legs.

With his stomach tightening, Denninger exclaimed "What's this?"

"Hello, *Old* Hot Boy," a curiously-high pitched voice at his elbow goaded.

Old Hot Boy? What the hell does that mean? he thought.

The doctor turned and saw a kid of about eighteen with his hair slicked back in the style of German movie star Willy Fritsch. His smile was flush with large white teeth that reminded Denninger of a palomino pony's. His pale blue eyes seemed to twinkle with a hint of violence, as if any wrong move on Denninger's part would result in the handle of the umbrella being removed from his crotch and buried in his skull instead.

Denninger creased his eyebrows. "Are you referring to me — and if you are, while you are at it, could you please remove this umbrella handle ... sir?"

The kid lowered the umbrella from between Denninger's legs, placed it over the crook of his arm and stepped in closer, taking Denninger's glasses from his face. "Maybe you should check your spectacles, hmm my friend?" the kid purred. He put them on and turned to his friends. "Well, what do you think, boys? Do I look like Benny Goodman?"

Out of the corner of his eye, he saw someone sidle up right beside him. "If you don't want to get fucked in the arse, Bobby, you should lose the glasses."

The kid whipped the spectacles off and turned swiftly to find himself face-to-face with Otto Rahn. The kid broke into a wide grin. "Why, Otto ... when did you get back in town?"

Otto took the glasses from the kid and handed them back to Denninger. "I think you should apologize to my friend here, Bobby." The kid gave a sideways smile to Otto and turned to Denninger. "Well, Old Hot Boy, I didn't know you were a friend of Otto's. Please accept my humble apologies," he said, punctuating his statement with a deep stage bow. Denninger put his glasses back on and glared at Rahn.

"Somehow I'm not surprised that you know these hooligans, Rahn — "

Rahn put up a hand and cut him off gently. "Gerhard," he began, "You should be a little more forgiving. These boys and girls who surround you here," he said, sweeping his arm towards the dance floor, "are the pride of Germany." His chest was puffed out like a bellows. Denninger wasn't sure if Rahn was kidding or not.

"Don't you listen to the Führer's speeches, my friend?" he said sarcastically. "This young man here is the hope of tomorrow." He placed his hand proudly on the kid's shoulder. "Say hello to Bobby, Gerhard." Bobby grinned and put out his hand. Denninger swore that he caught a whiff of women's cologne. Tentatively, he took the kid's hand and grudgingly said hello. "Come," said Rahn, "I have a table in the back where we can have a private conversation." Then turning to Bobby, he said, "Keep up the good fight."

Bobby smiled, put two fingers to his forehead and gave an informal salute, followed by the vee sign. Rahn put his arm on Denninger's shoulder as they made their way to the table.

As they sat down, Denninger turned to Rahn. "I don't understand. What kind of name is Bobby for a German? And 'Old Hot Boy?' What was *that*?" Denninger inquired.

Rahn laughed. "It's just an expression. His real name is Heinz. These kids ... they just do it to annoy the authorities. They take American and English names just to fuck with them. I love it. I'm actually thinking of changing my name to Franklin Delano Rahn. What do you think?"

Denninger's glasses had fogged up, so he removed them to give them a cleaning with his handkerchief. "I thought the authorities were cracking down on these types of establishments. Why hasn't this place been closed?" he asked as Rahn waved at a waitress.

"Oh, it has been — numerous times — but a well placed bribe here and there, well, you get the picture.

These Nazis, they huff and puff about a new world order, but a couple of marks in their pockets ... well, suddenly it's all right to be a capitalist." He then turned to the waitress and ordered two beers.

Denninger sighed and put his glasses back on. "All right, Rahn, what is it that you couldn't tell me in my office?"

Rahn leaned back, savoring the moment as the Cheshire Cat grin crept across his face again. He extracted a package of cigarettes from his inside pocket and pulled one out with his mouth. He offered the package to Denninger who declined. Rahn then flicked his lighter open with a flourish and lit the smoke.

Denninger straightaway began to cough. "That smells horrible!" he exclaimed with disgust.

Rahn just kept grinning. "It's a special blend that I have made just for me. It's made up of Turkish and Persian — "

"Look, Rahn ..." Denninger interrupted.

Rahn sighed and began, "All right, all right. Just what exactly do you know about the Cathar treasure?"

"You tell me. You're the one who supposedly found it."

"Come on, Gerhard. Humor me for a moment."

Denninger paused to gather his thoughts. "Well, I know that — " he began, but stopped when the waitress returned with their drinks.

Otto watched her carefully as she placed the heavy steins of beer in front of them. When she left, he turned back to Denninger. "Please continue," he said.

Denninger noticed that Rahn's demeanor had changed slightly. He seemed slightly less jovial and was acting in a more guarded manner. "You're awfully nervous, Otto."

Rahn ran his hand rapidly through his hair a number of times. "Please keep going," he reiterated.

Denninger shrugged and continued. "Well. It's never been found ... until now, of course," He waved a hand in mock reverence at Rahn. "During the siege of Montségur, some Cathars escaped with it before the rest were wiped out by the Catholics — "

Rahn interrupted Denninger. "Yes," he said, slowly nodding, "that is an interesting story, isn't it?"

Taking a long pull on his beer, Denninger replied, "No one knows what became of those mysterious Cathars. They have been lost to time I'm afraid."

Rahn sipped his beer and leaned in. "Do you think so?"

"What are you saying, Otto?" Denninger raised his eyebrows.

Rahn grabbed the seat of his chair and inched it closer. "What do you know about Rennes-le-Château?" he asked in a low voice.

"I thought we were talking about the Cathars?"

Rahn shook his head gently. "Please, Gerhard."

"Rennes-le-Château? You mean the story about the priest and the money and all that? What's that got to do with Montségur?"

"Do you know the story, Gerhard?"

Denninger scoffed. "Oh, it's all bunk. The priest ... I forget his name ... "

"Saunière," interjected Rahn.

"Yes, that's it ... he was renovating the church as I recall. He went to Paris where, not long after, he began to run with the upper class. When he returned to Rennes-le-Château, he was extremely wealthy — wealthy enough, as I remember, to finish the extensive work on the church and even to erect some new buildings." Rahn nodded as Denninger continued. "But in the end he was accused of selling masses, I think. That, apparently, was the source of his wealth."

Running his hand through his hair again, Rahn asked, "Are you sure about that?"

Denninger crossed his arms. "Oh, how would I know? I mean, who cares, Rahn. Is this why you brought me to this fascinating place? To rehash that old canard? Really, Otto, I have other things I could be doing, you know."

Rahn looked around, and put his hand inside his coat. Slowly, he pulled out a weather-beaten leather book that had obviously seen better days. Gently he placed it on the table and slid it towards Denninger.

"What's this?" he asked, looking up from the book to Rahn.

Otto smiled. "It's a diary. Open it to the second page," he instructed. Denninger did as he was told. Written neatly across the middle of the page was the inscription *Propriété de Abbé Rivière.* The name was unfamiliar to Denninger. "Who is Abbé Rivière?"

Rahn held his breath for a second before he finally sat back. "Abbé Rivière was the priest that went to Saunière's deathbed to give him last rites in 1917. The thing is, once Saunière confessed, Abbé Rivière refused to do so."

Denninger's knowledge of Catholicism and Christianity was shaky but functional. He was certainly surprised to hear that one Catholic priest had refused another the sacrament of absolution. Without it, according to their beliefs, Saunière would not be able to enter the Kingdom of Heaven.

Rahn sipped his beer and continued. "Apparently Saunière confessed something to Rivière that was so ... horrible, that Rivière felt he couldn't administer the rite. Something so terrible that it affected the poor abbé to such a degree that ... well, the rumor was that he never smiled again. Now, I'm not sure if that was entirely true — his not smiling again, I mean — but the fact is, something was revealed to him that had a profound effect on him. Something ... provocative."

The whole story had taken a left turn and Denninger was spellbound. "Is what Saunière confessed to in this book?"

Rahn only gave a sly smile. Denninger looked back at the diary. "Where did you get this anyway?" Denninger inquired. When Rahn didn't answer right away, Denninger looked up and was met with the Cheshire Cat grin again.

"I ... uh, borrowed it." Rahn cleared his throat and continued. "When I was in France, I happened to visit a small shop in the Rennes-le-Château area ... antiques and curios ... really quite nice ..."

Rahn paused to take another sip of beer.

"Anyway, the timing was, shall we say, fortuitous? The shopowner had just received a box of effects from the church where Abbé Rivière had been the parish priest. The owner was a very amiable fellow. It seems he knew all about the whole Saunière saga and was quite happy to go on at length about it. It was then that another customer came in, so ... I drifted over to one of the boxes. Since the shopkeeper was busy, I began to rummage through the box myself and I found it underneath some old clothes."

He held up the diary. "When I read what was inside, Gerhard..."

"But what does it say, Otto?"

Rahn patted the book with his finger. "I want you to read it for yourself," he said.

Scratching his head lightly, Denninger pulled the diary closer. "I cannot believe that the owner of the store parted with it," he said as began to thumb through the pages.

Rahn finished his beer and waved to the waitress, holding up two fingers. "Actually, I don't think he knew that it was in the box."

Denninger's mouth fell open slightly. "What do you mean, he didn't know?"

Rahn put his hands together and drummed his fingers against each other. "He'd only just received the boxes that day. I don't even think he knows about it."

Denninger couldn't believe his ears. "You mean you stole it! My God, Rahn, what were you thinking?"

Rahn put up his hand and shook his head. "When you read what's in it, Gerhard, you'll be thankful that I ... borrowed it. Trust me."

As the waitress brought the beers over, a commotion by the front entrance captured Rahn's attention. He noticed three men in trench coats, checking identification papers. "Fucking Gestapo," he muttered. "That's a really good way to blend in."

He quickly turned to Denninger. "I think it's time we left, my friend," he urged. He snatched up the diary with one hand and tried to button up his jacket with the other.

Denninger was puzzled and began to look around, not quite understanding what was happening. What is it? What is going on? Denninger wondered silently.

The Gestapo agents slowly waded into the crowd onto the dance floor. The dancers, suddenly aware of the unwanted guests in their midst, began to move a little more demonstratively, deliberately slowing down the progress of the intruders.

One of the Gestapo agents, scanning the back of the bar, spotted Rahn and started to make his way towards him. Rahn grabbed Denninger by the scruff of his coat and hissed. "Let's go!"

Denninger was completely bewildered. He was at the cloakroom, in the process of trying to get his hat from the shamelessly flirting transvestite, when he heard Rahn call out. Denninger turned just in time to see something flying straight at him. He had no time to react. The object, which turned out to be Rivière's diary, hit him squarely in the chest. The book flopped to the floor at his feet. More surprised than angry, he instinctively bent over to pick up the projectile, when suddenly he felt two legs crash into his backside at a high rate of speed.

The Gestapo agent who had just collided into Denninger sailed over the archeologist's back until he completed the parabola by landing on his ass with a loud crack, signifying a broken tailbone. Over on the dance floor, the other two agents, noticing the commotion by the cloakroom in the back, immediately reversed and tried to break through the crowd.

One of the agents managed to squeeze past two men, both dressed like Marlene Dietrich, but didn't notice the handle of an umbrella as it completed its vicious arc and smashed into his face. Blood and teeth sprayed onto the dress of the taller, uglier Marlene as the hapless agent crumpled to his knees. Ugly Marlene turned her head and saw a red splotch and a broken tooth on the white lace across her chest.

"Now, is that any way to treat a lady, swine?" she said hoarsely as she grabbed hold of the agent's hair with a large, hairy, knuckled mitt. A strangled yelp slipped between the lips of the Gestapo agent as he was raised a few inches off of the floor.

"Goddamned Gestapo," muttered the other Marlene as she connected a roundhouse smash to the rest of his teeth. Rahn winced. He's going to have to see a dentist, he thought. As the Gestapo agent slithered to the floor, Rahn saw the owner of the umbrella.

"Thank you, Bobby," Rahn called. Turning to the Marlenes, he gave a small bow. "Thank you too, girls."

Bobby tipped his hat to Rahn just before he took a huge cricket-bat swing at the other Gestapo agent who, at the moment, was being rendered immobile by a rather energetic swing doll, who had wrapped her legs around his neck like a boa constrictor.

Turning to Denninger, Rahn said, "You see Gerhard, they're really not such bad kids."

Picking up the pace, the two of them squeezed through what was rapidly becoming a riot of impressive proportions. The cloakroom "girl" had disappeared, no doubt engaged in the melee. Denninger saw his coat and grabbed it while Rahn yanked on his arm. As the first few ejections from the bar hit the street, news of the growing brawl had been brought to the attention of some members of the Hitler Youth. They quickly assembled in front of the bar, spoiling for a fight. The rest of the swing kids, upon hearing about the visitors waiting for them outside, were anxious to oblige them. There was no love lost between the two groups. The "überdiscipline" of the Youth contrasted deeply with the laissez-faire lifestyle of the swing kids, and Rahn could feel the electricity in the air. Excitedly, he grabbed Denninger by the arm and pulled him to the side of the building, out of the way of what was surely about to be a bloody clash.

"This is going to be ugly," whispered Rahn. "Don't move."

Denninger had pressed his back and face up against the wall, leaving an imprint of brick in his cheek. "Don't worry."

The Hitler Youth, decked out in their traditional brown shirts, short pants and leather belts were armed with rocks, lead pipes and two-by-fours. They stood in a phalanx across the road, effectively blocking any exits, while the kids, attired in their zoot suits and fedoras, were of a looser formation, with umbrellas and clasp knives at the ready.

No one made a move for at least a minute, as they sized each other up. One of the swing kids, a tall specimen in a chalk-white dust coat stepped forward. "Hello *boys,*" he began, "Isn't it past your bedtime? Everyone I know in short pants is asleep by now." There were assorted chuckles from the kids behind him. "You know," he continued, "We don't fight with children ... why don't you come back in a couple of years when you are ... Hitler *Men*?"

More guffaws.

There was suddenly a loud crack and the kid in the dust coat fell to the ground. A bloodied rock with flesh and hair stuck to it clattered across the pavement.

Rahn held his breath.

"Here we go ... ," he breathed.

Someone in the crowd yelled. All hell broke loose. Both sides charged simultaneously and crashed into each other with sickening thuds. The sounds of screams were punctuated by solid thwacks of lead pipe and board on bone. In the middle of the melee, Rahn saw Bobby giving one thug a two handed chop to his head with his umbrella handle.

Rahn was just itching to join in. It wouldn't be the first time, but he knew it would be foolish. Suddenly, a few blocks away, the sound of a whistle split the air. Rahn turned to Denninger, who was still pressed against the bricks. "We have to move. Now."

Denninger grabbed Rahn's arm. "But we have done nothing wrong, Otto. The authorities will leave us alone."

"You think so, eh?" he hissed, and added more ominously, "What do you think the Gestapo was doing in there anyway?"

Denninger blinked. "What are you saying?"

Otto pulled Denninger to the left, and headed through an opening in the flank of the mob. As Denninger shot forward, he clutched at his jacket and realized that he didn't have the diary. He stopped short. A feeling of horror punched him deep into the pit of his stomach. He suddenly felt sick. "Otto ... stop! *Stop!*" he yelled, "I lost the diary!"

Rahn turned and grabbed Denninger's jacket. "Keep going," Rahn shouted.

"But Otto — "

"Run!" Rahn commanded. The two of them bolted, heads down, diagonally across the war zone. Rocks narrowly missed them as they tried to weave through the crush around them. One stone caught Rahn in the shoulder, causing him to stumble slightly. Denninger sidestepped a two-by-four that came tumbling towards him from out of nowhere, the whole time cursing Rahn and himself over the fact that he had lost the diary. They turned down an alleyway, dodging trash bins and two alcoholics passed out in their own vomit. After they had put the better part of five blocks behind them, they slowed down, catching their breath. Denninger collapsed to his knees and then fell forward to the pavement, all the while coughing and wheezing.

Rahn squatted beside his companion and began to chuckle. "Well, Gerhard, did you ever think you'd see so much action tonight?" He looked down at his sputtering partner.

Denninger gradually turned over. When his breathing finally slowed, he grabbed at Rahn's legs. "I lost ... the diary!" he gasped. "I ... told you ... to stop! I had it inside Carlotta's ... but I must have dropped it. We'll have to go back!" Denninger's voice became weaker and he started to cough again.

Rahn remained impassive.

When he saw that Rahn wasn't reacting, Denninger became angry. "Did you hear what I said? I lost the fucking diary!" he screamed hoarsely.

Rahn grinned. Dramatically, he reached into his jacket and pulled out the leather book. "You mean ... this?"

Denninger stared mutely at Rahn and the book.

Rahn chuckled and stood up slowly. "After I threw it at you — oh, sorry about that, by the way —," he said, noticing Denninger's glare, "you bent over to pick it up. That's when the Gestapo agent fell on top of you. Your foot bumped it right back at me — no problem at all."

Denninger shook his head and took off his glasses. As he began to wipe them with his handkerchief, he looked up at Rahn who was lighting up another of his horrible-smelling private-blend cigarettes.

"What *were* the Gestapo doing in there, Otto?"

The Cheshire Cat just grinned.

3

IT WAS PAST MIDNIGHT when they arrived at Rahn's apartment. The stairway was ominously dark as Denninger and Rahn made their way towards Rahn's flat, and the first thing Denninger noticed as he climbed the stairs was an overpowering smell. He couldn't place it at first, but the higher he climbed, it seemed to become more familiar. Rahn happened to turn around and observed Denninger's look of puzzlement. "Ah, so you notice the sweet aroma, yes? The locals that can't afford rooms use the stairway for their business. C'est la vie!"

Denninger was starting to realize that there was probably nothing in the world that caused any sort of discomfort or outrage in Rahn's life. Men and women having sex in his hallway was just a matter of course in a normal day, it seemed. Denninger took a deep breath, held it, and followed Rahn upwards. When they reached his apartment, Rahn reached up and felt along the lintel until he found the key.

The whole time they had been heading to his flat, Denninger had been picturing in his head what it would look like inside. He figured a flamboyant world traveler like Otto Rahn would have bamboo furniture from China, or maybe Persian rugs, or possibly West African headdresses mounted on the walls. When Rahn switched on the light, Denninger stared into a nearly vacant room. A sorry-looking wooden table with a solitary chair was lumped in one corner near a decrepit icebox, and, above a torn throw rug, a skeletal sofa with irregular patchwork to keep the stuffing in was leaning on three legs and a book that served for a fourth.

Denninger stared at Rahn in disbelief. "Did you just move in?" he asked. Rahn looked back at Denninger and answered confusedly, "No, I've been here for just over a year — why?"

Denninger just shrugged.

Rahn directed him to the sofa while he grabbed the wooden chair and brought it over. He pulled the diary out from the inside of his coat and handed it to the archeologist.

As Denninger took it from the researcher he said, "You still haven't told me why the Gestapo were after you — I mean us — tonight."

Rahn spun the chair around and straddled the seat, placing his folded arms across its back. "They have been watching me for the last year. I get the distinct feeling that they don't trust me." He ran his hand through his hair a few times.

Denninger had noticed that he would do that every time he was about to talk about something important. "Remember the story about the Cathars who escaped from Montségur with the supposed Cathar treasure? Well ..." He stopped himself for a second and seemed to reorganize his thoughts. "You have been to Montségur, haven't you, Gerhard?"

Denninger nodded.

"Well then, I don't have to tell you that the hill is like this." Rahn slanted his arms to form an almost perfect right angle. "The escaping Cathars supposedly carried off the treasure, right? But the slopes are too steep. It would have been impossible for anyone to take any kind of bulky object down those sheer sides. However ..."

Rahn paused for a moment. "What if the treasure wasn't within the walls of the fortress? What if the Cathars had carried off something else instead? Something that would have been easy to transport down the side of the mountain."

"Like what?"

"Like information, perhaps? A map, maybe? I do not believe that the treasure was ever in the fortress. I think that those Cathars escaped down the side of that mountain with information about the treasure and gave this information to the Knights Templar. The Templars then created a document with the information encoded so that no one but themselves could figure it out."

"Really," said Denninger skeptically. "An encoded document. By the Knights Templar, of all people."

Rahn nodded excitedly. Denninger harrumphed and said, "And you know this because ..."

Rahn said nothing, and then, almost comically, lifted his eyebrows. Denninger sat back on the sofa with his hands clasped across his chest, obviously finding Rahn's story a little lacking.

Suddenly it dawned on Denninger. "Don't tell me that you actually found this document?"

Rahn slowly spread his arms wide. "Brilliant deduction, Gerhard. Would you like to know where I found it?"

"I think I would rather see it, if you don't mind."

Rahn leaned back slightly in the chair. Denninger saw that if he didn't play it Rahn's way he would never get to see it. "All right, fine. Where did you find it, Otto?"

"That's better. I found it in Arcadia, of course."

"What?"

"To understand this, we have to look at the Saunière story again. According to my research, just before his incredible rise in wealth, he made a trip to Paris where he met a number of the city's elite, including Claude Debussy and the opera singer Emma Calvé — a very high class circle, to be sure."

"To be sure," murmured Denninger. "So?"

"You're so impatient, Gerhard. As I was saying, it appears that our friend Saunière was hobnobbing with the higher level of Parisian society. It was through them that he met a young monk named Emile Hoffet, and it was when he was with Hoffet that he saw it."

"Saw what?"

"*The Shepherds of Arcadia* by Nicolas Poussin. Have you ever heard of Poussin, Gerhard?"

Denninger nodded. "Of course I have ... although I don't know much about him, I'm afraid."

Rahn smiled. "Poussin was a baroque painter who had ties to the Knights Templar. When Saunière saw *The Shepherds of Arcadia,* I believe that he recognized the landmarks that Poussin had put in the painting."

"What landmarks?" asked Denninger.

"The mountains in the background matched the contours of the area around Rennes-le-Chateau. Even the tomb depicted in the painting matched one near Les Pontils, a few miles from his church."

"How do you know that?" Denninger scoffed.

"Because I recognized them too, Gerhard. Don't you see? A painting with a connection to the Templars, a document created by the Templars ... those warrior monks are everywhere in this story. Poussin obviously thought it necessary to leave these clues for some reason. Saunière must have speculated that perhaps there was a connection between this painting and the Cathar document, only I think he missed the real signifigance."

"Why do you say that, Otto?"

"Because he never left Rennes-le-Chateau. You see, Poussin had actually painted two versions of the subject, but it is the second one that is relevant. Both paintings depict a group of three shepherds and a shepherdess studying the tomb. The phrase on the tomb is '*Et In Arcadia Ego*' — 'Even In Arcadia, I Am.' You see, Arcadia or Arcady is — "

Denninger cut in. "A land of unspoiled beauty — paradise, if I'm not mistaken."

"Correct. Now, back to the Templars. When King Philip ordered the arrest of the Templar order, it was supposedly because they were becoming too powerful. I do not believe that was the real reason, though. I believe that Philip knew that the Templars had something of immense value and I believe that when some of the Templars escaped Philip's trap, the document wound up in Scotland."

Rahn paused for a moment and then leaned forward until the chair hit the floor. Denninger watched as the Cheshire Cat grin returned. He started to reach inside his coat for a cigarette.

"Please, Otto ... not in here," Denninger pleaded.

Rahn looked at the cigarettes, sighed and then put them away as he continued the tale. "Scotland had become something of a refuge for some of the remaining knights. For safekeeping, the document was kept at Rosslyn Chapel for a number of years until it was decided that it would be safer somewhere else — somewhere far away from anyone possibly getting their hands on it. I did some digging and I discovered that a descendant of one of the Templars, Sir Henry Sinclair, who was the Lord of Rosslyn, using a map provided by a pair of Italian navigators, took the document across the ocean in 1398. One hundred years before Columbus ever sailed across the Atlantic Ocean."

"Where did Sinclair ever manage to find such a map, Otto? It seems highly unlikely."

"The Italian navigators, Nicolo and Antonio Zeno, created the map from their travels in the fourteenth century. The story is that Sinclair himself may have financed their voyage."

"Where was Sinclair headed?"

Rahn smiled. "He was sailing for what would become New Scotland. That is, Nova Scotia, in Canada. He landed at the Gold River near a large island. Do you know what the native Micmac Indians called this area, Gerhard?"

The archeologist had no idea. Rahn stood up and walked around to the back of the chair. Placing his hands on the crossbar, he rocked on the balls of his feet building up Denninger's feeling of suspense. "Please, Otto, just tell me."

Leaning forward, he soberly said, "Acadia. The area where Sinclair made port was known as *Acadia*. Don't you see, Gerhard? The Micmac word *Acadia* became 'Arcadia'."

"Yes, but the theme of Arcadia in art has been around for years, Otto. It's a Greek ideal of paradise that's been cropping up in paintings for centuries. Arcadia is in Greece."

Rahn laughed. "That's the beauty of this, Gerhard. One would automatically think Greece, not Canada. '*Et In Arcadia Ego*' — Even In Arcadia I Am. The document exists in Arcadia — and that's exactly where it was."

Denninger was starting to become overwhelmed by all the information. His head actually began to hurt as he tried to keep the facts straight in his mind. "So let me see if I am following this," the archeologist said, holding up a finger. "When the Cathars were wiped out in 1244, someone escaped with the location of the Cathar treasure. He passed this information on to the Knights Templar who created a document — "

"A coded document," Rahn interrupted.

"A coded document that was kept in Scotland until it was taken away and hidden in 1398 somewhere in Nova Scotia." Denninger shook his head. "This is utterly fantastic, Otto," exclaimed Denninger.

Rahn continued. "Once I figured out the Arcadia riddle, I knew I had to make my way to Nova Scotia so I forged some 'secret orders' in Wiligut's name and commandeered a U-boat using the papers. No one would dare question orders from the SS. That, believe it or not, was the easy part. I also told them we had to run under radio silence so that there wouldn't be any pesky messages from headquarters to uncover my little subterfuge."

Rahn paused to collect his thoughts.

"According to the information I discovered about Sinclair, he had had a settlement built in the middle of the peninsula by the headwaters of two rivers, one to the north and one to the south. At the mouth of the southern river is an island called Oak Island. Oh, this is really good, too. The story there is that Captain Kidd, you know, the pirate, buried his treasure on the island, in a deep hole that's now known as — get this — 'the Money Pit'. For over two hundred years, people have been digging in this pit but have yet to find the treasure."

Denninger suddenly cut in. "What has that got to do with the document, Otto? I don't quite follow."

Rahn continued patiently. "Just listen, Gerhard. The pit itself was beautifully designed, you see. At a certain level, water gushes in, making it impossible to get to the bottom. Engineers have been wrestling with the problem for years, but even today, they still are unable to figure it out just how stem the tide. Genius! Sheer genius! Gerhard," Rahn sat back down across from Denninger and pulled the chair closer, "this pit — it is really an engineering marvel. It would have had to have been concocted by someone with skill — real engineering skill — and do you think that a simple pirate would be able to pull it off?"

"What does this have to do with the document, Otto? I don't understand."

Rahn smiled. "Then it dawned on me. Who would have had the skill? Who?"

Denninger suddenly clued in. "Henry Sinclair," he said softly.

"Right. The Knights Templar were great builders and engineers. They managed to expertly excavate Solomon's Temple in Jerusalem, and built huge castles and fortresses all over France. Sinclair, as a descendant of this tradition, would certainly have had the skill to pull it off. He and his crew would have been able to create such a perfect trap. I am convinced that they designed and built what is truly the world's greatest puzzle. Brilliant."

"But you got the document, didn't you? How on earth did you manage to succeed where others failed?"

Rahn slowly leaned back on the chair and grinned again. "I didn't. The document wasn't in the pit. It wasn't even on the goddamn island! I mean, it was on Oak Island, just not *that* Oak Island."

"Are you trying to confuse me? I'm having a hard enough time getting my head around all this without you making it more difficult."

"I'm sorry. What I mean to say is that there were *two* Oak Islands. I discovered this by studying Sinclair's records. There's one in the south which has the pit and another one in the north that has since become part of the mainland. Don't you see?"

"What are you saying, Otto?"

Rahn leaned in. "It's so obvious. There is no solution to the pit. It was designed to keep you digging and looking, looking and digging, understand?"

Yes, of course. Now I get it, thought Denninger. He smiled as he softly slapped his forehead. "The pit … the pit is a diversion, isn't it? The document wasn't *there* … because it was …"

"… on the other Oak Island," finished Rahn as he laughed out loud.

He stood up and began to pace again as he continued his story. "So that's where I went. I left the crew on board — it was a 'secret' mission, after all," he winked. "I spent two full days searching that goddamned island.

Nothing — not a fucking thing. Finally I came across this old disused graveyard, and didn't think anything of it, but I needed to rest. There was this big, old, oak tree, by far the oldest tree on the island, growing by a tumbled pile of rocks, so I headed for that thinking that I could use some shade. I sat there for a few minutes, wiping the sweat from my eyes, and tried to figure out where this thing could be. Gerhard, I was positive it was on that island." He ran his hand through his hair excitedly.

"I knew that Sinclair was a Templar and symbols were important to the Templar Knights. I needed to find a symbol, a sign — something that would tell me where it was. I sat there racking my brain, going over everything I could remember about Templar mythology. Finally at one point I stretched and looked up through the branches ..." He was looking up, as if there were branches above him, and then, slowly, he looked back down at Denninger. He then spread his arms, as if he had just completed a magic trick.

"It was staring me right in the face, Gerhard. Right in the face! The oak tree I was standing under was the biggest, oldest oak tree on the island. The tree was the answer! Gerhard, how is your Celtic mythology?"

Denninger looked at Rahn with an annoyed look as Rahn continued. "Did you know that the Celts worshipped the oak tree?" he asked "The words for 'oak' in the Celtic languages have the same root as the words for 'trust,' for 'truth' in the Germanic languages? Don't you see? The tree was the answer ... the truth, Gerhard. It was showing the way. It was telling me where to look." He dropped his hands and sat down on the chair. He smiled. "The biggest, oldest oak tree on the island was the clue to the location. The *true* location. It was right in front of me, Gerhard. I mean, if you saw that tumbled-down heap of stones, you wouldn't even give it a second thought. But when I looked down at that pile, it seemed to me that at one time it could have been a cairn. I began to rummage through the rocks and then ... I saw it — a stone with a skull and crossbones carved on it."

Denninger knew very well the significance of the skull and crossbones. Before it became a pirate symbol, the skull and crossbones had been a Templar motif.

It was all too unbelievable.

"I pulled up the stone — my God, Gerhard, it was heavier than I thought — and then I began to dig. About eight feet down, I hit something else that was solid. It was a smaller stone. When I removed this one, I discovered, to my astonishment, what looked like a metal box surrounded by a number of flat stones to protect it from the damp soil. My whole body, I swear, began to tremble. Slowly, I worked it out of the dirt until I could see it was an iron box, with the lock long rusted away."

"I opened the box, and saw something wrapped in strips of leather. I was confused at first, but when I removed the leather strips, there it was. My friend, it was like I was hit by a lightning bolt. It was easily seven hundred years old — from 1244 — I am sure of it, Gerhard. It was beautiful. It was a parchment which was covered in letters and Templar symbols. I had found it."

Denninger let out a low whistle and jumped up off of the sofa. He could feel the small hairs on his neck tingling. "Well, Otto, where is it? Let's have a look at it," he said excitedly.

Rahn shook his head. "It's not here," he said.

Denninger's mouth fell open. Rahn reached over and put his hand on the archeologist's shoulder. "Don't worry. It's safe. Things are beginning to heat up right now and these people following me — they can't know what I have, and I won't let them find it either. Make no mistake though, they are watching us. So that's why I want you to take this," he said, handing him the diary.

"They have no idea about the diary, and I believe that what is contained in it and what is in the document are linked somehow. Take it home, Gerhard. Keep it safe."

"But Otto, you never fully explained how the diary fits in."

"No time now. Take it to your apartment and read it for yourself. You'll figure it out."

As Denninger took the book, Rahn turned and went towards the makeshift kitchen and reached up into one of the cupboards. He extracted a revolver, checking the chambers to see if it was loaded.

Denninger jumped up. "Do you really need that? Are you expecting trouble?"

Rahn said nothing as he placed the revolver between his stomach and the waistband of his pants and covered it with his shirt. He opened the door of his apartment and motioned to Denninger to follow. As Denninger buttoned up his overcoat, he nervously fell into step with Rahn as he disappeared into the night.

4

As Rahn said goodbye, and disappeared down the road, Denninger had little idea what had been set into motion. Turning away, Denninger clutched the book as he made his way to his apartment, all the while trying to assimilate the fantastic story he had just heard. It was absolutely incredible. The legend of the Cathar treasure had dominated his whole adult life, and never once had he thought that he was close to actually finding it. He felt capricious, almost as if he was drunk.

As he walked along the narrow road, he kept thinking he heard strange noises, as if he were being followed.

He stopped.

Was that a footstep?

After a few moments of listening to his own breathing, he decided that it was probably just his imagination. Even so, he couldn't shake the feeling and so he clutched the diary more tightly. He desperately wanted to stop for a stiff drink, but he wanted to get to his apartment as soon as possible.

Suddenly, there it was again. A footstep. This time he *had* heard it.

Maybe.

Somebody is following me, he thought.

Then again ...

Deciding to not take any chances, Denninger picked up his pace, his footfalls echoing against the stone walls that lined the quiet, vacant street. His breathing was starting to become heavy as the tension built. He pressed the diary even closer to his chest with both hands, making his hurried pace even more awkward. Before he knew it, he was running.

Goddamn it, he thought, ever since I met Otto Rahn, all I do is run.

His breath was now coming in gulps and gasps, and for a brief moment the idea crossed his mind of an older man racing down a dark street late at night holding a book to his chest, being chased perhaps by no one. Not surprisingly, it made him feel more than a little foolish.

"What ... am ... I ... doing?" he gasped. He began to slow his pace, noticing with alarm that his heart was beating against his chest wall like a kettledrum. His feet flapped noisily against the road as his forward, out-of-control motion slowed to a stop. He doubled over, taking in deep breaths, like a man who had fallen overboard and just resurfaced.

"Easy," he said to himself. "Take it easy ... slowly."

His head throbbed and the blood pounding in his ears was making hearing difficult—so difficult that he was unaware of someone who had suddenly sidled up behind him and clamped a hand on his shoulder. Denninger screamed hoarsely and dropped the diary to the ground.

"Hello, Old Hot Boy," said a familiar, high-pitched voice in his ear. Denninger spun around to see Bobby smiling and twirling an umbrella. Denninger tried to speak but he couldn't get a breath. Bobby chuckled.

"Relax, old man, you'll give yourself a heart attack. I guess you thought I was the Gestapo, eh?"

The quivering archeologist reached out and grabbed Bobby by the arm, and at the same time, gulped for air. Slowly his breathing began to even out and the color came back to his face.

"Are you trying to frighten me to death?"

Bobby grinned. "Oh, I am sorry, Doctor. I did not intend to give you apoplexy, I assure you. Otto asked me to keep an eye on you until you got to your apartment. He didn't want any thing to happen to the diary," he said as he bent over to pick it up. He held the book out to Denninger who was obviously embarrassed.

"Nothing will happen to the diary, Bobby."

"Oh, I can see that. You've got it all under control. Here, you've got shit all over the cover of it," he told him, brushing at the loose dirt. Denninger yanked the book away angrily and said, "I wouldn't have dropped it in the first place if you hadn't scared me like that, you know."

"Oh, of course, of course," Bobby replied in a patronizingly dripping tone. He put his arm around Denninger and directed him down the street. "Shall we?"

They walked together for a few blocks, neither of them saying much, other than the minutest of small talk. Denninger wasn't in the mood for conversation. He pretended to listen as Bobby nattered on in his squeaky voice about the state of Germany and how Hitler was leading them to the brink of war. He gave cursory nods at all the right spots, and hoped that the swing kid would tire soon, but Bobby only seemed to be warming up. After another few minutes of self-righteous pontificating, Bobby said, "So ... what do you think of Otto?"

Denninger was slightly taken aback by the personal nature of the question, and he wasn't quite sure how to answer it. The question of Rahn's predilections quickly came to mind and Denninger was clearly uncomfortable with this line of questioning. "Uh ... I have only known him for a day or two, so ... it's a little hard for me to have much of an opinion. He seems like, uh ... a very *agreeable* fellow."

Bobby nodded. "Well he likes you — he wouldn't have taken you into his confidence if he didn't. You should feel honored. He is a very good man, you know."

That's what had Denninger worried. Why would someone like Otto Rahn, with whom he had very little in common, gravitate to someone like himself in the first place? It made little sense, however, deep down, he was glad that he had. For the first time in over forty years, he felt young and vital, excited about the hunt and what he would find at the end of it. Still, there was a nagging ...

Bobby suddenly grabbed Denninger's arm. "Keep walking," he said in a low voice. Denninger stared straight ahead and quickly fell into step with Bobby.

"Are we being followed?" Denninger whispered out of the side of his mouth. Bobby shot him a quick look. "Here — take this umbrella. You can use it as a weapon. When I count three, I want you to run as fast as you can go. Ready?"

Denninger tensed as Bobby began to count down.

"Run!" Bobby suddenly yelled and Denninger took off as fast as his already tired legs could carry him, the umbrella banging against his leg as he hurtled down the road like a wheezy locomotive. After only a few seconds, he became acutely aware that Bobby was not beside him and that the only noise he could hear was the sound of his own feet hitting the road beneath him. Slowing to a stop, he turned to find that Bobby had completely disappeared and that he was alone again. He spun completely around, his head whipping in all directions as he tried to see where Bobby had gone. There was no doubt about it. Bobby had vanished into the night. The doctor began to vibrate and he shook the umbrella that Bobby had somehow left in his possession.

"What in the holy hell is going on?" he yelled at the top of his lungs, ignoring the fact that it was well past two in the morning. A few windows slammed open with cries of "Get home, drunk!" and "I'm calling the police!" splitting the quiet night air. Denninger closed his eyes and seethed with rage for a few moments, until he regained his composure. He held the diary tightly in one hand and his new acquisition in the other, muttering to himself as he made the trek homeward.

—■—

Denninger's apartment was modestly furnished as befitted someone in the Heritage Bureau. He dropped the umbrella into a receptacle by the door and tossed the diary onto the small table in his kitchen. He was dying for a cup of tea. He opened the cupboard and grabbed a cup and the tin of tea. He filled the kettle with water and placed it upon the stove and then settled in at the table, waiting for the pot to boil. The diary lay in front of him. Opening it to the second page, he reread the inscription, "*Propriété de Abbé Rivière.*" The first twenty pages or so related to Rivière's work in the parish and was rather uneventful stuff. He continued to thumb through the diary until he found the passage about Saunière, just as the kettle began to whistle.

As he got up to make the tea, there was a shuffling noise just outside his door. The events of the past couple of hours had already put him on high alert, and of course, his imagination began to run wild. Gestapo? he thought fearfully.

Tiptoeing to the door, he reached into the receptacle to retrieve the umbrella in case he needed a weapon. He held the umbrella firmly in his right hand as he pressed his left ear to the door. He held his breath. A few seconds later he heard the noise again.

Someone was definitely in the hallway. Who would be up at this ungodly hour, he wondered, but he already knew the answer. The Gestapo must have followed him from Otto's apartment.

The shuffling grew louder. Deciding that an attack is the best form of defense, he gripped the doorknob and turned it slowly until he heard the click. As soon as he was sure that the shuffling was right outside his door, he yanked it open and leapt forward, screaming and waving the umbrella like a madman, right in an elderly woman's face.

In the fraction of a second before the umbrella opened, Denninger realized that his Gestapo assailant was actually Mrs. Gottfried, the superintendent's wife. The old woman gasped as the umbrella flew open with a flapping noise, obscuring her view of the deranged attacker. Cries of "Rape!" and "Are you crazy? I'm seventy-four!" were mixed with Denninger's attempts at an apology as he tried to close the errant umbrella.

"Forgive me, Mrs. Gottfried," he said through the umbrella. "It's only me, Gerhard Denninger. I am so sorry. I thought you were ... someone else."

Mrs. Gottfried was holding her hand to her ample chest, mumbling incoherently while Denninger wrestled with his makeshift weapon. He had caught it on the stair railing and was shaking it back and forth, ripping irreparable holes in the fabric as a result. He gave it a final yank, bending the ribs forward, as if a gale force gust of wind had caught it, turning the finely crafted umbrella into a piece of modern art in a matter of seconds.

"Of all the stupid ..." Denninger muttered angrily as he tried to disentangle the umbrella from the railing. Mrs. Gottfried gave a final shriek as Denninger dropped the twisted mess onto the floor. He rushed forward to comfort the babbling woman, kicking the umbrella into the wall in the process. As he put his arm around Mrs. Gottfried and began to console her, he happened to glance down and was instantly puzzled.

The ivory handle of the umbrella had come loose, and was detached from the rest of the contraption at an obtuse angle. On closer examination, he noticed something was sticking out of the remaining shaft.

Something light brown and leathery looking.

Denninger suddenly felt a chill as he realized what it was. Rahn had hidden the document in the handle of the umbrella.

He swiftly turned his attention back to Mrs. Gottfried, doing his best to placate her as quickly as possible. Inevitably, by this time heads had begun to peek out of doorways, curious and upset at the noise that had been emanating from the hallway at close to three in the morning.

"Is everything all right, Mrs. Gottfried?" asked a young man, who stared at Denninger with a look and a curled fist that said he would be happy to take care of the situation if she so desired. Denninger did his best to stare down the would-be rescuer, at the same time trying to pull the broken umbrella closer with his foot without drawing any attention to it. As he tapped it with his foot, the document slid back inside the handle.

"Go back to your homes," he ordered. "It is just a misunderstanding. Everything is fine. I am sorry that you were awakened by the noise, but as you can see," he said with his arms outstretched, disheveled hair, and coat askew, "it is all under control now."

Just then, Mrs. Gottfried fainted and fell forward into Denninger's waiting arms, causing him to stumble backwards through the open door of his apartment.

"Mrs ... Gottfried ..." Denninger grunted. The two of them fell to the floor in a heap, her heavy chest landing right on his solar plexus, knocking the wind out of him. He tried to lift her off, but the angle was awkward and it was obvious they were both down for the count.

"Someone ... please ... ," he wheezed.

Two tenants came into the room, each taking one of her arms and lifted. One of them was laughing so hard that he had a hard time managing the job at hand.

"Keep quiet, Gunther," ordered the other. "This isn't funny."

"Oh yes it is," replied Gunther.

They finally managed to hoist the unconscious woman up, enabling the flattened doctor beneath to rise. As they unceremoniously dragged Mrs. Gottfried out, Denninger shut the door and went to retrieve the umbrella.

His heart leapt into his throat when he saw that it had disappeared.

The crowd had begun to dissipate as Gunther and his friend were finally able to get Mrs. Gottfried back into her apartment. She was coming to, and mumbling incoherently about socialists, fascists, and decent women on the street.

Denninger began scouring the hallway, absolutely beside himself with panic, at the idea that the scroll had somehow disappeared from right under his nose. It was in his hands! How could he have lost it?

He rubbed his temples in frustration. Up and down the hallway he searched, but to no avail. Maybe, he thought hopefully, someone put it back inside his apartment. He hurried back down the hall and was immediately disturbed by the fact that his door — which he knew he had just shut — was now slightly ajar.

Denninger braced himself as he gently pushed it open. The door swung wide with a slight creak, revealing a medium-built individual sitting at the table holding a lit cigarette in one hand and the diary in the other.

The umbrella lay in two pieces on the floor beside the intruder's shoe.

His thick, blond hair was slicked back with a tiny wisp hanging strategically over his right eye, seemingly not by chance but by design. He had the look of a teenager but his baby face belied his age, and his pale, blue eyes reminded Denninger of a timber wolf's.

He had been followed after all.

"Who are you?" demanded the archeologist, puffing himself up in an attempt to try and take control of a situation that was so obviously not in his control.

The blue-eyed man lifted his head from the diary, turned to Denninger and scowled. "I will ask the questions here, Herr Doctor, if you don't mind."

"Ah," said Denninger, "Blond hair, blue eyes, prerequisite trench coat, rude manner. You must be Gestapo." Denninger let the last word drip with sarcasm. "You are aware, I am sure, that I work for the Ahnenerbe and that, of course, means I work for your boss, Heinrich Himmler. And *that*," he said, pointing at the diary, "is private property."

The Gestapo agent nodded and stood slowly, crushing out the cigarette on Denninger's table. "Oh, I can see that it is private property, Dr. Denninger. My French is not so good, but I can tell that it belongs to an Abbé Rivière — whom you, clearly, are not."

"I received that book from Otto Rahn. He — "

The Gestapo agent put up his hand, interrupting Denninger. "Yes, we know all about Otto Rahn. He is a thief, a liar, most likely a homosexual, and most certainly a Jew. When we catch him, we will ... *speak* to him, to be sure. Now, what else did he tell you?"

Denninger froze and fought the urge to look at the umbrella lying by his foot. "Tell me?"

The Gestapo agent put his hand into his pocket and removed a pistol. He pointed it square at Denninger and took a step forward towards him. "Look here," he began menacingly, "you will tell us what we want to know." Denninger kept backing up until he plopped into a chair behind him.

"Tell you what?" he asked exasperatedly. "I really have no idea what it is you want. The only thing we ever talked about was the Cathars, a subject we are both interested in, and that would certainly bore a cretin like you."

As the Gestapo agent tossed the diary onto the table, it was clear to Denninger that this dullard had very little idea about what was going on. He was just an errand boy sent to pick up the goods, which, unknown to him, were lying just a few inches away from his right foot. Denninger started to stand up.

The Gestapo agent leaned back to let Denninger rise out of the chair but he kept his cold eyes trained on the doctor as he spoke. "Do not misunderstand, doctor. We have men following Rahn as we speak. We will find out what he's up to. In the meantime, perhaps we should take a little trip to Prinz-Albrecht-Strasse, eh? Gestapo headquarters? I am sure you have heard of it. Maybe there you can tell us exactly what you know. We are a little more persuasive there."

5

THE INTERROGATION TOOK THE rest of the night and part of the next morning. The Gestapo was certainly thorough, but clearly they had nothing and were merely fishing for information. The document would remain a secret, at least for now.

Denninger stepped out of the building and promptly shielded his eyes from the incessant brightness of the sun as he was still accustomed to the dark, dank interrogation room in the basement. His head hurt but he wanted to get to his apartment as quickly as possible. He prayed that the umbrella was where he had left it. Flagging down a passing taxi, he hopped in and gave the driver directions to his apartment. As he sank into the seat, he rubbed his legs, trying to get the circulation pumping again. He had been sitting in the same chair for seven hours, and his legs were throbbing.

The car was rounding the corner near his home when he saw a familiar figure in a duster coat loitering outside. Wonderful, thought Denninger. What does *he* want?

Denninger gingerly stepped out of the cab and paid the fare as Bobby sauntered over. As he watched Bobby's demeanor, however, Denninger sensed that there was something wrong. Bobby's piano-like smile, the one that Denninger found so agitating, was conspicuously missing now. The kid leaned in close to Denninger.

"Otto's missing," he said in a low voice. Denninger's heart skipped a beat.

"What do you mean he's missing? I just saw him a few hours ago."

Bobby took hold of Denninger's elbow and pushed him towards the door of his building. "Let's talk inside. It will be more private."

As they made their way up the stairs, some of the tenants who were involved in the previous night's escapades, looked disapprovingly at Denninger. He ignored the stares as he fumbled for his keys. He put the key into the lock and was about to turn it when he heard the door behind him open. He turned to see Herr Gottfried, the superintendent. Denninger gave a tiny bow as a greeting. As he bent forward, he felt Herr Gottfried's fist hit him square on the chin. Denninger had always thought seeing stars was something that only happened in the funny papers, but he actually saw little star-like lights when he got tagged.

"Filthy pervert," muttered Herr Gottfried as he shuffled past the two of them.

"Hmmm," intoned Bobby. "Did I miss out on something last night?"

Denninger rubbed his chin and said nothing as he opened the door. Once inside he looked toward the kitchen table and noticed the diary, still open, and was horrified to see that the broken umbrella was missing. A small gasp escaped from his mouth.

Bobby tapped Denninger on the shoulder. "Looking for this?"

Denninger turned to see Bobby with his jacket open and the broken umbrella inside. He felt the blood rush to his head like he was going to faint as Bobby pulled out the umbrella and handed it to him. "I saw the Gestapo taking you away," he said. "I was worried that they had the umbrella so I decided to check your apartment. Thank God I saw it on the floor — so I took it. You seem to have trouble holding on to things, eh?"

A wistful look came over Bobby as he gazed at the broken umbrella, then he sighed. "It was such a beautiful umbrella, too"

Denninger closed his eyes in relief, then said, "What is this about Otto?"

Bobby casually meandered over to the sofa and slumped into it. He took one hand out of his coat pocket and ran it through his hair. The gesture immediately reminded Denninger of Rahn.

"I was supposed to meet him this morning, to let him know that I had given the umbrella to you." He shrugged his shoulders. "But he never showed up. I checked with everyone who would know where he would be, but nobody has seen him. He just ... vanished." Bobby frowned morosely. "I am afraid the Gestapo or the SS got him. That's why he had me give you the umbrella. He was afraid of something like this happening."

The Gestapo agent had told Denninger that they were after Rahn. If they had actually found him, they may have found out about the document. If that had happened, then Denninger knew it wouldn't be safe at his apartment. He would have to hide it until things died down.

But where?

"Bobby, we've got to hurry. I'm sure they will be coming back here soon." Denninger grabbed the diary from the table and put it into one of the pockets of his overcoat and clutching the remains of the umbrella, jerked his head towards the door. "Let's go," he ordered. Bobby jumped up and followed him out into the hall.

They raced down the stairs, but as soon as they got to the front door, Denninger put his arm out to halt Bobby's progress.

"What is it?" Bobby asked.

Denninger was peeking through the window, trying to see down both sides of the street. His head was pounding like a snare drum. After a few moments' inspection, he thrust the umbrella into Bobby's hands. "Here," he said. "Hide this inside your jacket. I'm going to go out alone. You wait for a few minutes, then leave. I'll meet you later tonight at Carlotta's."

Denninger carefully opened the door and nonchalantly stepped outside. He turned right and started to walk towards his office. He figured he would just continue on as if nothing were the matter. If he were to be searched, they would find the diary, but they had no idea of its importance or else the Gestapo agent would have taken it last night.

He arrived at the Ahnenerbe within twenty minutes and climbed the stairs. He was vaguely aware that as he made his way down the hall, his co-workers seemed to give him a wide berth and avoided eye contact. He found it a little disconcerting but chalked it up to a slight paranoia, no doubt the result of being taken in and interrogated by the Gestapo the previous night.

He opened the door to his office to find his immediate superior, Karl Schlosser, stretched out in a chair, waiting for him. Denninger would normally have been surprised, as he and Schlosser rarely spoke, let alone had face-to-face conversations, but nothing seemed to surprise him much lately.

"Karl," he said in mock astonishment. "What brings you to the bowels of the building today?"

Schlosser didn't say anything. He waited until Denninger had hung up his coat and sat down at his desk before he spoke. "Gerhard," Schlosser began, "I have orders from above that require me to reassign you."

"You have orders from God? That is impressive."

Schlosser smirked. "Don't be flippant. You're being sent to Tibet."

Denninger suddenly felt a pain in the pit of his stomach. Tibet? This could not be happening.

Not now.

"What is the reason for this reassignment, Karl?"

Schlosser shrugged. "It's out of my hands, Gerhard. I was told that Bruno Beger asked for you personally."

"Beger?" said Denninger with no small amount of surprise. "That lunatic? He hates me. I told him once that his ideas were moronic. Do you have any idea what he does?"

Schlosser remained silent, his mouth a tight slash across the bottom of his face.

Denninger's eyes were wide like roulette wheels. "He's looking for Shangri-La! *Shangri-La!* He thinks the Tibetans are descendants of the Aryan race, so you know what he does? He measures their skulls! He's been in Tibet for two years now. Two years, and he hasn't been able to find anything remotely of value to further his asinine theories. Karl, you know how I feel about this Aryan race shit. It's ludicrous." He stood up and began to pace frenetically.

Schlosser smiled wanly. "Oh, I know. His theories make Ernst Gräfenberg's ideas about the female orgasm look like a scientific probability," he remarked.

Denninger moved around the room in a panic. "Isn't there anything you can do, Karl? I can't leave now."

Schlosser eyed him suspiciously. "Why not?"

"Well, I ... I am really busy right at this moment."

"Busy? Oh, you mean the *Aesinas Codex*? Please Gerhard, I've been extremely lenient, but enough is enough. You have been requested to join Beger and Ernst Schäfer in Tibet."

Schäfer too, thought Denninger. Wonderful. The list of absurdities gets longer.

"Karl, I must insist that you — "

Schlosser cut in. "There will be no discussion, Gerhard. My hands are tied. These orders are from Himmler himself. There is nothing I can do."

Denninger's heart sank as he slumped into his chair.

Schlosser sighed. "I am sorry, Gerhard," he said. "I did what I could, but they insisted."

Denninger just stared at the desk, and said nothing.

"It's really for your own good, Gerhard. So, you'll go to Tibet. Maybe for six months, maybe a year. Then you'll come back. I promise."

Denninger seethed inside. He knew there was no way out at this point. "When do I leave?"

Schlosser stood up. "Right away. The Bureau has taken care of everything. There is a car waiting for you downstairs to take you to the airport."

"But what about my apartment?"

"All taken care of. In fact, your superintendent — Mr. Gottfried is it? — he seemed happy that you were going away for a while."

Denninger began to rub his head again. How was he going to get word to Bobby? So many thoughts began bombarding his brain. Six months to a year! He was feeling a little dizzy. "Could you get me some water, please?" he asked Schlosser as he sat down. Schlosser nodded and got up. He told Denninger to take it easy and he would be back in a few minutes. As soon as he left the room, Denninger began to rummage through his pockets.

"Where the hell is it?"

Panicking, he started to turn out his pockets. Coins and little pieces of paper fell to the floor as he shook the clutter free. Then, something bright caught his eye.

"Ah ... ha!" he exclaimed as he noticed the pink claim ticket from Carlotta's just under his chair. He picked it up and turned it over to read the telephone number. The archeologist dialed rapidly and waited for what seemed to be a lifetime for someone to pick up.

"Carlotta's" said an oddly familiar, raspy voice on the other end. Denninger realized that he was talking to the cloakroom "girl." Denninger made a face and pressed on. There was no time for pleasantries.

"Uh, yes, I was wondering ... are you ... are you going to be working tonight?"

"Who is this?"

"Oh, I'm sorry ... I happened to be there last night ... during the excitement? Umm, my name is ..." He paused. He knew that he couldn't give his real name. Scratching his head he finally said, "I'm usually known as ..." He lowered his voice, as if he didn't want anyone to hear what he was about to say. " ... 'Old Hot Boy'." He winced as he said it.

There was no reaction from the other end. Denninger thought for a moment that the line had gone dead. "Hello? Are you still there?"

The raspy voice cut in. Denninger thought that he could detect a smirk in the voice on the other end of the phone. "What is this all about ... Old Hot Boy?"

Denninger did a slow burn. "Are you working there tonight?" he said in a flat voice.

"Are you looking for a date?"

Denninger almost dropped the receiver. "Of course not," he retorted. "I was just wondering if you can deliver a message for me. I was supposed to be there tonight, but I can't make it."

The raspy voice huffed, obviously irritated at the inconvenience. "Who is the message for?"

Denninger suddenly realized that he didn't know Bobby's last name. "It's, uh for ... Bobby," he stammered. "Do you know Bobby?"

The voice on the other end became annoyed. "The whole fucking place is filled with Bobbys. What is his last name?"

Heaving a sigh, Dennnger said, "I don't know — you must know him. He's there every night. He wears one of those, uh ... oh, what are they called?" Suddenly it came to him. "Zoot suits, I believe they're called."

"They *all* wear zoot suits."

"Well, he looks like that movie star ... what's his name?"

"Willy Fritsch?" offered the raspy voice.

"Yes! That's it. He looks like Willy Fritsch!" he exclaimed.

"They *all* look like — "

" — Willy Fritsch, right, of course," Denninger muttered, finishing the sentence. "You must know this fellow ... he's got teeth like a horse ... "

The raspy voice chuckled. "Oh, you must mean Heinz Hofner. Yes, I do know him. *Very* well, in fact." The insinuation that Denninger sensed in the raspy voice gave him a distinctly creepy feeling. "What is the message?"

Denninger repeated what he had said earlier, and added, "Tell him to keep a close watch on the present I gave him. It's very important. Also tell him ... that I'll see him when I get back."

"Oh honey, you should forget about him," said the voice. "He would just break your heart anyway."

Denninger fought the impulse to gag and thanked the raspy voice for "her" time. He was just replacing the receiver when Schlosser arrived with the water. Denninger took the glass gratefully and drained it in one gulp. Schlosser watched him with a bemused look and said, "There's a car waiting downstairs to take you to the airport. A bag has been packed for you and has been loaded aboard the aircraft. Anything else you need, just invoice the Bureau." He held out his hand. Denninger took it tentatively.

"Good luck," offered Schlosser, and then he added, "I'm sorry."

Denninger gave a half smile and walked slowly to the door. He put his hands in his coat pockets and oddly, felt reassured by the feel of the leather cover of the diary. As he headed down the long hallway to the front doors and the waiting car, he thought to himself, Six months. I guess I'll just have to wait six months."

6

July 16, 1944

SIX MONTHS, HE HAD been told.

That was in 1939.

Hitler then did what everyone expected him to do — he invaded Poland in September of that year and Denninger's heart sank. He knew he could not get back to Germany now. He would have to wait it out in Tibet.

It was truly mind-numbing to think how six months could turn into five years.

Five years.

Five years of measuring Tibetan heads, noses, ears, and eyes. Five years of looking for an Aryan Utopia and *not* looking for the Cathar treasure. Five years that he would never get back thanks to a war that Germany now had no hope of winning.

The worst part was getting the news soon after his arrival that Otto Rahn had died in the Tyrolean Mountains. Although Denninger had hardly known the man, he had been stunned nonetheless. In the few days that they had been together, he hadn't felt any particular closeness to the man, although there certainly was a bond of sorts there that he couldn't deny. Perhaps it was because they shared the same passion for the Cathars, or perhaps because Rahn had started him on his journey for the treasure. Whatever the reason, Denninger felt a loss.

The time in Tibet held only one saving grace. It gave the archeologist plenty of time to read and to try to understand the diary. Of one thing he was certain — all the answers he was looking for would be found in France. Everything pointed there. He remembered Rahn's reference to Carcassonne and Rennes-le-Château in his office that day. The Cathars and Montségur, and the Knights

Templar — everything indicated a French location. The question was precisely where.

At first the diary puzzled him, as the abbé did not go into any details about Bérenger Saunière's confession. But there were subtle hints. The more he read the diary, the more it seemed that Abbé Rivière was having a crisis of conscience. What could Saunière have told him?

The first part of the diary was fairly inconsequential, with stories about Rivière's parish and discussions he had had with Saunière, religious and otherwise. There was one humorous passage about Rivière trying to get the older abbé to quit smoking, a habit the older priest had picked up while in Paris. Apparently Saunière had trouble rolling the cigarettes himself and would try to get anyone else to do it for him, promising a place in heaven for whoever aided him. But the last ten pages or so were rambling, incoherent, and bordered on lunacy. One passage in particular kept coming back to him.

I am in hell and I know that is where Saunière is as well. All my life I have dedicated myself to God and the Word of God. As a child I was indoctrinated in the faith and I believed every word, every letter, every dot. When Christ was before Pilate, he said 'Everyone on the side of truth listens to me,' to which Pilate replies 'What is truth?' What is truth, indeed!

I cannot express the conflict that racks my soul. Has it all been for nothing? Again I say 'What is truth?'

Denninger pondered this passage for a long time. He soon acquired a Bible and reacquainted himself with the four Gospels and the Acts of the Apostles. He had studied them years ago when he first became interested in the Cathars. As time dragged on at the top of the world, he became quite knowledgeable in the Gospels, yet he still couldn't figure out what Rivière was alluding to.

What *is* truth, indeed?

—■—

As his six month hiatus stretched into five years of damnation, Denninger's will to continue his search for the Cathar treasure never diminished. In fact, it only became stronger. There were many times he thought of just jumping on a plane and continuing the search but the war and the possibility of being arrested by the SS kept him grounded in Tibet. He would have to bide his time.

However, by the time 1944 rolled around, he had had enough; enough of Beger and Schäfer and measuring heads and the quest for "the Northern Race."

The time to act, he finally decided, was now.

In June, the Allied assault at Normandy had ripped a hole in the German defenses and it would not be long before the mighty Wehrmacht would fold like a tent in the wind. Just over a month following the invasion, Ernst Schäfer assembled everyone together outside the mess tent.

"I will make this brief," he began. "The Allies are beginning to make inroads into France, but I have been assured by Berlin that this is only temporary."

Denninger smirked. He knew the beginning of a propaganda speech when he heard one. The only question was, when he could slip away without being noticed by Schäfer and Beger. As Schäfer droned on, Denninger looked at his watch, and started to take baby steps backwards, hoping to meld into the crowd. Suddenly, something Schäfer said caught his attention.

"... so we are wrapping up our studies here. Unfortunately, we will not be able to return to Berlin just yet ..." Noticing Denninger backing up through the crowd, his voice became louder. "Can you hear me, Dr. Denninger?"

Denninger looked at Schäfer and waved. "Asshole," he muttered.

Schäfer turned back to the crowd and continued, "Everyone must be ready to move out within a fortnight. Any questions?"

The man next to Denninger raised his hand. "Where will we be going, Dr. Schäfer?"

"We will be relocating to Waischenfeld in Franconia until further notice; however the plan is to return here as soon as possible. Our work is not yet over but we will finish it, I assure you."

A small cheer went up as thoughts began racing through Denninger's head. Franconia. At last they were going back to Germany. Getting to Berlin would be tough, but he would have to try.

And there was still another problem. He had no idea where Bobby and the document were. Even if he managed to get to Berlin, finding them would be like finding the proverbial needle in the haystack.

And still, even if he did manage to get to Berlin, and even if he did find Bobby and the document, getting to France in the middle of an Allied invasion during a war seemed to be a near impossibility.

7

THE TWO WEEKS SPED by like molasses in January. Outwardly, Denninger exuded a sense of calm but inside he was a churning mass of nerves. He felt like a ten-year-old child waiting for Christmas Day when still only mid-July.

He was in his tent packing away his things when there was a noise at the door. Looking up, he saw the bulky form of Bruno Beger in the doorway. Beger had a sideways grin that most women thought adorable and most men thought dashing, but not Denninger. It always looked to the archeologist like Beger had something nasty on whomever he was speaking to, which Denninger found nauseating.

Beger stood in the doorway for a few moments, his arms crossed and one leg crossed lazily over the other. “Well,” he said, “packing up, are we?”

Denninger kept folding his clothes without looking up. “Very observant, Bruno. The Bureau is lucky to have a man with impeccable vision. It’s a pity you can’t see how idiotic you are.”

Beger let the jab go and continued to smile. “Five years, eh?” he murmured. “I can’t believe we made it through five years together, Gerhard. It is a testimony to our professionalism, don’t you think?”

Denninger choked. He looked up at Beger with obvious distaste. “Define professionalism, Beger. I would be curious to hear your interpretation of that term. I would find it highly fascinating, as I am an avid fan of science fiction.”

Beger leaned away from his perch and slowly walked into the hut. He was tall, with the palest of blue eyes which appeared almost white, and slicked, jet-black hair. A fitness nut, he was well built, emanating confidence in his swagger, and Denninger had no doubt that if Beger wanted to, he could snap the archeologist in half. As Beger got closer, Denninger started to feel a little uneasy.

"I get the distinct impression that you don't like me very much, Gerhard." He leaned in until his face was about two inches from Denninger's. Denninger could smell the onions from Beger's lunch and it made him queasy. "Have I done anything to offend you, Doctor?" he breathed in an insinuating tone.

Denninger stood up quickly, dropping the shirt he was packing onto the floor. "Yes," he said, his voice rising, "You have offended me. You and Schäfer, and every other nutcase that believes in this Aryan race nonsense. You call yourselves men of science! How dare you!" Denninger picked up another item of clothing and threw it against the wall in frustration. "You and your kind. Your arrogance sickens me. It's no wonder we are losing the war."

Beger stopped smiling and brought himself up to his full height. His eyes narrowed to slits and he clenched one hand into a fist. "For someone who is on thin ice here, I would watch what I say if I were you. Treason is punishable by death, you know," he warned.

"Treason?" Denninger's voice was becoming hoarse. "You make me laugh. How long do you think it will be before the Allies land on Hitler's doorstep? Soon there will be no Germany to speak of, much less to be treasonous of."

Beger's hand suddenly shot out towards Denninger in a vicious arc. He grabbed the front of his shirt, ripping both buttons and cloth in a single swipe. Denninger felt himself lifted off the floor until he was nose to nose with the larger man.

"You want to know something, you piece of shit?" he muttered through clenched teeth, the last word spraying spittle on to Denninger's cheek. "This is going to feel so good. I've wanted to do this for a long time." He flung the older man with tremendous force against the wall of the tent, tearing a wide hole in the fabric. Denninger gasped as he slipped backwards through the opening and found that he couldn't move his legs because Beger had grabbed his ankles and was pulling him back inside.

"Are you crazy?" cried Denninger.

The commotion turned a couple of heads in their general direction. One of the researchers looked at another and smiled. "I was wondering when this was going to happen," he laughed as they hurried over to the tent, just in time to prevent Beger from pummeling Denninger into the dirt. It took three of them to pull the bigger man off of the older one, with one of the rescuers taking an errant fist to the eye in the process. Denninger, his hands covering his face, was gasping for air as he was hauled up to his feet. Beger lunged again at the archeologist, but this time he was well restrained. Denninger started to regain his regular breathing rhythm and rubbed his neck and chest where Beger had grabbed him.

"The man is a lunatic!" Denninger rasped, his mouth frothing like a mad dog's. "He should be locked up!"

A voice from right behind Denninger startled him. "Who should be locked up, Dr. Denninger?"

Denninger turned to see Ernst Schäfer in the doorway. Denninger blinked a couple of times trying to get the dust out of his eyes. "Your gorilla. Beger attacked me. He's insane."

Schäfer looked from Denninger to Beger. "Is this true, Bruno?"

Beger never took his eyes off of Denninger. "He's damned lucky I didn't kill him," he seethed. Schäfer said nothing for a moment, then told Beger and the others to step outside.

Once they were removed from the hut Schäfer told Denninger to sit down. Schäfer moved slowly around the tent, looking absently at the various things around the room. "Would you like to tell me what that was all about?" he finally asked.

Denninger shook his head. "Not really. It was a private matter."

"There are no secrets on my team, Dr. Denninger. It would be in your best interest to tell me."

Denninger stared back at Schäfer. He took a deep breath and said, "Or else what, Ernst? Are you going to have me arrested? It's really just a disagreement between me and that idiot. That's all."

Schäfer pulled lightly on his bottom lip before he reached into his breast pocket and fished out a cigarette. He knew Denninger didn't smoke, so he made sure that when he lit the cigarette, he blew the first puff of smoke in his direction. Denninger closed his eyes and swallowed the cough that tickled at his lips.

"Ah, Gerhard," he began, "What am I to do with you? I am well aware of your feelings regarding our work here, not to mention how you feel about Bruno and me. I have overlooked your shitty attitude for the past couple of years because I felt you could be a valuable member of the team." He took another drag off the cigarette. "Perhaps I have been wrong about you after all."

Denninger puffed out his chest slightly. "Just what are you saying, Ernst?" Schäfer was now leaning in the doorway again with the sun behind him, casting his whole body into shadow. Denninger moved his head, trying to get a better look at Schäfer's face. All he could discern was more smoke heading in his direction.

"Could you please stop blowing smoke at me?" asked Denninger. "It's very rude you know."

Schäfer turned around so that he could feel the sunshine on his face. He dropped the cigarette to the ground and asked "Are you packed yet?"

Denninger looked around at his clothes strewn about everywhere. "Almost," he said sarcastically as he knelt down to pick up a dirt-covered shirt. Schäfer then said, "You had better hurry—your plane will be here shortly."

Denninger looked confused. "What do you mean?" he asked suspiciously.

Schäfer continued, "You are leaving within the hour for Berlin. There will be a brief fuel stop, and then on to the naval base in Bremerhaven. From there you will board a U-boat that will take you to Brazil."

Denninger stopped packing and stood up quickly. "Brazil?" he exclaimed in horrified surprise. "I thought we were going back to Germany."

Schäfer nodded. "Yes," he said. "*We* are returning to Germany. *You* are not. Your presence has been requested in Brazil by Konrad Brucher," he said rather lackadaisically. "Apparently he's on the trail of a crystal skull ... or something...in some jungle somewhere. I am sure you will enjoy it."

It was obvious to Denninger what was going on. They were going to bury him. He would be sent away to the jungles of Brazil until God knew when, until the war was over or maybe longer. But why?

Denninger slowly began to pick up his clothes and drop them into his pack. Just then a thought occurred to him. He sat down on the edge of his bunk, and slowly the thought became an idea.

A good idea.

8

Denninger was packed in less than fifteen minutes. He made his way to the air field's hangar to wait for the Junkers 290 aircraft to take him to Berlin. He felt that his only chance would be to escape when the airplane landed to refuel. He would look up Bobby and get the scroll back from him, and if he accomplished that seemingly impossible feat, he would then have to make his way to the south of France. That was the idea, anyway.

As he approached the hangar, Denninger smiled. He caught a glimpse of just the man he had been hoping to see slouching behind the desk. It was Felix Metzger. He was reading a book and seemed to be having trouble concentrating as was evidenced by his ceaselessly nodding head. Denninger had seen Metzger the night before and it was quite clear that the man had been blotto. Denninger had known the effect would be a massive hangover in the morning. As he got closer he noticed what the lieutenant was reading.

"How do you like it?" Denninger asked innocently. Felix peered over his copy of Adolf Hitler's *Mein Kampf* to gaze through bloodshot eyes at the doctor. Putting the book down, he looked around, making sure no one else was in the hangar. In a sleepy, drawn-out voice he said, "Do we really have to read this shit?" He yawned.

Denninger grinned. "Late night last night, Felix?"

Felix took a moment to answer. "Oh, God, yes," he muttered. "There was a bit of a soirée, you could say. My head is pounding and this ... " he said, holding up the book, " ... isn't helping." He leaned over and dropped the volume onto the desk with a soft plop.

Denninger could see that Metzger was sweating, despite the cool temperature in the hangar. "You don't look so good, Felix," offered Denninger. Metzger rolled his eyes upwards and nodded. "I've already thrown up twice. I want to puke again but there's nothing left in my stomach." He leaned in close to Denninger. "Hey, Doctor," he whispered, his breath reeking of vomit, "do you have anything in your little black bag there that could ... you know, take the edge off?"

As Metzger was speaking, Denninger noticed a file on his desk with his own name on it. Interesting, he thought. He backed off a bit then walked over to his pack. He rummaged around for a minute until he found the pill bottle he was looking for. He knocked two small capsules into his hand and then filled a cup full of water from a nearby jug. "Here," he said, handing the pills to Metzger with the water. "These should help your head."

Gratefully, Metzger took the pills and swallowed them like a starving man, downing the water in a single gulp. "Thank you, Doctor. I can't tell you how much I appreciate this." He slumped down in his chair and belched quietly into his hand. Denninger smiled and headed back to his chair to wait for his flight.

Metzger rubbed his temples and then looked at Denninger quizzically. "Hey, Doctor — what are you doing here anyway?"

Denninger shrugged. "I'm being sent to Brazil, apparently. It seems my services are not needed here anymore."

Metzger whistled. "Brazil? What's in Brazil?"

"A crystal skull ... or something like that."

Metzger tried to open his eyes wider, but his eyelids felt very heavy. He yawned again. "Boy," he said, stretching. "I'm so stired ... ha! Sorry ... I mean *tired*." Another yawn. He stretched out his arms and legs, making a protracted grunting noise that seemed to pitch upward the longer he stretched. When he was finished, he turned his head slowly to Denninger.

"Hey, Doctor," he started to say but he found his lips numb and barely moving. "Whab dib you gib — ?" He stopped in mid sentence, his eyes rolling back in their sockets. His head slowly fell forward and his mouth hung open like that of a sea bass. Denninger waited a few minutes until he was sure Metzger was asleep. Upon hearing the heavy breathing associated with deep somnolence, he softly padded over to the desk. He examined Metzger and was satisfied that the Veronal had done the trick.

"Sleep tight, Felix," he smiled as he snatched the file from off the desk and began to leaf through it. There were no real surprises inside. There was the usual data, work reports, his biography and work evaluations. He saw the order for his transfer to Brazil but as he lifted the order out of the file, a loose page fell to the floor. As he bent over to pick it up, something caught his eye. Near the bottom of the page, he noticed that someone had written something in a sloppy scrawl, but then had scratched it out. Raising the sheet, he saw that there was a piece of carbon paper affixed to it. Gently lifting the carbon paper, he saw that whoever had scratched out the information hadn't had the carbon lined up properly. A portion of it was still legible. Faint, but legible. Denninger tried to make it out. It looked to him like *nzHof.* In spite of the cryptic nature of the letters, something stirred in the back of his memory.

As he was trying to make sense of them, he looked up in time to see Schäfer making his way to the hangar. No doubt to see me off, thought Denninger sarcastically. He quickly closed the file and bounded around the desk back to his chair.

Schäfer strode in and gave a curt nod to Denninger. He slowed his pace when he noticed Metzger, flopped in his chair quietly napping. Schäfer stared at the sleeping lieutenant and then slowly turned his head in Denninger's direction. Denninger shrugged. "Apparently, Felix had a busy night," he said.

Schäfer turned his attention back to Metzger. "No doubt," he muttered. He then lifted his fist high into the air and slammed it as hard as he could down on the desk. Denninger jumped at the noise but Metzger only stirred slightly and continued to snooze. Schäfer gritted his teeth and, swearing under his breath, he wheeled around the desk and delivered a kick to Metzger, knocking him out of the chair. The unconscious Metzger fell sideways, landing on the side of his face and shoulder, his buttocks raised in the air, making a perfect three-point pyramid.

"Is this man drunk?" Schäfer demanded.

Denninger sauntered over and knelt down beside Metzger. He leaned in for a few moments and then looked up at Schäfer. "I don't think so. Maybe he is a narcoleptic."

Schäfer grunted and grabbed Denninger's file from off the desk. He took one more disgusted look at Metzger and thought about kicking him again. Instead, he shot Denninger one last withering grimace and quickly left the hangar.

When Denninger decided that Schäfer was far enough away, he reached inside his jacket. He pulled out the crumpled piece of paper with the mysterious carbon-copied letters. Sitting down in the chair again, he racked his brain, trying to decipher what the letters meant.

In the distance, Denninger could hear the engines of the Junkers growing steadily louder. He folded the paper and quickly shoved it back into his pocket. Bending over, he picked up his pack, and slowly walked out of the hangar towards the area where the large aircraft was going to land.

The massive, four-engined Junkers landed with a couple of hops and slowed almost immediately as the brakes were applied. It lumbered toward the end of the runway and then began a slow 180-degree turn to taxi up to the hangar.

Denninger looked behind him and marveled at the fact that even with the high-decibel scream of the Junkers' massive motors, Metzger remained blissfully unaware of the commotion and continued his oblivious dozing.

A hatch opened in the rear of the Junkers, providing entry into the aircraft, and Denninger climbed the stairway and took one of the available seats. He noticed with mild surprise that, along with the two pilots, he was the only one on board. He placed his pack on the seat beside him, strapped himself in, and began the wait for takeoff. After a few minutes, the engines revved up once more and the airplane began to taxi down the runway.

Once airborne, Denninger closed his eyes, took a deep breath, laid his head back against the top of the seat and before he knew it, he had fallen into a deep sleep.

After what seemed to be only moments, but was in reality a number of hours, Denninger awoke. He stretched and yawned. He checked his watch and was surprised at how much time had passed. I must have been more tired than I thought, he said to himself. They must have refuelled while I was asleep.

The nap had done him good. After rubbing his eyes, he reached into his jacket and once again extracted the paper which he had found at the hangar. He looked at the letters.

Those letters.

The letters were so familiar.

As he tried to piece them together, memories of the past few years came flooding back. Out of nowhere he thought of Rahn. He then thought of Bobby, how he had given Denninger the document when …

He sat up quickly. "Of *course*," he said, banging the heel of his hand against his head.

Bobby.

Denninger suddenly knew what the letters were. He looked down at the scribble on the paper.

nzHof.

Hei*nz Hof*ner. Bobby's real name.

It was Bobby's name on the paper.

But why? Had they somehow linked Rahn to Bobby and then to himself? Something then dawned on him. If they interrogated Bobby, it's possible that he could have told them about the parchment. Could they now have it? Was this why he was being sent to Brazil? To get rid of him?

He started to get a very bad feeling.

As his worrying began to take a firm hold in his brain, he failed to notice a higher-pitched engine whine somewhere in the distance. The Junkers suddenly banked to the left, abruptly throwing Denninger to his side, causing his open pack to hit the floor. He watched with alarm as the diary fell out and slid away from him towards the cockpit. The whine got louder and as the aircraft began to bank to the right, a line of machine-gun bullets ripped through the fuselage, one bullet barely missing Denninger's head. The Junkers was climbing fast, trying to outmaneuver whatever was firing at it. Leaning to the right, he managed to catch a glimpse through the window as two British Spitfires shot past, tearing up a good portion of the right wing, and causing one of the engines to explode into flames.

"This can't be happening!" he yelled in a panicky voice.

Denninger unbuckled his seatbelt and was attempting to get out of his seat when the Junkers shook violently, knocking him to the floor. As he lay there, he looked up and spied the diary just under a seat a few feet away. He tried to get up, but the Junkers suddenly banked left and upward, sending the archeologist backwards towards the rear of the plane. Denninger landed hard on his tailbone, the wind being knocked out of him as the diary came whizzing down the aisle towards his feet. Another burst of gunfire from outside the aircraft was followed by a muffled boom signaling the defeat of another engine.

We are going down, he thought as his stomach lurched violently.

As the plane leveled out somewhat, he was able to reach the diary, and scrambled to get his pack and the various items that had spilled out of it. The aircraft suddenly pitched and Denninger found himself, for a brief moment, airborne. The airplane tilted forward slightly and Denninger crashed to the floor only to begin the inexorable decline towards the cockpit again. This time, however, he knew he wouldn't stop until he hit the door.

The inside of the aircraft began to fill with noxious fumes and smoke, temporarily blinding Denninger. He grasped for the cockpit's door handle, flailing helplessly through the acrid smoke until he managed to snag it. The door flew open and he tumbled forward, landing at the feet of one of the pilots who was quite obviously dead, the side of his head a tangled mass of bone and flesh, torn apart by the deadly bullets from one of the Spitfires. The remaining pilot had his hands full, trying to level out the downward spiral of the Junkers, with the wind ripping through the shattered window slapping both of their faces with fury.

"Is there anything I can do?" yelled Denninger above the sound of the wind and the engines. The pilot shot Denninger a sideways look and through clenched teeth asked him if he was a praying man.

In an attempt to keep out of his eyes the wind that was ripping through the broken window, Denninger held his hands in front of his face. Once the wind had been blocked, he was able to see through his squinting eyes the rapidly approaching ground. His stomach began to flip-flop once again.

"Hold on," barked the pilot. He yanked the controls back with terrific force, causing the aircraft to shudder violently. The plane suddenly pulled out of the deadly dive and Denninger felt his whole body vibrating as he clutched the back of the dead pilot's seat in an effort to anchor himself. It felt as though his teeth were about to crumble apart in his mouth. The Junkers' motors screamed as the plane began to skim across the tops of the trees at about two hundred and eighty miles an hour, grinding limbs and leaves into a pulpy mulch. Denninger let go of the seat and managed to pull himself through the cockpit door and slowly began to inch his way to the rear of the plane. If we're going to crash, he thought, I don't want to be in the cockpit. He buckled himself into his original seat and holding his pack against his face and chest, he waited for the inevitable as the roar of the doomed plane filled his ears.

9

SILENCE.

The first thing Denninger was aware of was the silence. The eerie quiet was both serene and unsettling at the same time. The first thought that crossed his mind was that he was dead. But if he were dead, why was he thinking about being dead?

He slowly opened his eyes and looked around. He tried to move but found he couldn't. He was still buckled into his seat, and was squeezed up against his pack and the seat ahead of him. He started to wiggle back-and-forth in an effort to dislodge the pack so that he could liberate himself from his seat. After a minute the pack became loose enough for him to have it drop to the floor. As it fell, he let out a huge grunt. Because he was able to unbuckle his seatbelt, he realized that his arms weren't broken. Breathing a sigh of relief, he set about carefully moving his legs to see if they were injured. They felt stiff and achy but at least they moved. Feeling exactly like a man who had just gone through an airplane crash, Denninger reached down to pick up his pack and then pulled himself up out of the seat. He half-walked, half-dragged himself towards the cockpit, in the faint hope that the remaining pilot had somehow made it.

He hadn't. A large tree branch had broken through the windshield and imbedded itself into his upper chest and neck area. A sickened Denninger could see the pilot's head was hanging precipitously to the left, the tendons and skin the only things keeping it from hitting the floor of the cockpit. Denninger turned away from the carnage and attempted to open the side door that had become wedged shut from the crash. With each push, sharp needles of pain zipped up and down his arm. Wincing, he continued to throw his weight into the door until finally it opened slightly.

One more push, he thought. Stepping a few feet back, he took a deep breath and launched himself into the door. He caught it full force, making it pop open with a metallic screech and causing him to tumble out, somersaulting over the bumpy ground like a convulsive acrobat. He rolled to a stop and sprawled out for a few moments, waiting for his eyes to focus. When they didn't, he realized with mounting horror that he had lost his glasses. Panicked, he threw his hands up to his face. Without his glasses, he was practically blind, and being in the middle of nowhere, surrounded by plane wreckage and all alone left Denninger with a sick, sinking feeling. Afraid of breaking his only hope of seeing clearly, he got down on all fours and began to lightly pat the ground with the tips of his fingers, almost as if the soil was too hot to touch. After a few minutes of hunting and cursing, he collapsed in a heap by a piece of the wing.

In spite of the fact that he couldn't see, Denninger knew he would have to somehow make it to Berlin. But which way to go? Narrowing his eyes and cupping his hands over his eyebrows, he thought he could discern what looked like a path. Throwing his pack over his shoulder, he started out on what was probably going to be a fairly long trek, since he had no idea where to find the nearest town.

He had been walking for about an hour when he finally came to what looked to be, to his unfocused eyes, an actual road. Somewhere off in the distance, the sound of a motor steadily grew louder. He squinted in a vain attempt to see who or what was coming his way. A few minutes later, a patrol in a *Kübelwagen* pulled up alongside of him. It slowed to a stop and one of the soldiers got out and went over to Denninger. The soldier took a moment to take in the disheveled appearance of the archeologist and then exchanged a questioning look with the driver. Turning back to Denninger, he asked to see his papers. Denninger squinted once more and then reached into his jacket and handed him his papers.

The soldier perused them for a few seconds and then gave them back. "May I inquire as to what you are doing way out here, in the middle of nowhere Dr. Denninger?" he asked. Denninger blinked a few times and said, "Yes, well ... I, uh, was visiting my nephew near Strausberg and I was on a hike when I uh, lost my footing and fell, as you can tell from my ... disorderly appearance. In the process I seemed to have lost my glasses and I'm having a devil of a time finding my way. If you could possibly give me a lift into Berlin, I could retrieve my spare set of specs from my apartment, I mean if it is not too much trouble Herr ... ?"

"Corporal Schmidt," finished the soldier as he looked at his watch. "We may have a little time to help you out," he said. He went around to the other side of the vehicle and opened the door. Denninger waited for a few seconds to see if the corporal was going to help him into the vehicle. Sensing that he wasn't, Denninger reached out, helplessly groping for the side of the bucket-shaped jeep. He managed to find the back of the vehicle and followed the contour until he reached the open door. Corporal Schmidt stood by impassively until Denninger had wedged himself into the back, grunting as he settled in. Schmidt then got into the front and shut the door with a slam as they started off.

They drove in comparative quiet, the silence stabbed by the occasional oath from the driver, who couldn't get the two-way radio to work. "Goddamn cheap shit," he muttered. Schmidt made a face and looked out the window as they drove towards the city.

They arrived at Denninger's apartment within twenty minutes. Corporal Schmidt opened the door and helped the doctor out of the back of the vehicle. Denninger squinted at the façade of the building and could just make out the damage inflicted upon it by the nightly RAF bombings.

He entered the building with the two soldiers and they slowly made their way up the stairs to his apartment. At the landing on the second floor, Denninger heard a familiar voice from the past.

"Doctor Denninger? I thought you were dead," said the voice.

It was Mr. Gottfried, the superintendent.

"Hello, Herr Gottfried," he said, putting out his hand vaguely in the direction of the voice. "How have you been?"

"It could be worse, I suppose. The building is still standing. Goddamn RAF." He snorted and finally took the outstretched hand. "You're not here about your apartment, are you? It's rented."

Denninger had known that it would be. There was no way that his old apartment would remain vacant for five years. "Of course. Is there any chance, however, that you kept my things? I know it's been a long time, but — "

Gottfried cut in. "Did you think I would throw out someone's personal property?" he said indignantly. "What kind of insensitive clod do you think I am? There's a box of your things in the cellar."

Corporal Schmidt stepped forward. "If everything is fine here, we must get back to our patrol." Schmidt cocked his head towards the other soldier and said "Let's go." Denninger waited until he heard their boots on the stairs and then let out a low breath. "Herr Gottfried, could you help me? I need to find my spare glasses." Gottfried grunted. Denninger put his hand on the superintendent's shoulder and followed him down to the cellar.

Once there, Gottfried began to haphazardly toss boxes around, trying to find Denninger's things. He narrowly missed the half-blind doctor, who held his watch inches from his face in an attempt to see what time it was.

"Excuse me, Herr Gottfried, but do you have the time?"

Gottfried paused to look at his watch. "It's ... eleven fifteen."

Eleven fifteen. The office, if things still ran the same way as they had before he left, would break for lunch in about an hour. If he could get to the Bureau while everyone was out ...

"Have you found my possessions yet?" he inquired, squinting in the superintendent's direction. Gottfried grunted again. After a few minutes, Gottfried pulled out a large, faded-looking box and declared, "Here it is." Denninger leaned in close so that he could try to get a better look. Gottfried opened the top and pushed it over to Denninger. The doctor had reached in and began to rummage around when abruptly he yanked his hand out in pain and stuck his finger in his mouth. Detecting a coppery taste, he knew at once that he was bleeding.

"*Verdammt!*" he exclaimed as he licked his finger. Gottfried gave Denninger an odd look and then peered into the box himself. Removing books, papers and clothing, he soon found what had stabbed the doctor. Slowly he pulled out the remnants of an umbrella.

Bobby's umbrella.

Even with his weak sight, Denninger recognized it. Gottfried stood up and said, "Piece of junk. I'll throw it out."

Denninger leaped up and shouted, "No!"

Gottfried looked at him with surprise. "What is it?"

Denninger quickly affected a calm expression as he shook his throbbing finger. "I am sorry, Herr Gottfried. Please, may I have that? It's the only thing I have left from my friend. He died a few years ago and I thought I had lost it for good. I am very thrilled that I have it still."

Gottfried shrugged. "What do I care? A broken umbrella? Here. You'd better hope it doesn't rain." He handed the rattling remains of the umbrella to Denninger who, carefully taking it, surreptitiously ran his hand over the handle until he came across the opening. He put his finger inside it, but to his horror, he couldn't feel the document. His elation at finding the umbrella quickly dissipated. Gottfried reached into the box and pulled out a small spectacle case.

"Is this what you were looking for?" he said, handing the case to Denninger.

"Thank you," he said quietly.

The doctor took the case and opened it, extracting the spare pair of specs. He put them on and looked at the umbrella. So close, he thought sadly.

Gottfried stood up and stretched. "If you have everything you need, then I must get back to work. You can leave your things here until you find someplace else to live, I suppose." He turned and headed for the stairs.

Denninger remained sitting on the floor examining the umbrella. As he moved it around, the light from the dim bulb above his head seemed to reveal something inside the handle. Denninger optimistically placed his middle finger inside. The tip of his finger brushed across what felt like paper. His heart skipped a beat. He stuck his finger in further, but he couldn't get a good grip on the paper. "Come on," he said through clenched teeth. He pulled out his finger, licked it and then stuck it back inside. This time, the moisture allowed the paper to adhere to his finger. Gently he pulled it out. As it came free, Denninger saw that it wasn't the document at all, but a folded slip of yellow paper. Denninger unfolded it and read what was written on it.

A.B. 719

What did *that* mean?

While he pondered the meaning of the cryptic message, he became aware of a rattle inside the umbrella handle as he moved it around. He gave it a little shake and the rattle became more pronounced. Something was loose inside the handle. Denninger, turning it over, shook it a little more forcefully. A small key slid out and bounced lightly across the floor. He went over to where it had fallen and picked it up. It looked as if it would open a small box of some sort. He turned it over in his hands, but there were no markings on it to give a clue as to what it was used for. Denninger looked at the paper again.

"A.B. 719." It was obvious that they were connected.

Denninger put the paper and key into his pocket. He made another quick search through the box to see if there was anything else he would need. Finding nothing else of use, he stood up and headed for the stairs.

Once outside the building, he turned to his right and headed towards the Bureau office. If he timed it right, it should be just about empty for lunch.

At least, he hoped it would be.

10

DENNINGER SLOWED HIS APPROACH as he got closer to the office. His eyes darted up one side of the street and down the other. It looked safe enough. He took a deep breath, mounted the steps of the building and went through the door with no small amount of trepidation. He saw a few people in the hall and didn't recognize any of the faces, but then again, probably a lot had changed over the last five years. He headed down the hall with his head down, and made his way towards his office.

"Excuse me."

The voice was clearly aimed at Denninger. He stopped and turned around to see someone dressed in what looked like a security uniform. Denninger put on his best disarming smile. "Yes?"

The security guard sauntered over to Denninger. He was young, probably about twenty, with slicked-back blond hair and blue eyes. One of the master race, thought Denninger. And he was so young. With the war going the way it was, it seemed the Fatherland was pressing children into service now.

The guard, trying to affect an air of authority, looked at Denninger warily. To Denninger, however, he just looked petulant. The young man held out his hand. "This is a secure building for authorized personnel," he said in a bored voice. "I assume you have your papers?"

Denninger looked at the guard with an irritated look and reached into his jacket. "Of course." He handed the papers to the guard who scanned them hastily.

"Dr. Gerhard Denninger, eh? Never heard of you," he huffed as he handed them back to Denninger. The guard gave a modest nod and continued his little patrol down the hallway. Denninger stuffed the papers back inside his jacket and headed towards his office.

He should have known. When he arrived at what had been his office, he saw that his name had been removed and replaced with that of a Dr. Albrecht Neumann. Apparently, they had decided that Denninger was not going to be returning and had given his office to someone else.

That's just wonderful, he thought. He knocked lightly on the door and receiving no response, tried the doorknob. It was unlocked. He slowly pushed the door open and peered around. The first thing that caught his eye was that his broken picture of Himmler had been replaced with an identical one. Denninger reflected that the monkey picture would have been infinitely more amusing.

It seemed to Denninger that Neumann was probably out for lunch so Denninger took the opportunity to make a search of the office, but after a few minutes it became apparent that there was nothing of his own remaining in the room. He hadn't really expected to find anything anyway. He slipped back out into the hall and turned towards Karl Schlosser's office. Everything that he would need would be found there. His only hope was that Schlosser would be out as well. Denninger then wondered if Schlosser knew what was going on. Undoubtedly, he would know about the flight, and it would only be a matter of time for him to figure out that there had been a crash and that he had escaped.

The door to Schlosser's office was slightly ajar when he arrived. That's odd, he thought. Schlosser's door was always closed whether he was in his office or not. It was as if he had left in a hurry. Denninger looked furtively up and down the hallway but couldn't see anyone so he decided to go inside.

—■—

On the third floor, Karl Schlosser had just entered Armin Reiter's office. Reiter was Schlosser's immediate superior, and had summoned Schlosser to discuss the information he had just received. When Schlosser sat down Reiter handed him a communiqué. "Read this," he said. Schlosser scanned the paper and then looked at Reiter. The communiqué was from Ernst Schäfer, stating that Denninger was on the aircraft and en route to Berlin. Schlosser handed it back to Reiter.

"When is he due to arrive?" he asked, taking a seat. Reiter looked at his watch.

"Soon." He rubbed his forehead wearily. "We really missed the boat on this one, you know." Schlosser nodded slightly as Reiter continued.

"Goddamned Rahn. He really played us for fools. All this time he had us searching in Spain for nothing. He was a very clever man. He left just enough clues for us to fall for it. I must say it really was genius using Himmler's interest in the Cathar treasure."

"What gave it away?"

"You mean other than five years of empty excavations in the wrong country?" he chuckled mirthlessly. "We actually caught a break a few weeks ago. The Gestapo were in one of their regular crackdown modes and raided an establishment where known degenerates hang out. One of those arrested was a man by the name of Heinz Hofner."

"Who is this Hofner?" asked Schlosser

"A nobody, really. Just one of those jazz kids. You know the type. Loud suits, ugly umbrellas, big hats, smart mouths. He likes to call himself Bobby. As luck would have it he was in a cell with someone the Gestapo regularly pays for information, when the little shit started mouthing off. He mentioned Otto Rahn's name. Our informant didn't know who Rahn was, but when the

Gestapo pumped him afterward, he repeated the name. That's when we were called in."

Schlosser nodded again. "How did Denninger's name come up?"

Reiter smiled. "You know the Gestapo — they really have a knack for persuasion. And eventually Hofner did talk. While we did know that he and Rahn were together a few nights before Rahn's disappearance, it was always assumed that Rahn was a lone wolf, so to speak. And when Denninger was interrogated by the Gestapo earlier, nothing about Rahn came up so we had no reason to tie the two of them together."

"So what do you think?"

Reiter shook his head and looked at his watch. "I won't know what to think until Denninger gets here. But I'll tell you this — he *will* talk."

Denninger figured that he only had a minute or two before Schlosser got back. He hurried over to the large oak desk and opened the top left-hand drawer. He patted his hand along the bottom until he heard a telltale rattle. Denninger smiled. He removed the false covering and felt around until he found the key that he knew had to be there.

"Aha!"

Taking the key, he headed over to the filing cabinet and opened the second drawer. Quickly, he thumbed through the files until he found a large black binder entitled "Enigma Codes."

He was going to need an Enigma code. Each vessel in the German navy was equipped with an Enigma code machine, an extremely complex device that had proved to be nearly impossible for the Allies to crack. It worked by letter substitution through a number of wheels and rotors that never encoded a message the same way twice. To decode a message, you had to have the correct key from a key sheet. Enigma operators were issued a key sheet every month, and the keys themselves were changed daily by the operators. Denninger was not only going to need a code key, but a specific code key. He flipped through the pages until he found what he was looking for. Carefully he removed the page. It was a sturdy piece of paper that certainly looked and felt resilient. Smiling, he placed it on the desk and opened another drawer and removed a few pieces of Ahnenerbe letterhead. He picked up the papers and stuffed the sheets inside his coat. Patting his jacket down, he returned the binder to the cabinet and then took a cursory look around the office to make sure that everything was still in its place. Once again, the perfect crime, he thought to himself and headed for the door.

He took a peek out the doorway and seeing it empty, slipped into the hallway. He had just turned the corner when right behind him he heard his name being called out. "Gerhard!"

Denninger stopped cold.

"When did you get back?"

Slowly he turned to see Rupert Zumwald.

Not now, thought Denninger impatiently. He forced a smile and put out his hand. "Hello Rupert. How have you been?" Zumwald took Denninger's hand in his own fat, sweaty one. Denninger noticed that Zumwald hadn't changed much in five years, other than he looked like he had gotten fatter, if that was at all possible. Denninger wiped his hand on his jacket as Zumwald giggled.

"How was Tibet? Five years — my word, that's a lifetime!" he said.

"In truth, it was a colossal waste of time, Rupert. In fact, I have to see Schlosser to give him a report ..."

Zumwald giggled again and pointed. "You *have* been away for a long time. You just passed his office back there."

Denninger cleared his throat. "Oh, I know, I know," Denninger fired back. He had to think quickly. "I was just there, but he wasn't in. As a matter of fact, I was just trying to find him."

"Well then, come and wait in my office until he returns. We'll have some tea and get caught up," Zumwald enthused, his puffy eyes twinkling brightly. He put his arm around Denninger's shoulder and began to guide him down the hallway. Denninger half-heartedly smiled and inwardly cursed his bad luck.

In Zumwald's office, Denninger sat in the chair just opposite his desk, in spite of the fact that there was a massively overstuffed sofa against the west wall. Although it looked comfortable, he was put off by the multitude of stains, no doubt the result of Zumwald's gastronomic passions. Denninger noticed that Zumwald's desk was also covered in many stains that he could only assume were food related. His wastepaper basket was overflowing with garbage and the sweet odor of strudel carpeted the whole office like a sugary blanket. Zumwald took off his lab coat, flopped into his chair and giggled again. Denninger shuddered. He could not stand the way Zumwald giggled all the time. He was like a little girl being tickled by an overly friendly uncle. Denninger looked at his watch.

"The tea will be here momentarily," Zumwald said. "Do you still take it with honey?"

Denninger didn't respond. The Rheinmetall typewriter on the shelf just over Zumwald's shoulder had caught his eye. "Actually, with milk. Listen, Rupert, would you do me a favor? It's been a rough couple of days and I was wondering if you could get me something for a headache." Denninger rubbed his head and closed his eyes as if in pain.

"Oh I'm sorry to hear that, Gerhard, but I don't have anything here in my office. Do you remember, I don't use any kind of pharmaceutical medicines. I prefer herbal remedies."

Denninger nodded. "Oh, of course, that's right. I forgot." He began to rub his head harder. "It's really throbbing," he moaned.

Zumwald stood up. "Well, there's a chemist's shop about a block away. Would you like me to go and get you something? I hate to see you like this." He reached down and opened a drawer of his desk. "I have this preparation here made from willow bark that — "

Gerhard moaned even more loudly. Zumwald shut the drawer and hurried out, saying that he would be back in ten minutes. As soon as the large man shut the door, Denninger sprung out of the chair and grabbed the Rheinmetall from off the shelf. He pulled one of the sheets of letterhead out of his jacket, quickly loaded it into the typewriter and began to type. In a matter of minutes, he was finished. He ripped the paper from out of the machine and surveyed his work. Perfect, he thought. Now all he needed was Heinrich Himmler's signature.

Zumwald had just returned from the pharmacy when he spied Schlosser coming down the hallway. Zumwald waved excitedly at Schlosser who turned away, pretending that he didn't see him.

Not that giggling idiot, he thought. I have no time for this. He quickly started down the hallway in the other direction.

Zumwald ran after him. "Karl!" he called out. "Oh, Karl!"

Schlosser picked up the pace as Zumwald broke into a run. Schlosser turned the corner and tried to duck into a closet just as Zumwald came panting into view. Wheezing, he said, "I guess ... you didn't ... hear me ..." Schlosser rolled his eyes and said "Oh, hello Rupert. Were you calling me?" Zumwald was taking deep breaths and clutched at his shirt which had become quite damp. "Yes … I was … you'll never guess who … "

He blinked and then a strange look came over his face. The medicine in his right hand fell to the floor, the little pills rolling around like ball bearings. Schlosser had seen this look before when his father had had a heart attack. Zumwald started to gasp for air as he collapsed to the floor. Immediately, Schlosser called out for a doctor. Four heads peeked out of offices along the hallway.

"*Medical* doctors" corrected Schlosser as he tried to elevate Zumwald's feet. "I think he's having a heart attack here." Zumwald tried to speak, but Schlosser shushed him. "Take it easy, Rupert," he urged. "Save your strength."

But Zumwald still tried to speak. "De … De-in … ," he breathed painfully.

"That's enough, Rupert. There's a doctor coming."

Denninger heard the commotion and stuck his head out of Zumwald's office door. He could see Zumwald sprawled on the floor with Schlosser hovering over him. A small crowd had gathered to get a look at what was happening.

"All those professionals and no one knows what to do," he muttered bitterly. It was going to be nearly impossible to get away without someone seeing him. He looked at his watch again as a slight wave of panic started to set in.

Come on, he thought. Just move the man out of the damned hallway. I have a train to — "

All at once a thought struck him. Quickly, he fished the yellow piece of paper that he had found in the umbrella handle out of his pocket. He read it again.

A.B. 719. He pulled out the key and took a better look at it. It was a small, innocuous looking key, one that would maybe open …

Denninger smiled.

Would it open a locker, perhaps?

A.B.—*Anhalter Bahnhof*? The name of the train station was the Anhalter Bahnhof. A.B.719 must be a locker in the terminal. The scroll must be in locker 719 at the Anhalter Bahnhof train station.

Well, thought Denninger. That's just great. How the hell am I going to get out of here and down to the train station? Denninger stuck his head back inside and looked around the windowless room, in a vague, desperate hope that somehow an escape would present itself.

As his eyes fell on Zumwald's desk, Denninger straightaway broke out into a grin.

Escape had just presented itself.

11

Zumwald's breathing was becoming shallower, and it looked to Schlosser like he wasn't going to make it. "Has anyone called a doctor yet?" Schlosser shouted. He did his best to work crowd control as one of the secretaries ministered to the motionless man on the floor. Where the hell did all these people come from? he wondered. Surely to God they can't all work here?

"He needs air!" someone shouted.

"He *needs* a doctor!" responded Schlosser with annoyance.

"Yes, we know that."

Schlosser was beginning to lose his patience. "Would you all please go back to your offices? If a doctor has been sent for, everything will be fine! Please! Excuse me, Ma'am, could you please step back?" Schlosser was now physically pushing people out of the way. One extremely heavyset individual in a white lab coat, who made Zumwald look undernourished, was hopelessly trying to slide between the wall and the crowd in a desperate attempt to get out of the way.

For Christ's sakes, is this guy kidding? Schlosser thought incredulously as he watched the behemoth trying to wedge himself between the wall and an onlooker.

Finally reaching the end of his endurance, Schlosser went over and put his shoulder into the obese man giving him a shove. He was taken aback at just how puffy and soft his gargantuan belly was. "There's another heart attack ready to happen," he muttered with distaste.

Schlosser continued to pound the crowd into some semblance of submission. Suddenly there was a noise coming up from behind the mob.

"The doctor's here!"

Schlosser's crowd control went into overdrive. "Make way, make way. What's the matter with all of you? Let the doctor by! Go back to your goddamned offices, will you?"

The doctor managed to wend his way through the mob and knelt down beside Zumwald. After a few tense moments, the doctor ordered Schlosser and another man, Dietz Melman, to take the patient to someone's office.

"Zumwald's office!" shouted Schlosser. "Take him to his own office. He's got that big sofa!" Schlosser took hold of Zumwald's beefy legs and the other one took his arms. "On three, we lift. Ready?" Schlosser counted off and with an enormous grunt they lifted Zumwald's massive frame. Schlosser's face drained as he felt something pop in his back. Gasping, he immediately dropped his end, causing Zumwald's body to fall backward like a felled sequoia on top of the hapless Melman, whose breath shot out of his lungs like an airy geyser.

"Get ... him ... *off* ...," Dietz gasped.

Schlosser bellowed like a water buffalo stuck in a bog and writhed on the floor beside Melman, who was speedily turning blue as Zumwald made gassy noises. "Somebody should really do something," said a voice in the crowd.

The secretary who had been helping Zumwald while he was on the floor, had gone into his office to prepare the sofa. A moment later she stuck her head out of the doorway with a confused look. "Does anyone know where the sofa pillows are?"

Denninger squinted in the sunlight as he ducked around the building into the adjoining alley. As he removed Zumwald's lab coat, the sofa pillows that filled it out fell to the ground in a heap. Denninger kicked them away and then threw the coat on top of them. Straightening his jacket and smoothing his hair, he lifted his wrist to look at his watch.

"Time to catch a train," he said to himself.

He arrived at the Anhalter Bahnhof train station within twenty minutes. Although it had been badly damaged by Allied bombing raids, the station still managed to keep the trains running on time with customary German effiency. He paid for the cab and hurried inside to the ticket counter. "I would like a ticket to Bremerhaven, and could you tell me where I could find locker 719 please?" The ticket seller, a bored, pock-marked man in his thirties, pointed to the back of the station without looking up. Denninger paid for his ticket and then strode to the line of lockers in the back, nervously fingering the key in his now sweaty hand. The events of the last five years began to flash through his head with each step. He thought of Otto and Bobby, and the sacrifices they had made so that he could be where he was right now. He felt elated and terribly sad at the same time.

He then saw the locker.

It was an ordinary looking locker, just like all the other lockers around it. Some contained clothes, some personal effects, some were empty. And behind the door of locker 719 was what could be, for Dr. Gerhard Denninger, the culmination of his life's dream. The key in his hand suddenly felt very heavy. Drawing a deep breath, he slowly placed the small key into the lock and turned it until he heard a click. He closed his eyes and took another deep breath as he opened the locker door.

At first, he didn't see anything and his heart fell. Tentatively he put his hand inside the locker until his fingers brushed up against something cool and round.

His heart began to beat faster.

Slowly, he pulled the object towards the mouth of the locker until he could see what it was. The object turned out to be a tube, the kind that typically holds blueprints.

It was light, giving Denninger the impression that it might be empty. Gingerly he turned the lid and looked inside. Under the yellow train-station lights he saw what looked like a piece of parchment. He touched it lightly, almost timidly.

It *was* the parchment.

His eyes began to tear up as he swiftly put the lid back on the tube and checked his watch. He had ten minutes to catch his train.

He hurried along the platform looking for his car, carefully keeping an eye out for the Gestapo agents that routinely skulked about the station. Locating his car, he furtively boarded and searched for his seat. With the parchment safely tucked away in his pack and firmly held on his lap, Denninger was settling in for the trip to Bremerhaven when he heard a hoarse but familiar voice by his ear.

"Hello … Old Hot Boy." Denninger turned around to see Bobby sitting in the seat behind. The archeologist was shocked to see that Bobby's eye was bruised and his left cheek was swollen.

""Bobby … what are you doing here? What happened to your face?"

Bobby smiled his big horse grin and sluggishly shrugged his shoulders. "The Gestapo had a few questions for me," he said. Denninger got up out of his seat and sat down next to him. He took a closer look at his wounds. "You should probably see a doctor for those cuts, Bobby. They could get infected."

"Well, Doctor, you're looking at them right now, aren't you? That should be good enough."

"You shouldn't be so frivolous Bobby — "

Bobby gently cut him off in a quiet voice. "Really, I'm fine. Not to worry."

Denninger could tell that he was really hurt but understanding that he didn't wish to discuss it any further, he changed the subject. "What are you doing on this train, Bobby?"

Bobby took a deep and evidently painful breath. "I'm originally from Bremerhaven. I'm going to stay with my relatives. To convalesce." He winced. He opened one eye and looked at Denninger. "So ... might I ask you the same question?"

Denninger tapped his pack. "I have the scroll — but you knew I would find it, didn't you?" Bobby shrugged as Denninger continued. "I need to get to France, specifically the south of France. That's where I need to start looking. That is, once I figure out what's in the scroll, of course. And to get to France, I'll need to somehow get myself aboard a U-boat."

"Sounds like you have a full day planned," Bobby grinned. He winced again and held his ribs tightly as he coughed. Leaning over, he spit on the floor. Denninger noticed it was mostly blood.

"Bobby, your ribs are broken."

Bobby waved him off. "How will you get aboard the U-boat?"

Denninger's look of concern turned into a smile. "Look at this." He pulled out a sheet of paper. Bobby looked at it with interest and said "That's fantastic ... um, just what am I looking at, anyway?"

Denninger made a face and then told him it was an Enigma code key.

"What's it for?"

"Well, all U-boat operators use an Enigma coding machine to send messages back and forth. If they have to send an emergency message, the code key I'm providing them with is a year old. It won't work."

Bobby looked confused. "But … if you provide them with the wrong code, won't they know what you're up to?"

Denninger grinned. He reached into his jacket, pulled out another sheet and handed it to Bobby. Bobby took the sheet and quickly scanned it. He looked up at Denninger, impressed with the paper. "Signed by Himmler himself? Where did you get this?" he said handing it back to the doctor.

"I wrote it myself. I've seen Himmler's signature often enough that I could forge it in my sleep. This one says that we must run under radio silence — ergo, no messages. And if they do have to send one, this code won't work, so hopefully it will buy me enough time to get to my destination. Otto gave me that idea." Bobby chuckled.

Denninger went on. "The letter also says that my mission is top secret and that I have virtual carte blanche to do what ever I need to do to facilitate my mission. No one will go against Heinrich Himmler's orders."

Bobby started to laugh but then doubled over in pain. Denninger put his arm on Bobby's shoulder. "You *really* need to see a doctor, Bobby."

"Please, I'm fine. I just need some sleep, that's all." Bobby laid his head back against the seat and closed his eyes. Denninger watched him for a few minutes, looking at his pale face and the sweat that slowly dripped down his red swollen cheek. He took out his handkerchief and mopped the young man's face lightly and then settled back for the long trip to Bremerhaven.

Denninger awoke with a start as he heard the conductor's voice announcing that the train was now arriving in Bremerhaven. He rubbed his eyes and gave Bobby a little shake to wake him. He received no response and then noticed a small trickle of dried blood that trailed down to Bobby's chin from the corner of his mouth, the dark crimson contrasting against the alabaster white of his cold skin.

Denninger knew that Bobby would not be waking up.

He didn't want to leave Bobby alone, but he couldn't risk drawing any attention to himself. He turned Bobby's head away towards the window and covered his chest with his duster jacket, making it look like he was still asleep. He slowly made his way to the exit, trying to be as inconspicuous as he could. As he stepped onto the platform he turned his head and looked at Bobby one last time. "Goodbye Bobby," he whispered and headed into the station.

Spotting a phone, Denninger made a beeline for it, at the same time pulling his little notebook out of his jacket. Flipping through the pages, he looked for the notes that he had jotted down at Schlosser's office. As the operator put the call through, Denninger looked at his watch. Once he was connected, he cleared his throat.

"Hello? Yes, my name is Dr. Gerhard Denninger. I work for the Ahnenerbe. I believe you were expecting my call. I wish to speak to ..." His eyes wandered down the page until he found the name he was looking for. "I wish to speak to Captain Meuller please."

The submarine U-2516 was fueled up and ready to go. Standing on the dock by the submarine, Captain Franz Meuller took another drag on his cigarette. He watched through half-closed eyes as the last of the supplies were loaded aboard. He looked at his watch and decided he would give this clown from the Ahnenerbe just twenty more minutes to show up or he would leave without him, orders from Himmler or not. Meuller had a safe, regular patrol route, and he was not particularly happy about the change in plans. Anytime *that* happened, it only meant trouble. Sailing the relatively safe waters off the coast of Germany was one thing but heading to France just after a major Allied invasion, well that was another, and he was none too thrilled with that prospect.

Meuller was stubbing out his smoke when a taxi skidded to a stop near the docks. Denninger put his head out of the window and called out to the U-boat captain. "Are you Captain Meuller?" he shouted. Meuller stared silently as the archeologist stepped out of the cab. Denninger paid the driver and, with his hand out, went over to the brooding sailor. "I am Dr. Denninger. I will be joining you on your trip," he said, smiling. Meuller remained silent.

Although he wasn't very tall, Captain Meuller was an imposing figure nonetheless. He had a perfectly round head, with small, ice-blue eyes on a pair of broadly square shoulders that narrowed down to a thirty-two-inch waist. Physically, he was a geometric marvel. He had joined the German navy when he was sixteen, dreaming of adventure on the high seas, and twenty years later, after doing just about every horrible job imaginable on just about every single vessel there was, he had managed to rise to the rank of captain in Admiral Doenitz's *Kriegsmarine,* or war navy. Not yet forty years old, the U-boat captain's face had the weathered, sere look that four years of war gives to a person, not to mention what it does to a person's soul.

He warily looked the doctor over. "Don't you have any bags?" he asked nonchalantly. Denninger shook his head and held up his pack. "This is all I need, Captain. I also have these for you." He pulled the orders and the Enigma code from out of his jacket and handed them to Meuller, who quickly scanned them and noticed the radio-silence order.

"What's this? Why are we to run under radio silence?"

Denninger suddenly affected an air of importance. "It's all right there, Captain. The mission, I'm afraid, is secret. By orders of Heinrich Himmler. I'm really very sorry, but I cannot speak about it." He forced a smile but Meuller remained unfazed.

He handed the orders back to Denninger and placed the code sheet inside his coat as he jerked his head towards the gangplank. "We leave in twenty minutes," he said gruffly. "I suggest you get on board right now." Denninger nodded and smiled again. He threw his pack over his shoulder and ambled over to the gangplank.

Meuller watched him make his way up onto the submarine and pulled out another cigarette. "Fucking bureaucrats," he muttered as he lit up. Out of the corner of his eye he saw his first mate Willi Koenig coming toward him. Meuller nodded as he got close.

Koenig watched as Denninger went inside the U-boat and then turned to the captain. "Is that him?" Meuller nodded again. "What do you think he's up to?"

Meuller took a pull on the cigarette and blew a perfect smoke ring. He turned to Koenig. "I'm about to find out," he muttered.

12

THEY WERE A FEW hours from their destination and Denninger was stretched out on his bunk with the diary when the door to his cabin suddenly slid open. He jumped up and quickly slid the diary under his pillow just as Captain Meuller stepped inside. Clad in a grey turtleneck that had been washed too many times, he moved towards the little table, not acknowledging Denninger in the least.

The doctor, despite his aching legs, angrily leaped off his bunk. "Just what do you think you're doing?" he barked.

The unwanted visitor was already at the table. "It's my boat, Doctor. I go anywhere I please."

He stared at the document. "What's that?" He asked, gesturing at the textured parchment.

Denninger continued to glare at the captain.

Meuller leaned over the manuscript and he pulled out a cigarette.

"I thought you didn't allow smoking on board?" Denninger challenged as he put his arm in front of the document.

Meuller narrowed his eyes. "*My* boat, remember?"

Denninger forced a smile. "Could you not smoke in here, please? It's ... that is, the document is very fragile ... we ... don't want to damage it."

Meuller slowly pulled the cigarette out of his mouth as he gave the archeologist a withering look. Denninger took the cigarette and placed it on the desk, away from the parchment. Meuller turned his attention back to the document. Leaning against the table, he studied the letters on the document, and turned to the archeologist. "Is this the reason why we're out here? For an old piece of paper?"

Denninger said nothing.

"It looks ancient," Meuller asked. "Do you know what it says?"

Again Denninger remained mute. Denninger was angry with himself for not putting the document away. Why hadn't he locked his door? "Not yet. I need more time to decipher it. It's not written in any language that I — "

"Yeah, yeah," Meuller interrupted, clearly not interested in the details as he ran his stubby fingers along the torn corner. Denninger began to sweat slightly. "Probably some sort of prehistoric recipe for goats' balls soup or something, eh?"

Denninger smirked at the lame attempt at humor and rolled his eyes. "Hardly," he muttered.

Meuller grunted and changed his tone slightly. "Is it valuable?"

Denninger was starting to get impatient. "Look ... Captain Meuller. I am sure you understand that I am on a classified mission. I am under orders not to discuss it with anyone. Your orders are to make sure I reach my destination safely." Denninger inched forward and put his hand on the document, placing himself between it and Meuller. "And that is all."

Meuller slowly stood up and turned to face Denninger. His eyes narrowed as he studied the doctor's face. Jabbing his index finger roughly at his chest, he pushed Denninger towards his bunk. "You had better watch your step, Doctor," Meuller said in a low, menacing tone. "You could find yourself floating the rest of the way to France."

Denninger collapsed onto his bunk as the captain headed towards the door. "I'm late for my chess game with Koenig, anyway. Do you play chess, Doctor?"

Denninger took his glasses off and began to clean them with a handkerchief.

Suddenly something stirred in his mind.

Chess ...

"Why, uh, yes. I was never very good at it, however."

He sneered. "Really? An educated man like yourself, not good at an intellectual pursuit like chess?" He huffed sarcastically, pulled out a cigarette and lit it, blowing the smoke in Denninger's direction. "Well, it is a difficult game, after all. Not for everyone, obviously." He briskly tipped his cap to Denninger. "Goodnight, Doctor. You'll be informed when we reach the beach."

Denninger watched him disappear down the corridor before he shut the door. He clicked home the lock and returned to his bunk. Sitting on the edge of the bed, he dragged the glasses off his face and pulling out a handkerchief, he wiped his forehead. He replaced his glasses and took a long look at the parchment on his desk.

Chess ...

13

As the submarine continued its silent passage, Denninger headed down the passageway to the galley. He sensed that he was close, as a pungent odor of something he thought might be soup, mixed with perspiration, hit his nose like a grimy mallet. As he entered the kitchen, his glasses instantly fogged up from the stove's heat which blasted out like a furnace. He cleaned his glasses and noticed that the cook, overweight and sweaty, was hovering over a large pot of broth, trying to coax flavor out of the concoction by dropping massive amounts of onions and beets into it. As Denninger stared at the cook, what struck him was that the man seemed to have no neck. It just seemed to be a head stuck on a pair of concave shoulders. Denninger's eyes began to water as he sidled up to him and he coughed slightly.

Without looking up, the cook barked. "What the hell do you want?"

Taken slightly aback, Denninger stammered "I was wondering if I could get some tea?" The cook turned his whole body to Denninger with a sneer and cocked his head in the direction of the pantry. "Make it yourself. I'm busy".

Denninger thanked him, took a deep breath and squeezed himself over to the small cupboard. He opened the door, removed a teacup and a saucer, and then began his search for the tea. Moving packages of food back and forth, he looked over his shoulder at the cook. "Excuse me, I really hate to bother you, but where exactly is the tea?"

The cook, annoyed at Denninger's constant interruptions, dropped his ladle, nudged Denninger out of the way, and removed a number of packages and tins. He then grabbed a box and slammed it on the counter. "Here," he grunted, "Open your eyes. It was right behind the flour tins." Denninger took the tin of tea, poured some water into the kettle and set it on the stove to boil.

"Would you like me to put these things away for you?'" he inquired.

The cook grunted wearily. "It's been a long day," he mumbled. "Ach! I can't seem to make anything that Meuller likes. Such a picky bastard."

Denninger chuckled. "He is a hard man to warm up to, isn't he?"

The kettle began to whistle. Denninger poured the boiling water into the cup and put the kettle on a cooler part of the stove. He swiftly took his cup and thanked the other man once again. Without looking up, the cook muttered something incomprehensible and continued on with his soup experimentation.

Back in his cabin, Denninger put his tea on the table and reached inside his coat. By the cup, he put the small tin of flour he had liberated from the galley and then turned to his bunk. Thrusting his hand into his pack which lay on the pillow, he pulled out a copy of *Lucifer's Court* that Rahn had given him. He opened it to the first page and read the inscription: "To Gerhard: couldn't find the chimp with the cigarette. Hope this will do. Otto."

Yes, thought Denninger, I think this *will* do.

He placed the book on the table and started to look through the drawers of the night stand by the tiny table. Not finding what he was looking for, he searched throughout the cabin. In the small cabinet just over the table, Denninger spied a small cardboard box. He reached in and removed it, then placed it on the table next to the book. Rummaging around inside, he discovered a knife, a dirty shirt, spare radio parts, and an outdated training manual inside.

"Exactly what the doctor ordered." He smiled.

He took the knife and the manifest out of the box and placed them next to the book and the tin of flour. He then picked up the cup of tea and took a long drink. It wasn't the greatest cup of tea he had ever had, but it would do. He placed the remainder of the tea next to the flour and turned his attention to the manual. He thumbed through the pages of charts, transactions, and numbers, until he found a blank page.

Holding the knife by the point like a pencil against the spine of the manual, he slowly dragged it downwards until the paper came free. Reaching over, he picked up *Lucifer's Court*, turned to the back cover, placing the paper against it, measuring the difference between them.

"Just a little trim," he murmured, as he began to cut the paper.

14

DENNINGER LOOKED AT HIS watch and saw that they were about ten minutes from landing. He grabbed his pack and the tube, and began to make his way to the control room. Except for the normal noise of the machinery, the passageway was eerily devoid of any human sounds. As Denninger's mission was "top secret," only a skeleton crew had been deployed. The archeologist had been on a submarine only once before, but the quiet of this one, a long range XXI type, gave him a profound sense of trepidation that he couldn't shake. With his head lowered, he hurried down the passage and ran headlong into a large, hulking sailor in a ratty pea-coat. It was Koenig, Meuller's first mate. He thrust out his massive hands and grabbed ahold of Denninger as his pack hit the floor.

"Excuse me, Doctor" he said in a sonorous voice. Koenig bent down to pick up Denninger's pack. It looked comically small in Koenig's gorilla-like grasp. Denninger forced a smile and took it from Koenig. As he turned it over in his hands, one of the books fell out. Denninger froze as the first mate watched it hit the floor. Koenig bent over once again and picked up the book. He turned it over to look at the title.

"*Lucifer's Court*?" He then looked at the author's name. "Otto Rahn, eh?" Koenig thumbed through the pages and noticing the inscription, said, "Oh, you knew him?"

Denninger put the pack over one shoulder. "I did. He was a friend of mine."

"Really?" Koenig smirked. "Is it true he was a fairy?"

Denninger felt his skin start to get very warm as he fought his anger and he forced a shrug. "I wouldn't know about that," he said through gritted teeth. "May I have my book, please?" He held out his hand. Koenig continued to flip through the pages. He got to the back of the book, and noticed that the paper covering the inside cover was a little loose.

Denninger nervously cleared his throat. Slowly, Koenig flicked at the slightly curled paper. He looked at Denninger. "It seems that your book is falling apart, Doctor."

"It was...uh ... it was a small run. Otto had it printed through a small publisher in France. They cut corners to save money. It ... uh ... actually started to fall apart a few days after he gave it to me," Denninger grinned awkwardly.

As Koenig continued to pick at the loose paper with a large thumbnail, Denninger made a big show of looking at his watch. "It's almost time," he said. "We must hurry."

Koenig looked at Denninger and finally handed the book to him, then looked around quizzically. "Do you smell tea?"

Denninger quickly snatched the book from the sailor's hand and hurried up the ladder to the bridge.

Dawn was breaking as the periscope cut the surface of the water. Meuller scanned the horizon as Denninger anxiously looked at his watch for the fifth time in half an hour. Meuller closed up the periscope and turned to Denninger. "All right, let's go up top. I have a feeling we're not going to be alone for long."

Standing on the deck, Denninger took in a deep breath of salt air. He began to cough, but he felt better anyway, knowing that he would soon be on dry land and finally beginning the search. Buttoning up his coat, he turned to Meuller, who was sipping a cup of coffee.

"Thank you for your help, Captain Meuller. I will be letting my superiors know that you and your crew were of great help." He put out his hand but Meuller didn't move.

He gazed coldly at the archeologist. "Will you, now?" he murmured.

Denninger stared at him with a look of puzzlement. Meuller handed his coffee to Koenig and then pulled out a folded piece of paper from one of his pockets. Slowly he opened it in front of Denninger. "Do you recognize this, Herr Doctor?"

Denninger could see that it was the Enigma code key that he had provided Meuller with at the beginning of the trip. He wasn't sure why Meuller was showing it to him.

The U-boat captain moved in closer to Denninger. "Here," he said, "Could you hold it for a minute, please?"

Denninger took the sheet from the sub captain as Meuller turned to Koenig for his cup of coffee. Suddenly and without warning, Meuller tossed the remainder of the coffee at Denninger. The brown liquid sprayed all over the doctor and the key sheet. Denninger stumbled backwards, alarmed by the sudden assault. "Are you crazy?" he shouted indignantly at Meuller. The captain raised an eyebrow and pointed to the key sheet dripping in Denninger's hand.

"Dr. Denninger, would you mind reading the top line for me, please?"

"What!?"

"Please — humor me, won't you?"

Denninger angrily shook the key sheet free of the remaining coffee, and shooting a dirty look at Mueller, quickly began to recite the top line in a venomous tone. "*Kampfflugzeuge*," he began, practically spitting out the words, "*Schlüssel-Nummer 561* — "

Meuller held up his hand. "That's interesting ... I can see you have no trouble reading the code key."

Denninger lowered the sheet. "Of course not. Why would I?"

Meuller grinned humorlessly. "Key sheets, Doctor, are written in soluble ink." Meuller leveled his gaze at Denninger. "If we were to be captured, pouring liquid on the key sheet would render it illegible to enemy eyes — that is, if that was a proper key sheet."

Denninger closed his eyes and cursed himself. Although he had been extra careful to take a code that was inoperable, the sheet he had taken was written in waterproof ink. He should have copied it out in soluble ink.

Meuller reached out and snatched the key sheet out of the doctor's hand, crumpled it up and tossed it to Koenig then reached inside his jacket to remove a pistol. He aimed it at Denninger's chest. "It was very clever. With the orders to sail under radio silence and a useless key sheet, we would have been kept off guard for days — long after we had dropped you off.

He held out his free hand. "I'll be taking that document of yours now."

Denninger's eyes grew wide. He held up a hand in protest. "I told you it wasn't valuable. It's purely a historic — "

Meuller cut him off. "Yes, I know, you told me." His finger beckoned as he steadied the pistol. "Don't make me ask again."

Denninger glared at the submarine captain, who, tired of waiting, bent over and pulled out the tube from out of the pack. Denninger shot out his hands in desperation and tried to grab it.

"You can't. You're making a big mistake, you know," the archeologist warned. "You have no idea what you're doing."

Meuller chuckled and yanked the case from his hand. “Oh, I think I do. You know, I have the distinct feeling that no one at the Heritage Bureau has any idea where you are. But why are you so upset? You wanted to get to France, and so — here we are!”

Meuller put the pistol barrel up against Denninger’s chest.

“Get in the dinghy,” he ordered.

Denninger backed up slowly towards the ladder. He looked up at Meuller as he began to descend to the dinghy.

“You see, Doctor, this is my last mission, although no one back in Berlin knows it yet. I’m not going back to Germany. This war is almost over and I have a feeling that we are not going to be coming out on top. So, I am going to retire from this war — alive and rich. I figure if you’ve gone to the trouble to go through this charade to keep this little item from the SS, then it must be extremely valuable,” he said raising the cylindrical case.

Meuller stood up and tossed Denninger his pack. It hit him square in the chest and knocked him to the bottom of the dinghy.

“Good luck, Doctor Denninger,” the captain called as the submarine pulled away from the dinghy. He waved from the deck. *“Lebewohl, Herr Doktor …* and good luck.”

Denninger looked at the U-boat through narrowed eyes as he began to drift towards shore.

As the submarine slipped below the surface, Meuller left orders with Koenig that he was not to be disturbed. He closed the door to his quarters, tossed the case on his bunk and removed his topcoat. He picked up the case and started to remove the top when a strange hissing noise caught his attention. Meuller saw a small puff of smoke escape from inside the tube. He closed his eyes and swore as the smell of burning tobacco and sulfur hit his nostrils.

"Ah, Doctor— "

Denninger felt the explosion before he heard it. He watched as a plume of water and debris flew several feet into the air. Denninger smiled to himself as he hauled the dinghy up onto the beach. He hadn't thought that the destruction would be so massive, considering the small amount of time he'd had to improvise the device from explosives he had found in the munitions room along with the cigarette left by Meuller in his cabin.

Checkmate, he thought smugly.

He lifted his pack out of the boat and pulled *Lucifer's Court* from its protective cover. He turned to the back and lifted the envelope-like covering he had constructed using the paper from the training manual and the simple glue made with the flour and tea. The parchment inside was dry and untouched. Well, that worked out well, he said to himself. He replaced the book and removed the diary. It too was dry.

The current eventually carried him to shore, where he disembarked. He dragged the boat as far up onto the beach as he could and began the long trek inland. No one would stand in his way now. The only link to the document would soon be resting on the ocean floor, and there would be no way to find him once he disappeared into the French forest.

15

IT WAS WELL PAST dark when Denninger came upon the farmhouse. There were no lights on at all, but still, he remained cautious. He stopped and listened for any signs of life. He was fairly sure the farmhouse was deserted, but nonetheless, he carefully made his way around the perimeter of the house. It was deathly quiet. He crept forward, trying to make as little noise as possible, until he found himself under a windowsill. Slowly he raised his head and peered through one of the lower panes of glass. With the help of the moonlight, he was able to make out what looked like a kitchen table in the middle of a common room. Deciding to take a chance, he circled the house until he found the door. He checked the doorknob and found it turned easily in his hand. He opened the door a tiny crack. Pausing, he waited for any kind of sound or movement that would betray the presence of inhabitants within.

Nothing. All was quiet.

Convinced that he was alone, he finally mustered up the courage to light a match. Under the soft light of the flame, he got a better look at the surroundings and he was impressed by the general tidiness of the home, even though it was obvious that the owners had left in a hurry. Just before the match went out, he noticed a stairway. He lit a second match and slowly began to climb the stairs. He peeked around one corner then the other and saw that the hallway was deserted.

Turning left, he struck another match and entered the room at the end of the hall. He tapped the wall gently as he groped for a light switch. "There must be something here," he muttered. As the third match went out, he bumped into a table and dropped the box of matches all over the floor. Uttering an oath, he dropped down to his hands and knees, feeling blindly for the scattered matches. It was then that he heard it.

A creak.

From downstairs.

He stopped moving.

There it was again. Denninger at once could feel his heart pounding in his ears.

Someone else was in the house.

Downstairs, flashlight beams split the darkness as four American soldiers moved carefully throughout the room. The lead soldier unexpectedly stopped and then turned to the others. "Hey Phil, do you smell that?" he asked, shining the light right into the other soldier's eyes. Phil, temporarily blinded, put his hand up to block the light and nodded.

The first soldier turned to the other two behind him. "Someone's been burning matches," he said. He wheeled around and said excitedly, "Doug, I don't think we're alone here."

Doug glowered at them in disbelief and put his finger to his lips. He pointed to the stairs. "Matty, Sam." he whispered, and pointed up the stairs. "Phil, the kitchen — and for Chrissakes everybody, be quiet!" he hissed. Matty nodded, gave Sam a bemused look and pushed him towards the landing. "C'mon, rube," he ordered.

As they made their way up the stairs, Corporal Doug Markham exhaled nervously, leaned against the door jamb and rubbed his right temple with his thumb. Not exactly what you'd call a career soldier, Markham had been drafted in 1942, a few months after Pearl Harbor. He had breezed through basic training, and in spite of his less-than-stellar attitude with authority, he'd wound up a corporal. A tough New Englander with a lanky physique, his seemingly laconic façade hid a fierce temper that was constantly percolating just below the surface. It had been two months since the four of them had landed at Omaha Beach, and they still acted like they were at Fort Lewis. When they had become separated from their unit, Markham, officially because of his rank and unofficially because of his character, had taken charge.

He cocked his head as Phil Lucas came out of the kitchen shaking his head. Markham thought that of the four men, Lucas was the sharpest of the bunch. He was educated, cool and levelheaded. A soft-spoken West Virginian by birth, he had an ingratiating personality that Markham found too submissive at times, but which he relied on nonetheless. Markham wouldn't have been at all surprised if Lucas had been a teacher's pet in school.

He was also devoutly religious. Luckily for Markham, Lucas didn't overtly foist his views on anyone and on the outside he seemed to be a "live-and-let-live" kind of guy but Markham remained guarded. He had always been wary of this type. Growing up a Catholic in Boston, Markham had delighted his family when he became an altar boy and they had hoped that he'd become a priest. That is, until he came back home one Sunday, announcing heatedly that it had been his last day as an altar boy. He wouldn't go into any details other than that he had had a "disagreement" with Father Justin, the parish priest. His parents were understandably dumbfounded.

While his mother and father were terribly upset over the turn of events, it was nothing compared to the shock of hearing later that night that Father Justin, on his way to a restaurant for a late dinner, had been beaten so severely that he eventually lost his hearing in one ear. It was true that Doug had been out that night, and mysteriously, he had busted two fingers in a door, but he did have an alibi and besides, he *was* an altar boy after all.

No one was ever arrested since the priest couldn't remember much about the beating. The last anyone had ever heard of Father Justin was that he had been sent to a boys' reform school in Canada, where he was later convicted of fondling a twelve-year-old pupil.

When questions of faith arose, Markham usually shut them down straightaway by announcing he was an agnostic. He had no use for God and really didn't trust the role that faith played in some people's lives, but he figured that as long as God didn't fuck things up for him, then it was all right. If Lucas wanted to be Mister Religion and as long as he was a good soldier that Doug could count on, then great. If he had Lucas's will, he couldn't give a shit about his soul.

Matty Rourke on the other hand, was something else.

In Markham's opinion, if you ever wanted an argument against God, all you had to do was to take a good look at this guy. Rourke was a punk who was just begging for a bullet. He was a greaser from Chicago who ran with the Italian gangs until he got nailed for robbing a store when he was sixteen. He spent a year in juvenile hall, where he knifed another guy for coming on to him in the showers. He was all set up for a long stretch in the state penitentiary, but lucky for him, the war broke out. After considering his dismal circumstances, a judge gave him a choice ... either join the army, or bust rocks at the pen. He signed up the next day.

Or so he said. Doug didn't buy a lot of what came out of Rourke. He was a walking, talking Warner Brothers movie cliché who was a first class little bullshitter, troublemaker, and asshole. To Markham, it was like listening to an Our Gang version of Jimmy Cagney. He felt that it was all part of the image Rourke wanted to portray because Matty was just a little guy, and sometimes little guys had to sound tough and act tough to survive. Markham was also keenly aware however, that it just reeked of desperation, and worse, it made Rourke just that much harder to trust. He wouldn't have been the least bit surprised if the little prick had been drafted just like any other mug and made up all that garbage about almost going to prison, just to sound hard-boiled. A little shit like Rourke would last about two seconds with some of those guys at Joliet. On the battlefield you had to trust your buddies, and Markham wouldn't trust Rourke to piss even if his bladder was busting. Markham believed that the little creep would screw you six ways to Sunday if he was in over his head, because he didn't give a shit about anyone but himself. He was a hothead with a big mouth and a small brain, and Markham had to consistently keep him in line. Guys like Rourke were dangerous, and Markham was never quite sure if the bullet that he was certain would ultimately find the little punk would come from a German machine gun or Markham's own rifle.

Markham tilted his head slightly and could just see the bottom of Johnson's enormous boots at the top of the stairs. He watched as they disappeared down the hallway with Rourke's smaller boots following close behind. It's a good thing Sam is easygoing, or Rourke would be dead by now, he thought.

Sam Johnson was a quiet farm boy from Oklahoma. He was gigantic, just the way they grew them out there, and along with six brothers and sisters, he helped run the family farm. In school, he had played for the football team, but even with his size, he had proved to be a terrible player. He just couldn't bring himself to hit anybody. He was afraid of hurting someone. When he was eventually called up for the army, he tried to beg off as a conscientious objector. In order to accomplish this, it was necessary for the big Oklahoman to fill out a questionnaire explaining the nature of his objections. When Johnson returned the form, his inept attempt at answering the questions, (due in no small part to his poor schooling) resulted in the draft office denying his request. Thanks to this petition for exemption, he was pegged as a potential troublemaker, an unfair characterization that seemed to follow him wherever he went. He was actually a good soldier and followed orders, yet Markham was still wary of the gentle Okie. He sensed Johnson had a good heart, but a good heart and pacifist tendencies made for a potentially enormous problem in the middle of a war. While he had his doubts, Markham always told himself that when the chips were down, Johnson would come through.

It's what he kept telling himself, anyway.

Markham watched Lucas as the latter softly made his way over towards the corporal. "Watch my back," cautioned Markham as he headed for the stairs. "I'm going up."

16

IN THE BLACKNESS OF the room, Denninger was conscious of the visitors and had moved to hide behind a large chair when he realized, to his horror, that he had dropped his pack. Shit, he thought. Tentatively putting his hand forward, he began to feel for it in the darkness.

His fingers suddenly brushed across a boot.

"Cripes!" yelped Johnson, as he involuntarily squeezed the trigger of his weapon. A burst of gunfire sprayed the ceiling as he stumbled backwards, crashing heavily into Rourke.

"Motherf— "

Rourke's oath was cut off as Johnson's flailing elbow caught him square in the mouth. Denninger leapt up quickly and dove in what, he hoped, was the direction of his pack. Markham, upon hearing the noise, skipped three stairs at a time on his way towards the commotion.

Denninger's hand snagged his pack and in one swift movement, swiped it up and breezed past the snarl of soldiers by the doorway. In the darkness Markham could just see the outlines of Rourke and Johnson wrestling with each other and a third body coming his way fast. Between spitting up gobs of blood, Rourke was swearing at Johnson.

"Phil!" Markham yelled as he wheeled around, "He's coming down!"

Markham forgot about Rourke and Johnson and made chase. Denninger was running full tilt, his pack clutched tightly to his chest. As he rounded the corner, he felt his balance start to go. He hit the stairs hard but he missed the second step and began a headlong descent into Lucas who was running up the stairway. Denninger struck him like a boulder square in the chest. Lucas felt the air punched out of his lungs just before the two men rolled the remaining way down the stairs. Denninger skidded across the floor as Lucas clutched at his ribs. Rourke and Johnson had by now untangled themselves and headed for the stairs. Markham reached the bottom and ran to Lucas.

"Phil, you OK?" he asked.

"Just ... the wind..." Lucas gasped. Markham looked over at Denninger and saw that the older man wasn't moving. Johnson and Rourke had reached the landing and were already heading towards him. Rourke reached him first.

He suddenly brought his boot back and delivered a vicious kick to Denninger's midsection. "You piece of shit, get up!" Rourke screamed.

Johnson instantly grabbed Rourke's shoulder and spun him around. "You hit him again, you deal with me," he told the smaller soldier.

Rourke's eyes narrowed and he pointed a finger at Johnson. "What the hell are *you* gonna do, rube? Threaten to *not* punch me?" Johnson stared at the smaller man without saying anything. Rourke put his hand up to his mouth and gingerly touched his lip.

He looked at the blood on his finger and then touched his tooth. "Nice...it's loose, you idiot." He spat on the floor. "One of the front ones too — that's just fuckin' great."

Johnson smiled to himself. It had been an accident and Johnson felt bad at first, but considering it was Rourke, the feeling had passed rather quickly.

Markham picked up a candle he saw on a shelf, lit it and then joined them. "Knock that shit off, Matty," he ordered, and then, nodding towards Johnson, told him to get a chair.

They picked Denninger up and put him in a rocking chair which Johnson had dragged over from the corner. Delicately rubbing his ribs, Lucas was slowly walking towards the group when he noticed Denninger's pack on the floor. He picked it up and brought it over. Handing it to Markham, he said he would take a look around to try and get the lights on. Markham agreed and placed the candle in the middle of the table then leaned in towards Denninger.

The older man was breathing heavily but remained still. Markham moved in closer and began rummaging through Denninger's pockets. Finding nothing, he went to the table and looked up at Johnson. "Keep an eye on him for a minute, Sam" he ordered. He placed Denninger's pack on the table as Rourke lit a lantern that he had found in another room. Suddenly the room brightened all around them.

Lucas came around the corner with a grin. "Let there be light," he joked.

As Markham picked up the pack and dumped it unceremoniously onto the table, Lucas noticed the books. He picked up *Lucifer's Court* and began to casually thumb through it.

Denninger stirred slightly and then gradually opened his eyes. His head and his chest throbbed. As the cloud in his head cleared, he began to get a more comprehensible picture of his dilemma. Slowly looking around, he counted the soldiers surrounding him. He wondered how many more of them were nearby or outside. He wasn't able to make a run for it, so he would have to bide his time. He would need his pack. His pack …

Looking around, he saw that its contents were spilled all over the table, and the book containing the document was in one of the soldier's hands.

He gripped the arms of the chair tightly and began to grind his teeth. Markham and Lucas noticed that their prisoner had awakened. Denninger tried to clear his throat. "*Wasser,*" he croaked.

Markham looked at Rourke. "Aha! A German," Markham remarked. He crooked a finger at Rourke. "Get him some water, Matty."

Rourke, who was rummaging through the pack's contents on the table, raised his head slightly. He sneered, giving Denninger a dirty look. "Fuck him—"

"Right now, Matty—right this fucking second."

Rourke slowly looked up at Markham.

Matty Rourke had a malevolent stare that could burn right through you. His brown eyes would take on an almost black, dilated look that exuded unbridled hate, and unsettling as it was, Markham remained impassive.

He'd seen this look before.

When on the beach at Normandy.

"Water, Matty. Right—fuckin'—now," he ordered.

For a moment it seemed like a Mexican standoff, but then, oddly, Rourke slowly began to grin. His penetrating eyes however, remained coldly trained on Markham. "Sure Doug, whatever you say." Rourke contemptously spat some more blood on the floor, and went to the kitchen as Markham put his hand firmly on Denninger's shoulder. Denninger looked up at him.

"So you're a German, huh? *Sprechen Sie Englisch?*"

Denninger just stared. "Well," he said looking around, "That's it for my German. What about you, Phil?"

Lucas shook his head and noticed that Markham was clicking his fingernail and his thumbnail together again. He had seen him do it before when he was either nervous or deep in thought. Lucas also observed that Denninger would not take his eyes off the book.

"Let me see that," Markham ordered Lucas, motioning to the book. Lucas handed it to Markham. The corporal took it and turned it over in his hands. He thumbed through the pages and then shook it so that anything within the pages would fall out. Through his peripheral vision he watched Denninger's reaction but the archeologist remained cool and unmoving.

Markham finally reached the end of the book and was about to drop it on the table when he noticed the loose paper on the back cover. "Huh," he grunted. "That's funny ..." He scratched at the paper.

Denninger tensed.

Markham cast a sideways glance at Lucas.

When Markham turned his head, Denninger made his move. *"No!"* he yelped, swiping madly at the book. Caught by surprise at the sudden assault, Markham dropped the book to the floor and put up his hands in self-defense. Denninger lunged forward, but springing suddenly from a rocking chair probably wasn't the best way of making a clean escape. The forward momentum caused his body to drop lower than he expected and both of them tumbled to the floor. Johnson made a feeble attempt at catching Denninger but missed him completely. The rocking chair, free of its occupant, swung smartly backwards and, continuing the parabola, smacked Johnson in the ear. Upon hearing the commotion, Rourke came rushing back in from the kitchen. By this time, Lucas had managed to train his weapon against Denninger's head. Denninger rolled onto his back, wincing in pain, his glasses hanging by one arm from his ear. Markham pulled himself up into a sitting position and rubbed his shoulder.

He picked up the book and held it out in front of the German. "Okay ... Let's try this again. *Sprechen Sie Englisch*, buddy?"

Markham and Lucas picked up Denninger and roughly threw him into the chair as Johnson rubbed his own rapidly swelling ear.

"Look," Markham began, "I got a pretty good idea that you can understand me. We don't want anything from you, understand? We're just a few guys who got separated from our unit and we need to know what you're doing here." As Markham waited for a response, Denninger continued to stare at the table. Markham reached out and grabbed the archeologist's shoulders firmly. "This isn't a game, buddy" he warned.

Denninger gave Markham a vexed look. He opened his mouth slightly and, after a long, slow, excruciating moment, he spoke in heavily accented but plain English. "Please stop calling me 'Buddy.'"

Rourke gave out a short hyena like laugh. "Why you dirty phony ..."

Markham exchanged glances with Lucas again and then turned back to Denninger. "Okay, friend ... what are you doing here?"

Denninger refused his to meet his eyes, and looked back down. Rourke leaned in towards Markham. "Lemme have a couple of minutes with him, Doug, and I'll make him talk," he said in a low voice. Markham cast a look of annoyance at Rourke who just shrugged. "Hey, it's your call," he muttered.

Markham turned back to Denninger. "Look, I know you can understand me and I'm not going to ask again. You either tell me what you're doing here, or I *make* you tell me. Your choice." Lucas was surprised. He'd never heard Doug make a threat before, so he wasn't quite sure what would happen next. He nervously shifted from his left foot to his right foot.

Denninger ran a number of scenarios through his head, all with dismal outcomes. Realizing that he didn't have much of a choice, his shoulders shrank in resignation and then cleared his throat. "You have nothing to worry about," he began in clipped English. "I am not a soldier or a spy or anything like that."

Rourke inched forward. "So says you, Fritz — "

Markham whipped around. "What the fuck is wrong with you?" he barked at Rourke. "Are you that fuckin' stupid that you can't see that I'm talkin' here?"

Rourke opened his mouth to speak, but Markham quickly jumped in. "Close it," he warned. "Close it. Now."

Rourke remained impassive. "You're pushin' it, Doug. We're all the same here"

Markham moved closer. "No, Matty, we're not. You guys would be in pieces on the fuckin' beach if it wasn't for me." Markham was now a few inches from Rourke's nose and poked his finger roughly into the smaller man's chest. "You especially."

For a moment, Rourke's eyes flashed darkly and a noisy image flickered through his mind.

The pandemonium on the beach. The deafening roar of the surf and bombs combined, drowning out the bullets and the screams.

The smell of smoke and blood as flesh and bone sprayed all around him. Gasping in the fetid air, a hand suddenly grabbing at his collar and yanking him down. The sound of the mortar shell exploding a few feet from where he had been and the realization that he should have been fragmented all over the beach.

Rourke vigorously pushed Markham's hand down and slunk away. Markham started to follow but Lucas stepped in and shook his head. "Doug ..."

Markham stopped, and without taking his eyes off of Rourke, barked at Denninger. "So ... what's it gonna be, buddy?"

Denninger clenched and unclenched his teeth. His eyes wandered from Markham to Lucas and then to Johnson. Rourke stood quietly brooding in the shadows. Denninger tried to think, but the blood pounded in his ears and his head throbbed. His shoulders slumped a bit more and he cleared his throat again.

He had to get the book back. He held out his hand.

"May I have that book, please? It was a gift from a close friend."

Markham started to give the book to Denninger, but at the last second, he pulled it away.

"First things first. Name?"

Denninger nodded. "I will tell you everything. My name is Gerhard Denninger. I am a member of the Ahnenerbe — "

Markham cut in. "Ahnenerbe?"

Denninger smiled. "Umm ... you might call it a Heritage Bureau. We study religious relics, artifacts, and documents. My role is decidedly ... umm ... unmilitary," he said.

He eyed the book for a moment, and then looked at Markham. "Truthfully, I am here alone. I am in this area studying the life of an extinct Christian sect called the Cathars. They..."

He trailed off as Lucas cocked his head towards Markham. They moved away from the archeologist.

"What do you think?" asked Markham in a low voice.

Lucas pulled at the bottom of his lip in thought. "I don't think I buy it. In the middle of a war zone, he's conducting a history lesson?" He glanced at Denninger. "I mean, look at the guy. He can't be army. But what's he doing this far south?"

Markham looked down at the book in his hand. "He seems really attached to this. He never takes his eyes off of it."

They went back over to Denninger and Markham placed the book on the table just out of the doctor's reach. The corporal grabbed another chair and spun it around. He straddled it with his arms resting on the back. "All right. Let's try this again."

"Honestly sir, I have nothing that would interest you, I assure you," Denninger pleaded. "I have no relevant military information. Please, I must ask that you let me go. I will say nothing of our meeting, I promise you. As I say, I am only here to study the Cathars."

He forced a feeble smile.

Markham pulled out a package of cigarettes. He took one and lit it then offered one to Denninger. The doctor waved it away with a look of disdain. "No thank you, I don't smoke."

Markham shrugged and put the pack back into his pocket. He took a long pull on his cigarette then exhaled, leaning forward, letting the smoke drift toward his captive.

"All right," Markham directed, "here's what we're gonna do. We need to rest, so we're gonna stay here tonight. I kinda believe you, but I can't risk letting you go just yet."

Denninger's hopes began to fade.

Markham continued. "We'll spend the night here, and in the morning we'll let you go. I'm sorry, but it's the best I can do."

Markham then got up and turned to Johnson. "Tie him up in one of the rooms upstairs, Sam. You take the first watch then I'll spell you in a couple of hours." Turning to Rourke, he said, "All right Matty, you take the perimeter and Lucas will take over later."

Rourke began to protest. "Why do I gotta go outside? Why can't Lucas or the rube do it? I'm tired after all that walkin' we've done today. If Sam hadn'ta fucked up the truck back there … ."

Markham spun around, reaching out and roughly grabbing Rourke by the front of his uniform. "Look, you little shit, I've had enough bellyaching outta you. The next sound comin' out of your mouth better be breathing, or I swear to Christ I'll tie your tongue around your fuckin' face."

Rourke's mouth started to open in protest as Markham threw him backwards. "I was a fuckin' Boy Scout, Matty," Markham warned.

"That means he's good with knots," Johnson chuckled.

"I get it, rube," Rourke said acidly.

Hoping to diffuse the situation, Lucas went over to Rourke. "Relax, Matty," he said calmly. Rourke turned to confront him. "Fuck you, Phil," he spat out.

Lucas' eyes narrowed. "I've told you before, I don't like that word."

"I ... don't ... *fuck*-ing ... care, Phil," Rourke growled, deliberately emphasizing the offensive word.

Lucas let one hand drop from his rifle. Markham could have sworn that he thought he saw Lucas' hand balling up into a fist, but then he saw his fingers splay outwards instead.

C'mon Phil, do it, thought Markham. Take a shot at the little prick.

Lucas took a step backwards to let Rourke pick up his rifle. Rourke then yanked the door open, letting it bang loudly against the wall causing a small, white puff of dust to fly up as the doorknob embedded itself in the plaster. No one moved as Rourke stalked out into the night.

Denninger glanced warily at the other soldiers then cleared his throat. "That young man has a lot of anger," he opined.

Markham shook his head. "Actually he's got a lot of hate. There's a difference."

"C'mon, let's go," Johnson said to Denninger. The archeologist hesitated for a moment then they both gradually made their way upstairs. Markham went into the main living area while Lucas rummaged through the cupboards looking for any food or coffee.

—■—

In one of the bedrooms, Johnson tied Denninger's hands together with a torn sheet, wrapping the free end around a bedpost. Once he was satisfied with the knot, he settled into a rocking chair in the corner, cradling his rifle on his lap.

"You may as well get some sleep," he told Denninger.

The archeologist lay on the bed and stared at the ceiling for a few minutes. Lifting his head, he looked at the large soldier. "You don't say much, do you?" remarked Denninger.

Johnson shrugged.

"I didn't catch your name," Denninger said. Johnson just stared back.

"Can you just go to sleep?" he asked.

Denninger smiled, and pulled himself up into a sitting position. "Your friend — the little one — he is a quite impetuous, yes?"

Johnson just looked down at his rifle and played with the sight. "He's a little excitable," Johnson finally conceded.

Denninger nodded. "He reminds me of a good friend of mine named Otto, although Otto wasn't quite as ... psychotic." Johnson shifted in his chair slightly as Denninger prattled on. "My friend Otto is the one who wrote those books, you know — the ones downstairs? He gave them to me personally."

Johnson bobbed his head a bit, in a noncommittal way. Why won't he go to sleep? he thought.

Denninger pressed on. "Do you think I could get my books?"

Johnson closed his eyes and rubbed his forehead fiercely. "Okay, enough already. You can get 'em in the morning, awright? Can't you just be quiet and go to sleep?"

17

LUCAS FOUND SOME COFFEE in the pantry and brewed a pot. As he brought it into the room, he saw that Markham was stretched out on the couch with his arm covering his face. "You want some coffee, Doug?" asked Lucas. Markham groaned and slowly sat up. He rubbed the back of his neck with unhurried, deliberate movements.

"How long's it been, Phil?" he asked.

"How long's what been?"

Markham stroked the stubble on his cheek. "Since we got to England ... since we landed at Omaha ... since we had a decent night's sleep ... since we got laid ... oh, sorry."

Lucas looked down at his coffee cup. Phil Lucas didn't like the "sex" stuff, what he called "the gutter talk." Lucas was aware that everyone used language like that, but there was an unwritten code between them that Markham would try to curb the curses and sex talk, at least around the sensitive soldier.

Markham stretched and yawned. He picked up the cup, put his feet on the table and drank some of the coffee. The thick, hot liquid cascading down his throat felt good. The two of them didn't speak for a few minutes.

Markham cleared his throat. "I gotta tell ya, Phil, I'm not sure what to do now," he confessed.

Lucas leaned forward. "What are you talking about, Doug?"

Markham continued, "I'm completely ... I don't know ... I feel like ... I feel like I'm a live wire, you know?" He dropped his feet to the floor and leaned forward. Markham's thumb and fingernail were going at it again,

Lucas noticed. He knew that Markham was really agitated.

"I'm ready to kill that prick Rourke. Sorry, Phil, but I swear to God, I'm gonna kill that sonofabitch."

Phil pushed forward. "Geez, Doug, you can't let that little jerk wind you up."

Markham took another gulp of coffee. "Yeah, I know, I know." He ran his hand roughly through his hair. "What do you think we should do? I mean, it was hard enough before, but now we got this Kraut here ..." He put up his outstretched hands. "I'm open to anything."

Markham started to put his feet back on the table, but he bumped Denninger's pack with his boot. It fell to the floor and spilled out all over the place. "Ah, crap," he said tiredly. He and Lucas bent over and began to pick up Denninger's things. Markham reached under the table and picked up one of the books that had fallen out. He looked at the cover. He showed it to Lucas. "Do you know what this says?"

Phil stared for a second and said "I think it says 'Lucifer's Servants,' or something like that. My German's not that good."

"Huh," mused Markham. "This was the book he was acting squirrelly about, wasn't it?" He began to flip through the pages and when he got to the back cover, he noticed the oddly sticky binding covering it. He flicked it with his fingernail. "Lemme see your knife, will ya?"

Lucas watched as Markham pressed the tip between the lip of the cardboard and paper and carefully peeled the sticky cover away. "Holy cow, would ya look at this," Markham mumbled as he gradually pulled out the parchment.

"What do you think it is?" asked Lucas. Markham said nothing as he opened the parchment and placed it on the table. "It looks old," mused Lucas. "It looks really old."

He ran his finger over the document, studying the letters. "Hey Doug, do you think it's worth something?"

Markham raised his eyebrows. "Beats me."

Lucas pursed his lips. "I wonder what it says? It doesn't look like it's written in any language I recognize. It's strange." He paused. "Maybe it's a code."

Markham looked at Lucas. "What do you mean?"

"Well," began Lucas, "For starters, there's no sentences, no paragraphs, no punctuation or anything. It just seems to be a whole bunch of random letters all bunched together in one big square pattern. And these symbols here ..." He pointed out what seemed to be a stylized cross and a bird of some sort. He also noted a skull and crossbones. "This here looks like maybe it might be a pirate map." He looked up at Markham with a crooked smile. "Buried treasure, maybe?"

Markham was still clicking his thumb and fingernails together and then cocked his head towards the ceiling. "I'm sure our buddy upstairs can enlighten us."

18

ROURKE SEETHED WITH ANGER with every step he took around the perimeter of the house. "Dirty fuckers," he muttered to himself. "They're worse than the goddamn Krauts." He kicked at a large stone that was in his path. Looking around in the light of the moon, he couldn't see anyone within miles of the place.

Fuck this, he thought. He spat between his feet, took his helmet off, and wiped his forehead with his forearm. He looked around furtively then reached inside his jacket and pulled out a small bottle that he had stolen from a dead German soldier. Rourke couldn't read what it said, but he had known very well what it was. All the German soldiers had bottles of this stuff. Kept 'em sharp. Back in Chicago, he used to sell shit like this to the dope fiends on 47th and South Parkway. He'd kicked the gong around a bit himself, but he never let it take him over. He was too smart for that. Let the other suckers get hooked. Not him. Once in a while, just to take the edge off. That was okay.

He knocked the bottle's mouth into his hand and a small white tablet dropped out. He popped it into his mouth and swallowed it quickly, feeling it fighting to slide down his dry throat. Putting up with the mild discomfort of the pill was worth it considering how he'd feel soon enough.

The Germans called methamphetamine Pervitin.

Amphetamine, marketed back in the States as Benzedrine and readily available to anyone by prescription for clearing stuffy noses, was often a cheap and easy substitute for cocaine addicts. Rourke knew it by its street name "hop" and Pervitin was pretty much the same stuff.

As he waited for the tablet to take effect, he sat on a flat rock and stewed about the developments over the last couple of days.

He was very good at brooding.

The day we landed at Omaha Beach, he said to himself. All that noise. So I'd got confused. So what? Everyone was confused. You'd think that I owed Markham my goddamn life, the way he tells it, for Chrissakes.

Rourke's breathing became a little more rapid and he was starting to feel warmer.

Goddamn Markham — he doesn't treat the others this way ...

Like a goddamn punk kid ...

Well, I ain't no kid ... could a kid do what I did when that Kraut patrol pulled up? They didn't know what hit 'em. It was a goddamn good thing that I was there or else they all woulda been killed. And Markham, that prick, what the hell was he so sore for? We're supposed to rub out Fritz, ain't we? They're the enemy, for Chrissakes.

He was starting to feel anxious again. He jumped to his feet, noticing his fatigue had completely disappeared. He was still pissed, but he really felt ... *alive.*

Markham had better fuckin' watch it, he thought.

Upstairs, Denninger was regaling Johnson with another boring historical tidbit when Markham and Lucas came through the door. When Johnson saw them come in, he was relieved. Denninger stopped in mid-sentence and became sullen when he saw the parchment in Markham's hand. Markham turned to Sam and said, "Gimmie a minute with this guy, woudja Sam?"

Johnson was out of the chair in an instant. "Anything you say, Doug."

As soon as Johnson left the room, Markham pulled a chair up close to Denninger and untied his hands while Lucas watched from the doorway. Denninger sat up and looked nervously at the two soldiers. Markham grinned.

"You look nervous ... Mister ... ?"

"My name is Gerhard, Dr. Gerhard Denninger," said the archeologist.

"All right Doc ..." Markham pulled the document from out of the inside of his uniform and held it up. Denninger looked at it with a stoney face. "... can you tell me what this is?"

He laid the parchment on Denninger's lap. Denninger glanced down at the parchment then back up at Markham. "Oh ... uh, where did you find this? It looks interesting ..." he began innocently. Markham said nothing while the doctor continued. "It certainly looks very old," the doctor prattled. "Where in the world did you find — ".

Markham cut him off. "All right, cut out the crap ..."

"Crap? What is crap?" Denninger looked confused.

Lucas shifted his feet uncomfortably as Markham reached out and snatched the parchment from off of Denninger's lap. The archeologist's tone abruptly changed. "Please be careful!" he pleaded. "It's — "

"It's what?" Markham cut in. "What is it? Is this some sort of code? Troop movements? You may as well tell us, 'cause we *will* find out ..." Markham leaned in threateningly and Lucas stepped forward.

"Look, we don't want to do anything — " began Lucas.

Denninger sat bolt upright and cut him off mid-sentence. "Are you threatening me?" he asked incredulously. "You can't threaten me. Under the Geneva convention ..."

Markham turned to look at Lucas and rolled his eyes as Denninger droned on.

" ... you can't harm me. I ... I am a prisoner of war and you can't ... "

Markham held up his hand. "Whoa, Fritz — "

"It's *Gerhard,* goddamn it!" Denninger shrieked.

Markham held up his hands towards the vibrating German. "Okay. Gerhard. Relax a second," he said soothingly. "Christ almighty. First, if you're not a soldier, you're not a prisoner of war. That means the Geneva convention can't do shit for you. Second, all I was going to say was that we're not going to do anything to hurt you. Trust me."

Denninger slowly sat back down. He was still trembling, partially from fear, but mostly in anger.

Markham continued, "But you gotta understand that we need to know why you were hiding this. So we're not leaving until you come clean. Do you understand me ... Gerhard?"

Denninger stared coldly at Markham. The archeologist thought for a moment. After all this time, had it truly come down to this instant? All these years he had searched for the treasure of the Cathars. Five lost years in Tibet. Surviving an air crash, for God's sake. And for what? To lose everything now? Not likely. Denninger took a deep breath. "I will tell you everything that you wish to know."

Lucas suddenly fell forward as Johnson burst through the doorway. Markham spun around. "What's going on, Sam?"

"Rourke's downstairs and he says there's a Kraut jeep heading this way!" he panted.

Markham immediately jumped up out of the chair as Lucas headed down the hallway. He quickly turned to Denninger, waving the parchment. "Stay here and don't fuckin' move!" he warned. Leaving on the heels of Lucas, Markham began barking orders before he got to the bottom of the stairs.

"Johnson, watch the front door. Matty, how far away are they?"

Rourke was pulsing from both the adrenaline rush and the Pervitin, and didn't hear Markham at first. He was hopping from foot to foot like he was on a hotplate.

"Rourke?"

No response.

"Hey! Rourke!"

Rourke, suddenly snapping out of it began to jabber excitedly. "Doug, there's a bunch of Krauts headin' this way!"

Markham looked at Lucas incredulously. "I already know that, Matty. How far away are they?" he yelled as he shoved the parchment inside his jacket.

"They'll ... they'll be here in less than a minute," he stammered.

Markham looked around quickly. There was no place to hide downstairs. "Quick," he ordered, "back up the stairs."

Lucas, Johnson and Rourke bounded up the stairs towards the bedrooms. Markham made a rapid sweep of the area before he followed the other three. Halfway up, he realized the lights were still on and then he caught something out of the corner of his eye.

Denninger's pack and book were still on the table, right next to their coffee cups.

"Awww shit."

Eyes wide, he made a 180-degree turn and was on his way back down when he heard voices just outside the door. There was no time to get the pack or kill the lights. Swiftly reversing, he leapt up the remaining stairs only to run straight into Lucas.

"What are you doing?" he whispered furiously. "They're at the door."

Lucas hissed back, "The Kraut's missing from the bedroom."

Markham swore under his breath and pushed Lucas back down the hall. Markham could see Johnson poking his head out from of one of the rooms. Markham aggressively waved him back but Johnson just stared oddly behind the corporal and pointed.

Markham turned his head just as Denninger quietly stepped out of the shadows and started for the stairway. Markham's jaw dropped. "That ... *dirty* ... fucker ..." he muttered. Turning back to Lucas and Johnson, he directed them to take cover. Markham, staying within the shadows speedily made his way back to the head of the stairs.

19

THE SQUAD OF GERMANS had already entered the house when Denninger stepped onto the landing. The soldier in front saw the doctor and leveled his pistol at him, barking orders in French. Denninger, looking startled, put up his hands and moved slowly towards them.

Markham could only see the wisps of the white hair on the back of Denninger's head, and the feet of the soldiers; he counted at least three of them, not including Denninger. He could hear their conversation, but he couldn't understand what they were saying. His nerves were tingling. All he could imagine was that the Kraut downstairs was turning them in. As he looked at the thinning patch of hair on Denninger's head through his telescopic sight he inhaled calmly. At least I'll take you out, he thought.

"Who are you?" demanded the sergeant in French. Denninger, his mouth set in a grim slash, looked deliberately at each of the three Germans and asked in a blustery tone, "What are you doing in my home? Do you think you can just burst into someone's home without permission? The question should be who are you?"

The sergeant, clearly unimpressed by the tone of Denninger's voice, carefully chose his words. "Ah … you speak German, eh? Well, I am Scharführer Dietrich … " he finally said.

Just what I need, thought Denninger.

The SS.

Dietrich continued, "We are checking all the houses around here. We believe there may be a guerrilla unit operating in the area." He eyed Denninger suspiciously. "Just what is a German civilian like you doing here anyway?"

Denninger puffed up slightly. "I believe," he intoned gravely, "that that is not of your concern."

The sergeant, a young man of twenty-five, was not in the least intimidated by the authoritative manner of the older man, and kept his cool, official exterior. "I am sorry Herr ..." he began in a mockingly obsequious manner.

"Denninger," finished the older man.

"Herr Denninger, but my job is to root out these troublemakers. I have orders from Standartenführer Dreisel to check everything and everyone in the area — including the occupant of this house — which, in this case, would be you."

Denninger was outraged. "I am a German citizen, sir!"

"Yes, a German citizen in the south of France, in the middle of a war zone. I assume you have your papers?"

Denninger paused for a moment, then he slowly reached into his jacket pocket.

Markham watched the scenario below and felt a small bead of sweat slowly cascading down the length of his nose. He tried to swallow, but his mouth was completely dry. His adrenaline picked up as Denninger made the move to the inside of his jacket.

Christ, he thought. He's goin' for a gun? How did we miss that?

Markham took deliberate aim at the back of Denninger's head and slowly began to squeeze the trigger.

Denninger pulled his papers from the inside pocket of his jacket and handed them to Sergeant Dietrich. As the German soldier took them from the doctor, Markham saw the papers and quickly let go of the trigger. Straight away he began flicking his thumb and fingernail together as his heart pounded in his ears. He rubbed the grimy sweat from his forehead and eyes.

Holy shit that was close … , he thought.

It started to dawn on him that his nerve, which had always been solid and steady since Normandy, had started to fray a little around the edges. As he wiped his forehead again, out of the corner of his eye he saw Lucas padding down the hallway towards him.

He bent down beside Markham. "What are they doin' down there?" Lucas whispered in his ear.

Markham shook his head and turned his attention back to the rifle's crosshairs. "I wish I knew." he replied, his voice trembling slightly.

20

ROURKE AND JOHNSON WERE holed up in the far bedroom at the end of the hall. Rourke took a peek through the blinds of the window and could see only one soldier smoking a cigarette near an empty half-track parked by the front of the house.

He closed the blinds and sidled up to Johnson and, in a low voice, said, "I can only see one truck out there so I think there's only a couple of those fuckers downstairs. C'mon rube, let's me and you take 'em out."

Johnson shook his head. "Doug said to wait here."

Rourke shot him a dirty look. "Are you shittin' me?" he hissed. "Markham's a boob. If you ain't comin', then — "

Johnson got up and stepped in front of the doorway. He raised his automatic rifle and blocked off Rourke's path. Rourke opened his mouth to protest, but the ever-expanding image of Johnson rising to his full height choked off his words in mid-diatribe.

"Doug said to wait," he warned.

Lucas heard the commotion and started back down the hallway to the room. He stood behind Johnson's large frame and had to stand on his tiptoes to see inside. "What the heck is going on here?" he angrily demanded in a loud whisper over Johnson's shoulder. "You guys better knock it off. We have a situation downstairs."

Johnson remained unmoving in the doorway, not taking his eyes off of Rourke. Rourke stared darkly at the massive soldier and moved his gun to his left hand as he slowly reached behind his back and lightly fingered the hilt of his hunting knife.

—■—

Sergeant Dietrich finished scanning Denninger's identification papers and then handed them back to Denninger. It was then that he spied the pack and the book on the table, next to Markham's and Lucas's coffee cups. Dietrich's eyes narrowed suspiciously. "I thought you said you were alone here, Doctor?"

Denninger continued to look at Dietrich. "Excuse me?"

"I said, I thought you were alone here, Herr Doctor. Do you often drink coffee from two cups?"

Denninger cleared his throat nervously then he lightly smacked the palm of his hand against his forehead. "As a matter of fact, I did have someone over. If it's any of your business."

Dietrich took a step towards the doctor.

"Of course it's my business — everything is the business of the S.S. You should know that."

The sergeant then nodded to one of the soldiers who went over to the table, picked up the items, and brought them over. Dietrich took the pack from the soldier, made a cursory look through it and finding nothing of interest, he exchanged the pack for the book. He looked at the cover and began to flip through it. "What's this?" he said, noticing the inscription.

"I knew the author," replied Denninger. The sergeant nodded and suddenly turned it upside down, letting the pages flap loosely. Denninger never took his eyes off of the sergeant. Seeing that nothing fell out, Dietrich snapped the book shut with one hand and started to give it over to Denninger when he caught sight of the loose paper covering the rear cover. Denninger swore quietly under his breath. Dietrich slowly brought it back toward himself.

He smiled humorlessly. "Interesting. I see the ending of this book is quite — revealing, eh?" He took hold of the paper and ripped it from the cover, revealing the improvised envelope underneath. Dietrich thrust two fingers inside, widening the slit in the process as he probed for whatever was inside. Finding nothing, he tossed the book away and raised his pistol at Denninger.

He menacingly placed the barrel under Denninger's chin. "Enough of this foolishness. What are you doing here and what are you hiding?"

Markham had moved down a few steps in order to get a better view and was stunned by what was developing. He watched the scene below in disbelief.

What the hell is goin' on now? Are they actually going to kill the old bastard? He looked back at Lucas who was still standing on his toes behind Johnson. Lucas turned his head and noticed Markham motioning him over. Lucas said something to Johnson, and then he hurried over to Markham.

"What's going on, Doug?" asked Lucas. Markham pointed downstairs. Lucas turned and watched the bizarre scene below.

"What in the heck ... ?"

Denninger held his hands up as the barrel of the pistol dug deeply into his chin. Dietrich repeated the question. Denninger said nothing at first, then asked to remove his belt.

Dietrich lowered the pistol slightly, a little confused by the request.

"Scharführer Dietrich, if you wish to know my ... uh, what I am doing here, then I must be allowed to remove my belt."

Dietrich thought for a moment, and then turned to one of the soldiers. "You," he ordered, "Remove his belt".

The soldier, who was clearly uncomfortable with the request, looked for support from the soldier next to him, who offered nothing but a shrug and an embarrassed smile.

Markham and Lucas exchanged bewildered looks as they watched the strange scene of the soldier unbuckling Denninger's trousers.

The soldier pulled the belt through the loops of Denninger's pants and once it was free, he handed it to Dietrich, who finally lowered his pistol. Denninger immediately began to rub the area of his chin where the sergeant's gun had been pressed. Turning the belt over in his hands, Dietrich discovered a series of small buttons on the inside. He thrust the belt at Denninger. "Open it," he ordered.

Denninger stopped rubbing his chin and took the belt from Dietrich. He unsnapped the buttons and, once it was open, removed a tightly folded piece of paper. He carefully unfolded it and handed it to Dietrich. As Dietrich scanned the paper, the color started to drain from his face. He let his hand drop slightly, still clutching the document. Denninger reached over and snatched the letter from the sergeant's hand and quickly folded it back into the belt. The two soldiers exchanged looks, and suddenly raised their guns to Denninger but Dietrich waved them off.

Denninger smiled to himself. It was simply amazing how anything with Heinrich Himmler's signature on it, real or forged, made everyone in the German army wet their pants. Denninger then stepped in close to the sergeant and whispered in his ear.

Dietrich gave a small nod and then turned to the two soldiers beside him. "You two wait outside. I need to have a word with the doctor."

The two soldiers went through the door as Dietrich stepped into the living area with Denninger following and readjusting his belt. Markham and Lucas watched unbelievably as Denninger turned to look at Markham and Lucas, and then cryptically, he crooked his finger at them. Markham couldn't believe it.

"Does he actually want us to follow him?" whispered Markham.

Lucas' mouth fell open. He could hear the blood pounding in his skull.

"Go and get the other guys," said Markham. "I'm not exactly sure what's going on here."

As Lucas began to make his way down the hallway, Markham carefully descended the stairs, keeping his eyes moving from where Denninger and the sergeant stood to the front door, ever aware of the soldiers stationed only a few feet away.

21

LUCAS WAS HALFWAY DOWN the hall when he heard a loud thumping coming from the last bedroom. Eyes wide with panic, he sped down the hall to the room in time to see Johnson lying on top of Rourke. The smaller soldier was trying to cut the bigger man with a knife, but Johnson had twisted Rourke's arm so that the blade was dangerously close to Rourke's own throat.

"Oh my God!" Lucas gasped as he threw himself into the melee. "Hey … stop … " he hissed loudly as he tried to wedge himself between the wrestling soldiers.

Rourke had waited until Lucas had gone back to Markham before he'd pulled his knife on Johnson. Grinning, he gingerly put his gun down and slowly advanced on the big Oklahoman, waving the knife threateningly. "Okay rube," he grunted, "Just you and me now."

Johnson stared back at Rourke "Are you nuts?"

Rourke just grinned maniacally.

Johnson placed his weapon quietly on the floor as well, and prepared himself for the crazed soldier's inevitable attack.

Rourke waited until Johnson made the first move, and then leapt like a jaguar at the large soldier, swinging his knife in a wild arc.

Although Johnson was larger than most normal individuals, his huge size camouflaged a cat-like agility. Feinting to the right, Rourke's berserk slash cut a harmless swath through open air. Off balance, Rourke fell forward and slammed into the door jamb. Johnson spun around and, with his huge reach, grabbed ahold of Rourke's knife hand to prevent a further attack. He yanked hard, causing the smaller man to bounce around like a rag doll back into the middle of the room. Rourke spun like a drunken ballroom dancer, and landed in a tangled heap on the floor. With lightning speed, Johnson was on top of Rourke having one hand on the wrist of Rourke's knife hand and the other just under the smaller man's jaw line.

After a few seconds, Johnson carefully removed his hand from Rourke's throat, and using a small amount of strength, managed to get Rourke's knife hand closer to Rourke's own neck. Johnson hoped the feel of the cold steel pressed against Rourke's own Adam's apple would turn the tide, but Rourke's frenzy only seemed to get stronger, in spite of the fact that he had little chance against the huge Okie. He grunted as he tried to get Johnson to release his grip by twisting his hands around Johnson's wrist.

The whole time he was on the floor, Rourke couldn't help thinking how he had fucked this up. He still couldn't believe that he'd let Johnson turn the knife against him, like a goddamn baby. Some street fighter, he thought. It's lucky the boys in Chicago didn't see that.

Johnson continued to press the edge of the knife closer against Rourke's flesh. Come on, Johnson thought, drop it.

It was at that moment that Lucas had come rushing in to break the two combatants apart. He surged forward and wrapped his hands around Johnson's beefy wrist, trying to get the big soldier to release his hold on the smaller man. "Sam," he wheezed as he lugged at his vise-like grip, "Stop."

Downstairs, Sergeant Dietrich and Denninger were startled by the unexpected noise directly above them. Dietrich promptly looked up and then as he turned to

Denninger, he was shocked to see the doctor leaping towards him with his arm out.

"*Was ist das*?" was the last thing the sergeant said as Denninger plunged into Dietrich's throat the knife that he had taken from the box on the U-boat. Dietrich dropped his pistol and tried to yell but the knife had pierced his windpipe, cutting off all sound and oxygen. The momentum of his attack had carried Denninger over the top of the German sergeant as the latter fell, and he slid across the floor into the table. In blinding pain, Dietrich clutched at his bleeding throat, and fighting for air, yanked out the knife, spraying blood in a two-foot arc across the table. The knife clattered to the floor. Although he was fatally wounded, Dietrich, buoyed by the adrenaline coursing throughout his body, stumbled towards the prone figure of Denninger lying askew halfway under the table. Dropping to the floor, Dietrich held one hand to his punctured throat and with the other hand, grabbed hold of Denninger's right leg, yanking as hard as he could. Denninger grasped the table leg and held on fast.

Why isn't he dead? The thought raced through Denninger's mind as he balled himself up under the table with his head under his hands and his knees up to his chest.

At last, the pressure being exerted on Denninger's leg began to dissipate, but he remained under the table, not wanting to move just in case Dietrich was faking it. He finally felt Dietrich's hand let go of his leg, but unexpectedly, another, stronger pair of hands began pulling him with such force, that Denninger banged his head on the way out.

"*Gottverdammt!*" Denninger screamed as he grabbed at his head. He then heard a voice in English telling him to get up. Opening his eyes he saw that it was Markham holding on to his legs. Abruptly, the American soldier dropped Denninger's feet as he whipped around to see the three remaining Germans burst through the front door. Firing a few shots from his rifle, he nimbly side stepped to the left, avoiding Dietrich's bloody body and Denninger, who had instinctively pulled his arms and legs in close to his body like a turtle.

The sound of the gunfire below jolted Lucas, Johnson, and Rourke back to reality. "Holy Mother of God!" Lucas yelled. Johnson seized the moment to give Rourke's wrist a final twist, causing him to yelp loudly and release the blade. Johnson shoved his huge frame off of Rourke and snagged the knife. Rourke was on his feet in a flash. He gave the big man a vicious look and rubbed his hand along his neck where the blade had been held. "This ain't over, rube," threatened Rourke in a low voice.

Johnson ignored the comment as he grabbed his weapon and ran for the stairway. Lucas hit the stairs first and, seeing the Germans ducking for cover near the doorway, began to fire his submachine gun indiscriminately in their general direction. The Germans, surprised by the gunfire on their flank, began to back up to the front door. One of the soldiers got his feet caught up in a floor rug and fell backwards smacking his head against the wall. His neck snapped sideways with a sickening crack. On his way down, he'd squeezed off a final burst of fire from his MP40 into the ceiling, narrowly missing Rourke, who was just heading out of the bedroom. Bullets splintered the floor right by Rourke's feet, causing him to hop like a frog on a hot rock.

"You wanna play, fuckers?" he yelled as he charged down the hallway towards the stairs. With nerves raw, burning, and Pervitin-fuelled, he blew past Johnson and Lucas at full tilt, barreling down the stairway and screaming like a banshee, right at the perplexed Germans.

"Matty!" yelled Lucas, as Rourke screamed "Dirty fuckers!" above the deafening gunfire. Lucas and Johnson were both thrust aside by Rourke's frenzied attack. Lucas fell forward and caught the barrel of his gun in the stairway railing. As he spun around, Johnson, who was in full flight behind Lucas, tripped over Lucas's splayed legs. Johnson's huge bulk shot forward like a cannonball over Lucas and into the small of Rourke's back, accelerating Rourke's headlong charge towards the Germans.

Markham watched the whole thing in awe.

Un*be*lievable, he thought as he bounded out into view. He attempted to divert attention away from Rourke, but the crazed soldier was already on top of the Germans. Somehow Rourke, by sheer dumb luck, managed to fly right between the two, evading even the smallest nick from a bullet, and crashed shoulder first into the half-track parked outside the door.

Lucas was still trying to free himself from the railing and Johnson, completing his slide down the stairway, was lying in a heap by a chair, at which point he finally began to fire. One of the Germans crumpled when three of Johnson's bullets somehow managed to find their target.

Markham, with a clear shot now that "Rourke's Charge" was over, carefully aimed his weapon at the remaining German and prepared to shoot. He pulled the trigger, only to hear the faint click of the hammer against the empty chamber.

It was like a scene out of a B Western, where the protagonists squared off for the inevitable gunfight. It appeared to Markham as though everything was moving in slow motion, and he watched as the lone German raised his own weapon with deliberation at the helpless American.

Markham had always wondered what he would do in a situation like this. He'd faced death a number of times since they hit the beaches at Normandy, but this was altogether different. Defending yourself in the heat of battle is one thing, but this was not the same.

This was certain death and there wasn't a goddamn thing he could do.

He suddenly went cold.

"This is it," he said to himself. He closed his eyes and waited for the sound of the gunfire.

Then suddenly he was aware of a whistling sound that went right by his left ear. He opened his eyes to see the German soldier with his eyes wide and weapon dipped forward. Markham was confused for a second, only then realizing that the widening patch of blood on the German's uniform that had seemed to appear out of nowhere was the result of a knife sticking out of his chest.

Markham and the German both fell to their knees at the same time, one in his death throes, the other out of fear and exhaustion. Markham watched with grim fascination as the dying soldier fell forward, the hilt of the knife which protruded from his chest hitting the wooden floorboards with a hollow thonk. He then teetered momentarily, and finally listed to the right with a breathy groan.

Behind him, Denninger, who had by now risen to a sitting position, was rubbing his right shoulder and wincing. Markham turned around and realized immediately that it was Denninger who had thrown the knife at the German soldier. He crawled over to the older man, avoiding Dietrich's body and said in a soft voice, "Are you okay?"

Denninger let out a short laugh and grimaced. "I'm not as young as I used to be," he breathed.

Markham sat down beside Denninger and became aware of an uncomfortable wetness in his crotch area. To his horror and embarrassment, Markham realized that he had pissed his pants. Oh that's just great, he thought miserably.

Lucas had, by this time, finally untangled himself from the railing and Johnson came over to see if everyone was all right. Markham had surreptitiously removed his helmet and placed it on his lap, camouflaging his unfortunate accident. He looked up at Johnson and nodded slowly. Lucas went over to check on Denninger.

"He's hurt his arm, Phil, so be careful," he said. Lucas nodded and helped up the injured archeologist. Johnson bent down to help Markham, but he waved it off. He stood up slowly under his own power, being careful to cover the front of his pants, and stated that he needed some water. He ambled slowly to the kitchen.

"I smell pee," mumbled Johnson as he sniffed and made a face.

Rourke at last staggered in, smiling from ear to ear, holding his shoulder with one hand and his gun in the other. "What a bunch of saps!" he chortled. "They had the bulge there for a second but I showed 'em! You guys see me empty my chopper into those Kraut lemons? Just like George Raft!"

Denninger looked confused. "What did he say? I'm confused by this language. Is it English?"

"Nevermind, he's just a moron," muttered Johnson as he went over to inspect Dietrich's body.

Markham returned with a half glass of water. Noticing that everyone was looking at his crotch, he explained that he had spilled some water in the kitchen. He then went over to the sofa and flopped onto the soft cushions. "Okay boys," he began in a deliberate tone, "Could you tell me what in the fuck was goin' on up there?"

Rourke immediately stepped forward to say something, but was stopped cold by Markham's upheld hand. "Not you."

Rourke glared at Markham. "What are you sayin' Doug? You sayin' this is my fault?"

Markham just stared silently at Rourke.

"Fuck you. If it wasn't for me, we all woulda been dead!" he protested.

Johnson suddenly stepped forward. "You know Matty, you're right," he said. "If it wasn't for you pullin' that knife on me upstairs and makin' all that noise, if it wasn't for you doin' all that shooting, if it wasn't for you acting like a complete idiot, then yeah, we all coulda been killed."

Markham sat up quickly. "What was that?" He looked at Rourke. "He pulled a knife on you?"

Johnson nodded solemnly.

A dark, threatening look crept across Rourke's features. He took a step towards Johnson.

Lucas suddenly jumped in between them, pushing them apart. "Enough of this shit!" he yelled. "You jerks want to go at each other, you gotta go through me first!" Johnson and Rourke stopped staring each other down for a moment and both turned to Lucas.

"What was that?" said Rourke. Lucas was breathing harder now, and Markham, because of Lucas's rare use of invective, knew that he was serious.

Denninger shook his head in disbelief as Markham finally told everyone to shut the hell up. He turned to Rourke. "Matty ... what the fuck? You pulled a knife? On one of our guys? What in the fuck? Are you insane?"

Rourke looked away and wouldn't answer.

"Hey!" Markham yelled at the recalcitrant soldier. Rourke turned petulantly to meet Markham's gaze as the corporal stood up to make his point. "You reckless fucking asshole. You are this fuckin' close to having your head bashed in," he yelled, holding his thumb and forefinger close together. Rourke started to protest but Markham quickly closed the space between them.

He was soon within an inch of his face.

"You know, I don't know what your problem is, and frankly, I don't care — maybe you were dropped on your head as a baby, or maybe your first girlfriend stole your heart and broke it, or maybe your mother didn't love you enough — like I said, I don't fuckin' care, but as long as we're together, you will listen to me, you will toe the line, and above all, and this is for your fuckin' preservation, you will do as I say. And if you ever pull an asshole stunt like that again, I will put you down myself."

Rourke felt Markham's hot breath on his face and blinked.

Markham backed off. "Got it?"

Rourke, his mouth hanging open like the busted flap on a pair of hillbilly's underwear, began to say something, but then decided against it.

Markham then turned to Lucas and Johnson. They'd both seen this look before. "And *you* two — you *know* better," he said with bitterness.

Lucas stared at his feet and muttered an apology while Johnson remained quiet.

Markham then pointed at the dead Germans and said, "Get these bodies outside, and hide 'em in case somebody comes by. I need to talk to the Doctor here."

Lucas leaned down and grabbed a hold of one body while Johnson effortlessly pulled two of them across the floor.

Rourke hung back for a second, scratching roughly at a reddish patch just under his chin. He'd had enough of Markham's bullshit and briefly thought about settling his hash once and for all. He watched, raging quietly, as Markham went over to Denninger. Oh, it's coming Doug, thought Rourke as he picked up Dietrich's lifeless body and began to drag it unceremoniously across the floor.

Just you and me ...

Markham waited until everyone had gone outside, then he reached inside his jacket and removed the parchment. Denninger watched silently as Markham placed it on the table between them. Markham then looked up at Denninger. "All right, once and for all, what is this?"

Denninger shrugged and looked down at the document. "Well, I'm not quite sure yet. I haven't had time to decipher it, but I believe that it is a religious document from the fourteenth century. Its value is purely historical and — "

Denninger heard a click and glanced up from the document to see Markham's weapon trained at his face. He looked from the barrel to Markham.

"Don't give me that shit — you tell me what it is, pronto," Markham demanded.

"What do you mean? I don't understand."

Markham had had enough. "You are going to tell me what this is or I will blow your face off — right now."

22

OUTSIDE, ROURKE HAD JUST finished covering the dead soldier with leaves and branches, so he sat down on the running board of the half-track and pulled out a cigarette. Lighting it and taking a long drag, he attempted to blow a smoke ring in the direction of Johnson, who, pretending not to notice, sidled up to Lucas and slowly walked the perimeter of the house with him.

As they rounded the corner, Johnson put his huge hand on Lucas's shoulder, getting him to stop. Cocking a thumb behind him, he said, "Phil, I don't know how much longer I'm gonna put up with that guy. You know me, Phil. I mean, he almost got us all killed back there with that John Wayne crap. Remember when you came in the room and I had the knife up against his neck? I was this close to cuttin' his throat when you came in. This close!" He was shaking, and Lucas thought he could see his eyes tearing up a bit.

Lucas remembered then that he had seen that look before. He recalled the first week they were all together at Fort Lewis. Matty Rourke already had a reputation for being a punk and decided to let everyone know that, if they wanted trouble, he was more than happy to supply it. Most of the guys ignored him, figuring that it was just another case of a little guy trying to be a big shot, but Rourke, who had a real knack for figuring out who would and who wouldn't defend himself, wasn't content to let things be.

It had only been a matter of time before Rourke and Johnson would cross paths. Being a conscientious objector is an extremely difficult thing to hide in an army camp, and a predator like Rourke could smell blood.

One afternoon, Rourke saw Johnson in the chow line. He grabbed a tray and managed to push his way forward until he was right behind the large Oklahoman. In a low voice that only Johnson could hear, he started going on about the disgusting things he was going to do to Johnson's sister once he got out of the army. The big soldier refused to bite, so Rourke upped the ante, by exclaiming, in a louder voice, that how terrible it was that "a big daisy like Johnson wound up in a man's army," and that "dicky-lickers like him had no place with fighting men." Johnson remained impassive, but Lucas, who was in the same line, noticed Johnson's tray shaking slightly in the big man's grip. The abuse continued until they got to the table and all throughout lunch. Lucas told Rourke more than a few times to knock it off, but Rourke persisted. Johnson played deaf to the tirade, but Lucas could see something inexorably building within, and told Rourke to can it for good or he'd deal with him himself. Rourke, with a contemptuous look, finally decided that the "big lummox" was just "too fuckin' half-baked" to bother with anyway.

When Rourke finally got up, Lucas moved close to Johnson and told him to forget about the little troublemaker. Johnson never took his attention from his food, but Lucas could see a slight tremor as he raised the fork to his mouth.

I'd hate to see this guy if loses it, he had thought to himself at the time. A dip like Rourke was too dumb to know better, but someone as outwardly easygoing as Johnson could be a real time bomb, and pushing his buttons could be a sure way to the intensive-care ward.

Later that night, word was out that Rourke was in the infirmary. Someone had found him in the latrine with a huge lump on his forehead and facedown in a toilet bowl.

His mouth was full of feces. Rourke had had no recollection of what had happened. All he could remember was going to the latrine and then waking up in the infirmary with a mouthful of turds. No one was brought in for the attack even though there was no shortage of suspects. Rourke had pissed off just about everyone in the camp, but Lucas had had a pretty good idea who had done it. Although Johnson had an alibi, Lucas was convinced that the huge pacifist had somehow been responsible. When he was told about Rourke's condition, Johnson merely shrugged and said, rather cryptically, "Well, that's what happens to guys with dirty mouths."

Lucas saw the same look in Johnson's eye now that he had seen back at Fort Lewis. "We gotta stay cool, Sam. Doug is ready to kill him too, but we gotta stick together if we're gonna make it through this."

Johnson sighed, appreciating the effort, but remaining unconvinced. He had been very close to doing some serious harm to Rourke in that room, and he wasn't sure how long he could keep his emotions in check.

Lucas knew he was upset, so he decided to change focus. "What do you think's going on in there?" he said gesturing to the window they were just passing under. "What do you think the German's story is?"

Johnson shook his head. "Do you think he's a spy?" he asked Lucas.

Lucas shrugged. "If he was a spy, why would he kill his own soldiers? Maybe … I don't know. It's not making a whole lot of sense to me." He paused. "I wonder how Markham's doing?"

23

DENNINGER STARED DOWN THE barrel of the rifle aimed at his face.

"Are you gonna tell me or not?"

"You can't be serious." Denninger blustered.

Markham smiled humorlessly. "Obviously this document is worth a hell of a lot more than what you say it's worth — or else you wouldn't have killed those soldiers."

Denninger jumped up out of his chair. "What? I saved your life! And this is your gratitude? You are going to kill me?"

"Sit down," ordered Markham, "And cut the horseshit. You weren't saving me. Whatever this thing is, it's plain you would kill for it, and you did. And who knows, you might do it again. Now, I'll only say this one more time — tell me what this is or I promise you I will kill you."

Denninger took a small step backward. Defiantly he crossed his arms and stuck his chin out. "I will not."

Markham slowly stood up and tightened his grip on his rifle. His lip curled back like a mad dog's, revealing his teeth. "I'm going to count down from five. When I get to one, you had better be ready to tell me about this thing. If not ..." He leveled the rifle at Denninger's head.

Denninger went from appearing defiant to looking horrified. "Are you serious?" he stuttered.

"Five ... four ... three ..."

Denninger took another step back. "I saved your life!" he said coolly.

"Don't care ... two ... one ..." Markham closed the distance between them. The rifle barrel was inches from the German's forehead.

"Zero."

Denninger suddenly opened his eyes and looked evenly at Markham. Markham stared back and continued to hold the rifle in the doctor's face.

Neither moved.

"Corporal Markham?" Denninger said in a monotone voice. "Aren't you going to shoot me?"

Markham held fast for a few seconds, and then lowered the rifle. "Son of a bitch," muttered Markham. "You knew the rifle was empty, didn't you?"

Denninger shrugged. "I did not think that you would have done it anyway." He smiled. "Well, Corporal Markham, what do we do now?"

Markham lowered the rifle and a small smile crossed his lips. He sat back down on the sofa and chuckled softly. The sight of an American soldier with an empty gun and a wet crotch must have been truly terrifying, he thought sarcastically.

He motioned to the doctor to sit down. Denninger took his seat as Markham picked up the document. "Okay, you know you're not getting out of here with this unless you do tell me what it is. I may have an empty rifle, but you're not getting past the other guys. It's as simple as that. So if you want this, you're going to have to come clean."

Denninger sat back in the chair and sighed. His eyes felt heavy and his legs were aching. He knew that the American was right. He wasn't going anywhere. He briefly thought of Rahn. Rahn had brought him into this venture five years ago. Perhaps he would have to do the same with these soldiers.

Denninger pulled out his handkerchief and wiped his forehead. Staring at Markham he asked "What do you know about the Cathars?"

When Markham shook his head, Denninger continued. "I think that I may have to provide a little history first. The Cathars were a Christian sect that were wiped out by the Inquisition, actually not far from here. They were burned at the stake as heretics."

"Heretics? So they didn't believe in God?" Markham asked.

"No — it was more a question of how they believed in God."

Markham shook his head and slowly, a disgusted look crossed his face. "This is why I'm agnostic," he muttered.

Denninger looked mildly surprised. "You doubt the existence of God?"

Markham smirked sarcastically. "I just think that if there is a God, he could probably do a whole lot better than what he's been doing."

Denninger raised his eyebrows. "How old are you?" he asked.

"Twenty-eight."

"Such cynicism for one not yet thirty — how does one come to such a state, if I may ask?"

Markham rubbed his jaw and said, "When you've been fucked around your whole life by those who tell you what to do, what not to do, what to believe — I mean, when you're younger, and you want guidance, and, you need guidance — you seek out those you trust, and then you find out that they're just ..." He paused as he searched for the right word. "Well, they're just all ... liars — hucksters on the street, selling you a load of crap that they think will convince you that they're telling you the truth. *God's* truth."

He coughed and cleared his throat. "There's only one truth that I've learned, Doctor. There's no one watching out for you except for you yourself. I tell ya, if I get outta this war in one piece, it won't be with God's help, that's for sure."

The doctor didn't say anything for a moment as he looked at the American. Denninger had always believed that all soldiers, no matter what their core belief was, had faith in God, any God—if only for the idea that there was someone or something watching over them. It made them feel ... safe, comfortable.

Not this soldier.

"Everyone needs faith, Corporal Markham—"

Markham cut him off. "Faith is for the scared, Doctor. They want you to feel afraid so that they can control you. It's what they've been doing since the beginning of time. They tell you to be good or you go to hell. I mean, what does 'good' mean anyway? Explain good to me, would ya?"

Denninger noticed that Markham had begun to flick his nails together.

"I always saw myself as a 'good' guy. Maybe not great, but good, you know ... decent. But I like to gamble every once in a while. If I gamble, will I go to hell? If I kill someone in this war doing my duty, will I burn forever? I mean, just how good do you have to be to go to Heaven anyway? Who makes the decision? God, right? Whose God? Yours ... mine ... theirs?"

Markham suddenly realized he was practically shouting, and then let out a laugh. "Look, Doctor—I didn't mean to jump down your throat. It's just, I'm not so sure that ... religion is such a *good* thing, that's all. You're supposed to love God, right? But they don't want you to love God—they want you to be afraid of God. And being afraid of anything Doctor is, well, not very smart."

Denninger let his eyes drop to Markham's damp crotch. Markham smiled blandly. "*That* was nerves."

Denninger grinned. "Oh, of course, of course. Everyone is ... nervous these days. Shall I continue?"

Markham nodded.

"The Cathars made their last stand at Montségur, a mountain fortress, in 1244. They were accused of heresy. Two hundred Cathars refused to recant so they were burned at the stake." Noticing Markham's horrified expression, he said, "Cheerfully, I might add."

"What?"

"Oh yes, they couldn't wait to dive right into the flames. Now here's the interesting thing — there is a legend that a few months before the execution, a couple of Cathars escaped down the side of the mountain carrying something of value ... "

He paused for effect as Markham waited expectantly.

"The story was that they took a treasure with them — the Cathar treasure. I am not going too fast, am I?"

Markham leaned forward and shook his head. "Nope. What was this ... treasure, exactly?"

Denninger shrugged. "No one knows. Some believe it was the treasure stolen from the Jerusalem Temple by the Romans in AD 70. When the Roman Empire fell to the Visigoths, they looted the city and supposedly brought the treasure back with them."

"And where exactly did they bring it?" Markham asked expectantly.

The archeologist waited for a moment, relishing the drama of the situation, before he continued. "Somewhere in the south of France — somewhere near where we are right now." Denninger leaned back. He watched Markham's expression as he let it sink in.

Markham stood up and slowly walked across the room. He ran one hand through his hair and clicked his thumb and fingernails together faster. "Are you telling me that there's some sort of treasure out there somewhere and nobody's found it yet?"

Denninger picked up the parchment delicately and held it out to Markham. Smiling, he said, "No one has ever had *this* before." Markham took the parchment in his hands and studied it with new eyes.

"So this thing is like a treasure map, right? What does it say?"

"I don't know, yet" Denninger responded. "I haven't had any time to decipher the document as of yet, unfortunately. I have been, umm ... occupied."

"Do you think you can decipher it, though? I mean, do you think you can figure out what it says?" pressed Markham. Denninger smiled and took his off his glasses. He took the document from Markham and brought it up close to his face, peering at the mysterious letters, wondering not only what it said, but who created it.

Who created it?

Up until now, Denninger had never really thought about who had actually crafted the document. His eyes wandered across the letters and the symbols, trying to make sense of the whole thing. After a few moments, he looked over the top of the parchment at Markham. The American soldier had a strange look on his face.

Putting his finger on the parchment and pushing it down so that he could see Denninger's face better, Markham stared straight into the older man's eyes. "Here's the deal. Me and the other guys have been going off our nut since we hit the beach back in June. We've been shot at, pissed on, run off our feet, and gone days without a full night's sleep. We lost our unit and once we find the American army, or rather, once they find us, they'll just assign us to a new unit where we're gonna be shot at, pissed on, run off our feet, and get no sleep again.

"I can't speak for the other guys, but I know that I ain't no career soldier. I wanna survive this fuckin' war so I can go back home to my shitty little life where there's no one tryin' to kill me. Now, here's the thing ..." Markham plucked the parchment out of Denninger's hand and stood up as if to emphasize what he was saying. "I don't know what this is or if anything you've been telling me is crap or not. Let's say that this is true. You and me, and

Phil and Sam and the little shit are gonna go and find it. If we do find something, then we split it five ways."

Markham held out his hand to the archeologist. "Do we have a deal?"

Denninger paused. He looked down at the table and saw Rahn's book staring back at him.

Lucifer's Court.

The irony of making a deal with the devil was not lost on him. He had no choice, it seemed. He took Markham's hand and shook it.

Markham grinned and headed towards the front door. Sticking his head outside, he called to the others. As Lucas and Johnson came running from around the corner, Rourke stubbed out his smoke against the German halftrack. He methodically got up and slowly followed the other two into the farmhouse. He shot Markham a smug look as he brushed past him on his way into the living area.

"Are we bugging out Doug?" Lucas asked hesitatingly. Markham shook his head and walked over to Denninger.

Picking up the parchment he said, "Boys, have a seat. We've got something to tell you."

PART TWO

Judea
AD 33

IT WAS GROWING DARKER. As Yakob looked at the figure on the cross and watched his head beginning to loll to one side, he knew that it would not be long now. He bent over and surreptitiously removed a wineskin from the satchel. He placed it on the ground, reached back into the satchel, and removed a sponge.

"Find me a long stick," he whispered to Kipha. Kipha moved away as Yakob gently shook the wineskin.

The Roman guards sat below the cross, dividing up amongst themselves the meager belongings of the victims. Above them, they heard a cough. They looked up to see blood falling on them in a crimson spray. One of the guards angrily jumped up and struck him in the thigh.

"Pig!" he yelled. "Control yourself."

The other guard slowly stood, stretching himself to shake off the pins and needles that were stabbing at his lower back. He looked up and smiled arrogantly. "Where is your God now, Rabbi?"

The figure on the cross slowly opened his eyes and saw Yakob and Kipha hazily in the distance. He then, with all his remaining strength, called out, "My God ... my God ... why have you abandoned me?"

This is it, thought Yakob. It was time to move. He picked up the wineskin and sponge and motioned to Kipha. As they quickly moved towards the cross, Yakob drenched the sponge liberally with liquid from the wineskin. They approached the Roman guards meekly, hoping that they would be allowed to do what they intended.

When the guards saw them approach, one of them blocked their path. "What do you want?"

Yakob held out the sponge.

The guard stepped forward to inspect the sponge that was now affixed to the branch in Yakob's hands. A strong odor of vinegar from the sour-wine soaked sponge greeted the Roman. The guard, light-headed from the wine that he and his companion had been drinking, nodded and moved out of the way to let Yakob pass. Kipha was by now shaking and sweating and Yakob shot him a dirty look.

"Just the *posca,*" said the guard to the other as the two passed by.

Yakob now stood underneath the cross and looked up. He saw no movement at all. Slowly he raised the stick with the sponge until it was right in front of the condemned man's nose and mouth. Yakob pushed it gently forward into his face. The figure stirred slightly and finally seemed to take in the *posca*. After a few moments, Yakob lowered the sponge.

The man opened his eyes and seemed lucid, if just for a moment. Yakob held his breath while Kipha put his fists against his temples. Convulsing slightly, the condemned man suddenly cried out hoarsely, "It is accomplished!" He then went limp, and sagged downward.

Yakob dropped the stick with the sponge to the ground and looked at Kipha, who had fallen to his knees. Turning towards the guards, he pointed. "Look … ."

The guards looked up at the unmoving form above them. One of them nudged his leg but there was no reaction. They exchanged confused looks with each other. The *posca*, instead of hastening his death, should have revived him. Perhaps the initial scourging took too much out of him. Suddenly, without warning, one of them thrust his spear into the unmoving man's right side.

Yakob gasped and Kipha almost passed out. After a few seconds, the guard roughly yanked the spear out.

The figure never stirred.

The guard turned to Yakob and shrugged. "Well," he said, "He is dead. At least we won't have to break his legs."

Yakob insisted that he be allowed to take down the body. The guard swiftly became threatening. "He stays where he is until the birds and dogs are done with him." Yakob, upset and anxious, repeated his demand.

The guard remained impassive. "Talk to Pilate," he muttered. "Until then, he stays where he is."

Yakob trembled with quiet rage, but he knew not to push it. He and Kipha hurried away from the scene, taking care to retrieve the sponge. Yakob then turned to Kipha. "Hurry. Go see Yosef — tell him to go to Pilate to see what he can do, and remember, we do not have much time," he told him.

Kipha nodded and hurried away as Yakob sat back down on the ground, warily keeping an eye on the situation.

At his palatial home on the outskirts of the city, Pontius Pilate paced the floor and fumed. To be sure, he had been upset when he was sent to Judea to be the governor of a desert wasteland, but the anger he had felt then was nothing compared to this. He could not believe that he had let himself lose control, especially with an itinerant preacher.

It was those Jews, he thought malevolently. This was their issue, not Rome's. He should have sent them away when they had come to him with their complaint. Was it his business that a Jewish preacher caused problems at the Temple? Passover was their holiday, not Rome's. It was their temple. It was their problem.

If only they had not insisted this man was a seditionist, then he would have been free and clear. They claimed that this preacher had called himself the "King of the Jews." Anyone claiming to be king, *any* king, would be in violation of Roman law, even if he had only said he was the "King of the Jews."

Pilate was the one who would have to deal with it. He was in a tough spot, to be sure, but he decided that he would not get caught up in what he believed to be, essentially, a Jewish spat. He would hear the case, and then give the preacher a token punishment. Everyone would be happy.

That had been the plan.

When the preacher had been brought before him, he did not make much of an impression at first. They had dressed him in a dirty robe, and it looked to Pilate that he had not bathed in days, although he knew this was due to the beating he had received when he had been arrested. Pilate was anxious to get it over with, so he'd ushered the others out and removed the preacher to his quarters for questioning.

The interrogation was uneventful until Pilate asked in a bored voice, "So ... are you the King of the Jews?" He was completely unprepared for the answer.

The preacher paused, then methodically responded in a quiet, even voice. "Is that your own idea or did someone tell you that?"

For a few moments Pilate could not find his voice and his mind reeled. Have I just heard correctly? Did this man just ask if it was my own idea? *My idea*?

As the implication of the statement sunk in, Pilate's eyes narrowed. Only one Jew would call another Jew the "King of the Jews." Did this criminal just call me a *Jew*?

Pilate sensed his face flushing with anger and he felt his blood beginning to boil.

Ever since he had been appointed governor of Judea, his hatred for the Jewish population had been no secret to anyone, least of all to those in Rome. He had had no qualms about ill-treating them whenever he felt like it and because of this attitude, he had been in trouble numerous times with Rome and the emperor, Tiberius. Tiberius knew Rome could not afford to aggravate the largely Jewish local population if they were to have any success there. Thanks to Pilate's numerous indiscretions, a hands-off policy with the Jews was instituted in the region and Pilate had been told to consider himself warned for the last time. His patience, however, had grown extremely thin with these people.

And now, this preacher, this criminal, had just accused him of being one of them.

Pilate was beside himself with rage. His eyes flashed as he asked with venom and a clear anti-Jewish malevolence, "What? Am I *a Jew*?"

The preacher, unmoved by Pilate's menacing tone, had actually seemed to enjoy Pilate's response. It was as if this was the reaction the prisoner had been hoping for.

Pilate quickly composed himself, but inside he seethed. He continued the questioning but his mind was made up. No one insults Pontius Pilate, he said to himself. No matter what happens, he vowed, this man will pay, and pay dearly.

When Pilate was finished, he called for a guard. "Remove this man to his cell. Prepare him for punishment."

Kipha found Yosef with the others at the meeting place where they had broken bread together the night before. He related to Yosef the events of the last hour and that things had not gone as hoped. They had wanted to get the body from the cross, but the guards had refused the request. Kipha told Yosef that it would have to be up to him to speak to Pilate. Yosef nodded solemnly, but he was not sure if Pilate would acquiesce so easily. The governor was rabidly anti-Jewish, notorious for following the letter of the law, and the law stated that all who are crucified are to remain on the cross until there is nothing left but bone. Yosef was not sure what he could do.

But he would have to try.

The noise in the hall was disturbing Pilate. He had ordered quiet, but it seemed that no one was listening to him. When he demanded to know what was happening, his servant came hurriedly into the room. "Someone insists on seeing you, sir," he announced.

"Tell him I am busy," responded Pilate, irritated at the interruption.

Yosef, outside in the hall, heard the exchange and stepped just inside the doorway. "I think you should see me, Governor," he said in a measured tone. "It is very important."

Pilate rubbed his temples in fatigue. "It is always important. I told you, I am busy."

Yosef began to feel agitated. He had to conduct his business quickly, as he knew that every minute counted. He spoke again from just outside the doorway, his voice a little more urgent. "My name is Yosef. I am a tin merchant from Arimethea and just recently back from Rome. I should like to speak to you for a moment."

Pilate continued to rub his temples and sighed. "What is this about, and will it take very long?" he finally asked.

"It should not. It is about my nephew, Yeshuah."

Pilate paused. He looked at Yosef with a bored look. "Yeshuah? I know no Yeshuah."

"You should ... you killed him today."

Pilate looked at Yosef again, this time with considerably more interest. "Come in," he said.

Yosef entered the room and bowed slightly. Pilate showed him to a chair and told him to sit down. As Yosef settled in, Pilate poured a glass of wine for himself, and then offered Yosef a glass. Yosef shook his head and said

"I mean no disrespect to Rome or the law, but I come to ask a favor."

Pilate drained the glass and poured himself another. "What is it you want, tin merchant?"

Yosef shifted in his seat slightly and cleared his throat. This man is a pig, he thought. "I wish you to release my nephew's body to me. He is dead and I would like to put him in my family's tomb. I hope you will grant me this wish."

Pilate looked a little confused. "He is dead? Already? Impossible! Crucifixion takes days, not hours," he said, waving his hand dismissively.

Yosef looked grim and said "I believe the beatings and torture may have had something to do with it. You Romans are very thorough. He was very weak when he was ..." Yosef paused for a moment. " ... when he was nailed to the cross."

Pilate shrugged and put a finger to his lips. "You say his name was Yeshuah? There was a crowd here yesterday making much noise about him, but they called him by another name, as I recall."

"Barabbas," said Yosef. "He was also known as Yeshuah Barabbas. It means 'Son of the Father.'"

"Ah, yes ... the Son of the Father — your Messiah. Did you know we execute a Messiah a day? You Jews seem to have a number of them."

Yosef's patience was wearing thin, yet he was aware that getting mad at this bigoted dog would do no good. He stood up, keeping his anger in check. He knew that if he was to succeed, he would have to humble himself to this arrogant Roman. "Be that as it may, it would be a great personal favor if you would release his body to me."

Pilate waved his hand. "Out of the question. His body stays where it is. That is the law."

Yosef thought for a moment, then said, "I see. I am, of course, saddened by your decision." He turned towards the door and on his way out he remarked, "I must depart for Rome immediately. I'm sure my friends there would be very interested to hear about my nephew's death. Good day."

Pilate told Yosef to wait for a moment. "Friends in Rome? You have friends in the capital?"

Yosef turned back to Pilate. "Of course. I even have friends in the Senate."

A cold chill rapidly swept down Pilate's spine. This Jewish tin merchant probably *was* well connected. If word got back to Tiberius that he had just killed a Jew in direct violation of his order ...

Quickly, he jumped up out of his seat, smiling obsequiously. "Perhaps I have been hasty after all," Pilate said as he scribbled something on a piece of parchment. "I think that it may be a good idea to let you take the body."

Yosef smiled humorlessly. He wasn't surprised. Pilate really was a repugnant creature.

Pilate put one arm on Yosef's shoulder and handed him the parchment with the other hand. Yosef shuddered at his touch as he read it and saw that it was a notice of release for Yeshuah's body.

"Anyway," Pilate continued, "What's one Messiah, more or less? I am sure there will be another to take his place tomorrow."

Yosef ignored the comment. "Thank you Governor," he said over his shoulder on the way out. "God will smile on you for what you have done."

Pilate slumped down into his chair after Yosef left and heaved a heavy sigh. He poured himself another glass of wine and began to drink it slowly, this time savoring the liquid as it traveled down his throat.

A smile from God, he thought sarcastically.

Whose God?

—■—

With the parchment in hand, Yosef and Kipha headed to the Hill of Skulls where they joined Yakob who was still keeping watch. They approached the guards who, after viewing the parchment from Pilate, finally agreed to let them take the body. They refused to help, but remained to keep an eye on the procedure.

"We must hurry. It is almost dark," whispered Yakob. Gently, they were able to lower the cross, and then set about removing the nails. Kipha laid out a burial shroud on the ground so that they could place the body upon it to transport it to Yosef's tomb. Once he was removed from the beams, they laid him gently on the cloth and covered him. Yakob then took one end of the shroud and Kipha the other. The trek to the tomb wasn't far and within minutes they had moved the sealing stone out of the way of the entrance and went in. Carefully, they placed the body upon a flat rock inside. They left the tomb and once outside, rolled the big rock back into its place.

It was done.

The guards, satisfied with the burial, moved off, back to their positions. Once they were out of earshot, Yosef then turned to the others. "All right. Everyone meet back here at midnight and remember, not a word to anybody."

Kipha took hold of Yosef's arm. "Will he be—?" he began, but Yosef held up his other hand to silence him. "Remember," he warned. "At midnight, and not a word to anybody."

Arles, France
October 16, 1307

"JACQUES DE MOLAY HAS been arrested!"

Eudes Roux looked up from the document he was working on, with a look of utter shock. Jacques de Molay, the Grand Master of the Knights Templar had been apprehended in Paris.

"When?"

The bearer of the news, Gratien Lambert, collapsed into a chair by the fire. He had made it out of Paris a few nights previous, knowing that he had to make it to Roux as soon as possible. If he had been caught, it would have been the stake for him.

"On Friday the thirteenth. All the Templars in the area were rounded up and thrown in prison." He closed his eyes. "It is exactly what we've feared, Eudes. They are arresting all of the Templars. I fear they will be coming for us next."

Roux put the quill down and stood up. He ran a hand through the tufts of red hair that sprouted up just above his ears, framing his bald head. His brown eyes widened as he looked at the young knight who was visibly shaking. "So he has actually done it," Roux said quietly.

"He" was the king of France, Philip IV, also known as Philip the Fair. For years Philip had been trying to get his hands on the Templars' legendary wealth. The royal coffers had been bankrupted by the excessive spending of Philip's grandfather and father and it was up to Philip to pull the crown out of debt. He had tried taxing the Church, but that failed miserably. He had also devalued the coinage of the realm, but that caused riots in the streets.

He had to do something else. He turned to his councillor Guillaume de Nogaret who devised a plan whereby they would remove the Pope and install a puppet in the see of Rome at Avignon, where the papal court would be free from the interference of the Roman families. He also developed a scheme whereby the Templars would be found guilty of crimes against the Church and Philip would then be able to confiscate their wealth with impunity. He would have everything he wanted. Including the Cathar treasure.

Philip had heard about the treasure of the Cathars, the rumors of what it actually was. If they were true, it would explain how the Templars had held sway over the Church for so long.

The stories of the escape of the treasure-laden Cathars during the siege of Montségur had abounded in the Languedoc area for over sixty years, and the possibility that the heretics may have met up with the Templars was not lost on Philip. The fortress at Montségur had been completely empty of anything of value when the Inquisition had searched it, leaving the obvious question as to what exactly had been removed.

What had the escaping Cathars taken? And what had they given to the Templars?

Philip was finally about to find out.

Roux sat back down at the table and took a long drink from his glass of brandy. The candle cast a dim light upon the parchment that he had been working on. He glanced up at Lambert with a stern look. "How long before the rest are captured?"

Lambert figured it wouldn't be long. "I've been told that the *Knight of St. John* will be ready to sail from Marseilles by midday tomorrow. They are waiting for this. When will you be finished?" he asked hopefully, gesturing to the parchment on the table.

Roux nodded. "It is ready now."

He picked up the finely scripted page and checked to see if the ink was completely dry. Satisfied that it was, he carefully rolled it up and reached across the table to pull a small oak box towards him. He opened the box and extracted a number of cloths that were inside. He then laid the document on the cloths and folded them over, so that the scroll was completely covered, and placed it into the box. Roux locked it and then handed it to Lambert. "Take it and leave now. We cannot take any chances."

Lambert took the box from Roux and wordlessly headed for the door without looking back. Roux waited for the door to close and watched Lambert through the window as he disappeared into the night.

Once he was gone, Roux locked the door and checked the table where he had been working. He grabbed all of the scrap pieces of parchment and threw them into the fire. Satisfied that any evidence of the text had been destroyed, Roux then dragged the chair by the table into the middle of the room. Roux thought about what was in store for the captured Templars in Paris. The Inquisition was extremely adept at extracting information from their prisoners.

As a Knight Templar, Eudes Roux was a Catholic and had always lived his life according to the tenets of the Church and the code of the Templars, but now it seemed so hopeless. He took a length of rope which he had obtained from the stable earlier and threw one end over the beam just above him. He carefully stepped on to the chair and tied one end firmly to the beam. Once he was satisfied that the rope was tight, he fashioned a noose from the other end and quickly placed it around his neck. As a Catholic, he knew that suicide would prevent him from going to heaven.

Not that that mattered much now. Heaven seemed so ... pointless.

It was more important that he not be captured alive.

In the seconds before he kicked the chair out, he remembered a passage from the Bible. It was from the fifteenth chapter of Paul's first letter to the Corinthians. *Si autem Christus* ... Somehow, in the instant before the drop snapped his neck, the fourteenth verse had more resonance to him now, than it ever had before.

Lambert reached Marseilles an hour before the ship was about to set sail. He leapt from his horse and he saw the *Knight of St. John* anchored in the harbor. It was a cog, a small, single masted ship used primarily for exploring shallow coastal waters, but since this ship had been rigged with large, Atlantic type sails, it was apparent that she was set for the long voyage along the French and Spanish coasts to Scotland.

Lambert hurried up the gangplank with the oak box and looked desperately for the captain. A large mountain of a man with a full growth of beard practically enveloping his face, gruffly directed Lambert to have a seat and told him to wait. The captain was below deck, doing final checks.

Lambert shivered in spite of the warmth from the midday sun, and ran his hands nervously over the box. His leg shook. He furtively looked around at the sparsely populated deck, trying to ignore the suspicious glances of the crew. One of the sailors, a small, but wide and thickly muscled character waddled over. Lambert, pretending not to notice, watched him out of the corner of his eye, and as the sailor got closer, his grip on the box got tighter, draining his knuckles of color.

The sailor stood over Lambert, his shadow cutting across the young knight's face and body. Lambert looked up and saw the sailor pointing at the oak box. "What have you got there, boy?" he demanded in a cracked, guttural voice. Lambert noticed that the throat of the sailor had a hideously jagged scar that ran from his left ear to just below his right jaw. Lambert did his best to muster up an air of bravado.

"This is for the captain — only he is allowed to have it," he answered as intimidatingly as he could. The sailor just smiled, exposing his yellowed teeth and held out his hand.

"Well then, that would be me — hand it over, son."

As the sailor reached forward to snatch the box out of Lambert's hands, there was a quick movement behind him and a thunderous crack that unmistakably signified wood connecting with bone. The sailor's hands quickly grabbed at the top of his head and his eyes snapped closed in pain as he dropped to his knees. Behind the fallen sailor, Lambert saw a large individual with what looked like an ax handle in his right hand.

"Someone come and get rid of this thing here," he said with authority, kicking the wriggling form at his feet. Two sailors quickly ran over and began pulling the semi-coherent creature across the deck.

This must be the captain, he thought as he stood up. For a Knight Templar, Gratien Lambert was admittedly shorter than requirements demanded, but in recent years, that particular demand had seemed to fall by the wayside. Lambert was nonetheless a little surprised to see that he only came up to the captain's chest. The captain was at least six and a half feet tall. He also seemed to be of a very different sort from the others on board. He was immaculately dressed and seemed to carry himself with a regal comportment. He had a long brown beard and closely cropped hair. His face was ridged with hard lines and his eyes were deeply set. His huge arms were crossed in a defiant manner, and Lambert noticed that on one of his fingers was a gold ring with a Maltese cross insignia.

There was no doubt that the man before him was a Templar.

Lambert gave the box to the captain who took it with a small nod and then handed it to someone that Lambert presumed was his first mate. The captain then turned back to the diminutive knight. “Do you have any idea what this is?” he inquired, jerking his thumb at the box. His voice, in spite of his size, was fairly melodious, but Lambert could still detect a hint of menace.

Lambert cleared his throat nervously. “No sir, I do not. I was just told to deliver it to you as soon as possible,”

In truth, Lambert did know exactly what was in the text. He had helped Roux draft it before he’d gone to Paris. He was also acutely aware that to admit that he knew what it contained would mean his death.

The captain continued to stare at Lambert, his eyes boring into the smaller man’s, making Lambert squirm. Without saying a word, he pulled a dagger from out of his belt and with his other hand, grabbed the smaller knight and brought him to within an inch of the blade. Lambert quickly took a breath as he felt the razor edge of the dagger press against his throat. He could sense the captain’s warm breath against his cheek as the blade began to dig deeper into his skin. The small man involuntarily let out a small whimper.

At the sound of the whimper, the captain let go of Lambert, letting him fall to the deck with a light thud. The first mate chuckled. The captain looked down at Lambert and said derisively, “Somehow, I don’t think that they would have told you anything, little boy,” and put the dagger back into his belt. Lambert rubbed his neck as he slowly got up.

The captain gestured to the gangplank. “You are free to leave, my friend. Go home to your mother.”

Lambert shot him a dirty look as he hurried down the gangplank. As he ran to his horse, he watched over his shoulder as the Templar flag, a skull with two crossed bones underneath on a field of black, was hoisted.

He made the ride to his hometown of Rennes-le-Château in a few days. Upon his arrival, he dismounted and entered his house quietly. He didn't want to wake up his parents who were fast asleep in a nearby bedroom. Lighting a candle, he sat down at his desk and took up a quill near the inkstand. He dipped the nib in the ink and, in spite of knowing the dangerous course of action he was about to undertake, he began to write. He knew what he was doing could very well put their whole plan in jeopardy, but since the scroll on board the *Knight of St. John* was the only copy, and would be sent across the ocean to New Scotland, he was afraid that if something happened on the way, the secret would be lost forever.

Lambert would not, could not let that happen.

He had mentioned to Roux that there should be another copy in the event that the original got lost or destroyed but Roux was vehemently opposed to this. They had argued many times over the existence of other copies until Lambert finally acquiesced to only having a single key. It was the only way, Roux had insisted. Lambert reluctantly agreed.

For the time being.

Now that Roux was certainly dead, Lambert could do what he knew deep in his heart he had to do.

Once he was finished, he surveyed his handiwork. It certainly wasn't as elaborate as the original, but it followed the same pattern albeit on a much smaller scale. He was satisfied.

Lambert blew out the candle, put the parchment inside his coat and left the house. It was still dark and he figured it was only an hour until daylight. He mounted the horse and spurred it on towards the village church. As he rode, he smiled to himself.

It would be the one place where they would never look.

24

As Markham filled in the others with the details, Denninger studied the document for what was really the first time since he had received it. He adjusted his glasses and began to analyze the symbols in earnest.

In the top left hand corner was a faintly drawn circle. Denninger could see that inside the circle was a depiction of two riders on one horse. Recognizing the Templar seal, he knew that it signified that what he held was indeed a genuine Templar document, and it sent chills down his spine. There was little doubt now in Denninger's mind that the parchment in his hand contained the information provided by the escaping Cathars seven hundred years ago.

Denninger felt a profound humility as he held the manuscript. He thought of the Cathars who were sacrificed in order to protect what was hidden on the page that he now held in his hands. He removed his glasses and cleaned them with his handkerchief then moved on to study the body of the document.

The letters were grouped in a large sixty-four letter by sixty-four letter square. The letters seemed random and there were no sentences or paragraphs.

It was truly mind-boggling to look at.

Behind him, the discussion between the soldiers began to get heated and he was finding it increasingly hard to concentrate. He looked over his shoulder and called out to Markham. The corporal nodded and told Lucas to get the others ready as they would be leaving momentarily.

"We cannot leave just yet, Corporal. It's imperative that we decipher this," Denninger urged. "Otherwise we could wind up going in the wrong direction."

"Can't you make an educated guess, Doc? We really should be leaving before anyone finds us."

Out of the blue, something Otto Rahn had told him that day in his office a lifetime ago popped into Denninger's head.

"Ah ... the land of my beloved Cathars. Springtime in Paris is quite lovely, but Carcassonne and Rennes-le-Chateau ... well, I don't have to tell you, it's an absolute treasure."

Denninger glanced up at Markham with a faraway look in his eye. "Carcassonne. I think we should head towards Carcassonne."

Markham asked Lucas to bring over the map. They pored over the topography together as Denninger carefully rolled up the parchment and placed it inside his bag. Behind him, Rourke and Johnson stopped their bickering long enough to search out any supplies that might be left in the farmhouse that they could use.

When they got outside, Rourke was loading up the German half-track when Markham told him to stop what he was doing.

Rourke turned around with a petulant look. "Are you telling me that we're not taking this? Why?"

"God damn it Matty, I gotta say that nobody does stupid as good as you. Why do you think?"

When Rourke's response was only to shrug his shoulders, Markham lit into him. "This country's crawlin' with Krauts. Do you think that it's such a good idea to be zippin' up and down the countryside in one of their vehicles? For once could you use your fuckin' head?"

Rourke muttered something under his breath and began to roughly remove the things he had loaded into the back of the half-track.

Markham then turned to Lucas. "Okay, it's about seventy-five miles to Carcassonne, but we'll have to stay off of the main roads, so it'll be a little further than that."

Rourke groaned.

"All right boys, let's go," ordered Markham. He and Lucas took the lead, followed by Denninger and Johnson, with Rourke picking up the rear.

They had only been walking for a couple of hours when Markham suddenly told everyone to hold up. Lucas hurried to catch up with the corporal. "What is it, Doug?" he asked.

An odd feeling had come over Markham and he began to rub his finger and thumbnail together as he looked around. Something wasn't quite right. "I thought I heard something ... maybe ..." He lightly rubbed the side of his face. "Have you ever had the feeling that someone's watching you?"

Lucas hastily looked around. "Krauts?" he asked.

A strange look crossed Markham's face as he scanned the countryside. He'd had feelings like this before. He couldn't explain it very well, only that sometimes he would sense that something wasn't as it should be. "Maybe ... I don't know ... ah, it's probably nothing. It was like when we ran into that German patrol a few days ago. But I don't see anyone around, so ..."

He looked back at the others. "Any of you guys see or hear anything back there?" he asked.

Denninger turned to look at Rourke and Johnson, who both shrugged.

"The only thing I hear are my dogs barkin'," complained Rourke. "Can we take five?"

Markham looked at his watch and nodded. They all flopped to the ground where they had been standing.

Denninger pulled out his handkerchief and wiped his forehead, heading towards a nearby rock under a large tree. As he sat himself down on the rock, he reached into his pack and took out the parchment. All right, my friend, he thought as he studied the document. What are you hiding?

The symbols he knew, but it was the letters that had him perplexed. What was the pattern? Where was he supposed to start? There were no sentences, no paragraphs — just a big square, like a giant chessboard.

He blinked.

Like a giant chessboard ...

An image of Meuller talking about chess flashed through his mind. Something had stirred in his memory and all at once he was reminded of a riddle he had learned when he was younger.

A chess riddle ... Markham had wandered over, swigging water out of his canteen. He knelt down beside the doctor and offered him some. Denninger thanked him and took a drink while Markham looked down at the parchment. "Do you have any idea what it says yet, Doc?"

Denninger handed the canteen back to the American and raised an eyebrow. "Do you play chess Corporal?" he asked.

Markham nodded. "I used to play with my uncle when I was a kid. Why?"

Denninger continued to scan the document as he spoke. "I used to play quite often, but I haven't been able to do so in many years. A colleague of mine was very good at it, however. He studied famous matches and always tried to improve his game by indulging in chess puzzles."

Markham took another mouthful of water from the canteen and rolled his eyes. "I must say this is fascinating stuff, Doc."

Denninger shot Markham a mildly annoyed look. "Have you ever heard of a 'Knight's Tour' Corporal?"

When Markham shook his head, Denninger continued, "The Knight's Tour is a chess puzzle where you try to move the knight sixty-four times, landing on each square only once." As he spoke he drew the outline of a chessboard in the dirt with a stick. "You pick a starting point and move it around the board like this ..." He demonstrated by putting the stick on the bottom left corner of the makeshift chessboard and moved it as a knight would move, two squares up, one diagonally.

"You see? Now, imagine that there are letters on each square." He continued to move about the board.

Markham watched for a few moments and then it gradually dawned on him. "Yeah, I get it ... by moving around like that you're hitting each letter only once ..."

Denninger watched Markham's face as he warmed to the idea. "And if you only hit each letter only once, then you're actually .... ." His voice trailed off as Denninger nodded knowingly.

"Spelling out a message, perhaps?" He then sighed. "The only problem is to find out where to start." He started to pore over the letters again.

Markham leaned in and looked over his shoulder. After a few minutes, he murmured "What am I looking for, anyway?"

"I am not even sure," Denninger replied in a low voice.

Markham pointed at the circle with the two riders on the single horse. "What's that?"

"It is the Templar seal. The usual interpretation of the image of the two knights astride a single mount was that it represents their vow of poverty, the idea being that the members were so poor that each knight could not afford his own horse. It is actually ironic considering just how wealthy the order became later on."

"They were rich, huh?" queried Markham.

"Oh yes, very rich. They practically invented banking."

Markham looked mildly impressed. "Really? What ever happened to them anyway?"

Denninger put the parchment down for a moment and took off his glasses to clean them. "In 1307, King Philip of France felt that the Templars had grown too powerful and too wealthy. He ordered that they be arrested, and ultimately they were charged with a number of offences. Many were tortured and burned at the stake."

Markham blinked. "Holy shit — what the hell did they do?

"Well they were accused of many things including idolatry and homosexuality but the main charge was heresy."

"Heresy — what a surprise," muttered Markham sarcastically.

Denninger continued. "Yes, but what is interesting about the whole matter is that they confessed to everything, under torture of course, and then they recanted almost all of it — all except for the heresy charge."

"What was the heresy?"

"Mainly it was the denial of Christ. Apparently at their ceremonies, an initiate would be shown an image of Christ on the cross at which point the initiate was expected to spit on it. They were then told that Christ was a false prophet and not a god. Of all the accusations, this was the worst of the lot, and yet, it was this charge that they never recanted."

Markham stood up and adjusted his belt. "Do you think that they actually believed it? I mean, that Christ was a false prophet and wasn't a god?"

Denninger turned back to the parchment. "Do you know what the Templars were originally called?" he asked.

Markham shook his head.

"They were known as the 'Poor Fellow Soldiers of Christ.' They were warrior monks working for the Pope."

Markham laughed humorlessly. "Well, obviously something must have pissed them off." He looked at his watch. "Pack it up, Doc. We gotta head out."

25

BY THE END OF the day, Denninger and the Americans were about eight miles closer to Carcassonne. Lucas and Johnson headed deeper into the forest to scavenge for wood before it got too dark while Rourke measured out the rations for dinner. Markham sat down under a tree, loosened his boots and stretched, hearing the bones in his shoulders and neck crack. "Ahhh ... *ow!*" he moaned.

"Holy crap, Doug, I heard that over here," remarked Rourke. Denninger was kneeling beside Rourke, laying out a blanket he had taken from the farmhouse, intending to use it as a bedroll. Rourke looked at the German dismissively and pulled out a cigarette. "Hey Fritz — this is my spot," he muttered as he started to light the smoke.

Denninger looked up disdainfully at Rourke. "Oh I am sorry, Herr Rourke, I did not know that you owned the forest."

Rourke angrily tossed away the cigarette, reached down and roughly grabbed the archeologist by his jacket. "Look, fuckface, you had better watch it, or — "

"Or else what, Matty?" Markham had gotten behind the bullying soldier and spun him around. "Is there a problem here?"

Rourke, his face crimson with anger, knocked Markham's hand from off of his shoulder and, stumbling, took a step backward. "What the fuck, Doug? We're fighting these guys, remember? Why are you always stickin' up for him? Whose side you on anyways?"

Markham took a step forward towards Rourke and grabbed his shirtfront. "C'mere a second," he ordered, pulling the smaller soldier with him and away from

Denninger. Rourke was tripping over his feet as Markham yanked him forward.

"All right asshole, you want to know whose side I'm on? I'm on *my* side. Understand?" He pointed at Denninger. "We need that guy if we're gonna find whatever it is we're looking for. Do you want in on this or not?"

Markham was inches from Rourke's face at this point. Rourke absolutely hated it when Markham did this. He could see the sweat on his nose and could smell the fetid smoke from the cigarette on his breath. Rourke said nothing as Markham's grip got tighter.

"Well? I'm waiting."

Rourke growled like a caged animal and vigorously pushed away from Markham. He was breathing harder now, and to Markham, he looked like a churlish child who'd got caught with his hands down his pants. "Goddamn it, Doug — why you gotta keep pushing me around for?"

Markham put his hands on his hips. "I don't want to push you around, Matty. I just want you to smarten the fuck up, okay? Now, I want you — no, I *need* you to leave that guy alone. If you can't help yourself, then get as far away from the guy as you can, because, I promise you, I will not let you fuck this up."

Rourke was straightening his clothes brusquely with his hand and looked at Markham with a sideways glance. "Just don't fuckin' touch me no more," he said in a low voice.

"Okay. I'm taking the first watch. When the guys get back with the wood, make some grub for everybody. And stay cool, for Christ's sake."

Rourke watched Markham as he walked back towards the camp. As soon as he was out of sight, he reached into his pocket and pulled out the bottle of Pervitin.

—▪—

Lucas and Johnson returned with an armful of wood and had a small fire going when Markham reappeared. Denninger was spread out on his blanket studying the parchment. Markham said that he would be taking the first watch himself and that Lucas would take the next.

Rourke finally meandered over, taking a wide berth around Denninger, and started to set up his bedroll on the other side of the fire. As Markham passed by Lucas, he shot a glance in Rourke's direction, then back to Lucas. Lucas nodded, understanding Markham's non-verbal order to keep an eye on Rourke.

Denninger was rubbing his eyes when Lucas sat down beside him. "How is it going, Doc?" he asked.

The archeologist yawned and stretched before he responded. "I need to find the starting place," he said.

"Starting place?"

Denninger explained to Lucas the Knight's Tour puzzle and how he needed to discover the right spot to begin, but he had to admit he was starting to feel disheartened about it. "But perhaps I'm mistaken about this particular solution. Maybe it is not the Knight's Tour after all," Denninger grumbled. "What am I overlooking?"

Lucas scratched his head and asked, "Do you know who wrote it?"

Denninger nodded. "I believe that it was a Knight Templar, so the key would be something relevant to him ... something all the Templars would know." He banged his head with the palm of his hand. "Think, damn it, think!"

Lucas made a face. "Hey watch it Doc, you'll get a headache doing that to yourself." He smiled. "Have a little faith. I'm sure you'll figure it out."

Denninger watched Lucas for a moment. "You are much different from Corporal Markham, aren't you?"

"What do you mean?"

Denninger straightened up. "You seem more ... spiritual to me. Are you very religious?"

"I'm a Catholic, if that's what you mean. Church every Sunday, fish on Fridays—you know. I even went to a seminary for a few years, but ..." He trailed off.

Denninger pressed him to continue. Lucas sighed. "Well, I just didn't think I had the calling for the priesthood. I thought I did at first, but I didn't. I do still see myself as fairly religious, though."

"Do you regret not following through with it?"

"Sometimes. But then I console myself that maybe God has another plan for me."

Denninger nodded sagely and thought to himself that this group of Americans was quite a disparate bunch. He wondered how someone as anti-religious as Markham could bear to be with someone like Lucas, but such was the case with war, he supposed. "Does it bother you very much that Corporal Markham is an atheist?"

Lucas thought for a moment. Eventually he said, "Yes and no. I mean, I feel bad for him for not believing in God, because really, it's such a comfort to know that there's a higher being looking out for you. He's only hurting himself by not living in His love. Yet at the same time, I admire his fortitude, his force of will. If he chooses to live without God, well, that's his choice and come hell or high water, he's going to stick to his guns. It's foolish, and at the same time, very brave."

He winked. "I'll still pray for him though."

Denninger smiled. "*Non nobis, Domine, non nobis, sed nomini tuo da gloriam,*" he murmured as he studied the parchment.

Lucas looked questioningly at the doctor. "What did you say?"

Denninger looked up. "Oh, I'm sorry. It was the motto of the Knights Templar."

"What does it mean? I was never any good at Latin."

"It means 'Not unto us, Lord, not unto us, but to Thy name give glory.'"

Lucas grinned. "Oh I know that one. It's from Psalm 113, verse 9. I believe that the rest of it goes, 'For Thy mercy, and for Thy truth's sake: lest the Gentiles should say: Where is their God?'" Lucas then whistled.

Denninger furrowed his brow. "What is it?"

"I was just thinking ... I mean we were just talking about Doug ... you know, 'the Gentiles say, where is their God?' What they mean by Gentiles is *heathens*. It's kinda ironic, don't you think?"

But Denninger wasn't listening. He was thinking about the Cathars and Bérenger Saunière. He then contemplated the Templars and the accusations against them. Heathens and heretics all, it seemed, and they were all somehow tied together. The question was how?

"Dr. Denninger?"

Denninger was shaken back to the present. He looked at Lucas and smiled. "I'm so sorry. I was thinking of something else."

Lucas looked over at the campfire and sniffed the air. "Mmmm ... I think dinner's ready. Are you coming?" he asked.

Denninger nodded and then slowly glanced back down at the parchment. '*Non nobis, Domine, non nobis, sed nomini tuo da gloriam.*'

What are you telling me? he wondered.

26

THE FOOD WAS TERRIBLE but filling, and after dinner was over, each of them stretched out on their respective bedrolls to sack out. As soon as Markham finished his watch, he made sure to set up his bedroll near Rourke. Lucas picked up his rifle and began his patrol while Johnson collapsed on his bedroll near Denninger. He hoped that the archeologist wouldn't talk his ear off like he had at the farmhouse, so he made a big show of yawning just to show how tired he was. Denninger watched him and good-naturedly shook his head.

"Goodnight ... uh, Sam, isn't it?"

Johnson grunted and put his hands behind his head. Denninger went back to studying the parchment.

The crackle of the fire and the song of the cicadas filled the night air, soothing Denninger's nerves. He took off his glasses to clean them and remarked, "The cicadas are in fine form tonight."

Johnson turned over to look at Denninger. "The what?"

"The cicadas ... can't you hear them singing?"

Johnson propped himself up on his elbow and listened for a moment. "I thought those were crickets."

Denninger smiled. "Well they are very much like crickets. The locals in this area believe them to be good luck."

Johnson pondered that for a moment. "Huh ... if you believe in that kind of thing, I guess."

Denninger raised an eyebrow. "You don't believe in luck, Sam?"

Johnson just shrugged. "I think that if I was lucky, I wouldn't be here right now. I'd be back in Elmore helping out my family," he said.

"Where is Elmore?" asked Denninger.

"It's in Oklahoma. My family has a farm there."

Denninger tried to encourage the conversation. He was getting annoyed at not being able to figure out the riddle of the parchment and he badly needed a break. "They must be very proud of you back home, I would think."

Johnson closed his eyes and sighed. "Not really. They're what you'd call 'conscientious objectors.' They're against killing and wars and such, so they weren't too happy about my being in the army."

Denninger sat up. "Are you a conscientious objector as well?"

"You could say that, but my pastor explained to me. He said that even though the Bible is against war and killing, I have to do what's right for my country—just like Sergeant York did back in 1918."

"Sergeant York?"

"Oh he was in the Great War. He was a conscientious objector too, but he became a big hero. During one battle he killed over twenty Krauts ... oh, sorry ... I mean Germans, and captured over a hundred of 'em. They made a movie about him and everything—with Gary Cooper."

Denninger was truly intrigued by the big man. Here was someone who could crush you with one hand but he really didn't want to hurt anybody. Yet ... something about him told Denninger that if this gargantuan man was pushed hard enough his conscientious objections could be overlooked.

Johnson gestured towards the parchment in Denninger's hands. "What's the deal with that, anyway?"

Denninger's mood immediately changed to one of frustration, as his attention went back to the scroll. "I am having a devil of a time trying to decipher this." Denninger ran through a brief Templar history and his theory about the chess puzzle. A lot of it was over the big Okie's head, but he gamely followed as best he could. "I should be able to figure it out but, it's a stalemate right at the moment." He smiled at his own joke, but it was obviously lost on Johnson.

"Well I wish I could help you, Doc, but I think this stuff's a little beyond me. Sorry."

He rolled over in his bedroll and said goodnight.

"Goodnight Sam," responded Denninger quietly.

Denninger yawned and gently rolled up the parchment. He put it inside his jacket and slithered awkwardly into his makeshift bed. As he closed his eyes he thought of Cathars, Templars, and chess riddles.

"What the heck are you doing?"

At the sound of the urgent voice, Denninger's eyes snapped open to observe Rourke hovering over him with his hand shoved inside the archeologist's jacket. Lucas had just returned from his post and saw what was going on. He shouted at the thieving soldier, making Rourke freeze in position.

Markham and Johnson were out of their bedrolls and on Rourke before Denninger had even gotten up.

"*Was ist los*?" exclaimed Denninger sleepily as he turned to see Markham and Johnson pinning the smaller soldier to a tree.

"You little fucker! What the fuck was that?" yelled Markham.

Rourke squirmed like a greased snake and whimpered. "I wasn't doin' nothing wrong! I swear! I swear!"

As he wriggled, Denninger checked inside his jacket and was relieved to find the parchment was still there.

He stood up and wandered over to where Rourke was being held.

By now Markham's hand had a grip on Rourke's neck, and the smaller man was starting to turn red. "Stop it! I can't breathe! I can't br — "

Lucas saw that Markham's eyes had gone completely dark. If he didn't stop, Lucas thought, Rourke would either pass out or die. He rushed over and grabbed Markham's arm and began to pull. "Doug! Stop it! You're killing him!" Lucas glanced over at Johnson. "Sam! Pull him off!"

Johnson let go of Rourke and slid his hand in between Markham's hand and Rourke's throat. Lucas switched from Markham's arm and began to pull on his shoulders instead. As Johnson pried Markham's hand away, Rourke slipped out of the hold and fell to the ground, gasping for air. Denninger leaned down to look at Rourke to make sure that he was all right.

It took a minute or two to completely calm the corporal down. Lucas told Johnson to get Markham some water. Rourke was rubbing his raw throat and turned to Lucas with clenched teeth. "Hey — what about me?" he wheezed.

Lucas shot him a dirty look and said, "You're lucky you're not dead. Wait your turn." Rourke petulantly continued to rub his neck.

Markham spoke to Lucas in hushed tones, and then asked Denninger to come over. "Did he get the document, Doc?" he asked.

"No, I still have it," Denninger said as he patted his jacket.

"I don't get it," wondered Lucas. "Why would he want to take it? What was he planning on doing with it?"

Markham's face grew dark again. "Well, let's go ask the little prick then," he muttered.

They moved over to Rourke, who was still sprawled on the ground, trying to get some kind of feeling back in his neck. He looked up at the three of them just as Johnson returned with a canteen. Markham crouched down until he was face-to-face with Rourke. He stared at him without speaking, his eyes burning into Rourke's with a fiery intensity.

Rourke shifted uncomfortably on the ground. "I wasn't trying to steal it, you know," he finally mumbled irritably.

"Really? Then what were you doing? Looking for a rubber?"

Rourke stared coldly at Markham. "You gonna let me talk or are you just gonna hit me again?"

Markham spread out his hands in a grand gesture. "Oh please — enlighten all of us, would you?"

Rourke looked around at Lucas, Johnson and Denninger and cleared his throat. "I think I can figger out that paper," he said calmly.

27

MARKHAM GLANCED OVER AT Denninger with surprise on his face as Lucas coughed nervously. Johnson stifled a smile. Rourke noticed Johnson and lashed out at him. "What the fuck are you laughin' at, rube?"

Markham eyed Johnson and shook his head softly then turned back to Rourke. "Hey, Doc," Markham said, his eyes trained coolly on Rourke. "You got that paper handy?"

Denninger blinked, then reluctantly pulled the parchment from out of his jacket and handed it to Markham. The corporal took the document and unfolded it slowly and then to the surprise of everyone, handed it to Rourke who diffidently took it.

Markham pointed at the paper in Rourke's hand. "All right, hot shot — what's it say?"

Rourke cleared his throat again. He looked at each of them nervously, and then began to speak. "Okay ... I heard everything you guys were saying earlier ... about the knights and the chess puzzle ... the Knight's Tour. You probably won't believe this, but when I was a kid I was a pretty good chess player."

"Hey, I thought you said you were in reform school when you were a kid," Lucas said.

"I guess they had quite a chess club at Boy's Town, huh?" added Johnson.

"Hey, fuck you, rube — "

"Enough!" exclaimed Markham with exasperation. He turned back to Rourke. "What do you know about chess?"

Still glaring at Johnson, Rourke continued. "The Knight's Tour is a famous chess puzzle. I solved it a bunch of times but that's not what I want to tell you guys. It's what Phil said before."

Lucas looked confused. "What I said?"

"Hear me out a sec. You see, when I was thirteen, I used to play chess with this priest, Father Jerry, in juvie—yeah, that's right, rube—he taught me all about chess. He thought that if I followed 'intellectual pursuits' I could make something of myself—"

"Well, that really worked out for you, didn't it?" quipped Johnson.

"Why don't you learn to drive a fuckin' truck…"

"Knock it off, you two," Markham warned softly.

"As I was sayin'," Rourke groused, "Father Jerry taught me all about chess. He showed me the Knight's Tour. He also said there was a whole bunch of ways to solve it. The bigger the board, the more solutions there are. Father Jerry said that on a regular chessboard there could be tons of solutions—and this thing you got here looks just like a chessboard only bigger."

Markham cut in. "So, what are you saying, Matty? It's impossible to figure this out?"

Rourke huffed. "You gonna let me finish?" Markham waved him on.

"Okay… when Father Jerry would test me, he would give me a Bible passage—you know, like 'Blessed are the meek, for they shall inherit the earth.'"

Markham looked confused. "So…?"

Rourke looked at Lucas. "Phil?"

"Matthew 5, verse 4," said Lucas. "In the Vulgate, of course."

Rourke rolled his eyes. "Yeah, okay… whatever you say. Matthew 5, verse 4—what he was saying was *row* 5, *square* 4… you see?"

Markham looked at Denninger who was rubbing his head in thought.

Rourke went on. "I got real good at figgering out that shit, man. So Father Jerry made this bigger board for me — sixteen-by-sixteen. I tell ya, some of those puzzles were a bitch to do, but I figgered 'em all out."

Rourke paused.

"And then I remembered a tough one after overhearing you guys — 'How long will you judge unjustly: and accept the persons of the wicked?' — Phil?"

"Psalm 80, verse 2," responded Lucas.

"Right again. But the problem was, it was only a sixteen-by-sixteen board ... "

Something in Denninger's brain stirred. Rourke watched the archeologist's face as the answer finally dawned on him.

Denninger stepped forward slowly and said in a soft voice, "Row 8, square 2 ... "

Rourke nodded. A chill ran down Denninger's spine as Rourke gave him a knowing look. "Do you get it now, Fritz?"

Denninger stared into the distance as he murmured, "*Non nobis, Domine, non nobis, sed nomini tuo da gloriam.*"

The archeologist turned to Lucas who murmured, "Psalm 113, verse 9 in the Vulgate."

Denninger reached out and snatched the parchment out of Rourke's hands. He quickly scanned the document. He whipped his finger down the first column until he found the eleventh row and then counted in thirty nine letters.

"Row eleven, square thirty nine ... " he said excitedly.

He looked down at the letter *D*.

He had found the starting point.

28

DENNINGER WAS TOO EXCITED to sleep. Why couldn't he see it before? It seemed so obvious now. He was well aware, however, that it would still take some time to decipher the rest of the document as there were over four thousand letters to go through, but at least he knew where to start. He looked at his watch and saw that it was only a few hours to sunrise. He forced himself back into his bedroll, knowing that he would have to be sharp in the morning if he was going to break the cipher.

Markham and Lucas were resting by the fire, discussing the events of the past hour and looking at Rourke who had fallen asleep with a self-satisfied smile on his face. Lucas was somewhat stunned by Rourke's revelations. He'd had no idea that *he* would be the key to solving the riddle. "Who woulda thunk it, eh Doug?"

Markham, on the other hand, was still wary. "I still don't trust the little bastard, Phil," he grumbled. "I know he figured it out, but, he was trying to steal it while the guy was asleep."

Lucas nodded. "Yeah, I know, Doug, but think about this ... if he had said that he wanted to look at the document, or that he could solve it, would you or the Doc have given it to him?"

Markham grimaced. "Probably not."

Lucas looked surprised. "*Probably* not? There's no way that you would. Maybe he knew the only way to get a look at it would be to take it when everyone was asleep. I mean, come on Doug — where the heck would he go if he did steal it?"

Markham pondered this for a few minutes. Lucas was right. It's not like the little shit could take it to some black-market dealer in the middle of a French forest and sell it, but even yet he had his doubts.

On top of that, he still had that nagging feeling that they were being followed. He hadn't seen anyone on his patrol and neither had Lucas. He realized to his chagrin that he was flicking his nails together again. "Well, I'm still gonna keep my eye on him," Markham vowed. "From here on in, I think we should have one of us watching him all the time. Just in case."

Within an hour of sunup, they were once again trudging across the fields and through the forest towards Carcassonne. Lucas had the point, followed by Johnson, Denninger and then Rourke. Markham was bringing up the rear just behind him. It was a fairly uneventful trek until they were just outside the town of Fabrezan. Lucas was out of sight, just over a rise, when he suddenly came rushing back. "Someone's coming!" he yelled. Markham hissed at the others to scramble for cover. Lucas and Markham ran straight for the woods while Denninger, Rourke, and Johnson dove into a ditch by the side of the road.

Markham crouched low behind a bush and shot a look over at Lucas. "What did you see, Phil?" he whispered loudly.

Lucas was peering out from behind a tree, looking up the road. He turned to Markham. "It was a truck. I didn't stop to see if it belonged to the Krauts or not."

The low rumble of the truck got louder as it rounded the corner. Markham waited anxiously for a good look at the vehicle and breathed a sigh of relief when he saw what it appeared to be a farmer's Citroën with a single occupant. The truck, which had obviously seen better days, slowly drove by the soldiers and then pulled up to a stop about one hundred and fifty yards past them. The driver, a man that looked to be in his seventies, clambered out of the cab and wandered over to the other side of the road. Rourke popped his head up out of the ditch and watched as the man began to relieve himself. He turned and looked at Markham and Lucas, giggling like a school kid. The two of them left their positions and joined up with the others in the ditch.

"I think we can make use of that truck, boys," said Markham. "Let's move."

They stealthily made their way down the road towards the truck. The driver, who had just finished his business, turned to go back into his truck but was met by the barrel of Johnson's weapon.

"*Qu'est-ce qui se passe*?" the farmer blurted out in surprise as he raised his hands. Markham came around the other side of the truck with Rourke and Denninger.

"Sam, tell him that we're not going to hurt him — tell him we just need a ride."

Johnson slowly shifted his gaze from the farmer to Markham. "Uh, Doug ..."

Markham suddenly grinned sheepishly, and then looked at the others. "Yeah ... right ... French." Lucas stepped forward. "Do you want me to try Doug?" Markham shook his head.

"Not after what happened when Sam drove the truck into that ditch on that farm near Montazels. I don't know what you said to that farmer, and I don't think you know either, but we're lucky he didn't shoot us all."

From behind Rourke, a hand went up and Denninger stepped forward. "I can speak French," he offered.

Lucas stood next to Markham and whispered, "Can we trust him?" Markham rubbed his chin and cast him a sideways glance. "Do we have a choice?"

He told Denninger to speak to the farmer but to withhold any relevant details about what they were actually doing there.

Denninger spoke with the old man for a few minutes and then hurried back to the group. "Well, he says his name is Etienne, and apparently he is not thrilled with the German army. He says he can take us to Carcassonne."

"Tell him thanks a heap," Markham said as he tossed his weapon and pack into the back of the truck and motioned to the others to get in. He then told Denninger to sit up front with the driver as he climbed into the back with the others. "Everybody, for Chrissakes, keep your heads down," he ordered.

The truck slowly started to move and made a 180-degree turn as it began its journey toward Carcassonne.

Inside the cab of the truck, Denninger had the parchment on his lap and had begun the arduous process of trying to decode the message again, this time from the correct starting point. Etienne glanced over at Denninger a few times as the archeologist traced his finger across the document. "*Qu'est-ce que c'est*?" he asked.

Denninger looked over at him. "I am an archeologist," he replied in French. "This is a historical document and I am trying to translate it but I am having some difficulty."

The farmer looked blandly at the document then turned his attention back to the road. The bumpy ride of the truck and the frustration of trying to decode the document were starting to make Denninger feel a little bit nauseous. He turned his head and looked out towards the horizon in an attempt to soothe his queasy stomach. Etienne smiled.

"Are you feeling ill? You look pale."

Denninger returned the smile weakly. "Just a little. I'll be all right in a few minutes." He rolled down the window, letting the breeze blow through the cab. Etienne rolled his window down as well, creating a crosswind.

"Can I ask you a question?" he asked.

Denninger nodded and closed his eyes as he laid his head against the seat.

"What is a *boche* ... sorry ... I mean a German, doing with American soldiers?"

Denninger looked at him out of the corner of his left eye. "I suppose," he said, "that it is a little odd. It's very hard to explain."

"You don't seem to act like a German ... I mean like the soldiers ... you know," Etienne said. "You are not army, no?"

"No, not at all. I am a historian, and my passion is the Cathars." He turned his head to face the farmer. "Didn't you tell me earlier that you were descended from the Cathars?"

Etienne nodded. "Yes. My family has lived in this area for hundreds of years," he said proudly. Denninger let the wind caress his face for a few moments then asked, "What about your immediate family? Are you married?"

Etienne didn't respond immediately. He stared straight ahead, studying the road and then he spoke. "I was married to my Collette for fifty-three years. She was seventeen and I was twenty when we met. You know, she was the most beautiful girl I had ever seen. She had long dark hair and the most gorgeous blue eyes. My God, she looked like a painting come to life."

Denninger noticed that his eyes were becoming moist.

Etienne took a deep breath and continued. "She ... got sick about nine months ago. She didn't tell me. She kept it to herself. That was so like her, you see. She never burdened me with her troubles. I, on the other hand ... well, I don't know how she put up with me, but she did." He looked at Denninger and he smiled warmly at him. "She was an angel. A real angel." He turned back to the road. "I miss her very much."

"She sounds like she was very special," Denninger agreed.

Etienne just nodded. "Yes, she was special. I'm sure God must have had a good reason for taking her from me," he said quietly.

"May I ask," Denninger inquired tentatively, "did you have any children?"

"I have two sons, Edouard and Remi. And three grandsons ... well, two. Edouard's son Theo was killed last year. He was a member of the CEF."

"The CEF?" asked Denninger.

"Yes. *Le Corps expéditionnaire français*. They were made up of Free French and ex-Vichy French. He was captured and eventually tortured to death for information but he refused to talk to *les boches*. I am very proud of the boy."

"So he was a member of the Free French then," said Denninger. Etienne nodded. "Are you not at all worried to be telling a German that you or your family may have ties to the resistance movement? How do you know I am not a Nazi?"

Etienne turned and eyed Denninger with a crooked smile. "You say you are not in the army and you are traveling with American soldiers. Besides, you don't seem stupid enough to be a Nazi."

They drove in silence for a few more miles and Denninger resumed studying the scroll. Suddenly something caught his eye. "Eh? What's this?" he wondered out loud.

Taking a closer look at the document he noticed that there was a pattern to the letters after all. It was very subtle, but it was definitely there. He noticed that there was a spacing anomaly after every eighth letter, across the top and down. It was almost imperceptible.

Almost ...

The spacing provided eight squares across the top by eight squares down, for a total of sixty-four individual squares, all within one large square. Eight-by-eight squares — like chessboards within a larger chessboard, he thought.

He took another look at row eleven, square fifty-one with new eyes.

If there were sixty-four squares, or chessboards, then the starting letter was now found in the seventh chessboard in the second row.

Denninger smiled to himself. He now had only one eight-by-eight chessboard to work with.

He had just removed over four thousand letters from the riddle.

29

BY THE TIME THE truck had pulled to a stop just outside the city of Carcassonne, Denninger had the message figured out.

He just didn't know what it meant.

Markham and the others had emptied out the back of the truck when Denninger came up to him with the parchment in one hand and a piece of paper with some scribbling on it in the other. He thrust it towards Markham. "I believe I have it figured out," he said confidently.

Markham quickly turned his head to the archeologist. "Are you shittin' me?" he blurted out. Denninger didn't understand what Markham meant, but handed him the paper anyway.

Du visage dernier fils au coeur dieu dels aussors entressim au pierre droite.

Markham handed it back to Denninger. "This is French, Doc. I can't read French. What's it say in English?"

Denninger took the paper back from the corporal. "Well, it looks to me like it is in four parts. If you read it literally, the first two parts say 'from the face last son' and then 'to the heart god,' and the very last part reads 'to the right stone,' but I'm having trouble with '*dels aussors entressim*.' I am confident that it is French, but I do not recognize the words."

Markham jerked his thumb towards the driver. "Didja ask him? He might know."

Denninger nodded and went over to the farmer to show him the paper. Etienne studied it for a minute then looked at the archeologist. "What is this?" asked the farmer.

Denninger explained to him that it was a riddle that he was trying to figure out, but he was having trouble with one of the phrases. He pointed to *dels aussors entrissim*. "I don't understand this particular French phrase," he said.

The old man smiled. "That's because it is Provençal," he responded.

Denninger furrowed his brow slightly and looked at the phrase again. Provençal. Of course, he thought. He should have known that. Provençal was the language in this region of France. At one time it was one of the most popular languages in Europe, the language of the troubadours, and more than likely the vernacular language spoken by the Knights Templar situated in the south of France.

"Do you know what it means?" asked Denninger.

The farmer nodded. "It says 'from the height among the peaks.'"

"From the height among the peaks," he murmured. He thanked the farmer and went back to the group.

Markham spread out his hands when he saw him coming. "Well? Does he know?" he asked.

"Yes he does. Apparently it says: 'From the face last son to the heart god; from the height among the peaks to the right stone.'"

They all looked at each other in confusion. "Well … that's as clear as mud," Lucas said to himself.

The three men were conferring together when Rourke crept up next to them. "What are we gonna do with the Frog?" he asked, jerking his thumb at the farmer.

Lucas turned and made a disgusted face at the slur. "Are you referring to the person who drove us here? He's French. Show a little respect."

Rourke shrugged. "Po-*tay*-to, po-*tah*-to."

Markham told Rourke to knock it off and to keep unpacking the truck and then turned back to Denninger. "So what you're saying is that you don't know what this means ..."

The archeologist scratched his head and sighed. "The way it reads, it doesn't make much sense." He closed one eye and pursed his lips as he studied the phrase. After a few moments he mumbled, "'The height among the peaks' ... maybe we need to add a few words, eh?" He then opened his eye and turned to Markham with a smile on his face. "How about this: 'From the face *of the* last son to the heart *of* God; from the height among the peaks to the right stone.'"

Markham nodded. "Okay ... that sounds good. Now ... what the hell does that mean?"

Denninger shrugged. "Ah well, that I don't know yet. My first inclination is to think that they could be landmarks, but they could also refer to something else entirely. We have to be sure what this means before we rush off in all directions."

Markham put his hands over his eyes to shield them from the sun as he surveyed the countryside. There were mountains and farmlands as far as he could see, but nothing that stuck out like an obvious signpost. He put his hands on his hips and turned to Lucas. "All right, let's make camp here. Put Johnson on guard." He asked Denninger to thank the farmer for his help. "We can manage on our own from here," he said.

Denninger was deep in thought and didn't hear Markham. He was staring at the paper in his hands.

"Uh, Doc? Hello?"

Denninger snapped out of it. He looked at Markham with that look that the corporal was starting to recognize as meaning that the archeologist was on to something. "I'm sorry, Corporal ... it's just ..."

He gazed at the paper. "Something is coming to me ... something I read somewhere ..." He tapped his temple lightly and silently cursed his age. His once infallible memory, he noticed, was becoming increasingly fallible. The things that used to be second nature to him were becoming harder and harder to recall.

Markham repeated his request about the farmer but Denninger shook his head. "I think it may be a good idea to keep this man around for a while."

Markham looked skeptical. "Why?"

"I really do think that this message refers to landmarks around here. He may be able to help us."

Markham shook his head. "We don't need anyone else in on this deal, Doc."

Denninger seemed a little defeated. "Well, I have to tell you, Corporal, that I may not be able to decipher this alone, unfortunately."

Markham scratched his head furiously and looked at the farmer. "Fuck it. Go see what he knows."

Denninger went to speak with the farmer while Lucas sat on a small rise and stretched. Rourke smoked a cigarette and blew smoke rings as Markham read and reread the translated paper that Denninger had given him, trying to, but knowing that he wouldn't be able to, figure it out.

After about ten minutes of speaking to Etienne, Denninger came over to see Markham. The archeologist seemed excited. "All right. I only let him in on what I had to. He says his family has lived here for many generations. He says he can trace his great-, great-, great- ... whatever, grandfather back to the siege at Montségur. Apparently rumors of the Cathar treasure have lingered in this area for hundreds of years."

"They didn't find it, did they?"

Denninger shook his head happily. "Of course not. They didn't have this," he declared, holding up the manuscript proudly.

"But we don't know what it means," protested Markham.

Denninger suddenly smiled knowingly. "Don't we?"

Markham grabbed Denninger by the shoulders, crumpling up the notepaper in the process. "What are you saying? What did he tell you?"

He took the paper from Markham, smoothed it out and pointed at the first line. "He knows what *that* means."

From the face of the last son...

Markham looked at Denninger intently. "Well?" he asked. "Are you going to tell me?"

"The reference to the 'face of the son' was very cryptic, but I knew it had to be a landmark. Remember when I said something was nagging at me? It was this. Etienne ... that's the farmer's name ... reminded me. I really should have remembered this — "

"Doc!" cut in Markham impatiently.

"Yes ... sorry ... 'the face of the last son' — the son ... is a *castle*."

"A castle?" Markham asked dubiously.

"Yes — the castle of Quéribus. You see, there are five Cathar castles that make up what are known as 'The Five Sons of Carcassonne': Aguilar, Peyrepertuse, Termes, Puilaurens and Quéribus. They all eventually fell to the French and Quéribus was the last castle to fall — hence, the 'last son.'"

Markham whistled. "So what's the deal with the 'face'? It says 'from the face of the last son.'"

"Well, Quéribus sits on a mountain, so I would assume it means the face of the mountain."

"But it says '*from* the face' What the hell does that mean? It sounds to me like this is only the first of maybe four places," Markham said with exasperation. "What do you think, Doc?"

Denninger shrugged. "I don't know, but I think if we can decipher 'the heart of God,' we may find out."

30

HE WAS ABOUT FIVE hundred yards away and could see the truck through the binoculars. He only saw three soldiers and knew that one of them was on patrol. He lowered the binoculars, wiped his brow and took a long drink of water from his canteen. When he finished, he checked his watch and figured that they would be settling in for the night.

Since he had been following them from the farmhouse, he had begun to recognize their patterns very well. They had thrown him for a loop by commandeering the truck, but luckily for him, a two-man German motorcycle patrol had come along. Since he had been dressed as a farmer, and could speak French fluently, the patrol, thinking he was an ignorant peasant, gave him the usual hard time they gave all the locals. When they were done, he thanked them in the only way he knew how — a bullet to the face for each of them. After he pulled their bodies from off the road, a task made more difficult because of a painful limp (the result of a near-fatal fall he'd survived a few years before), he tossed his supplies into the sidecar and was soon back on the hunt.

He raised the binoculars to his eyes again and watched as Denninger pored over the papers.

"Very good, my friend," he murmured.

Just then, something caught his attention. Looking to the left he saw what looked like a patrol heading towards the group. He gnashed his teeth in frustration. "Goddamn German efficiency," he muttered.

Lowering the binoculars, he threw them into his pack and pulled out his pistol.

31

THE HEART OF GOD; the height among the peaks; the right stone ...

Denninger was going over in his head every Cathar and Templar reference he could remember. He grilled Etienne again, but the farmer couldn't help.

"Think, Gerhard," he said to himself. "You *know* this."

He was roused from his thoughts by Johnson calling out to everyone to take cover. Markham saw that there wasn't enough time to put out the fire, so he yelled at Denninger to tell the farmer to sit by it, as if he had built it himself. Denninger quickly related Markham's orders to Etienne, who understood. He was just sitting down beside the fire when the four German soldiers rolled to a stop.

Etienne looked up in feigned surprise at the intrusion. "*Qu'est-ce que vous voulez*?" he asked the lead soldier. The German, who knew a little French, ordered Etienne to stand up.

The farmer then became belligerent. "Who do you think you are? You don't tell me what to do," he replied indignantly. "I'm not doing anything wrong here."

The German, a little startled, looked briefly at his comrades and then back at the farmer. "What are you doing here? Where do you live?"

Etienne spit between his feet and looked up at the soldier. "I live wherever I stop. Tonight I live here. What is the problem?"

"The problem, old man, is that this is a war zone. Do you want to get killed?"

"I can take care of myself."

The German was clearly becoming irritated. “Right. I assume that is your truck over there,” he said, gesturing towards the road.

“Of course — am I not allowed to drive in my own country now?”

Watching from the safety of the trees, Markham told Denninger to listen to what they were saying. Denninger leaned out and strained to hear the conversation as Lucas, Rourke and Johnson trained their weapons on the Germans. After a minute, he turned to Markham. “He is not making any friends out there,” Denninger whispered.

Now, annoyed at the attitude of the farmer, the soldier became more menacing towards him. “You French had better understand something. *We* are in charge. Get used to the idea, and things will go much better for you in the long run.” He paused. “You are alone?”

Etienne spread his hands theatrically. “Do you see anyone else around here?”

“Do you think I am stupid, old man?”

“Well, yes ... yes I do.”

Ignoring the retort, yet growing more angry by the minute, the German continued. “You Free French think yourselves very clever and heroic, don’t you? Well you’re not.”

“You think I am *Free* French? Then you *are* as stupid as I thought.”

‘Where did all these footprints come from?”

Etienne grinned. “My guess would be feet.”

The German finally snapped. “Enough! Tell me where the others are or I will put a bullet in your head right now!”

Etienne put his hands up. “I told you, there are no others. I am all alone.”

The German stepped closer to Etienne and put the barrel of his pistol up against the farmer's temple. "Then why don't I believe you, old man?"

Etienne closed his eyes and waited for the bullet.

A second later he heard the shot.

He opened his eyes and looked down at the German crumpled at his feet with blood running from of a hole in his forehead.

Markham looked with panic at the others and loudly hissed, "Who fired that shot?!" as the other German soldiers fanned out and began firing into the woods erratically. Etienne immediately dropped to the ground as Markham and the others began to fire back. The woods were suddenly filled with the acrid smell of burnt gunpowder, and the trees seemed to explode in a shower of splinters and bark. Excited shouts in German and English along with an occasional French oath from Etienne filled the air. A fiery trail of lead followed the farmer as he slithered towards the relative safety of the woods, the last two bullets ricocheting off a rock. One of the ricochets caught Markham in the shoulder, causing him to scream out and drop his rifle.

Rourke nailed one of the soldiers point blank when he burst through a bush and caught the American by surprise. The momentum of the German soldier carried him forward, striking Rourke and knocking him to the ground. The German was lying across the smaller soldier and, in his dying moments, pushed the weight of his machine gun into Rourke's neck. Rourke was on the verge of passing out when Denninger came out of nowhere and kicked the German in the side of the head, knocking him away. A hail of bullets ripped into a nearby tree, causing Denninger drop to the ground beside Rourke.

Rourke gave Denninger a look of relief that was quickly replaced with resentment. "Thanks for nothin', Fritz," he muttered as he got up. Denninger watched as Rourke disappeared into the woods. Suddenly, another volley of bullets just over his head sent the archeologist quickly in the same direction as Rourke.

The two German soldiers who were left had found cover behind a thicket of trees about three hundred feet away. They popped out at uneven and swiftly paced intervals, taking shots in the direction of the Americans. Markham was leaning against an elm tree with his right hand pressed against his left shoulder. He could feel the sharp, hot needles traveling up and down his arm. Lucas had a first aid pack open and was trying to tend to the injury when Markham saw Johnson. The corporal jerked his head to the left, indicating that he wanted the big soldier to try and outflank the remaining Germans.

Once Johnson went forward he saw someone else moving just about a hundred feet behind. "Rourke!" he yelled. "Get over here!"

Lucas had found the disinfectant and applied it to Markham's wound. Markham screamed in pain as the antiseptic salve burned into the torn flesh. "*Je*sus Christ! What is that? Gasoline?" he spit out through gnashed teeth as Lucas ministered to the wound.

Rourke and Denninger crouched alongside some bushes until they had come up behind Markham and Lucas. Lucas heard the shuffling and turned around. "Where did you guys come from?" he asked with surprise. "I thought you were over there," he said, gesturing forward with his head. Another barrage caused the group to rapidly duck their heads.

"Spread out!" ordered Markham. Rourke immediately headed off to the left. Markham looked over at Denninger and told Lucas to give the archeologist a pistol. Lucas glanced up from dressing Markham's wound, with a concerned look. "It's okay," assured Markham.

Lucas hesitated momentarily, then handed Denninger a pistol which the latter took somewhat reluctantly. "I've never used a gun before — " he began.

"Now's not the time for bullshit, Doc."

"No ... I am not lying, Corporal. I have never used a gun before," he reiterated.

Markham gave him a sideways glance. "I guess knives are your weapon of choice, right? Just take the fuckin' thing and follow Matty, would ya?"

Denninger made a face and crouched lower, trailing Rourke.

Lucas handed Markham his weapon. The corporal winced but managed to hold on to it. Lucas moved off to the right as Markham began to fire. Each recoil from the rifle caused his whole body to shudder in pain.

Denninger continued making his way to the left, gripping the pistol tightly in his right hand. He had been telling the truth when he informed Markham that he had never fired a gun before. He was much handier with knives.

He was looking around when he noticed the large form of Johnson about seventy-five feet away. He was just standing in the clearing, not moving. Why isn't he firing? he wondered. He tried to get the large soldier's attention by hissing at him but another fusillade of bullets made him hit the dirt. Once they stopped, he took another peek and saw that Johnson was gone. Denninger figured that he had either ducked or moved.

The firing had died down to intermittent spurts, during which Denninger heard snippets of heated conversation in German. "I think there's one over there," said one voice. Denninger peeked through a bush and saw the two remaining German soldiers. He pulled his head back and hastily looked around. Where had Rourke gone?

—■—

Rourke was out of Denninger's sight twenty feet away, near an oak stump. He slowly raised his head and saw the doctor slightly off to his left. He laid his weapon across the stump and carefully aimed. "I got you now Fritz," he said to himself as he placed Denninger in his crosshairs.

32

THE REMAINING GERMAN SOLDIERS stepped into view and were caught by surprise at the sound of another German voice coming from a bush directly in front of them. "Who's there?" one of them called out. Denninger put the pistol in his pocket and quickly stood up with his hands in the air.

Rourke's mouth fell open as he saw the soldiers step into the clearing. "What the fuck? Where did they come from?"

Denninger pushed his way through the bush towards the stunned Germans. "Don't shoot. I am German."

The Germans steadied their machine guns but kept them pointed at the archeologist. "Who was shooting at us?" yelled one of them. "Was that you? Keep your hands where I can see them!"

The German was clearly rattled, but Denninger kept walking towards them. "I was captured by some Americans. When the shooting started I was able to escape. Thank heavens you are here." The Germans just looked at each other.

Rourke had no idea what was happening. He crouched behind the stump and watched intently. He couldn't risk taking on three of them so he would have to wait it out.

In the sudden quiet, Markham could hear German voices faint in the distance. What the hell? he wondered. That sounds like the Doc.

He was too far away to see anything, so he headed to make his way towards the voices. As he got closer, he noticed Rourke, who seemed to be aiming his weapon at Denninger rather than the German soldiers.

"Son of a bitch!" he cursed. He began to run towards Denninger.

Lucas, who had been moving around the other side, caught sight of Denninger with his hands up. He couldn't see the Germans, as they were hidden by a clump of trees, but he surmised that they must be close by. He started to move slowly forward towards the trees.

As Denninger neared the soldiers, he caught a movement out of the corner of his right eye. He hesitated.

One of the Germans saw the movement too. "It's a trap!" the German called out excitedly and he rapidly raised his gun towards Denninger. A second later Denninger heard the shot behind him and instinctively fell to the ground. The soldier was hit in the chest and he dropped, cursing as he went down. The other German soldier began to fire in the direction that he believed the shot had come from.

Markham had made it to where Denninger and the Germans were, just in time to see the first soldier fall. He'd heard the shot but couldn't see who had fired it.

Lucas, at the sound of the shooting, burst through the trees and to his horror found himself suddenly standing next to the last German soldier, who spun around and gaped at the American. Lucas was just as surprised as the German and began to fire but the only thing that emanated from his weapon was a series of clicks.

His gun had jammed.

Impulsively, he thrust the barrel forward like a battering ram straight into the midsection of the German, who was immediately thrown backwards. Rourke saw Markham closing in on Denninger so he leapt up from his hiding place and made a rush towards the battling soldiers. Denninger had retrieved the pistol from his pocket and was firing it indiscriminately upwards from the ground, the bullets flying harmlessly, yards over the soldier's head.

Lucas now held his weapon by the barrel like a baseball bat and swung it full force at the German soldier. The stock smacked against his helmet with a sonorous clang, sending the dazed soldier into a bramble bush.

Markham watched Denninger, his eyes closed, clicking an empty pistol and turned to see Lucas on one knee, face red and gasping for air. The German soldier was hopelessly caught up in the bramble and Rourke stood his ground, grinning like a village idiot. Markham rushed over to Lucas to see if he was all right.

Lucas nodded and then went over to Denninger to relieve him of the pistol. He took it from the archeologist and began to reload it. "I guess you were right. You never did fire a gun, did you?" asked Lucas.

Markham then looked around and noticed that both Johnson and the farmer were missing. "Sam!" Markham called out. He looked over at Rourke. "Do you know where Sam is?" he asked. Rourke shrugged.

"Ici!"

Markham swung around and saw Etienne about a hundred feet away, waving. Turning to Lucas he said, "Keep an eye on the Kraut," as both he and Rourke swiftly headed over to the farmer. As they got closer they saw Etienne motioning towards his feet. Lying face down in the dirt was the body of Sam Johnson, the back of his uniform torn, wet, and red from machine-gun fire. Markham turned him over and saw that his eyes were open but glazed and there was a trickle of blood at the corner of his mouth.

"Ah, shit, Sam," Markham sighed.

Rourke stood very still. "Shoulda ducked, rube," he said quietly. Markham reached down and slowly closed Johnson's vacant eyes. He looked up at Rourke and told him to grab a hold of Johnson's legs. The two of them carried the big man out to the clearing where Lucas had untangled the German soldier and was guarding him.

Denninger was sitting by a tree and quickly got to his feet when he saw the group emerge from the thicket.

"Oh no," murmured Lucas as he momentarily lowered his pistol. The German soldier, noticing that Lucas's attention had shifted, leapt to his feet and started to make a run for it.

"Phil! The Kraut!" yelled Markham. Phil swung his head around and shouted for the soldier to stop. He quickly raised his pistol, but suddenly he hesitated.

Markham called out to Lucas again. "Phil! He's gettin' away!"

Etienne, who had been carrying Johnson's weapon, quickly chambered a bullet, took aim and pulled the trigger. The German's head abruptly snapped to one side as the bullet smashed through his spine at the neck. He was dead before he hit the dirt.

Etienne shucked the empty cartridge as Rourke looked at Markham with a look of amazement. "Holy shit, Doug! Didja see that?" They lowered Johnson's body to the ground. Rourke turned to the farmer. "Where'd a half-baked clown like you learn to burn powder like that? Fuckin' unbelievable!"

"Hey, shithead! Johnson, remember?" Markham muttered. "Besides, he doesn't understand English ... or whatever that crap is that you speak."

Rourke turned back to Markham. "All I was sayin' was that was some shootin' by the Frog — "

Markham's fist unexpectedly shot out and hit Rourke square in the chin. Rourke fell back and landed on his ass. He sat there, not moving for a few moments, as Markham hovered over him. Finally reaching down, Markham grabbed the smaller soldier and hauled him up roughly. "You and me have to talk. *Right now,*" he intoned threateningly. He ordered Lucas to get Denninger and Etienne to help hide the German bodies and then dragged the gasping Rourke away from the group towards the thicket where they'd found Johnson.

Once they were far enough away from the rest, he threw the sputtering Rourke forcefully to the ground.

"What the fuck, Doug?"

"You little turd! You were gonna shoot the Doc back there, weren't you? What did I fuckin' tell you before?"

Rourke began to protest. "I wasn't aimin' at him Doug. I was gonna shoot the Krauts! Honest!"

Markham's eyes were as dark as they had been the last time he attacked Rourke. The smaller soldier swallowed hard as Markham menacingly stepped towards him. "All right. I'm gonna ask you this once and only once — and you'd better give me the right answer."

"Are you goofy?" Rourke asked with a trace of defiance.

"Okay! Enough of the George Raft shit!" Markham screamed. He was shaking, and his thumb and finger were rubbing together as fast as a cricket's legs on a summer evening. Rourke started to scramble back, away from the out-of-control corporal.

"Jesus, take it easy, for Chrissakes."

Markham took a deep breath and closed his eyes. In measured tones he said, "Listen to me carefully. Did you fire the first shot?"

Rourke blinked. "What?"

Markham slowly opened his eyes. "Did ... you ... fire ... the ... first ... *shot*?"

Rourke sat still for a second, his eyes darting from his own feet to Markham's face. He's really gonna kill me, thought Rourke. Nervously, he cleared his throat. "No — I didn't," he finally choked out.

Markham stared coldly at the cowering soldier. He then reached behind his back and pulled out a Colt pistol. Methodically he checked the weapon and when he was satisfied he carefully aimed it at Rourke and cocked the hammer.

Rourke's eyes went wide as tears welled up in them. He started to hyperventilate. "I told ya — I never fired first! I swear to Christ I didn't!" His hands went up in front of his face and he began to weep hysterically.

A few moments later Rourke heard a click and through his splayed fingers he saw that Markham had uncocked the pistol. Rourke's heart was jackhammering and he felt as if it was going to break a few ribs in his chest.

Markham lowered the pistol and squatted down beside Rourke, satisfied that Rourke hadn't fired the first shot. "Well then," Markham said quietly, "who did?"

33

ROURKE SLOWLY PUT HIS hands down. His nose was running like that of a little kid who's been out in the cold too long, and his breathing was shallow and edgy. "Maybe it was Johnson," he said tentatively.

Markham shook his head. "Doubt it. He was a pacifist. There's no way he would've fired first. Remember back at the farmhouse? He was the last one to start shooting."

"Well, what about Lucas?"

Markham scoffed. "Did you see him react when that Kraut took off? It's lucky that the farmer was there."

"Well then, who do you think did it?" he asked.

Markham didn't speak. He stared off in the distance, his eyes scanning the trees and bushes. Rourke then saw the corporal's finger and thumb twitching. Something's up, he thought uneasily.

Back at the camp, Markham ordered the others to clean up the area and hide the bodies. Denninger was lost in thought as he looked around at the landscape. Just to the east, he saw a gentle slope that seemed to get progressively steeper the higher it went. He decided to get a more elevated view if he could, so as to gain a better lay of the land. He moved off up the rise and after a few minutes, found himself standing on a crest of land overlooking the expansive countryside. As he gazed at Mount Bugarach, the highest mountain in the area, he could hear the faint voices of the soldiers below him.

"We're going to bury Sam, right? He needs a Christian burial," Lucas asked.

Markham scratched his head and looked at each one of them. He saw their concerned looks, including Rourke's, so he shrugged in resignation. "Fine, whatever you say. Phil, c'mere a minute."

Lucas stood next to Markham as he whispered to him that he thought they were being followed. Lucas gave him a curious look. "You still have that feeling, huh?"

Markham nodded solemnly.

"Think it's the Germans?"

The corporal shook his head. "I'm not sure. If it were Krauts, they would just come at us like this patrol just did." Markham scanned the horizon for any hint of a possible pursuer. He then became aware that Denninger was missing. "Where's the doc?" he asked.

Lucas pointed up towards the rise. "He went up there."

Markham started up the slope with Lucas closely following. A few minutes later they were standing next to Denninger who was looking intently up into the sky. He had his hand on his forehead, shielding the sun from his eyes. A grin began to creep across his lips.

Lucas watched the archeologist for a moment then he too, looked skyward. All he could see was a lone bird, circling above them. He looked back at Denninger. "Whatcha lookin' at Doc?" he inquired.

Denninger kept grinning and pointed at the sky. "A bird — I think it is an eagle," he murmured.

Lucas turned his face back up to the sky. He was soon able to identify that it was indeed an eagle. It glided majestically across the sky until it finally disappeared as it flew towards a distant mountain peak. Denninger put his hand down, lowered his gaze and then beamed at Lucas. Lucas was starting to get a little annoyed at the cryptic behavior of the archeologist. He swung around to look at Markham and then jerked his head towards the older man.

Markham decided to find out what was going on. "What is it Doc?" he asked.

Denninger's grin turned into a huge smile as he pointed to the mountain toward which the eagle had flown. "Gentlemen ... ' from the height among the peaks.'"

Markham and Lucas looked to where he was pointing.

"That ..." said Denninger dramatically, " ... is 'le Pech de Bugarach' ... Mount Bugarach. It is the highest mountain in the area ... from the height among the peaks." He shook his head, patently upset with himself. "So obvious," he mumbled.

Markham was looking at the peak and then slowly turned to face Denninger. A faraway look was creeping across the corporal's face. He reached into his pack and pulled out his map of the area. "Doc, c'mere a second," he said excitedly. "Okay, look here. This mountain — what did you call it?"

"Bugarach."

"Yeah, Bugarach ... uh ... yeah, here it is," he said pointing at a formation on the map. He looked up. "Phil! You got a pencil?"

Lucas reached into his breast pocket, took out a pencil and tossed it over to Markham. The corporal caught it and made a circle on the map around the site of the mountain. "Okay Doc ... the first part of the clue that we figured out — the castle?"

"Quéribus," ventured Denninger.

"Okay, where would that be on this map?"

Denninger studied the map for a few moments and then pointed at a spot about twelve miles southeast of Bugarach. "I would say in around here, in this general area."

Markham quickly shook his head. "No, it's gotta be exact. *Exactly* where would it be?"

Denninger looked at Markham and then studied the map again. After a minute he pointed to another mountain formation. "Here — I'm almost positive," he finally stated.

Markham turned the map around and stared at the spot where Denninger pointed. "Are you sure?"

Denninger nodded. "It is the highest of the peaks in that particular area. Quéribus is located on the highest peak."

Markham circled the spot and lightly bit his lip. "What's the clue again? The whole thing, I mean?"

Denninger fished the paper out of his pocket and read it out loud. "'From the face of the last son to the heart of God; from the height among the peaks to the right stone,'" Denninger stated. "'From Quéribus to the heart of God' and 'from Bugarach to the right stone.'"

"Yeah, but what about those other places. I mean, they're places, right? We still need 'the heart of God' and 'the right stone.'"

Denninger turned the map around again. "All right ... Bugarach is here, and Quéribus is south ..." He pointed his finger at one site then to the other. "Now — where is the heart of God?"

34

THEY BURIED SAM A few hundred feet back in the thicket, so that the grave wouldn't be seen from the road. Lucas said a few words, with Denninger translating the whole time for Etienne. Markham refused to be part of the makeshift service, so he sat by the truck and smoked a cigarette while they conducted the ceremony. He noticed that his thumb and finger were going at it again. Tossing the cigarette away, he got up and once more scanned the area. Someone is following us, sure as shit, he thought.

The others finished the ceremony and began to get ready to leave. Lucas looked down at Markham's hand and saw his twitching.

Denninger noticed it as well. "Can I ask where we are going, Corporal?"

"Anywhere but here, Doc," he replied. "We gotta keep moving."

A look of concern crossed Denninger's face. "We cannot just drive around aimlessly, hoping to come across 'the heart of God' or 'the right stone.'"

Markham grunted. "Well, I'm open to suggestions. What do you think, Phil?"

Lucas thought for a moment. "Maybe the farmer here knows where we can go."

"But I already questioned him about this — " began Denninger.

Lucas cut in. "No, what I mean is that maybe there's somewhere around here that may have the information we're looking for — like a library, or maybe a church, or something."

Denninger thought it was a good idea. He beckoned to Etienne and he asked if there were such a place in the area.

"There is a church about four miles from here," said Etienne. "Except for two years which the abbé spent in Dijon, he has been the parish priest there for over forty years. He knows very much about this area. He might be able to tell you something."

Denninger related to the others what Etienne had told him.

"Okay," Markham ordered, "everyone into the truck and put on your Sunday best. We're going to church."

Ste. Marie de la Mer was an old building, more of a chapel than a church. It was built of brick on the site of another church that had burned down over three hundred years before. A stable containing an old wagon and a pair of workhorses was about ten yards to the rear of the rectory. Although the church had weathered much over the centuries, it was a very sound structure.

The truck pulled up to the front of the church where they saw a hunched-over old man puttering around in what was presumably a garden but looked more like a bed of weeds. Etienne hopped out of the cab of the truck and headed over to him.

"*Bonjour, Père Ambroise,*" exclaimed Etienne. The old priest looked up and, recognizing the farmer, gave him a broad smile. They exchanged a warm hug and then the priest asked Etienne who his friends were. Etienne hesitated. He didn't want to tell the priest what they were really doing there. He swung around and gave a worried look to the rest of the group.

Denninger immediately stepped forward with his hand extended. "Hello, Father," he began in French. "I am Doctor Denninger and I am a historian. Etienne here has told me that you may be of great help to my work," he said, smiling.

The priest stared at him warily and motioned towards the soldiers standing behind him. "Do you always travel with an army?" he asked. Denninger smiled wanly as the priest looked guardedly at the soldiers and then back to him. "Are you aware that this is occupied territory — by the Germans, I mean? What exactly are American soldiers doing this far behind enemy lines, if I may ask?"

Denninger cleared his throat. "Well, yes, you may ask, of course, uh ... you see, the reason ..." His voice trailed off and then he looked helplessly at Markham.

The corporal couldn't understand the dialogue between the two, but sensed something was amiss. "What's going on?" he demanded quietly.

"He wants to know why I am traveling with American soldiers," he hissed rigidly. "It is a perfectly valid question. Why would I be traveling with American soldiers? We should have thought of this!"

Markham put one hand on the excited archeologist's shoulder, trying to calm him down and rubbed his own face in frustration with the other. "All right ... stay calm. Just tell him the truth. Tell him we got separated from our unit and we're trying to get back, and you guys have offered to help us."

Denninger took a deep breath and exhaled quietly. He turned back to the priest who was eying the situation with a bemused look. Denninger smiled weakly and proceeded to tell the priest exactly what Markham had told him to say.

It seemed to work, in spite of the inquisitive stare he received from the elderly cleric. Ambroise invited them inside the rectory where he could find out what it was they wanted. As they filed in, Markham told Rourke to stay outside to keep watch. "Keep an eye out and for

Chrissakes don't do anything stupid." Markham started into the rectory but then he paused and added, "Please?"

"Relax," Rourke said calmly. "Everything is fine. I got it under control."

Markham rubbed the stubble on his chin and gave Rourke a labored look before he went inside. Rourke waited until the door shut before he popped another Pervitin.

Father Ambroise directed them to have a seat at the large table in the rectory kitchen and then set a pot on the stove to boil water for tea. He then opened a tin of biscuits and put them out for the men to share. "So gentlemen," he said in French, "How can I help you?"

When Denninger asked him if he spoke any English the priest shook his head. Denninger turned to Markham. "He doesn't speak English—I'll have to converse with him in French."

Markham nodded and Denninger began to speak to Father Ambroise. "As I told you outside, Father, I am a historian. My area of study is the Cathars."

The priest suddenly lit up. "Ah, the Cathars, very interesting. This whole area was Cathar country once, many centuries ago."

"Oh yes, I do know that. I have been researching their history for a book I am writing and have come across a number of references that I have been unable to ... decipher, if you will. Etienne here assures me that you are the person who can help me."

The priest looked at Denninger quizzically. "References? References to what?"

"Well, I was hoping that you could tell me. I have a feeling that they may be landmarks of some sort. One of the ones I am having trouble with is 'the heart of God."

Father Ambroise's face didn't move, though Markham, in spite of the language barrier, detected a trace of recognition in response to what Denninger had asked. The pot on the stove then began to whistle, so the abbé got up to make the tea. They watched him keenly as he methodically went about the task. Markham shot Denninger a questioning look but the doctor just shrugged his shoulders.

Father Ambroise turned to the men at the table and placed a cup of tea in front of each of them. "I'm afraid I only have milk for your tea. Little luxuries like sugar or honey are very hard to come by these days."

Denninger told the priest that everything was fine as he sat back down. "Please, Father, do you know or have you ever heard this expression before?"

Father Ambroise stirred his tea and then tapped the spoon against the saucer, much to the annoyance of Markham.

"You are writing a book, you say?' he asked Denninger.

The archeologist was becoming a little exasperated. "Yes, a treatise on the Cathars and the Albigensian Crusade. Any help would be greatly appreciated."

The priest took a long sip from his teacup. "You know," he finally said, "I have not thought about the Cathars in many, many years ... the last time was about thirty years ago ..." His voice trailed off. Denninger watched him for a few seconds, then cast a sideways glance at Markham.

"Father Ambroise?" Denninger prompted.

The abbé shook his head slightly and smiled. "Excuse me ... I drifted off there for a moment. You were asking about the Cathars?"

Denninger smiled. "Yes ... specifically about the expression 'the heart of God.' Have you ever heard it before?"

Ambroise pursed his lips and furrowed his brow, as if deep in thought. "'The heart of God,' eh? Well now, that's very lyrical, isn't it? Very poetic."

As Ambroise spoke, Denninger noticed two paintings and a framed photograph over the abbé's shoulder. One of the paintings was of a woman with long reddish hair, her arms across her chest and her hands on her shoulders. She was draped in a mantle of red and a jar of oil was at her feet. Denninger recognized it as a Renaissance depiction of Mary Magdalene. The name of the church, Ste. Marie de la Mer, was a reference to the legend that Mary Magdalene had crossed the Mediterranean Sea and landed in Provençe after the death of Jesus Christ. In this region there were many representations of the Magdalene. Next to it was a watercolor of a large mountain and the word 'Cardou' painted beneath it, with another phrase that Denninger couldn't read from where he was.

On the other hand, the subject of the photograph Denninger immediately recognized. The sitter was a priest who had a strong-featured face with a trace of a whimsical smile. He had seen it many times before. "I am sorry to interrupt Father, but that photograph on the wall — it is Bérenger Saunière, isn't it?"

Father Ambroise never took his eyes from the archeologist. "You know of Father Saunière?" Ambroise asked warily.

"I know he was the parish priest at Rennes-le-Château," responded Denninger.

Father Ambroise sniffed. "I suppose you are going to ask about the treasure, now. Well, everything you ever heard about it is false. It was, and is, just a story."

"So Father Saunière's source of wealth — "

"Simony," Ambroise cut in. "He was selling masses. I know this because I knew the man. He confessed to it when he had his last rites given to him."

Denninger sat forward with a start, but the priest didn't seem to notice.

"It was a very sad story for such an interesting and witty man," remarked Ambroise. "As a tribute to him, I had the stations of the cross in our church done the same way as he had them done at Rennes-le-Château."

Denninger nodded. He had immersed himself in Catholicism while he languished away in Tibet. He knew that the stations of the cross depicted the story of Christ's Passion.

"Getting back to the information I need, Father. I have identified a number of Cathar landmarks such as Bugarach and Quéribus, but I am having trouble with a couple more. Are you absolutely sure that you have never heard the expression 'the heart of God' before?"

The old priest put a finger to his lips, as if in thought. After a few moments, he repeated the phrase. "'The heart of God,' eh? No, I'm sorry."

"What about 'the right stone?' Did you ever hear of anything called 'the right stone'?"

Father Ambroise got up and walked with deliberation around the table with his hands clasped behind his back. He stopped by Denninger's chair and finally said, "I'm sorry, Monsieur. I'm afraid I can't help you. It is too bad that you came all the way here for nothing." He put his hand out towards Denninger. The archeologist smiled resignedly as he shook it.

As they stood up to leave, Denninger stretched and as he turned, he happened to get a better look at the photograph and the paintings. This time, something about the watercolor of the mountain caught his eye. As he moved away from the table, Denninger surreptitiously gave his pack, which was under the chair, a little kick. It slid quietly under the table. He looked around and, to his satisfaction, nobody had noticed. They went outside where Rourke reported that he had seen no one. Markham started to ask Denninger what the priest had to say but the doctor gave him a look that implied that they shouldn't speak yet. Etienne was behind the wheel and was speaking with Father Ambroise when Denninger suddenly exclaimed, "Oh ... I've forgotten my pack inside. I'll just be a minute."

Once inside the rectory he retrieved his pack and then hurried over to the artwork to get a good look at the words on the watercolor painting. "Aha," he murmured. He headed outside and started towards the truck and on the way thanked the priest for his time.

Father Ambroise smiled. "I wish I could have been more help to you, Monsieur Denninger," he said as Denninger climbed into the cab of the truck.

He smiled back. "Oh, you have been, Father," he said to himself as the truck pulled away.

35

THEY HAD ONLY BEEN driving for a few minutes when Denninger asked Etienne to stop the truck. Markham asked what the problem was as Denninger hopped out of the vehicle.

"Did you happen to see the paintings in the rectory?" Denninger asked as Markham joined him.

Markham shook his head.

"There were two paintings on the back wall; one was of Mary Magdalene and the other was of a mountain called Cardou."

"So?"

"Do you know what was written beneath it?" he asked.

"I didn't see the paintings, remember?"

Denninger took a breath. "'*Le Coeur de Dieu.*' Cardou is 'the heart of God.'"

Markham's eyes went wide. "Well that's great! But why didn't you say something when we were back there?"

Denninger frowned. "Something odd happened when I was speaking to the priest. He was talking about Bérenger Saunière — "

Markham interrupted him. "Who?"

Denninger quickly filled in Markham about Saunière. He then reached into his pack and pulled out Rivière's diary. "This was written by Father Rivière, the priest who was supposed to give Father Saunière absolution on his deathbed. Father Rivière, however, refused to give the rite to him."

"Why?"

"Nobody knows. It's not even in here," he said holding up the diary. "But Father Ambroise said that Rivière *had* given Saunière absolution. Ambroise lied."

Markham shrugged and rubbed his left shoulder, wincing slightly. "Maybe he made a mistake."

Denninger shook his head. "He told me that he knew him. He would have known the truth for sure. He also said that he never heard of 'the heart of God', yet he has a painting of it on his wall! I'll bet you that he knows what 'the right stone' is as well." Denninger stroked his chin thoughtfully. "The question is, why did he lie?"

Markham was quiet for a moment and then said, "Well, let's go find out."

Just off the side of the road about a half a mile back, the man on the motorcycle was watching keenly through his binoculars. He saw Markham and Denninger speaking for a few minutes then get back into the truck.

What are they doing? he wondered.

He watched curiously as the truck turned around and started to head back the way they had come. They were now coming straight towards him. He hastily mounted the motorbike and sped off, staying just out of sight of the truck. As he came to a crossroads, he made a quick right and then turned off the road into a thicket. He watched as the truck passed by and waited for a few moments before he gunned the motorcycle back down the road just behind the truck.

The sun was starting to go down when the truck pulled up to the church again. Markham leapt out of the back before it completely came to a stop. Lucas and Rourke followed, with Denninger coming up behind. Etienne, not quite understanding what was happening, decided to wait in the truck. Markham tried the door of the rectory but it was locked. They then circled around to the doors of the church, which they found open. They went in and discovered that it was empty. Except for some candles on the altar and burning in a number of niches along the walls, the church was dark.

"That priest must be around here somewhere," muttered Markham. "Everyone spread out." He turned to Lucas. "You're the Bible guy. Do you think there's another way into the rectory from here?"

Lucas shrugged. "Could be. It looks like there's a hallway off to the right of the altar."

The corporal started for the hallway as Rourke stood guard by the doors and Lucas headed for the vestry.

Denninger stepped up to the altar and looked around at the statues in the niches of the reredos which were casting strange shadows in the candlelight. As his eyes travelled along the walls of the church he noticed the stations of the cross. Father Ambroise had mentioned that he had replicated what Saunière had done at his church but something was perplexing about them. Something wasn't quite right.

Particularly station fourteen.

He went over to one of the niches where he picked up a candle and then made his way over to the relief. He held the candle up to it and made a closer inspection. The fourteenth station showed the removal of Christ's body from the cross and its internment in the tomb in the middle of the night.

At night? That isn't right, he thought.

As he tried to make sense of the image, his attention was diverted by a loud noise in the hallway. He turned around to see Father Ambroise in a dressing gown, being pushed by the barrel of Markham's weapon. Lucas rapidly returned from the vestry when he heard the commotion.

"Hey, guess what? I found a way into the rectory, and look what I found in the bathroom," said Markham proudly. The priest was sputtering in heated bursts of French. He spotted Denninger inspecting the relief and strode angrily over to him demanding to know what was going on.

"What is the meaning of this, Monsieur Denninger? This is a house of God!" he raged. His face was drained of color.

Denninger turned from the station to face the priest. "Hello Father Ambroise. We are very sorry to disturb you again, but I have a few more questions."

"I answered your questions already," Ambroise seethed.

"Not this one. Why did you lie?"

Father Ambroise was taken aback. He stared with wide eyes at Denninger. "Lie? How dare you accuse me of lying! What did I lie about?"

Denninger took a few steps closer to the priest. "That painting in the rectory. The one of Cardou. It says right on it 'The Heart of God.' When I asked you if you knew what the phrase meant, you told me you didn't know. Why?"

The only sound that came from Father Ambroise was heavy breathing. Denninger was studying the priest's face when he heard the sound of a bullet being chambered in a rifle. He looked behind Ambroise to see Markham walking over with his weapon pointed directly at the priest.

"Tell Father Frenchy here that if he doesn't come clean, he'll be visiting God very soon," uttered Markham in a low voice.

Father Ambroise turned deliberately at the sound of Markham's voice. His eyes narrowed. "You would actually kill a priest in God's house?" he said in heavily accented English.

Markham did a double take. "Does everyone around here lie about speaking English?" he asked with exasperated astonishment.

"Please Father," Denninger said in English, "just tell us what we need to know, and we'll leave you alone."

Father Ambroise glared coldly at Denninger. Markham stood next to him with his rifle trained on the priest's chest. "It's your call, Father," warned Markham. Ambroise's heavy breathing began to slow and his shoulders sank. Finally, he told them to follow him back to the rectory.

At the table, Denninger took the sheet of paper with the translated clues out of his pocket. Taking a pencil, he wrote the word 'Cardou' and looked up at the priest. "All right Father. Why the lies?"

Father Ambroise looked cynically at Denninger. "You are not writing a book, are you? You're looking for the treasure," he stated.

Denninger cast a quick glance at Markham who held his rifle, aimed threateningly at the priest, on his lap.

"So what if we are?" said Markham.

"I told you there is no treasure."

Markham raised his eyebrows doubtfully. "Forgive me Father, but for some reason I think you're full of shit — with all due respect, of course."

Father Ambroise scoffed. "What do you think you are going to find? A big treasure chest brimming with booty, no doubt."

He lowered his voice and shifted his gaze from Markham to Denninger.

"You have no idea what you are getting into."

Rourke stepped forward. "Oh, I think we do, pal. Just tell the Doc here what he wants to know, and we're outta here like a couple of bangtails shootin' out of the starting gate."

Ambroise shook his head in disgust. "Saunière didn't listen either."

"Father Ambroise, I need to know something," said Denninger. "When you were speaking about Father Saunière, you mentioned that he received last rites. That wasn't true, was it? Father Rivière refused to administer the rite."

The priest raised his eyebrows. "Ah, so you do know the story. Who lies now?"

Denninger pressed on. "Do you know why Rivière refused absolution?"

"I do."

"How do you know?"

"I knew Saunière. I also knew Father Rivière. He was the one who told me."

"Well could you tell me the reason why he was refused absolution? What was so terrible that one priest denied another the last rite?"

Ambroise sighed. "Abbé Gélis," he at last said quietly.

"Abbé Gélis? Who was Abbé Gélis?"

After a moment of silence Father Ambroise began. "Abbé Gélis was the parish priest of Coustaussa, a small village very close to Rennes-le-Château. He and Saunière were colleauges and had lunched and dined together many times. They had, however, very different personalities. Once Saunière became wealthy, he liked to surround himself with the nicer things in life. He was very much a spendthrift, as opposed to Gélis who preferred a more ... Spartan lifestyle, if you will. I am not sure if this caused any friction between the two of them, but you never know, eh? Considering what happened, there may have been more friction than met the eye."

"On the last night of October in 1897, Gélis was entertaining someone at the rectory. No one knows who it was but the next morning, he was found on the floor of the kitchen, in a pool of blood, with his head bashed in."

Father Ambroise at once became more animated. In spite of the fact that he was a priest he seemed to relish the gory details of the story, and enjoyed Denninger's appalled look even more.

"Someone had smashed him in the head with the fire tongs and then finished off the job with a small axe. He was lying on his back, with his arms crossed on his chest, as if he were in a casket, and he was wearing his biretta. Upstairs in his bedroom, his briefcase had been pried open, as if the killer were looking for something. Robbery was not a motive, as the abbé had over 200 francs still in his possession. The most puzzling bit of evidence though, was a package of cigarette papers with the brand name The Tzar found nearby. It was very odd."

"Why is that?" wondered Denninger.

Ambroise shook his head. "Gélis didn't smoke. Whoever murdered him more than likely dropped the cigarette papers."

Denninger was suddenly reminded of a passage in Rivière's diary. It was the story about Abbé Saunière trying to get Rivière to roll his cigarettes for him. Denninger understood immediately the implication.

"The abbé's nephew was the prime suspect at the time, but there was no evidence. They eventually let him go, and the crime remained unsolved."

Denninger was quiet for a moment and then said, "It was Saunière, wasn't it?"

Ambroise nodded. "Gélis knew that Saunière was selling masses and threatened to go to the church with the information. On his deathbed, he confessed this to Rivière. This is why he refused the rite."

"I see," said Denninger.

There was still something missing. Denninger recalled the passage in Rivière's diary which he had read many times.

I am in hell and I know that is where Saunière is as well. All my life I have dedicated myself to God and the Word of God. As a child I was indoctrinated in the faith and I believed every word, every letter, every dot. When Christ was before Pilate, he said 'Everyone on the side of truth listens to me,' to which Pilate replies 'What is truth?' What is truth, indeed!

I cannot express the conflict that racks my soul. Has it all been for nothing? Again I say 'What is truth?'

Something didn't make sense. Saunière's confession to a murder would not prevent him from receiving last rites, and Rivière's allusion to Pilate seemed irrelevant. Rivière had written: "Has it all been for nothing?"

Has *what* been for nothing?

"All right—enough of the history lesson," declared Markham. "We got three of these clues figured out. We just need the last one and we're out of here." He stood up and walked around the table until he was hovering over Ambroise, the rifle inches from the old priest's face. "Where or what is 'the right stone'?"

Father Ambroise stared at Markham defiantly. Slowly he pushed the chair away from the table, and with deliberate intent went face-to-face with Markham. "I am not afraid to die, you know," he told the soldier defiantly.

Markham grunted. "Well, I am certainly prepared to help you out with that."

Denninger quickly stood up. "Father Ambroise, please ..." Without taking his eyes from Markham's, Ambroise said in a low voice, "St. Salvayre—the right stone is on a peak in St. Salvayre."

Markham lowered his rifle and slowly smiled at the priest. "There. Was that so hard now?" He turned to Rourke. "Matty, get the map."

Denninger wrote St. Salvayre underneath Cardou on the sheet and then read the clues aloud. "From the face of the last son to the heart of God; from the height among the peaks to the right stone."

Rourke put the map on the table and began to spread it out. Markham laid his rifle against his chair and leaned over the map. "Okay—where's that pencil?" Denninger took it out of his pocket and handed it to the corporal.

"Let's see ... Cardou, right? Okay, there it is." He put a circle around the mountain's location just to the north of the other locations. After a moment or two he found the hamlet of St. Salvayre and circled that as well.

"All right," said Lucas, who had come over to scrutinize the map. "What do we do now? Do you suppose we have to go to these places for more clues?"

"Well, it's too late to go anywhere tonight," said Markham. "We'll have to stay here and leave in the morning. All right, Father ..."

Markham looked around. He realized too late that no one had been paying any attention to Father Ambroise.

The priest had disappeared.

36

OUTSIDE THE CHURCH, THE men heard the truck as it started to drive off.

"Shit!" yelled Markham. "The truck!"

They raced outside just in time to see the truck disappearing down the road. Lying on the ground where the truck had been was Etienne, face down in the dirt. Lucas ran over to the farmer and saw a small laceration on the back of his head with a small trickle of blood oozing out. He moaned slightly.

"I think he's okay. Ambroise must have hit him in the head with a rock or something."

Markham told Rourke and Lucas to bring the wounded farmer inside the rectory. They carried him into Ambroise's room and laid him on the bed. Lucas went to get a towel and water to clean up the old man's injury as Markham, Rourke and Denninger went back into the kitchen.

Markham rubbed the side of his face roughly and slumped into a chair. Rourke stood by the door while Denninger looked at the map again.

Markham watched him for a few minutes and then sighed. "What's the point, Doc? Without the truck, how are we going to get to all those places?"

Denninger cocked his head to one side and reread the clues. Markham noticed that his mouth was moving soundlessly until it became a knowing grin. "Corporal Markham, could I have that pencil back for a minute?"

Markham tossed the pencil to the Denninger, who began to sketch something on the map. When he was done he called the soldiers over. "Look at this," instructed Denninger. Markham and Rourke saw that he had drawn lines connecting Cardou, Bugarach, Quéribus and St. Salvayre.

"Remember what the clues said ... from the face of the last son to the heart of God ..." Denninger had drawn a line joining Quéribus to Cardou. "And from the height among the peaks ..." he said, putting the pencil on Bugarach, " ... to the right stone." He dragged the pencil from Bugarach to St. Salvayre.

"There you have it," he said triumphantly.

Markham and Rourke looked at what Denninger had done.

"Well whattya know?" declared Rourke. "*X* marks the spot!"

The lines between the four points created an irregular cross, but there was no doubt that it marked a spot about two miles from where they were.

"It couldn't be that easy, could it?" wondered Markham out loud.

Denninger sniffed. "It's easy when you know the clues. It just happened to be hard to decipher them. Now gentlemen, we have a problem. Obviously Ambroise knows about this, otherwise he would not have fled. My guess is that he's heading here right now," he said, pointing at the center of the *X*.

He looked gravely at the two soldiers. "We have to get there now."

"Yeah? How? Are we just gonna fly out there on gossamer wings?" jeered Rourke as he fluttered his hands like a small bird.

Markham ignored him and was looked out of the window, towards the back of the building. He suddenly spun around and called out to Lucas who was still in the bedroom with Etienne. Lucas came into the kitchen. "How's the old guy?" Markham asked.

"He's awake. He's got a pretty good knot on the back of his head but I think he'll be okay," Lucas responded.

Markham scooped up his rifle and told Denninger to get the map. "Saddle up boys," he ordered as he headed for the door. "We're forming a posse."

Denninger glanced at Lucas with a confused look. "A what?"

Markham was already behind the church when the others eventually made their way outside. Rourke looked around. "Where the hell did he go? It's gettin' real dark out here," he complained.

They suddenly heard a strange noise coming from the rear of the building. Lucas cocked his head. "Do you guys hear that?" he asked.

There was a clicking metallic sound immediately followed by a snorting noise coming from behind the church.

"You must be shitting me," Rourke blurted out as Markham led the two workhorses out from the stable.

"Matty, Phil, pull out the wagon," he directed.

Denninger tapped Markham's arm. "Do you know anything about horses, Corporal?"

"Not a goddamn thing," he replied, steadying the nervous beasts as best as he could.

Lucas and Rourke pulled the wagon up to the horses. Rourke looked at the horses, then at the wagon and then at Markham and Lucas. "Okay genius ... how do we do this?"

Lucas went back into the barn and returned with a harness, which he then set about hooking up to the horses. When he noticed the others looking at him he explained, "My grandfather had a farm in Roane County, West Virginia."

Within minutes, the team was hooked up and Lucas jumped up front, taking the reins while the others piled into the back of the wagon. Markham leaned in towards

Lucas. “Ambroise has about a fifteen minute lead on us. How fast can you get these horses going?”

Lucas shrugged. “They’re workhorses, but I’ll get ‘em going like it’s the Kentucky Derby,” he promised.

He snapped the reins, urging the horses forward.

37

THE FADED RED CLAY bricks that remained at the site were covered with weeds and tall grass. Part of the west wall near the entrance had crumbled to the ground years before, and the rest of it seemed to be threatening to follow. The glass from the windows had disappeared long ago and the cross that had adorned the roof of the bell tower was missing its horizontal beam. No one would ever take a second look at the ruins of the ancient church, even if anyone managed to make it that far in from the road. The landscape was dotted with dozens of old ruins like this one, yet this one was unlike any other in the country.

Or in the world, for that matter.

Ambroise had parked the truck off the road behind some bushes and ran to the church. He was still wearing his dressing gown and it flapped against his legs as he raced down the nave towards the altar. As soon as he reached it, he fell against it, sweating and suffering from a panic attack.

He could not let anyone find it. He reached inside his pocket and extracted a pistol he had taken from one of the drawers in the rectory kitchen before he got away. He knew they would be here soon.

"May God have mercy on my soul," he prayed, as he took a position behind a section of wall that was still standing.

His breathing was out of control. It was coming in short gasps and he was feeling light-headed. He felt the same way he had that night forty-seven years ago, when he was nineteen years old.

The night that Bérenger Saunière told him about the document.

Ambroise had been called to the priesthood at an early age and spent his formative years at Rennes-le-Château. Father Saunière had taken a liking to the intelligent, quick-witted lad and took him under his wing. Ambroise was a frequent visitor at Saunière's home, and Saunière's housekeeper, Marie Denarnaud, kept him well fed.

Once, the young seminary student asked Father Saunière how a poor parish priest could afford to do the extensive renovations that he had done to his church. Saunière was angry at the impertinence of the question, and chastised Ambroise, but Ambroise could somehow sense that the older priest was hiding something. Saunière, however, refused to divulge the source of his wealth.

It was a cool October night when Ambroise arrived at Saunière's home to find Saunière in an inconsolable state. It was apparent that he had been drinking heavily and was having a hard time standing. He had a badly rolled cigarette in his hand which was burning his fingers, but he appeared not to notice. His eyes were red-rimmed, though Ambroise couldn't tell if it was from the drinking or from crying.

Ambroise took the cigarette from the older priest's hand and led him to the table, where he poured a glass of water. He handed the glass to Saunière, who took a small sip and then began to sob uncontrollably.

"Father Saunière, what is the matter?" Ambroise asked worriedly. Saunière took a moment to collect himself, and then grabbed a hold of Ambroise's arm. His fingers dug in deep into the young man's flesh, causing it to bleed.

"Father Saunière, you're hurting me!" Ambroise cried out. Saunière pulled Ambroise closer and stared at him through bleary, tear-filled eyes.

"I am going ... to tell you something ...," he gasped. "You think ... that *this* hurts?" He held up Ambroise's arm and then flung it to the table. He then paused to catch his breath. "I am going to tell you a secret — one that will hurt more than a few scratches on your skin." Ambroise rubbed his arm as Saunière continued. "Tell me — your calling to the Church, is it a strong one?"

Ambroise nodded. "Yes, Father. I love God with all my heart."

Saunière smiled but there was no humor in it. "Well then, please, roll me a cigarette and let us find out."

He began to relate to Ambroise the story of the renovation of the church almost ten years ago. It was when workers were removing the altar that the parchment which Gratien Lambert had concealed over six hundred years before was discovered.

As Saunière's eyes pored over the parchment, he tried to understand just what it was that he was looking at. It was certainly an odd document, and he wondered just who could have hidden it away in the first place. And why.

Going to Paris was certainly enlightening.

He met up with the young monk Emile Hoffet and the two of them spent two days trying to decipher the document, but with no luck. They had decided to take a day at the Louvres when one particular piece of art caught Saunière's eye. It was a painting of some shepherds crowded around a tomb that caused the priest's heart to beat faster.

"What is this called, Emile?" he asked breathlessly.

"*The Shepherds of Arcadia*," the young monk responded. "It's interesting that you ask about this particular piece."

Saunière turned his head and looked at Hoffet. "Why is that?"

"The artist, Nicolas Poussin ... he had Templar connections, you know."

Saunière looked back at the painting. "I don't follow you," he said. Hoffet smiled.

"Well, that document of yours. It was undoubtedly created by the Templars. Remember the symbols on it? The Maltese cross, the two riders on one horse? They are all symbols of the Knights Templar."

Saunière didn't respond. He eyes remained glued to the painting but he wasn't looking at the shepherds. He was looking beyond them. He was staring at the outline of Blanchefort and Cordou and the depiction of the tomb that lay only a few miles from his church.

He was looking at Rennes-le-Chateau.

A Templar document and a painting of his home by a Templar artist. He recalled the legends about the Cathars and the Knights Templar. Was it possible that it could all have had something to do with the famed Cathar treasure?

It was only after he returned from Paris that it all became clear.

Saunière, who was an avid game-player, finally recognized the chess-like pattern on the document, although it took him many days after that to eventually decode the manuscript. Once he had, he immediately understood the landmark references as he had grown up and lived in the area for most of his life.

Armed with a shovel and pick, he was soon at the church ruin. Saunière spent hours exploring the site until he happened to move a screen behind the altar and saw something that caught his attention. There was a figure carved into the base of the eastern wall. He knelt down to get a better look. In the faint light streaming through the broken window, it looked like a bird. Upon closer inspection, he could see that it was a dove.

The dove was a Cathar symbol. He knew immediately what it meant. The ruin he was standing in, before it was a Catholic church, once belonged to the Cathars.

Saunière suddenly felt a chill that enveloped his whole body.

The Cathar treasure. Every schoolboy in Languedoc knew of the Cathar treasure.

It couldn't be here, could it? he thought.

He felt a rush of heat from his head to his toes replace the chill that had gripped him earlier. He used the pick and began to chip away at the floor right in front of the stone with the carving. The going was slow, but he persevered. He labored for a good part of the day and after he had dug down a few feet, he hit something softer than the stone. He brushed away the dust and discovered a rotted oak platform. He ran his hands along the surface until he found an edge, and taking the pick, he inserted the tip and began to pry up the board. The softened wood gave way easily as Saunière pushed the handle of the pick forward. The oak came up, revealing a dark hole beneath.

Saunière took a minute to catch his breath, then lit a kerosene lantern and lowered it into the blackness below.

A gasp caught in his throat when he saw a stone stairway.

Making the sign of the cross, he slowly stepped onto the first stair and began to descend.

The light of the lamp showed that he was in a bricked room, which seemed to be built before the church had gone up. How old it was, Saunière couldn't even hazard a guess. He quickly shone the light all around but within seconds he could see that it was completely empty. He had been positive that the Cathar treasure was here, yet the room was bare. Perhaps it was just a church cellar, used in years past, and had been emptied when the church was abandoned.

Dejected, he turned and was about to head back up the main floor when he saw something on the wall by the stairs. In his haste he hadn't noticed it before. He moved the light closer and discovered that there was a painting of a fish on the wall with a small ringed handle set into the stone just below its tail. In ancient times, the fish was a symbol for Jesus Christ's followers.

As Saunière went closer to inspect the fresco, he looked down and noticed that the wall wasn't completely flush with the floor. Kneeling down, he lowered the lantern for a better look. There was a thin gap that ran for about five feet along the base of the wall. He placed his little finger into the space and was able to slide it along the length of the gap.

This wall must move, he thought excitedly to himself. Standing back up, he grabbed the handle and pulled on it. At first, nothing happened. He pulled again but the wall was steadfast. He fiddled with the ring, gave it a turn, and heard a click. He pulled it again, but it still wouldn't budge. Changing tack, he then tried pushing against the wall.

It moved a few inches.

He pushed again, this time putting his shoulder into it. The wall moved forward a few more inches. Saunière lifted the lantern and upon closer inspection saw that the corner of the wall had iron projections on the right-hand side and were fixed into circular impressions at the top and bottom on a pivot system.

He wondered who had designed and built it. It was both simple and ingenious. He pushed against it once again and managed to get an opening large enough to go through. Saunière picked up the lantern and stepped inside.

The room had an old, musty smell and was larger than the one he had just come from. Holding up the lantern in front of his face, he was able to see in the glow of the yellow light, three stone boxes about two feet in length, twelve inches high and twelve inches wide. A small clay pot stood next to the box on the right.

Saunière stared at the boxes for a minute, confused. The boxes, if they contained the Cathar treasure, looked far too heavy and unwieldy to have been carried down the side of the mountain at Montségur. He stood transfixed in front of the boxes, trying to determine what exactly they were. He went over to the clay pot and removed the lid. Reaching inside he felt something soft. Sensing that what he was touching was safe, he pulled it out. In the lantern's light, he could see that it was a leather-bound papyrus codex. As he carefully opened it, he saw at first glance the manuscript within was written in what seemed to be Hebrew. Not wanting to damage the codex, he put it back into the jar. He then went over to the nearest box, and after struggling with the stone lid, he managed to remove it. What in Heaven's name? he said to himself.

Although he didn't understand that at the time, what was inside the jar and the boxes would change the course of Bérenger Saunière's life forever.

He hurried back to his church in Rennes-le-Château, telling Marie Denarnaud that he would be going out again for the rest of the day and did not know when he would return. Marie nodded. She was used to the eccentricies of the priest and thought nothing of it. Saunière went into his study and began to search through his vast library of books.

"Aha!" he murmured as he pulled a large volume from the shelf. Thumbing quickly through the pages, he found what he was looking for. On the page before him was an example of an ancient language. It certainly looked similar to the writing in the codex and as Saunière realized what it was, his mouth went dry.

He reached under his desk and retrieved a soft bag which he often used when he went on long hikes around the area. He tossed the book and a few sheets of paper with some pencils into the bag. Throwing it over his shoulder, he quickly exited the house without even saying goodbye to Marie. Before he left the property, however, he went into the church and grabbed a few loose boards from the area where the renovations were being done.

At the site, Saunière spent a number of hours carefully copying, by the faint glow of the kerosene lamp, the text in the codex onto the sheets of paper he had brought with him. He had thought about taking the codex itself, but he didn't want anyone else to know of its existence just yet. It would definitely be safer to copy it and leave the original where it was.

Once he was finished, he pulled the wall closed and climbed the stairs. He then covered the opening with the loose boards he had brought with him. His next task would be to have the text translated, and he knew the perfect person to do it. He would visit his friend Abbé Antoine Gélis, the parish priest in nearby Coustaussa.

If anyone could decipher its meaning, it would be his old friend Antoine.

38

The next day, Saunière took the short walk to Coustaussa where he gave the curious abbé the transcribed papers to decipher. Once Gélis translated the text, both men sat, stunned, in the abbé's little study.

"Bérenger," Gélis said softly, "This is terrible. No one must know of this. The implications ..."

"Of course, I know," muttered Saunière. "Could it be *true,* though? I mean, what if they are forgeries ... something created to discredit the Church ..."

"They have been buried there for centuries, Bérenger! If shame or discredit was the aim, then why bury it? It makes no sense!" Gélis stood up and walked over to the window in the west wall of his study. He rested an arm against the glass and watched a horse and cart winding its way past the rectory.

"Then what do we do Antoine?" wondered Saunière.

"Forget about it," he said, his eyes still on the road outside. "Keep it buried where no one can ever find it. Without the document you found in your altar, no one will be able to discover the site anyway."

Saunière looked down at the translation on Gélis' desk and then looked at his friend.

Gélis turned and gestured towards the fireplace. "Burn it, Berenger. Get rid of that terrible document." He turned back to the window.

As Saunière picked up the translation from the desk, he was overcome with a number of emotions. He knew that Gélis was right, yet at the same time ...

He walked over to the fireplace with the translation in his hand. Watching the flames licking at the logs, he could feel the heat enveloping him, but at the same time, an icy cold finger traced its way down his back.

He knew what he had to do.

Gélis heard the crackling and turned to see Saunière with his hands by his sides and the orange flames turning the paper into a blackened ash.

"I suggest you do the same with your altar document when you get back."

Saunière watched the paper burn completely away and then headed for the door without saying anything to his friend. As Saunière strode across the church grounds away from the rectory, Gélis watched with a heavy heart. He looked up at the crucifix that hung by the door and began to weep.

Once Saunière was far enough away from Gélis's rectory, he slowed down his pace, taking smaller steps, and relished the moment. He put his hand into his jacket pocket and smiled to himself as his fingers closed over the translation.

He had looked around at the bare surroundings of Gélis's study and was reminded of his own Spartan lifestyle. Gélis may have taken a vow of poverty but Saunière had not.

A few days later he went to see Monsignor Félix-Arsène Billard, the Bishop of Carcassonne. In his hand was the translation of the codex.

"What's this?" asked the Monsignor when Saunière put them on his desk.

"Something I think you and the Church will be very interested in," responded Saunière. He watched the bishop's reaction as he took in the information that lay before him. Billard looked up slowly at Saunière when he was finished.

"What is the meaning of this, Saunière?"

"This is a translation of a document I have recently discovered. I knew immediately its religious importance, and so I knew you would have to be made aware of it," he said.

Billard put his hands up in the air in disbelief. "Where is this document now?" he asked. Saunière shrugged.

"It is safe — not to worry."

"Then get it!" demanded Billard. "The Church will want it right away. It cannot be allowed to fall into anyone else's hands."

Saunière smiled. "As I said, it is safe where it is now. No one will ever find it," he said softly. He then leaned over the desk towards the bishop and added, "I *assure* you."

Billard stared at Saunière with a look of mounting horror. "Are you saying that you will not turn them over to me? Or the Church?"

Saunière kept smiling. Billard got to his feet and came around the desk until he was a foot away from Saunière. The Monsignor was a good four inches shorter than Saunière so he got up on his toes to shorten the distance and to make himself seem more threatening. "Saunière ... you have been in trouble before. I stood up for you in the past but if you persist in this course of action, I will personally see to it that you will be removed from your position."

At this, Saunière stopped smiling and narrowed his eyes, making Billard take a step back. "I think, Monsignor, that it would be in the best interest of everyone if *I* take care of the document. All I ask, as compensation for the tremendous responsibility of looking after it, is a small monetary stipend — which I would, of course, use for the renovations of the church at Rennes-le-Château ... and other projects."

The color completely drained out of the bishop's face and his mouth fell open. "You ... you would actually ... *blackmail* the Church?" he hissed.

Saunière gave Billard a sinister look. "Blackmail? Please, Monsignor. Blackmail — it's not a pretty expression. Rather, think of it as an allowance or a gratuity — a consideration for services rendered." He seemed pleased with himself for the rationalization.

Billard couldn't believe what he was hearing. "What if the Church does not agree to this ... consideration, Saunière? What then?"

Saunière picked up his hat and started for the door. As he opened it, he turned to face Billard with a cold, stoney look. "Then the Church should be prepared to rewrite the Gospels."

Over the years, Saunière continued his renovations, thanks to the generous donations from the Church, and the projects eventually grew bigger and more extensive than originally planned.

Saunière knew the Church would keep quiet. He took many trips, sometimes to Paris where he met and became part of Parisian high society. He was also introduced to the composer, Claude Debussy, and rumors even had him romantically linked with the opera singer, Emma Calvé.

There was no doubt that Saunière made the most of his prosperity. The high life and Saunière went hand in glove for many years until Abbé Antoine Gélis was summoned to Carcassonne for a meeting with the Bishop Billard in late October of 1897.

Their meeting was short and explosive. When it was over, Gélis sent word to Saunière that he needed to see him at his earliest convenience. "On a matter of grave importance," he had said.

Saunière was beside himself. He knew Gélis had been to see the Bishop. Had he talked?

Saunière had become too accustomed to the good life to have everything fall apart on him now. He couldn't let that happen.

Early that night he made the short trip to Coustaussa, where Gélis met him outside the rectory, and Saunière could tell that the abbé was extremely distressed.

"Quickly," ordered Gélis. "Get inside. No one else is here."

Once the door was closed, Gélis began to berate Saunière. "What did you think you were doing, Bérenger? Are you out of your mind?"

"It is none of your concern, Antoine ..."

Gélis started to scream at him. "It is my concern! I knew about this! My God, Bérenger, do you realize what you have done? You have jeopardized our whole faith! For what? A few francs?!" He collapsed into the chair by the fireplace and began to weep. He balled his hands into fists and then jammed them against his temples. "I cannot live with this anymore! It is time to confess, Bérenger. I beg you, give the codex to the Bishop. Let the Church take care of it."

Saunière stepped forward and pointed his finger at him accusingly. "Antoine, you were the one who told me to keep it buried! It was your idea to keep it hidden — "

Gélis leapt out of the chair. "But you didn't do that, did you?" he shrieked. "It was a mistake! I admit that. We should have destroyed it. But now ..." His voice went quiet as he suddenly lost his passion. He looked utterly defeated. He looked at Saunière with imploring eyes. "This was my last day, you know ... I have a house already rented in Grèzes and after mass tomorrow, I am leaving to begin my retirement."

Saunière just stared as Gélis shook his head sadly. "I cannot risk losing that, Bérenger. I've worked too long and hard for this, only to lose it because of your greed and foolishness."

"What are you saying Antoine?" Saunière demanded in a low voice.

Gélis turned his head away from Saunière and looked at the fire. He couldn't bear to face him anymore. "The Bishop wants to keep it quiet. But I do not. I cannot do it anymore. I am going to go to the Archdiocese in Paris to speak with Archbishop Guibert," he said softly. He heaved a heavy sigh. "I am sorry Bérenger, but this is the only way."

Saunière's heart began to pound. He felt dizzy, as if he were going to pass out. "I need air … ," he gasped. Saunière reached for the door and left without saying goodbye. When he reached the rectory in Rennes-le-Château, Saunière saw that Marie had gone to bed. Good, he thought as he grabbed a bottle of brandy from out of the pantry. He had finished off two thirds of the bottle by the time Ambroise arrived.

As Saunière spoke, Ambroise began to feel ill. At the point when he revealed the contents of the codex, the young man jumped up out of his chair. "You lie!" he said with quiet intensity.

Saunière looked up at Ambroise with bloodshot eyes. He then glanced over at his Bible sitting on the counter by the stove. "I am not the one who lied."

His head began to loll to one side as the effect of the alcohol took greater hold of him. Ambroise began to rub his forehead.

It just couldn't be true could it?

His destiny was to be a priest. Religion was all he knew. What would he do now? Ambroise began to pace furiously across the kitchen floor, trying to think. He was starting to feel light-headed. In a matter of moments his whole world had fallen apart like rice paper in the wind.

"This can't be happening," he said to himself.

He thought of his mother. It was because of her that he was supposed to become a priest in the first place. His teenage years were spent in fervent religious instruction. Everyday she had thrust the love of God into him. It was for his own good, she told him. "You are *special*, son — you are meant to bask in the glory of God."

And that meant giving himself wholly to God. And that meant celibacy. His mother never failed to let him know about the evils of women, even if she had had to beat it into him.

Even if she had to do it every day.

He tried to think, but the blood rushing to his head deafened and confused him. So Abbé Gélis was going to Paris to let the Archbishop know the truth, was he? He could feel his anger rising. All rational thoughts were being replaced with rage. It was fine for Gélis, Ambroise said to himself. Gélis was retiring. He was going to be set for the rest of his life — but, thought Ambroise, what about me? Gélis was going to ruin everything. Everything he had hoped and prayed for. Everything his mother had hoped and prayed for.

He could not allow that happen.

Ambroise paused to look down at the passed out form of Father Saunière and the burned-down butt of the cigarette between his fingers. His eyes narrowed. "It's all your fault," he muttered at the slumberous abbé. "Why could you not leave well enough alone?" He reached down and extracted the packet of cigarette papers from Saunière's pocket. Taking a bit of tobacco from the bowl by the priest's arm, he expertly rolled himself a smoke and then pocketed the papers. As he lit the cigarette, he looked at the clock on the wall and saw that it was getting late.

It was time to pay a visit to Abbé Gélis.

39

STANDING BESIDE THE ALTAR in the ruined church, waiting for Denninger and the soldiers to arrive, Father Ambroise wiped the sweat from his eyes. He wasn't sure if he was perspiring because of the warm night, or if it was nerves. It had been forty-seven years since that horrible night, but he remembered every detail like it had just happened that morning.

The plan had not worked out in exactly the way he had hoped. Saunière's cigarette papers, a Parisian brand known as The Tzar, were found at the scene. Ambroise had planted them at Gélis' home and they should have pointed directly to the Paris-frequenting priest, yet everyone, including the police, had missed the clue.

That is, all except for Saunière. He knew that they were his cigarette papers and that they had been left there to make him look like the murderer. Although the crime went unsolved, Saunière had no doubt that it was a warning. He believed that certain powers could not let Gélis follow through with his confession and so he had been silenced. Saunière did not want to be next on the list. He met with Bishop Billard and assured him that the Church had his silence. Billard smiled and told him that he was doing the right thing. He also informed Saunière that the Church would not be funding his opulent lifestyle or any more renovations at Rennes-le-Château. Saunière humbly accepted the terms.

It had worked out in the end and Ambroise had become the priest that his mother wanted. The codex stayed hidden, and for forty-seven years the secret remained safe.

Until now. Ambroise knew that the German and the Americans would figure out the clues. It was only a matter of time. He checked his pistol again. He had clubbed Etienne pretty hard and felt sure the farmer wouldn't be with the group, so he figured that there would be just four of them.

With only six shots, it didn't leave much room for error. He would have to make each shot count.

Lucas was urging the horses on as best he could over the long overgrown road, but they weren't exactly thoroughbreds. With the wind whipping across his face, Markham held the map tightly while Denninger shone the beam from the flashlight at the spot they had marked. "I think we are very close, Corporal," said Denninger. "I would say we are about half a mile away."

Markham nodded. "Okay, I'm pretty sure that priest'll be there. God knows if he's armed, so I want you guys to keep your eyes peeled for him 'cause I don't want this fucked up."

Rourke sneered. "If he's smart he won't be there."

The wagon thundered along until Denninger called out to Lucas to stop. Lucas slowed the horses while Denninger shone the flashlight ahead. After a few moments he pointed. "There — do you see it?"

The light revealed what looked like a seldom used path just off to the left of the horses. Denninger cast the light back on the map and then turned to Lucas. "I am sure we must go that way," he said with confidence.

They got out of the wagon and started up the path with Markham in front, followed by Rourke, Denninger, and then Lucas. Markham began to flick his finger and thumb together. "I think we're close," he whispered.

Denninger grabbed at Markham's arm and pointed. "Closer than you think," he said quietly.

In the dim moonlight, they saw the outline of the church about a hundred yards away. Within a minute Markham, Rourke and Denninger were standing at the entrance of the church as Lucas searched the perimeter of the building with his flashlight. When he returned he shook his head.

"Okay, let's go in," ordered Markham. Once inside the church, Lucas shone the light around, giving the soldiers an idea of the layout. They could see the nave down the middle of the church leading to the altar, with two aisles along each wall. Many of the frescoes had long since worn away, leaving the surface of the walls nearly empty of decoration. To the left stood a pair of sorry looking confessional boxes, one of them missing its door, and to the right was a stairway leading to what Markham presumed was the bell tower. The bottom twelve steps were gone, making it impossible to climb.

"Well, he sure didn't go up there," he murmured. Lucas turned the light forward towards the eastern wall where they could see a carved screen behind the altar. He turned to Markham. "The vestry could be behind that screen. He might be hiding in there."

Markham nodded. "Okay, Phil, you go over there along the left aisle and I'll take the right. Matty, you up the middle. Doc, you stay here and keep an eye on the door." Denninger nodded as the three soldiers began the search.

Ambroise had moved behind the screen and watched the three lights of the Americans come closer as they moved up the aisles. The priest knew that it would be nearly impossible to take them all out, but he had an advantage. He knew this church inside and out. Even in the dark.

He saw the shape of one soldier coming coming up the aisle to his right.

Perfect, he thought.

Markham was moving to the left of Ambroise along the south wall. Rourke was slowly heading down the nave with Lucas along the north wall. A sudden movement just ahead caught Lucas's eye. He went quickly forward, with the flashlight shining on the east wall, calling out, "Father! Please we don't want — " His voice was cut off in mid-sentence as he abruptly fell headlong into complete blackness.

Markham heard the commotion and turned his head. "Phil!" he yelled. There was no answer. "Matty! Did you see what happened to Phil?"

Markham heard Rourke's voice off to his left somewhere. "My fuckin' flashlight's gone out! I can't see shit!"

Markham swore under his breath. He quickly shone the light in Rourke's direction, temporarily blinding the smaller soldier.

"Goddamn it!" he swore. "Matty, stay where you are. Don't move." Markham then aimed his flashlight in the direction of Lucas's last position. "Phil! Are you all right?" He could swear he'd heard a quiet moan. Markham shouted out to Rourke again. "Matty ... that way," he directed with the flashlight beam.

Rourke followed the direction of Markham's light and hurried down the length of one of the pews. Just as he got to the end of the bench, he saw a beam of light oddly coming from below and he heard a whimper near his feet. Looking down, Rourke saw that if he'd gone another six inches he would have toppled into the same hole that Lucas had just fallen into.

"Jesus!" he shouted. "Hey, Doug, he's in a hole!"

"Is he all right?"

Rourke peered into the opening. Although he couldn't see very well, Lucas's flashlight illuminated enough of the pit to show that Lucas was about ten feet down and not moving. "I don't know … I think he might be hurt."

Markham hurried over and shone his light into the hole. When he saw Lucas's prone form, he immediately leapt into the pit. He knelt down and turned Lucas over. His face was covered in dirt, and his forehead looked like it might be badly bruised. Markham checked for signs of breathing as he wiped away the dirt from Lucas's face. Looking up at Matty, he said, "He's out cold. We gotta get him out of here." He shone the light around the pit and realized that that was easier said than done. The hole was deeper than he'd thought. He looked back up at Rourke. "Go get the doc. We're gonna need his help, I think."

"Toss me up Phil's flashlight."

Markham grabbed the light and threw it up towards Rourke, who deftly caught it with one hand. He then doubled back to the entrance where Denninger had been waiting, only to find that the archeologist wasn't there. Rourke played the light around the area frantically. There was no sign of the archeologist. "Hey! Doc! Where'd ya go?" he called out.

No answer.

He turned around and saw someone just ahead, moving awkwardly near the altar. He aimed the flashlight in the direction of the movement, but whoever it was had disappeared. "Hey Doc!" he yelled again and ran down the southern aisle towards the man's last position. As he approached the altar, he suddenly felt the flashlight knocked from his hand and then a quick sharp pain to his face before everything went completely black.

Denninger was holding his hands high in the air as Ambroise pressed the pistol painfully deep against his neck. When Rourke and Markham had hurried to see what happened to Lucas, the priest had rushed along the southern aisle and was able to come up behind the archeologist. Denninger chastised himself for not being more vigilant. Ambroise roughly pushed Denninger towards the pit.

Markham, hearing the noise, directed his beam upwards, illuminating both Ambroise and Denninger. Markham swore and realized to his chagrin that he was unarmed. He had left his rifle above and Lucas must have dropped his before he'd fallen in the pit. "This is just lovely," he muttered as Ambroise smiled.

"Yes it is, isn't it?" he said smugly. He looked around and saw that Rourke had disappeared. "Where is your other friend?"

Markham looked around at the walls of the pit and then back up at the priest. "Now how the fuck would I know?" he barked.

Ambroise's smile faded. "There is no need for vulgarities. This is still a church, you know. Now, toss me your light."

Markham stared angrily back at the priest and noticed Denninger struggling slightly, but to no avail. "You okay, Doc?" Markham asked.

Denninger smiled weakly. "For the time being," he said softly.

Ambroise gestured with the pistol. "I won't ask again. Toss up your light to your friend here."

Markham threw the flashlight to Denninger who then handed it to Ambroise.

"All right buddy, what now?" Markham demanded of the priest.

Ambroise looked around nervously. "Where is the other soldier?" he asked again. Markham shrugged. "I told you, I don't know. He was supposed to go and get the Doc."

Ambroise lowered the pistol and then, without warning, hit Denninger with his shoulder, sending the archeologist into the pit. Markham jumped out of the way as Denninger's body slammed into the ground beside Lucas. Markham shot Ambroise an angry look, then grabbed Denninger's arm and helped the dirt-covered doctor to stand. "You're a prick," seethed Markham.

Ambroise ignored the barb and moved away from the pit. He had to find Rourke.

As soon as Ambroise moved off, the pit was plunged into darkness once again. "Goddamn it," cursed Markham. "This ain't good. Where the hell is — ?"

His sentence was cut off by the sound of a gunshot. Immediately Markham called out. "Matty!"

It was suddenly quiet. Markham strained to listen and could hear the unmistakable sounds of someone approaching. They heard the flicking of a lighter then smelled the smoke of a lit cigarette. It was a horrible odor which Denninger had not smelled for a long time.

Over five years, in fact.

"Oh my God … it *can't* be … ," he whispered. The cigarette smoker leaned forward and directed the flashlight beam into the pit. Denninger held a hand up in front of his eyes, trying to get a better look at the smoker. As his eyes adjusted he saw the man grin.

A Cheshire Cat grin.

"Hello, Gerhard," said Otto Rahn.

40

"I TRUST YOU ARE well, my old friend."

Denninger just stared up at Rahn, his mouth agape.

"You know this guy, Doc?" asked Markham. When he received no answer, he looked up at Rahn who was taking a long pull on his cigarette. "Hey, where's Matty?" he demanded.

Rahn exhaled and then grinned again. "You mean the other American?" he answered in accented English. He jerked a thumb behind him. "He's over there, resting."

"Resting? What did you do to him?" Markham demanded. Rahn shrugged and flicked the cigarette away. "He's fine. Don't worry. He's in better shape than the priest, I assure you. I assume you would like to get out of there?"

Denninger finally found his voice. "I thought you were dead!" he exclaimed.

Rahn chuckled and spread his arms wide. "I was. Now I am better," he smiled.

He reached into a small sack that was by his feet and pulled out a length of rope. He tossed one end into the hole and then he tied the other end to an arm of one of the pews.

"I am always prepared, eh Gerhard?" he asked giddily.

Markham gripped the rope and slowly pulled himself up in spite of the fact that his shoulder felt on fire from the gunshot wound. As he neared the top of the opening, Rahn grabbed hold of Markham's right hand and pulled him the rest of the way out. He winced and rubbed his wound as Rahn turned and shone the light back into the hole. "Who's next?" he asked cheerily as he threw down the rope.

Denninger took the rope and looped it around Lucas' chest. "All right … he's ready." Denninger lifted Lucas up as high as he could. Rahn and Markham pulled on the rope while Denninger pushed. As soon as Lucas was out, Rahn threw the rope back down to Denninger. The archeologist grabbed the line and began to haul himself up, with Rahn and Markham tugging at the same time.

Once they were all out of the hole, Markham could hear a muffled moaning and saw a barely moving Ambroise lying on the ground nearby. Markham shone the light on his face and saw it was screwed up in pain. He moved the light over the priest's body and saw a bleeding bullet wound in his thigh. He reached down and tore off a piece of Ambroise's dressing gown to act as a tourniquet. "Serves you right," he muttered. Once he had tied off the wound, he went to look for Rourke.

Denninger continued to stare unbelievingly at Rahn who was lighting a candle that he pulled out of his sack. "I don't understand … ," began Denninger. Rahn smiled and walked over to one of the pews. Denninger noticed that he was limping. "Are you all right, Otto?"

Rahn sat down with a grunt. "It's an old injury," he told him with a sigh.

Denninger collapsed beside him and put his hands on his knees. He cocked his head at Rahn and then shook it in disbelief. "Well?" he asked. "Are you going to tell me?"

Rahn looked tired. He put the candle on the back of the bench in front of him and reached into his jacket, pulling out his cigarettes. Denninger watched with fascination as he flicked the lighter with his customary flourish and lit the evil-smelling stick. He exhaled some brownish grey smoke. "Well, I won't go into *everything* that's happened over the last few years. I'll just hit the highlights." He took another drag on his smoke.

"I knew the Gestapo was on to me," he began. "I couldn't risk getting caught with the scroll. That's why I had Bobby get it to you ..." He paused, overcome with melancholy.

Denninger looked down and said "Bobby's dead, Otto."

Rahn nodded. "Yes, I know. Fucking Gestapo animals — he was a good boy."

He sighed then continued. "After you got the document I left. In a hurry, I tell you, but somehow they tracked me to Tyrol. I thought if I could get up into the mountains I could lose them. And I did ... but ..." He looked down at his leg.

Denninger stared at it as well and then looked up. "What happened?"

Rahn took another pull on the cigarette. "In my haste, I made a misstep — something you don't want to do when you're eight thousand feet up in the clouds. They were close behind me and somehow I found myself in a freefall down the side of the goddamn mountain. I fell over a hundred feet. A hundred feet — do you believe it? And I lived! I was injured quite badly, but the Gestapo thought I was dead. I was found a couple of hours later by some Italian monks who took me to their monastery. There was no St. Bernard with brandy, though," he chuckled.

"I had a broken back and my leg was shattered. It was two full years before I was back on my feet and another eight months of exercise so that I could walk. I had to learn how to walk again, Gerhard. By this time, the war had already started and I had lost track of you. It was too dangerous for me to go back to Germany, so I got word to Bobby who acted as my eyes and ears. He had heard of my 'demise' in the mountains, so imagine his surprise when he heard from me."

Denninger grinned. "Oh, I certainly can," he said.

Rahn nodded sagely. "Bobby told me that you had been sent to Tibet. I couldn't believe it. Everything was getting all fucked up! Bobby managed to get the scroll and hide it, but soon he was also under surveillance. So there we were, Gerhard. Me stuck in Italy, barely able to walk, you in Tibet, and Bobby unable to do a damn thing! I don't know about you, but I wasn't about to give up. Not after all this. War or no war, I was going to find the damn treasure."

Denninger nodded quickly. "I felt the same way, Otto. Tibet almost sapped my spirit. Did you know that I was in an airplane crash?"

Rahn looked surprised.

"We were shot down by two British fighters! It was both frightening and exhilarating at the same time," he exclaimed almost proudly.

"None the worse for wear I see," responded Rahn.

They were interrupted by the re-appearance of Markham with Rourke, who was rubbing his jaw. The corporal deposited the woozy soldier beside Denninger and then went to get the wounded priest.

Rourke winced. "Fuck, this hurts," he wheezed as he rubbed his chin. He looked over and saw Lucas lying on one of the benches.

"What's with him? Is he okay?"

Denninger nodded.

Rourke then turned his attention to Rahn and his eyes narrowed. "Are you the fucker who hit me?" he demanded accusingly.

Rahn spread his hands theatrically. "Guilty," he admitted. "I *am* sorry about that. You saw me and I couldn't let my presence be known at that juncture. My apologies."

Rourke started to get up just as Markham was dragging Ambroise over to the altar. "Sit down Matty," he ordered as he tied the priest to one of two small pillars behind the altar.

Rourke looked petulantly at the corporal. “Doug, he hit me!” he whined.

“Yeah, I know. Can’t say I blame him, though,” Markham responded. “Jesus, what’s that say about you? The guy doesn’t even know you and he punches you in the face.”

“It ain’t funny, Doug.”

“Who’s laughing, Matty? Just shut up and sit down, wouldja?”

Lucas finally began to stir. Denninger moved over to check on the injured soldier. “Ooooh my head,” Lucas moaned quietly.

Denninger cautioned him not to move around too much. “Does anything feel broken?” he asked, checking his limbs. Lucas began to shake his head but stopped almost immediately. “Oh, my head. My chest hurts too.”

Denninger ran his hands over his chest. “I don’t feel any broken ribs, but they might be bruised.” Lucas took a breath and winced. When he opened his eyes he saw Rahn. “Who’s that?”

Denninger stood up and presented Rahn to the soldiers. He quickly told them about their initial meeting and how the whole adventure began. When he finished, he turned to Rahn. “How did you find us Otto?”

“It was sheer luck. Bobby spotted you at the train station and contacted me before he boarded the train. I had a pretty good idea where you were going. I’d already hired a motorboat and landed in Marseilles. It was only a matter of time before we would meet up. We were going in the same direction.”

Markham suddenly stood up. “It was *you*, wasn’t it?” he said accusingly.

Rahn kept grinning, but looked at Markham questioningly. “It was I … what?” he asked innocently.

"*You* fired the first shot — back where Sam died."

Rahn raised his eyebrows. "Ah, you mean with the patrol. Yes I did — if I had not, your French friend with the truck would be dead."

Markham balled up his fists. "I had the situation contained. If you hadn'ta fired, I would have — "

Rahn cut him off authoritatively. "You would have what? Let the Germans kill the Frenchman and discover your whereabouts? As far as your friend getting killed, he let it happen. He froze. He just stood there and they shot him."

Denninger turned to Markham and confirmed what Rahn had said. "It's true, Corporal. I saw him standing in the clearing. When they started firing at us, I ducked. After it stopped I looked up. I had assumed he had ducked too. I am afraid he did not."

Markham glared at Denninger. "Why didn't you say anything before?"

Denninger glared back. "What would have been the point? Did you want to know that he froze? Would it have made you feel better if you knew that he didn't defend himself?"

"Besides," said Rahn, "Even if it had not been me who fired the first shot, do you think it would have changed the outcome?"

Markham was silent. He knew Rahn was right. It still didn't make things easier.

Everyone was quiet until Rahn started to talk to Denninger about the scroll. He grinned his Cheshire Cat grin again. "I had faith in you, Gerhard. I knew you would be able to decipher the scroll. How did you do it?"

Denninger explained how he had discovered the chess pattern on the document, but that it was Rourke who had actually figured out the Knight's Tour puzzle. Rahn glanced at Rourke with surprise as Denninger then explained what the clues were and how they found the site.

"Well then," said Rahn, turning to where Ambroise was tied and grimacing in pain. "Now that we are all here, perhaps our friend here can help us out." He limped over to the wounded priest. "Hello, Father. Are you prepared to make a confession?"

Ambroise looked up at Rahn with contempt and said nothing.

Rahn shrugged and went back to the others. "He doesn't seem to want to help us — how remarkably unchristian, eh? No matter. We'll wait until morning. I suggest everyone get some sleep. We may have a busy day tomorrow."

41

As the morning sun beamed through the windows of the church, Ambroise awoke with a start to see Rourke crouching in front of him and giving him a leering stare. He tried to get up but he discovered that he was still tied to the pillar. Rourke gave him a sideways grin. "How's it goin' there Frenchy?" he sneered. Markham, who had just awakened, told Rourke to leave the priest alone. Rourke glowered at Ambroise then stood up slowly and wandered back to the group. Rahn opened his eyes and stretched with a groan. He rubbed his leg and winced a little as he stood up.

Denninger was leaning against one of the walls and holding the scroll, poring over its contents. Rahn watched him for a few moments and then limped over. As he got closer, he cast a shadow over the archeologist. Denninger looked up and saw Rahn in silhouette in front of him.

"What are you thinking, Gerhard?" Rahn asked.

"There must be something in here that will tell us what we need to know," Denninger mused.

Rahn cocked his head in the direction of Ambroise. "I think there's something in *him* that will tell us what we need to know."

Markham went over and squatted on the ground near the recalcitrant priest. "All right, Father — we've been through this before. Just tell us what we want to know and we'll let you go."

Ambroise stared coldly at the corporal and refused to speak. Rourke started to get up but Markham shot him a particularly nasty glare that made him sit back down again.

"How is the leg, Father?" asked Rahn innocently.

Ambroise gave him a burning look. "You shot a man of the cloth. You will certainly rot in hell," he spat out.

Rahn raised an eyebrow. "Hell? Do you really think so?" He winked. "You Catholics are a very strange lot," How come anyone who doesn't do what you say will suffer the hellfires of damnation? I mean, you were ready to blow my friend's head off last night. Does that mean that you are going to hell, or do you have some sort of dispensation that allows you to murder?"

"Your flippancy is unseemly," retorted Ambroise.

Rahn stepped back as if shocked. "Flippant? Me? Oh, I am deadly serious, Father. You were ready to kill poor Gerhard. For what? To protect a treasure that doesn't even belong to the Catholic Church?"

Ambroise's face contorted into an ugly grimace. "You have no idea what you are talking about!" he snarled.

Markham stepped forward with his hands up. "Okay everybody, let's take it easy here."

Ambroise was struggling with the ropes. He was shaking with rage. "You may as well kill me now," he said in a trembling voice.

Rourke loudly chambered a bullet and aimed it at Ambroise's head. "No problem, Frenchy," he said.

Markham reached over and knocked the barrel away. "Normally I would just beat the shit outta Matty here for doing something stupid like that, but you know, I'm getting a little fuckin' tired of this game," muttered Markham. "We're gonna find what we're lookin' for with or without you. Truthfully, losin' a pain in the ass like you would probably make things a whole lot easier."

Lucas, who had just got unsteadily to his feet, was alarmed at Markham's treatment of the priest but remained silent.

Markham leaned in so that he was inches from Ambroise's face. "So, if you really want to die, you just let me know. I can accommodate you."

Denninger, who was still studying the scroll, suddenly called Rahn over. A few moments later, Markham was told to come over as well. The corporal told Rourke to keep an eye on Ambroise.

"What's up Doug?" asked Lucas.

"The doc might be on to something. What were you sayin' there, Doc?"

Denninger and Rahn showed Lucas a number of the symbols on the scroll. Ambroise strained to hear what they were saying but all he caught at first were the words "Templar" and "Cathar." When he heard the word "dove," his heart began to pound.

Denninger was pointing at the placement of the symbols around the document. "See here," he directed. "I thought these were randomly placed around the scroll — this is a Templar cross ... the skull and crossbones ..."

"I thought that was a pirate symbol," said Lucas sheepishly.

"Well, it is now. In fact, it's also an insignia of the SS, but originally it belonged to the Knights Templar. And this is the Templar seal. These are all Templar symbols."

"So?"

Denninger pointed at the depiction of the bird. "Do you know what this is?"

"It looks like a bird," Lucas responded.

"It *is* a bird. It's a dove. The dove is a Cathar symbol."

Lucas didn't quite understand.

Denninger continued patiently. "All the symbols on here are those of the Knights Templar. *All* of them — "

Rahn then cut in. "Except the dove. Now, look at this. Oh, I'm sorry Gerhard, would you continue please? This is your show."

Denninger smiled. "All right. Look at the Templar cross. Do you see that it is crooked? The top is off-center. That is a little odd don't you think?"

Lucas shrugged.

"Do you see the way the tips of the cross have two points? It's what is known as a Maltese cross. Now look here."

Lucas looked closely at where Denninger was pointing. One of the tips at the bottom of the cross seemed to be touching one of the letters in the body of the text.

The letter *N*.

The hair on the back of Lucas's neck stood up. "Oh my … it's a compass … " he breathed.

Denninger smiled again. "Right. So, if we turn the document this way … " He spun the scroll around so that the cross was orientated towards the north wall.

"Now, the seemingly random placement of the Templar symbols corresponds with … "

"Pillars inside the church," finished Lucas. He looked at the dove and then slowly he raised his eyes to the eastern wall. While each of the Templar symbols corresponded with a pillar, the dove aligned with the wall behind the altar.

They moved *en masse* to the eastern wall. Ambroise watched apprehensively as they moved past him and got closer to the secret entrance to the crypt. Markham shifted the screen about until Denninger suddenly gave a shout. "Look!" he pointed.

Markham squatted to get a better look at the carving. After a moment he turned his head to look at the others. "Yeah, it's a dove, all right. Now what?"

He stood up and took a step back as he put his hands on his hips. Ambroise craned his neck to see that Markham was standing directly on the boards which covered the entrance to the crypt. He held his breath.

Rahn was studying the carving when he caught Ambroise's fidgeting out of the corner of his eye. He followed the priest's gaze right to the spot where Markham was standing. "Father Ambroise," said Rahn.

Ambroise quickly averted his eyes from Markham and turned his attention to Rahn. "What do you want?" he asked sullenly.

Rahn grinned and sauntered over to the trussed up priest. Leaning casually on the altar he asked, "Just how old is this church?"

Ambroise looked confused. "What?"

"It's a simple question. You are the expert and I'm curious. How old is this church?"

Ambroise eyed him suspiciously. "Why do you want to know?"

Rahn pulled out his cigarettes and popped one into his mouth. He offered the package to Ambroise who just struggled with his bonds. Rahn shrugged and lit the cigarette, dramatically blowing the smoke upward. "Just naturally inquisitive. I suppose that's why I'm a genius, right Gerhard? Always wanting to know the answers, eh?"

"What are you saying, Otto?" Denninger inquired.

Rahn turned his attention back to Ambroise. "Would it be at least four hundred years old? Five hundred years old? Maybe more?"

Ambroise gave a bewildered shake of the head. "I don't know."

Rahn looked around at the decrepit state of the building. "I'd be willing to guess it's over six or seven hundred years old. I mean that wall there is coming down, the confessionals are turning to sawdust, why, the stairs to the bell tower are gone, for heaven's sake. And we're not fooled by the addition of the pews."

"Of course," Denninger said, "medieval churches didn't have pews. They didn't come into use until the Reformation."

Rahn nodded. "The pews were obviously added at a much later date. That's why the building might appear at first glance to be newer than it actually is." He turned to eye Ambroise who refused to meet his gaze. Rahn chuckled. "This place is full of surprises."

Markham headed over to the altar and stopped next to Rahn. "What are you getting at?"

Rahn grinned at the soldier, stepped around him, and walked over to the carving. In doing so, he stood directly beside the wooden planks. "If this building is at least five hundred years old, why do these boards here appear new?"

Denninger walked to where Rahn was pointing and knelt down. He rapped his knuckles on the wood and looked up at Rahn with a smile. "It sounds hollow," he said.

Lucas and Rourke rushed over to where the others were standing. Markham thumped the boards with his heel and confirmed what Denninger had said. He knelt down and tried to get his fingers in between the boards but it proved too difficult. "We're gonna need something to bust through this," he determined. Looking around, he spied what looked to be part of a statue's pedestal in the northeastern corner of the church. "Matty, go get that hunk of stone over there."

Rourke made a face. "Why me?" he whined.

"Because if you don't," Markham responded, "I'm gonna use you."

Rourke huffed and went resignedly into the corner. After a few seconds of struggling, manged to lift the heavy stone and waddled back to the group, grunting and swearing the whole way. "Here," he wheezed. "Somebody take it!" Unable to hold it any more, he let the stone slip out of his hands and it landed directly on the wood. It fell through the planks with a splintering crack and bounced down the stone stairs below.

"Well," said Markham, "that worked better than I thought." They soon had the remaining pieces of wood removed, exposing the steps and the blackness below.

Rahn grinned and clapped a hand on Denninger's shoulder. "Ah, Alice — are you ready to go through the looking glass?"

As they started to climb down, Markham told Rourke that he had to stay where he was. Rourke grabbed the corporal by the arm. "Why can't I go too?"

"Someone's gotta watch our friend over there," Markham said, indicating Ambroise.

Rourke shook his head. "We're all in this together, Doug."

"That's right, Matty. We're all in this together. You'll get your share. Just keep an eye on our buddy there."

When Rourke didn't immediately move, Markham grabbed one of the fingers still clutching his arm and started to bend it back. Pain shot across Rourke's face.

"I'm not telling you again."

Rourke let go straightaway and backed off. He sullenly headed back to where Ambroise was trussed up and leaned against one of the pillars.

One by one the other men entered the large room, the beams of the flashlights illuminating the dark emptiness around them. It wasn't long before they found the moveable wall. "Look Otto," directed Denninger, pointing at the carving of the fish. Rahn nodded knowingly. Markham saw the ring and pulled. When nothing happened, he looked at the others.

"Try twisting it," suggested Denninger. Markham followed the advice and turned the ring. They all heard the click. Markham grinned. He began to push and to everyone's delight, the wall began to move forward.

Once the wall was out of the way, they entered the other room. Markham aimed his flashlight forward and saw the three stone boxes and the clay jar that Bérenger Saunière had discovered over sixty years before.

Markham whistled when he saw the boxes. He looked at Lucas and a wide grin broke out across his face. "Look

Phil," he enthused. "Looks like we're gonna be set for life, huh?"

Rahn and Denninger exchanged glances. They both knew exactly what the boxes actually were.

They weren't treasure chests.

Rahn stepped forward and ran his fingers over the stone lid of one of the boxes. He looked up at Markham and Lucas and said, "I am afraid, gentlemen, that this is not what you think it is."

42

THE SMILE ON MARKHAM'S face faded somewhat at the statement. "What are you talking about?" he asked as he went over to one of the other boxes. "This is the treasure, isn't it?"

Rahn asked Lucas for his flashlight. He began to remove the lid of the box he was standing next to. Once the lid was off and the dust had cleared, Rahn reached in and removed one of the articles inside. He held up what looked like a leg bone for both Markham and Lucas to see.

Lucas looked confused. "It's a bone?"

Denninger nodded. "This box is an ossuary. The other two are ossuaries as well."

Markham looked stunned. "They're what?"

"Ossuaries," said Rahn. "They were used in the first century. Burial space was scarce, so bodies were placed in tombs for about a year until they were rendered to skeletons. The bones were then collected and placed in stone boxes just like these. Go ahead, Corporal. Open that box. You'll see that it contains bones."

Incredulously, Markham removed the lid. That box too, contained bones. Markham was both confused and angry. "I don't get it. Why all the secrecy for a bunch of goddamn bones?"

Denninger had by now moved over to the clay jar by the far ossuary. He carefully opened the lid of the jar and, after shining his flashlight inside, he reached in and gently pulled out the leather-bound codex.

"Otto," he called out softly. Rahn came over as Lucas was removing the lid of the third ossuary. Rahn aimed the flashlight at the codex. Denninger opened it and saw that it was written in what appeared to be an ancient script. He showed it to Rahn. "Is this what I think it is?"

Rahn nodded.

Markham had by this time removed all the bones from his ossuary, in the hopes that the Cathar treasure was perhaps hidden under the remains. Aiming the beam of the flashlight into the box, he was upset to find nothing else. In frustration, he kicked at the pile of bones at his feet. "All the shit we went through, and for what? A box of fuckin' bones!"

His dream of escaping the war a rich man became as dusty as the bones in the ossuary. His urge to leave had suddenly become overwhelming. "Are you guys about done over there? Can we get the hell outta here, please?"

Rahn and Denninger, however, were in deep discussion as they pored over the codex. Markham's patience was wearing thin. "Uh, fellas? Are you through?"

Rahn, with eyes wide, turned to Markham. "On the contrary, Corporal — we are just getting started."

Upstairs, Rourke was leaning lazily against one of the pillars, stroking the barrel of his weapon absentmindedly. Ambroise had long ceased struggling. Once the group had found the secret room, he knew that it was over.

He was thinking of the night when he went to see Abbé Gélis. The course of action he'd set in motion that night had resulted in where he was right now. He regretted killing Gélis and trying to frame Saunière. Ambroise had truly believed what he was doing was for God. He had had to prevent that terrible information from getting out. It was his duty.

If only he had just destroyed the evidence instead.

"So stupid," he muttered to himself.

At one time, Ambroise had actually come very close to destroying the evidence. A few years back, with the help of a demolitions expert, he had rigged the secret rooms with explosives, but in the end he found he just couldn't go through with it. Even knowing what was contained in the codex and what was in the boxes — and the fact that he had already killed for them — he'd found he could not, in good conscience, destroy them.

Ambroise's eyes wandered over to Rourke. Only about a yard away from the soldier's feet, hidden under an innocuous pile of bricks, was a small, flat piece of rubber. Under that, in a tiny hole in the floor, was the beginning of a powder fuse that ran underneath the length of the floor to the crypt below. Once lit, the two hundred pounds of explosives that were buried beneath and around the crypt would detonate within eight minutes. The resulting explosion would leave nothing but a hundred-foot hole where the church ruin now stood. The ossuaries and the codex, along with the body of the demolitions expert, buried with the explosives, would be vaporized. Ambroise regretted having killed the explosives expert. The man had, after all, done nothing wrong — but he knew too much.

If only Ambroise had lit the fuse then.

His arms ached where the rope was digging into his flesh. He shifted slightly and felt a sudden sharp pain in the area of his wrist.

Rourke heard Ambroise's yelp and told him to stop moving around. "You'll just make yourself more uncomfortable, Frenchy," he warned.

Ambroise tried to get his fingers close to where he had felt the sharpness. He soon realized it was a broken piece of brick that was jutting out from beneath the pillar he was tied to. Keeping one eye on Rourke, he hunkered down low and attempted to rub the rope against the sharpened edge of the brick.

43

ROURKE HAD JUST SWALLOWED another Pervitin when he heard the group coming up the stairs. He quickly stuffed the bottle back into his pocket seconds before Markham's head popped up through the hole. He was followed quickly by Denninger, Rahn and then Lucas. Rourke saw that they were empty-handed, save for the codex in Denninger's hand.

"What the ...?" he muttered. He rushed over and stopped in front of Markham. "Where's the loot?" Rourke demanded. His eyes darted from Markham to Denninger and then to Lucas and finally settled on Rahn. When no one spoke he turned back to Markham with an accusing look. "Are you guys are tryin' to put the Chinese squeeze on me?"

When Rahn looked at Denninger questioningly, the archeologist just shook his head and rolled his eyes.

Markham sat down on some bricks and rubbed his sore shoulder. "There's nothing down there but bones, Matty."

Rourke was incredulous. "Bones? But what about the treasure?"

Markham put his hands up in defeat. "What can I tell you? That's all there was. And that book thing there," he said, pointing at the codex in Denninger's hand.

Rourke's mouth hung open in disbelief for a moment and then his face distorted. He abruptly spun around and shot a searing look at Ambroise. "All right, Frenchy," he seethed. "Where is it?"

Ambroise just smirked at Rourke, which made the small soldier even angrier. He charged forward and delivered a kick to the priest's side, then reached down and pulled Ambroise towards him. "Where's the fuckin' treasure?" he screamed in his face.

Markham and Lucas rushed over and started to yank the crazed soldier from off of Ambroise. As they struggled with him, Rourke's bottle of Pervitin flew out of his pocket and crashed to the floor. It broke open, scattering the pills everywhere. Markham saw the tiny tablets rolling around and picked one up. He examined it carefully.

He knew what it was.

Markham went over to Rourke and held out the pill in front of Rourke.

"What the hell, Matty?"

Rourke was at once filled with terror and turned away. He was sure that Markham was going to kill him this time. He felt sick to his stomach and was certain he was about to vomit. Markham placed his hand firmly on Rourke's shoulder and Rourke, suddenly confused about what was happening, peered up through tear-filled eyes at the corporal.

Markham was looking at him very intensely but was uncharacteristically calm. "Where did you get these?" he asked quietly. Rourke sniffed and said that he got them from a dead German soldier a few days back. Markham clenched his teeth. He turned to Lucas and ordered him to help him gather up the rest of the pills.

Denninger had picked up one of the tablets, showed it to Rahn, and then turned to Markham. "You know what this is, don't you?" he queried.

Markham looked up and rubbed his shoulder again. "Yeah, I know what this shit is." he muttered. "I had this uncle ... he had some kinda health problem. His doctor prescribed this garbage for it and he wound up getting hooked on it." He shook his head disgustedly. "It was called Benzadrine. It was worse than anything you could get off the street, I swear." Markham sighed. "You know, my uncle used to be a real good guy, too. This shit made him paranoid and he thought everyone was out to get him ..." His voice trailed off.

"What happened to your uncle?' asked Denninger.

Markham took a large breath and didn't speak for a long time. "It got to the point where he always had to have it," he finally said. "He was having hallucinations and became very violent. He and another guy who was hooked on it too wound up robbing a store to get money to buy more of the shit. When the owner told them he had already made the bank deposit that day and didn't have any cash ..." He heaved a labored sigh. "... they beat him to a pulp. The store owner suffered some kind of brain damage and was never the same again. My uncle ended up in prison."

"I'm sorry to hear that, Corporal. Is he still in prison?"

Markham shook his head. "He's dead," he said quietly. "Someone cut his throat while he was working in the prison laundry." He held up the pill. "All because of this." He glanced over at Rourke who was curled up in a fetal position, holding his stomach.

"He'll have to be watched. Withdrawal from Pervitin could result in a number of scenarios," said Denninger.

"Like what?"

"Well, there could be fearfulness and hyperventilation. There also could be depression or extreme irritability."

Markham scoffed. "Well, he's always been irritable."

Rahn had by this time wandered over and was listening to the conversation. "There could also be outbursts of excessive violence," he added. "We're going to have to keep an eye on him."

Lucas went over to check on Rourke while Denninger and Rahn examined the codex more closely. The archeologist had opened it and was scrutinizing the letters when he realized something. He handed the book to Rahn. "Take a look at this, Otto," and mumbled something to him. Rahn took the codex and agreed. "I think you may be right, Gerhard."

Markham asked to see the codex. "Do you mind?"

Rahn grinned and handed it to the soldier. "Not at all. How is your grasp of ancient languages?"

Markham smiled. "Horrible. Why?"

"It would help in this case, I'm afraid."

Markham glanced down at the codex and raised his eyebrows at the jumble of unknown letters staring back at him. "Huh," he grunted. "You can't read this?" Rahn shook his head. He glanced over at Ambroise, who was obviously listening to them. Markham headed over to the priest with the codex, but Ambroise pretended not to notice his approach. The corporal knelt down next to Ambroise and put the open book in front of the priest's face. "Do you know what this is?" he asked.

Ambroise looked away. Markham glanced over at Denninger and Rahn and then back to Ambroise. "Do you know what it says?" he demanded.

Ambroise turned his face back to Markham and just glared at him. After a few seconds, Markham stood up. "Well boys, it looks like the good Father here doesn't know what it is either," he said to the others, "Maybe we should take this thing to a museum."

That got Ambroise's attention. He started to struggle again. "You cannot take it! You do not know what it is!" he pleaded.

Markham smiled and turned around. "You wanna try this again?" he asked.

"Let me loose," Ambroise bristled.

"Are you going to come clean?"

"Let me go!" he screamed, his face red with rage.

"Touchy," remarked Rahn.

"Look Father. One way or another, we will find out what this thing is," Markham warned.

Ambroise knew it was true. Even if they killed him, they would still have the codex and they would eventually learn the truth.

There had to be another way.

Rourke had vomited in the corner and that, coupled with the smell of Rahn's cigarettes, was overpowering the priest's senses. He shook his head in an attempt to clear his mind.

It was then that he got an idea.

"Untie me," he said. "I'll tell you what you want to know."

He would have to tell them everything, but he wasn't worried. They wouldn't be going anywhere.

44

"THE FIRST THING YOU should know is that the language of the document is Aramaic ... but I think you already surmised that," began Ambroise.

"Do you know what it says?" asked Denninger.

The priest looked sternly at each of the men. "Do any of you know what the term 'apocalypse' means?"

"It's Greek," responded Denninger. "It means the 'lifting of the veil' or 'taking off the cover', does it not?"

Ambroise nodded. "It's usually misunderstood as a prophetic revelation about the end of times, but the true meaning is much more like disclosure — a disclosure to certain privileged persons of something hidden from the rest of the world. May I see the codex, please?"

Markham handed the leather-clad document to Ambroise.

"What you are about to hear is apocalyptic in every sense of the world." He then opened it slowly and ran his hand softly across the papyrus. "This is a letter written by one of Christ's disciples," he said in a reverent voice. "The one whom Jesus loved best."

An energized Lucas stepped forward. "You mean, this was actually written by the apostle John?" he said excitedly.

"No. Not John." He paused. Pointing to the codex, he said, "This was written by Judas Iscariot."

Rahn and Denninger exchanged looks.

Lucas was shocked. "Is this some kind of joke?" he asked.

Ambroise merely stared at the soldier. "I wish it were a joke," Ambroise said sadly. "It breaks my heart now as it did forty years ago when I first learned of it."

Lucas started to move toward the priest but Markham stepped in. He put his hands on the shaking soldier. "Phil, relax. Let him finish," instructed Markham. "Let's hear what he has to say."

Ambroise cleared his throat and began to read as Rahn took notes.

I am Judah. I am one of the twelve.

What I will say to you is so that you will know. What I have done is what Yeshuah asked of me. Yeshuah spoke to me the night of the Passover meal and he said to me 'you will sacrifice the man that clothes me.' I understood what he wanted of me and said I would do so. The others were filled with sadness, but I said that I my happiness was in helping Yeshuah. He was prepared to go into the glory of God, but he could not leave Maryam heavy with child. He loved me best.

The night in the garden they came but they did not know Yeshuah. Yeshuah kissed me and they took me instead. They believed they had laid hold of the teacher. They took me to the high priest Caiaphas who delivered me to Pilate. I knew Pilate hated Jews, so I called him a Jew. I did this to make sure he would pass the sentence, and indeed Pilate grew angry and passed the sentence.

They led me to the Hill of Skulls where they put me to the cross. The others promised I would not die, and in truth I did not. At the appointed hour they gave me the drink. A sleep came over me and though they thought I was dead, I was not. That night they took me to Yakob, the brother of Yeshuah, who cared for me.

The days passed and Yeshuah saw me. He kissed me and wept. He put healing oils on my wounds and he wept. I begged him to weep not. I was his disciple. I followed Yeshuah and Maryam to Gaul where we lived. Yeshuah and Maryam spoke of God and the Law to many and they believed.

Ambroise paused to let what he had just read sink in. No one spoke. After a few minutes, Lucas finally broke the silence. "This is utter nonsense!" he said with disgust.

Denninger was in awe. "Yeshuah — that would be Jesus and Maryam would be Mary Magdalene."

"This is incredible," Rahn said in amazement.

"I have read to you what is written in the text," responded Ambroise. "You may draw your own conclusions."

"It sounds to me like Jesus asked Judas to take his place because Mary was pregnant and quite possibly did not want to risk leaving her a widow. Presumably the apostles somehow managed to get him off the cross before he died," surmised Rahn in a flat, analytical tone.

"This is fantasy," muttered Lucas. "*Jesus* was crucified. *Judas* betrayed him. That's what happened."

Rahn pursed his lips and remarked nonchalantly, "Not according to this."

Lucas suddenly lunged at Rahn. The two fell heavily to the floor, with Lucas's arm across Rahn's throat. Markham quickly jumped in and, despite his throbbing shoulder, he managed to squeeze his arm between the two and was able to separate them with the help of Denninger. Rahn put his hand to his throat and rubbed it while Markham pulled the angry soldier away.

"Fine Christian values there," muttered Rahn to Denninger.

Ambroise eyed the proceedings carefully, and tried to inch away slowly. Through the corner of his eye, Markham saw the movement and shot him a look which halted the priest immediately.

Lucas stood back and raged in silenced as Markham returned to the group. Denninger went over to Rahn.

Rahn rubbed his neck then cleared his throat as he looked down at his notes. "Look at what it says here: 'the man that clothes me'—what do you think that means, Gerhard?"

"Judas was the keeper of the group's purse ... and clothes ... you wear clothes to cover yourself, to protect yourself," he murmured.

"Yes. Protection. I believe that in this context, clothes mean protection. What Jesus was saying is that he wants Judas, 'the man that clothes me' or in fact, the man that 'protects me' to sacrifice himself. It seems they made the switch in the garden of Gethsemane when the Romans were brought there to arrest him."

"I see what you are saying," responded Denninger as it started to become clearer in his mind. "The Romans had no idea what Christ looked like. That's why they relied on him being identified by means of the infamous 'Judas kiss' when they came to arrest him. If the roles were reversed, Jesus would have kissed Judas and Judas would have been arrested instead."

Rahn nodded in agreement. "It is not so far-fetched, you know. There is an interpretation of the Muslim faith that holds that Jesus did not die on the cross. Their Koran speaks of another who took his place. I believe the phrase is something like 'they did not crucify him, but it appeared so.' I will have to look it up. It also sounds as though the apostles engaged in a little subterfuge as well. What did he say?" He checked his notes. "'The others promised I would not die' ... then there's that bit about the drink. Let me think ... Christ said something just before he died. It was ..."

"'*Eloi, Eloi, lama sabachthani*'?" muttered Ambroise.

Rahn turned to the priest with a look of surprise. "Thank you, Father. If I am not mistaken, that means 'My God, my God, why have you forsaken me?' And it is at this point he is given the sponge soaked with *posca*."

"Posca?" questioned Markham.

"It is a sour wine concoction. 'The drink' as he says. It was supposed to keep you awake, to prolong the torture when you are crucified." Rahn shook his head. "Those Romans were sadistic bastards." He paused and looked at his notes again. "'At the appointed hour they gave me the drink. A sleep came over me and though they thought I was dead, I was not.' Likely, they gave him something to render him unconscious instead."

Rourke, who had been sitting quietly by his puddle of vomit, suddenly brightened. "You mean they slipped him a Mickey!"

Rahn glanced at Markham, who told him to keep going. "I would think that a little bit of mandrake mixed in with the vinegar of the sour wine would be sufficient to do the trick. Mandrake was readily available in the area and was used medicinally as an anesthetic. What do you think Gerhard?"

Denninger wasn't listening. He was studying Rahn's notes and just then something caught his eye.

'That night they took me to Yakob, the brother of Yeshuah who cared for me ... '

He read it again.

'That night ... '

"Father Ambroise, when do they say Christ died?"

"At the ninth hour," Ambroise responded sullenly.

Denninger pulled at his lip thoughtfully. He turned to Rahn. "The ninth hour. Of course, that does *not* mean nine o'clock does it?"

Rahn shook his head. "In the classical era, the counting of the hours would begin at sunrise. So if the first hour had been at seven a.m., that means the ninth hour would be three in the afternoon.

"Three in the afternoon," Denninger repeated. "They would have taken him to the tomb before nightfall, wouldn't they?" He stared at Ambroise. "Wouldn't they, Father?"

The priest wouldn't meet his gaze.

"What are you getting at Gerhard?" asked Rahn.

"Back at Father Ambroise's church — the stations of the cross. The last station depicts Christ being taken to the tomb after death. It struck me as odd — until now."

"Why is that?" asked Markham.

"Jewish Law would have required that the body be interred before nightfall. There would have been plenty of time to accomplish this. Father Ambroise, you told me that the stations at your church were exactly the same as they were at Bérenger Saunière's church, correct?"

When he received no answer he went on.

"Saunière knew, didn't he?"

Ambroise was shaking slightly but still refused to speak.

"Saunière knew — the depiction showed the apostles with Christ. At *night*. They weren't placing the body *into* the tomb — they were taking it *out*. Later that night. Saunière knew the crucifixion was a hoax. He knew the truth, didn't he, Father?

"Judas took his place on the cross to save Jesus. The apostles then put him into a drug-induced coma to simulate death, and then later that night, they secreted him out of the tomb to recover."

Lucas, who had been seething quietly in the corner suddenly exploded. "Lies!" he screamed. The startled group turned to see Lucas with his weapon aimed squarely at them. "This is nothing but blasphemy."

"You cannot be serious. Are you actually going to shoot us?" asked Rahn with amazement. "We are not responsible for this text, my friend. Your anger is dangerously misplaced."

Markham swiftly rushed over to Lucas. "Phil, take it easy. I know this must be hard for you, but goddamn it … ," he said soothingly, putting his hand on the barrel of the weapon to lower it as Lucas stifled a sob.

"What do you even know about it, Doug? How the hell can you even comment on it?" he raged. "You don't even believe in God so this really doesn't affect you, does it?"

"You're right Phil. Okay, so it doesn't affect me. But, I mean, this is huge! Can you imagine what this thing is worth? Look at the big picture, would ya? We've come all this way to find a treasure and whatta we got? A bunch of bones and an old parchment. That's it. But what if this book is worth something? Did ya think about that? Who cares about what's in it, Phil. If it's a historical religious relic, it could be worth millions!"

Lucas brushed Markham's hand away. 'Do you think this is about money? I know, for someone like you who has no faith, this means nothing to you. But to me, Doug, this is awful! Do you have any idea what this means? Do you?

"Christianity is based on the fact that Jesus Christ died for our sins and then rose again. I know you were an altar boy once, so I'm sure you remember what Saint Paul said. If you don't, then I will remind you. Corinthians 1, chapter 15."

Markham shook his head. "It's been a long time, Phil. I don't remember that shit."

"Corinthians 1, chapter 15," he repeated. "The fourteenth verse. Still don't remember?"

"I'm sorry Phil."

Lucas blinked and the tears ran freely down his cheeks. "'And if Christ be not risen again, then is our preaching vain, and your faith is also vain.' If Christ didn't die and rise again, Doug, then there is no point to Christianity. Without the resurrection, there is nothing!" He wiped away the tears and felt his nose stuffing up. "I won't stay here and listen to this or be a part of it." He stepped around Markham and went outside.

"'And if Christ be not risen again, then is our preaching vain, and your faith is also in vain,'" repeated Rahn. "Very appropriate."

Ambroise cleared his throat and waved the codex.

"More than you think," he said solemnly. "Shall I continue?"

45

AMBROISE FOUND HIS PLACE in the codex and began to read again.

After many years Yeshuah went back to his home and I went with him. We heard of many terrible things that had passed. The one named Saul who worked for Rome attacked the Jews. Many were killed or arrested.

One day, Saul came to Yakob and told him he wanted to work for God. Yakob did not believe him at first, but Saul said he heard the word of the Lord. Yakob sent him away to preach to the Law. He did not. He preached saying to forget the Law and to forget Yakob. He said Yeshuah was the Son of God. He told of his calling to the church and that he heard Yeshuah's voice tell him to do so. He said Yeshuah performed many wonderous things. He said Yeshuah died and then rose to life again and many began to believe him. Yakob sent for Saul, now called Paul, and told him not to speak against the Law. Paul said he would not speak against the Law, but he did. He continued to speak of Yeshuah and against Yakob and the Law.

Yeshuah wept when he learned Yakob was killed by the Sadducee Ananus. Kipha was also dead and the church was gone. The others of the church had disappeared and the one in league with Rome did live.

They said Paul was dead but he was not. He lived in Rome. Yeshuah went to see Paul and I went with him. Paul did not know Yeshuah. Yeshuah had to tell Paul who he was and Paul then knew Yeshuah. Yeshuah asked why Paul lied and Paul laughed at him. He told Yeshuah this: "Why do you complain, Yeshuah? I made you a God."

Yeshuah wept. He went back to Gaul and I went with him.

I write these words in my own hand.
I am Judah

Rahn whistled and raised his eyebrows and murmured, "This ... is ... unbelievable."

If the first part was explosive, this was positively a time bomb. Ambroise sat down slowly and took a deep breath. "Do you see now why this has to remain hidden?" he asked quietly.

"Well," said Rahn. "It certainly casts Christianity in a whole new light, doesn't it?"

Ambroise hung his head low as Rourke looked from Rahn to Denninger. "Could somebody explain this to me? I don't get it."

Rahn was standing next to Ambroise and put his hand on the priest's shoulder. "Would you like to tell our little friend here about Saint Paul?"

Ambroise gave Rahn a sullen look. "I would rather not," he muttered.

Rahn lifted his hand from Ambroise's shoulder and smiled. "Well then, I will. You can correct me if I am wrong, Father. Now, let's see ..." He tapped his lips and thought for a moment. "Paul, originally known as Saul, was a persecutor of the Jerusalem church, the Jewish sect to which Jesus and his brother Yakob, or James, belonged. One day, on the road to Damascus, said Paul, he heard the voice of Jesus saying 'Saul, Saul, why are you persecuting me?' He fell to the ground, blinded by the light of God, and was immediately converted to Christianity. He then became a missionary and it was through him that the story of Jesus, his life, death and resurrection became known. Legend had it that he was killed by Rome shortly after James himself was murdered in AD 62. Is that right, Father?"

Ambroise nodded slightly. Rahn turned back to Rourke. "I guess you could say that without Paul, Christianity would not exist, at least in the form it is in today." Rahn then looked down at his notes. "Father, just how did Paul die?"

Ambroise blinked. "There are a number of traditions. One holds that he went to Spain where he eventually died. The more common tradition holds that he was beheaded during Emperor Nero's reign in AD 64. Another yet has him dying in prison."

Rahn read from his notes. "'They said Paul was dead but he was not. He lived in Rome.' According to this, Paul didn't die earlier. He was alive and well and living in Rome. No wonder there is no clear record of his death."

Ambroise looked like he was about to be sick and sat down on the floor near the pillar. His eyes were watering and his face had a death-like pallor to it. Rahn knelt down beside the priest and said, "Paul was a Roman agent, wasn't he Father?"

Ambroise heaved a great sigh and put his head in his hands. Rahn looked up at Denninger. "It all makes sense, Gerhard. Look at what was happening at the time. Judea was occupied by Rome and the Jews were not happy. There are many uprisings and Rome was getting fed up. They need to contain the problem. The Sadducees in the Sanhedrin who are in league with Rome are largely ineffective, so Rome needs to eliminate what they believe to be the root of the problem."

"The Jerusalem church," responded Denninger. Rahn nodded.

"Right. They need to neutralize the church, but they have to be careful about it. They don't want out-and-out bloodshed, so they come up with a plan to take down the church from the inside."

Rahn again referred to his notes. "All right. It says, 'One day Paul came to James, who is the leader of the church and told him he wanted to work for God. James did not believe him at first, but Paul said he heard the word of the Lord'—only there is a problem. Paul had for years been an openly hostile persecutor of the sect. So what does he do? He tells James that he has converted, literally 'seen the light.' James is naturally suspicious, so he decides on an interesting course of action. He sends Paul as far out of the country as possible to preach. He probably figures that if he converts anyone ... great, if he gets killed ... well, so be it.

"So now Paul is part of the Jerusalem church and his mission is to bring it down, and he feels the best way to do that is to bring down its leader James. But how? The letter says, 'James sent him away to preach to the Law. He did not. He preached saying to forget Jewish Law and to forget James.' Look, Gerhard. He begins preaching that James's brother, Jesus, the one who had been executed a few years back, is actually the Son of God. By elevating Jesus, he diminished James's role as leader. At first, there is much anger and resentment over this breach of Jewish Law and quite often, Paul was run out of the towns he preached in. In some cases he would just barely escape with his life, if I remember correctly.

"It is at this time that Paul has to make the story much more interesting. He's said that Jesus was the Son of God. He told of his calling to the church and that he heard Jesus's voice tell him to do so. He said that Jesus performed many wonders. He began speaking of the fact that his conversion was the result of Jesus actually talking directly to him. This is because Jesus was the Son of God! It was a perfectly natural extension of his preaching, and of course, with the prevalence of mystery religions at the time, it was relatively easy to convince people."

"Mystery religions?" asked Rourke.

"Yes, cults devoted to a particular god or gods, for which initiation was required and in which specific rituals, often incorporating mystical elements, were performed. Mystery religions were very popular in the Roman Empire, and quite a few shared some of the same characteristics. For example, virgin births and resurrections were commonplace motifs. By incorporating some of these aspects into the story of Jesus, particularly those from the legend of Mithras — "

"Mithras?" interjected Markham. "What's that?"

"Mithras was a figure from Persian myth. He was born of a virgin. He raised the dead, healed the sick, made the blind see, the lame walk, and cast out devils. He was even resurrected from the dead. Sound like anyone we know?"

Denninger smiled and nodded. It was easy to see why many were swayed. The story of Mithras was virtually identical to the story of Jesus.

"His birth was even celebrated on December 25. 'He said that Jesus died and then rose to life again.' So you see, Paul was very clever. By using these same elements, he created a story that would appeal to the Gentiles. The Jews were harder to convince, but Paul persisted and he eventually began to make some headway. Paul's propaganda was actually beginning to take hold: 'Many began to believe him.' He was actually converting people away from Judaism. James's authority was becoming completely undermined and the Jerusalem church found itself on shaky ground, so much so that in AD 62, James was finally taken out and murdered by the Roman-influenced, Sadducee-ruled Sanhedrin. A few years later, the Roman–Jewish war occurred. The Romans murdered almost a million-and-a-half Jews between AD 66 and AD 70. The Jerusalem church was effectively eradicated."

Rahn ran his hand through his hair and paused for a breath. "Look at the result, Gerhard. What was left when the dust settled?" Denninger looked down at Rahn's notes.

'The church was gone. The others of the church had disappeared and the one in league with Rome survived.' Denninger closed his eyes. "My God, Otto ..."

"You cannot deny it, Gerhard. The movement started by Paul to bring down the Jerusalem church, whether he intended it or not, resulted in the creation of the largest religion the world has ever seen."

'And if Christ be not risen, then is our preaching vain, and your faith is also vain.' Denninger thought of the passage in Abbé Rivière's diary, the one that had caused so much confusion for him those many years ago.

I am in hell and I know that is where Saunière is as well. All my life I have dedicated myself to God and the Word of God. As a child I was indoctrinated in the faith and I believed every word, every letter, every dot. When Christ was before Pilate, he said "Everyone on the side of truth listens to me," to which Pilate replies "What is truth?" What is truth, indeed! I cannot express the conflict that racks my soul. Has it all been for nothing? Again I say "What is truth?"

He now knew why Bérenger Saunière had not received absolution. He now knew why Rivière had refused to speak of it. Denninger's head was spinning as he read the last part of Rahn's notes.

Yeshuah went to see Paul and I went with him. Paul did not know Yeshuah. Yeshuah had to tell Paul who he was and Paul then knew Yeshuah. Yeshuah asked why Paul lied and Paul laughed at him. He told Yeshuah this: "Why do you complain, Yeshuah? I made you a God."

Ambroise was right. It was apocalyptic.

Paul truly was the Father of Christianity.

46

OUTSIDE THE CHURCH, LUCAS leaned against one of the partially standing walls. His head was pounding. He wiped his eyes and blew his nose. When they had begun this search, he never in his wildest dreams would have imagined this outcome. He was terribly conflicted. When he was younger, his faith had undergone a massive hit while he was at the seminary. He had decided to become a priest at the urging of his parents, both devout Catholics. His uncle was a priest and it was assumed that Phil Lucas would one day follow in his footsteps.

He remembered the day his mother, her face covered in bruises, came to see him at the seminary. She'd told him that she had slipped in the stairwell in their apartment building and had fallen. She was lucky that it wasn't worse, she had told him.

Lucas knew better. He had seen his father beat his mother unmercifully many times throughout his childhood, and no doubt this was the result of another beating. She had been urged many times to leave him, but she was a good Catholic, and good Catholics do not divorce. It was considered a sin.

The irony was not lost on Lucas. He would bury his head under his pillow to mask the sounds that came from the other room — not screams of agony, but the sound of fists against flesh and bone. His mother rarely called out in pain, stoically receiving the punishment in silence.

As he waited with his mother in the sitting room, studying the intense purple bruising around her eyes and the deep cut on her upper lip, he had wondered how this could be right. How could his mother be sentenced to endure this torture with no recourse? He had spoken to a number of the priests about the situation and was sternly rebuked on every occasion. He was told firmly that his mother had to obey her husband. They often quoted St. Paul who had said, "Wives, be subordinate to their husbands as to the Lord. For the husband is head of his wife just as Christ is head of the church, he himself the savior of the body. As the church is subordinate to Christ, so wives should be subordinate to their husbands in everything."

This can *not* be right, though, he had thought. His mother was being beaten to death and nothing could be done about it?

That night he made his decision. He confronted his father and told him not to touch his mother anymore. He recalled that his father, a large man with an Irish temper that became uncontrollable when he drank, had lumbered toward him. Lucas had seen the half empty bottle on the table and knew his father was having "one of his turns." His mother was in the kitchen pleading with Lucas's father but he, ignoring her, moved closer to his son.

"Well, well … Father Phil," he'd goaded. "Have you forgotten your lessons? Honor thy father — do ya remember that one, boy?"

His father had lunged at Lucas, who had put up his hands in self defense. They fell to the floor in a heap, and Lucas's struggling was more defensive than offensive. He didn't want to fight his father, but at the same time, he knew that he would surely be killed if he didn't fight back. He could smell the liquor on his father's breath and he could see his red eyes were black and dead.

"Do you want to see God, boy?" he growled.

Lucas closed his eyes and tensed, expecting to feel the fists raining down upon his face, when suddenly he felt his father go limp. The dead weight of the body made it difficult for him to get up, and he was aware of something thick and wet dripping from his father's face on to his own. His father was bleeding. Looking past him, he saw his mother standing above, holding his old baseball bat. He also saw a clump of hair and blood sticking to it. Later, when he had given it a closer look, he could see brain matter on the bat as well.

His mother had collapsed into a chair, weeping uncontrollably. Lucas tried to comfort her, but she shook him off. "Call the police," she told him.

When the police arrived, Lucas explained what had happened. He told them that his father had been trying to kill him, and that to prevent it, his mother had clubbed him. The policeman listened stone-faced to the story and then put the handcuffs on his mother.

On the way out the door, she had turned to him. "God will take care, son," she told him.

She was eventually found not guilty, and the people of her parish church, not wanting a killer in their flock, shunned her. It was as if she had been excommunicated. The only thing that kept her going was her faith and now it had turned its back on her.

It was then that she coldly told her son that, had she known the result, she would not have interfered that night.

Lucas left the seminary the next day.

His crisis of conscience lasted for a number of years, but in the end, somehow, his faith won out. He decided that it had been a test. God often tests his children, he'd told himself. He thanked God for making him worthy of his love, for this test. The death of his father, and the loss of his mother's love had to be a test.

And now he was being tested again, he decided. These lies could not be allowed to surface. God was testing him and he would not let him down.

—■—

Inside the church, Ambroise carefully watched the group as they discussed the contents of the codex. So now they knew. He had protected the secret for most of his life and he had even killed for it. And he would have to do it again. God would forgive him. It would not be the last time someone killed for God.

He saw that they weren't paying any attention to him. If he could somehow get to the fuse, only feet away from where he was, then all would be well. He just needed something to light it. God would surely provide.

He was shaken from his thoughts by Denninger's voice. "Father Ambroise, you said this codex is related to the bones in the ossuaries ... can you tell us how?"

Ambroise saw his chance. He nodded and said, "Perhaps we should go down there and I can explain it to you."

Congregating by the ossuaries, Markham, Rahn, Rourke, and Denninger began to extract the bones from the remaining boxes. When Ambroise had suggested they do so, he encountered some initial resistance from the soldiers, but he assured them he had a good reason. Once the bones were removed they began to lay them out in approximate anatomical order underneath the soft light provided by a pair of large candles that Rahn had brought with him. Markham, not being knowledgeable at all about such things, was having trouble, so Denninger came over to help.

One skeleton was smaller than the other two, and seemed to be female. One of the males had some broken bones, while the third seemed to be in fairly decent condition. When Denninger had finished emptying his ossuary, he noticed that there was something hard and smooth inside. Thinking that it might possibly be a jewel, he removed it, but when he held it under the flashlight, he could see that it was a stone. He noticed that the light bounced off the facets in a multitude of colors. He marveled at its polish. It was heavy, but not too heavy. He ran his thumb over the stone, over the dulled edges and thought that it was quite a beautiful stone. He placed the stone in his pocket and turned back to the bones.

Ambroise stood at the back of the room and asked Rahn for a cigarette. Rahn reached into his pocket and then threw the priest the package. Soon, the smell of the cigarette filled the air.

"Ugh!" muttered Denninger as he gave Ambroise a disgusted look and then fanned his hand at the smoke. He moved to stand over the remains that he had laid out and gingerly picked up two of the bones. What he saw made him take a startled breath. "Look Otto," he whispered. He placed them together and held them out towards Rahn. Rahn recognized the radius and ulna, seeing also that they were damaged. Both Rahn and Denninger understood the significance.

Rahn picked up one of the other bones. It was the tibia and he noticed that it was damaged at one end. Turning to Denninger he said, "Gerhard ... look at this."

Denninger nodded slowly and placed the bones carefully on the floor from where he had picked them up. "If it's what both you and I think it is ..." He turned and eyed Ambroise. " ... then something isn't right."

Rahn grinned, but without any trace of humor.

Markham overheard Denninger's statement and came over. "What did you say?" he asked urgently.

Rahn turned to Markham and held out the damaged bone. "There is something strange here, Corporal."

"What are you talking about?"

Rahn lightly rubbed his chin as he glanced at Denninger. "You *do* see what I am thinking don't you Gerhard?"

Denninger stared at the bones and said in a low voice "I do indeed."

"Okay you guys," a clearly exasperated Markham grunted. "Mind letting me in on what's going on? All I see here is a bunch of old bones. So fuckin' what?"

"Be patient Corporal," Rahn admonished. He then turned back to Denninger. "Well my friend, what are your thoughts?"

Denninger continued to study the bones. His eyes drifted from the remains of the body with the damaged bones to the second male and finally resting on the smaller female form. If what he was thinking was correct, then what he was looking at could quite possibly be the greatest archaeological find of all time. He slowly turned and faced a grinning Otto Rahn.

"Let's start with the codex first, shall we?" Rahn suggested. "Tell me, why on earth would the Cathars have this document in the first place?"

"It's very puzzling, isn't it?" replied Denninger.

"What's so puzzling?" Markham asked. Rahn gave Markham a weary look and shook his head.

"It has to do with the Cathar belief system, Corporal Markham" Denninger said patiently. "Although some may have called the Cathars Christian, they did not believe that Jesus Christ existed as a human being ... as a flesh and blood person. They thought he was a spiritual being, untainted by physical matter. So why would they have a manuscript that speaks of his human existence?"

"Perhaps," Rahn interjected, "they weren't fully aware of what was in it."

"Weren't aware?" countered Denninger.

"Possibly. I think it would be safe to assume that our venerable friends would not have known how to read Aramaic."

"True, but if they didn't know what was in it, why then would they have deemed it necessary to protect it, Otto?"

Rahn's eyebrows went up. "I said that perhaps they weren't *fully* aware. Let us look at what we can surmise from what we know and what we have just learned. First, we know from history that the Cathars didn't believe in a physical Jesus, therefore they did not believe in his death or resurrection; second, the codex states that Jesus wasn't crucified because third, the codex says that Judas took his place.

"Now let me ask you this: do you think that it might be possible that perhaps the Cathars may have been inheritors of a centuries-old oral tradition about Judas's participation in the crucifixion?"

Denninger thought for a moment. "Ah. That makes sense. If they had been aware initially that it was Judas who was crucified rather than Jesus, then it could explain why the Cathars wouldn't have believed in the literal resurrection. I guess that it is entirely possible that, over the years, the Gnostic and dualist elements that were central to their theology would have eventually overtaken or transformed the, shall we say, 'non-divine' parts of the story."

Rahn nodded in agreement. "All right then, let us suppose this. Let us assume that the Church was aware of this document. What would be their official view regarding it?"

"Heresy," responded Denninger. "In the eyes of the Church, this could be the most heretical document ever written. Judas and the resurrection subterfuge aside, there are the implications of Paul's mission to bring down James and the Jerusalem Church and the suspect beginnings of Christianity ... why, the Church would want to suppress it, of course."

"To be sure," Rahn concurred. "And how would the 'heretical' Cathars react to this course of action?"

Denninger spoke slowly. "They could not let it fall into the Church's hands, or rather, they *would not* let it fall into their hands. They would put their lives on the line to protect it."

Markham then stepped forward. "Whoa, wait a second here. Are you saying that these guys were killed protecting something that they didn't even understand? That's just crazy!"

"You have to appreciate, Corporal Markham, that for the Cathars, it was not about knowledge," Rahn stated. "It was about what they *believed*. Whether they knew what the document contained or not, they *must* have believed it to be sacred and true." He paused. "All that mattered to them was keeping and protecting it from their enemies."

Rahn noticed that Denninger's attention had shifted back to the skeletal remains on the floor. He realized that he was still holding one of the bones in his hand. "If you think the revelations of the codex were stunning, Corporal, you may find this earth-shattering." He held the tibia out to the soldier and told him to take it.

"What's this?"

Rahn and Denninger exchanged looks. "*That* may be the real Cathar treasure in your hand, Corporal Markham," Denninger said reverently.

Markham was confused. "I thought that book upstairs was the treasure."

"It is part of it, yes ...," began Denninger.

Markham swung his head around and mused, "It's just a bunch of dusty old bones."

"These are not just a bunch of bones, Corporal. Look," Denninger said as he reached over and picked up the radius and the ulna again. "See here?" He placed them against each other as if they were still joined together. "Look at this. These two bones along with the carpal bones make up the wrist. The radius and the ulna have been damaged. And do you see that bone that you are holding? It's called the tibia and, at the end, forms part of the ankle. At that end it is damaged as well."

"So what?"

"Otto, would you come here for a moment?" Denninger held the ulna and the radius together and then asked Rahn to stick his finger into the space where the damage was. A chill descended Markham's spine as he immediately understood the implication. Denninger was emulating a nail or spike going through the wrist. "I … I can't believe it," he uttered. He looked down at the remains on the floor, the two larger bodies next to the smaller one. "These bones — are you saying these are the bones of *Jesus Christ*?"

"Actually, no we are not," Rahn answered firmly.

"Well, what the hell are you saying then?"

"Corporal Markham," said Denninger in a calming tone. "It is virtually impossible to determine if these bones are indeed the skeletal remains of Jesus Christ — at least not without extensive study. However, we can make a guarded assumption thanks to the ironic providence of the codex."

"But who else could it possibly — " Markham protested.

"Corporal Markham," an exasperated Rahn interrupted. "Were you not paying attention earlier?" He pointed at the tibia in Markham's hand. "The codex tells us."

Markham swallowed hard. He looked down at the smooth white bone in his hand, noting the deep scratches and scrapes at one end where a crucifixion spike had damaged it. "Oh my God," he whispered. "Judas … "

"The fact that the codex was found with these bones does suggest that maybe these ossuaries contain the bones of Jesus and Mary, but we cannot be certain," Rahn said. "However, if Judas was indeed crucified, and these remains here certainly show clear indications of such treatment, then I think we can conjecture with some assurance that this is Judas."

"The one who 'clothed' Jesus," murmured Denninger as he pointed to the bone in the soldier's hand. "This is what they died to protect."

He bent down to take a closer look at the undamaged bones of the second male and the female. "I must say Otto, I am excited to examine these remains. If we can just connect them to the codex, then we — "

A scraping sound behind them suddenly caught their attention. They all turned to see the wall moving away from them, and moments later they heard the thud of the wall as it locked into place, telling them that they were now trapped.

47

"MOTHERFUCKER!" YELLED MARKHAM AS he flung himself towards the wall. It held fast. He quickly ran his hands along the surface, but couldn't find any kind of handle or grip that would indicate any way of opening it up from the inside. He kicked the wall in frustration. "Fuck, Matty—weren't you watching him?"

Rourke put his hands up helplessly. "I was watching you guys. I'm sorry Doug."

Rahn stood near the ossuaries and patted his hands against his jacket with a perturbed look. "He stole my cigarettes!"

"Thank God for small miracles," muttered Denninger.

Rahn held his hands out melodramatically. "What kind of world is it when you cannot trust a priest?"

"Uh, fellas," said Markham. "We got a situation here ..."

Rourke was panning his flashlight along the walls in the hopes of finding another way out. In the southeastern corner, near the floor, something caught his eye. He thought at first it was a shadow, but upon closer inspection, he saw that it was a hole just big enough to get two of his fingers inside. "Hey, Doug ... I think I found something here."

Markham hurried over and knelt down beside Rourke. He stuck his fingers into the large crack and wriggled them around. He pulled them out and said to the others, "I think there's something behind here."

—■—

Ambroise limped up the stairs and back into the church. He hobbled over to the altar and, picking up the codex, he headed back to the opening in the floor by the altar. He tossed the codex into the crypt, hearing it smack against the stone floor below. He then reached into the pocket of his dressing gown and ran his fingers over Rahn's lighter. As he eyed the hiding place of the detonator fuse, he noticed a movement in the back of the church and saw Lucas coming towards him. Damn it, he thought. I forgot about him.

Ambroise smiled and spread his hands in a welcoming gesture. Lucas, in response, unemotionally raised his weapon. "Where is the book of lies, Father?" he asked in a flat, soulless voice.

Ambroise was confused. The detached look that enveloped Lucas' face became more apparent to the priest as the soldier got closer. "The book? Oh, I do not have it. I believe that your corporal — "

The priest was suddenly flung backwards as three bullets slammed into his belly. As he fell, the lighter flew from his pocket and slid across the floor. Lucas continued towards the priest, who now lay in a puddle of blood which was spilling from his stomach and his mouth. Lucas reached down and grabbed Ambroise by the dressing gown and lifted him up to a sitting position.

"I'm going to ask you again, Father — where is the book of lies?"

"Did you hear that?" Denninger and Rahn spun around and looked up.

"That's gunfire!" exclaimed Rourke.

Markham meanwhile had managed to pull away some of the stonework that surrounded the chink in the corner. It was now big enough to get his hand inside. As he felt around the interior of the hole, his eyes instantly went wide as saucers.

"I don't know what the fuck is goin' on up there but we're in deep shit down here."

Ambroise was choking on the blood and flesh that filled his throat. Lucas turned him over like a bucket, enabling the wounded priest to clear the blockage to his breathing. His head was spinning and Lucas's words sounded very far away. "Where are the others? Tell me, goddamn it!" he raged.

This was God's toughest test yet, but Lucas was up to the task. He now understood what his role was. He was meant to find the book of lies. He would find and destroy it, and exterminate those who protected it.

He realized now that Markham and Rourke were not who they seemed to be. He was always taught that the devil would be attractive. Markham and Rourke weren't his friends. They were in league with those Germans.

Our enemies.

Lucas reached down and began to shake the priest like a rag doll. "Where are they?"

With his eyes rolling back in his head, Ambroise weakly pointed to the opening in the floor.

"And where is the book?"

Ambroise coughed up more blood and continued to point in the same direction. Lucas dropped Ambroise and moved over to the entrance to the crypt. He could see, in the faint light, the corner of the codex lying on the floor in the room below. He smiled to himself as he loaded another bullet into the chamber of his weapon and started down the stairs.

"What is it, Corporal?" Denninger asked heatedly. Markham had the flashlight up against the hole in the wall and he could see what looked like to him like dynamite. A whole lot of dynamite. It reminded him of a Bugs Bunny cartoon.

"Explosives," he said excitedly through clenched teeth. "This ain't good." He continued to probe the hole. "There has to be a detonator or a fuse somewhere."

"A fuse ..." murmured Rahn.

"Yes, something that would probably have to be lit by a ... ah, shit ..." He stopped and then he slowly turned to Rahn.

Rahn met the American's gaze with bewilderment. "What is it, Corporal?"

Markham stared grimly at him. With a poker face, he asked, "Got a cigarette?"

"No — the priest took my cigarettes and ..." His mouth fell open in stupefaction. " ... my lighter!"

Ambroise was almost dead. His ears pounded, and he was dizzy, and he knew he had only a short time left before the end, but he still had one last task to perform. He shook his head and although his vision was doubled, he saw, only inches away, Rahn's lighter lying within his grasp. He reached out for it, and after a couple of swipes, he managed to grab it.

Using every ounce of strength, he began to pull himself towards the fuse.

"Only another foot," he told himself. "Only another foot."

Lucas climbed down the stairs and picked up the leather-bound codex. He held it in one hand and the rifle in the other. He saw that the wall was closed and stepping near it he could hear their muffled voices.

How was he going to pull this off? he wondered. There were four of them and only one of him. They were armed too. He was sure they had heard the gunfire as well. Kneeling by the wall, Lucas made the sign of the cross. "Lord," he prayed, "into your hands I commend myself. You have my complete and utter faith."

He laid the codex on the floor by the wall and grabbed hold of the handle, turned it, and began to push.

Inside the room, they heard the click and saw the wall moving towards them. Markham and Rourke rushed over but just as suddenly as it had begun to move, it halted.

"What the hell?" Markham muttered. "Why did it stop? Hey — Phil! Phil!"

Lucas had been in the process of pushing against the wall when he'd heard the moan above him.

The priest, he thought anxiously.

It was the hissing sound that was more troubling however.

Scrambling up the stairs, he was greeted by the sight of Ambroise's dead body lying beside a small pile of bricks that was tipped over. In the priest's hands was Rahn's lighter, still lit beside a rapidly disappearing fuse. Lucas watched the flame as it followed the path of the fuse into the floor and quickly realized what was happening.

This place is wired, he thought. It's going to blow.

A small smile crept across his face.

"God certainly works in mysterious ways," he murmured.

48

INSIDE THE CRYPT, MARKHAM, Rourke, Denninger and Rahn were trying to get a grip on the protruding part of the wall. “On three,” ordered Markham. “One ... two ... three!” They dug in their heels and pulled at the stone obstruction. It moved slightly, giving them more of the wall to hold on to.

“Okay — once more.”

They each grabbed hold again and pulled. This time it moved about half a foot. Markham wiped his forehead. His shoulder throbbed.

“All right boys — third time’s the charm.”

Denninger could feel the strain in his neck and Markham’s shoulder burned like a white hot poker. Rahn was clenching his teeth so hard, he thought he was going to grind them down to the gums. This time the wall came all the way towards them. One by one they scrambled through the opening with Rourke bounding up the stairs in the lead. Seconds later, the sound of gunfire filled the air and Rourke’s body came tumbling down the stairway.

Half of his head was missing.

“Holy shit!” swore Markham. He may have never liked the little punk, but seeing him lying at the bottom of the stairs lying in his own blood and brains choked him up nontheless. “Sorry Matty,” he whispered. Moving towards the stairs, he carefully stepped over the corpse of Rourke and slowly started up. “Phil! You there? What’s going on?” he called out.

A few seconds later Lucas responded. “Hey Doug, I’m here. Come on up.”

Markham cautiously raised his head up through the opening. He was shocked to see Lucas sitting cross-legged by the bloody body of Father Ambroise. Right by the dead priest's hand he saw something shining in the sunlight that was streaming through one of the windows.

It took a second or two to realize it was Rahn's opened lighter.

"Holy Christ, Phil — " began Markham.

Lucas suddenly grimaced and fired a shot at Markham, just missing his head by inches. Markham fell to the bottom of the stairs.

"You shouldn't take the Lord's name in vain, Doug," warned Lucas in a flat monotone.

Markham exchanged a quick look with Denninger and Rahn. The corporal's bottom lip was quivering, and his finger and thumbnail were flicking together with lightning speed. "He's gone fuckin' nuts and I think he lit the fuse," he gasped.

Denninger began to rub his temples. "How much time before — "

"We get our heads and balls blown off?" finished Markham. "If the fuse began where Phil is sitting, I'd say about four minutes, tops."

"Well, then it is simple, Corporal — you are going to have to kill him," said Rahn matter-of-factly. Markham swung around savagely.

"That's easy for you to say, you prick," he spat out.

Rahn stepped in close to the American and narrowed his eyes. "Then give me the gun."

"Like fuck I will!"

The argument was interrupted by Lucas' voice. "Doug, aren't you coming up? You are being very rude," he called out.

Markham turned to the stairway and called back to him. "Sorry Phil, but you're being very homicidal," he responded. He turned back to Rahn who was looking disconcertedly at his watch.

"Corporal Markham," Rahn said in a modulated tone, "We simply do not have the time for this."

"I know that. He's my friend — let me think for a second, goddamn it."

They were interrupted by the sound of footsteps on the stairway. They both turned in time to see Denninger as he disappeared up the stairs.

"Shit. No, Doc!" yelled Markham but it was too late.

Denninger came into view with his hands high in the air. He was attempting to smile but the thought of either a bullet to the head or being blown to bits made it a difficult task. Once clear of the stairway, he started towards the American soldier.

"Hello, Doc," greeted Lucas, the barrel of his weapon trained right at the doctor's head. "How are you doing?" Denninger kept up his wavering smile. "Oh, I am doing well — I should be asking you the same question."

Lucas sighed. "Well Doc, I am a little upset. You see, I guess you could say that I am conflicted. The commandments say 'Thou shalt not kill,' but because of this test that God has thrust upon me, I must make sure that the book of lies doesn't see the light of day. And that means killing all of you. It is quite a conundrm, as you can see."

Denninger nodded bleakly. "Oh yes, I can see that it is a difficult problem, yes."

He figured they had less than four minutes.

"Uh ... Phil ... you are aware that this whole church is packed with explosives and is ready to ... uh, blow up, aren't you?"

Lucas nodded and gave a little kick to the body of the priest in front of him. "Father Ambroise here was kind enough to light the fuse for me. I wasn't sure how I was going to accomplish my test, but God, you see, has provided. You and the other blasphemers and the book of lies will be taken care of all at once."

Denninger heard a small creak behind him and out of the corner of his eye could see the barrel of Markham's rifle lined up along the floor, aimed at Lucas.

If I can just hit his gun, Markam said to himself.

Denninger then cleared his throat and said, "Is it part of God's test that you should die as well?"

Lucas smirked. "It is not my place to question the Lord. I am merely his instrument. If he wills me to die, so be it."

"Oh, I am not questioning God's will," responded Denninger. "I am merely questioning *your* will."

Lucas looked confused. "I don't understand."

Denninger continued. "If it is God's will that we blasphemers die, so be it. However, if you willingly stay to die with us, you will be, in effect, killing yourself—you will be committing suicide, a mortal sin in the Catholic Church, I believe."

Lucas blinked.

"God truly is testing you, isn't he?"

Lucas wavered. His gun, which had been aimed at Denninger, lowered slightly. His eyes dropped until they settled on Ambroise's blood-soaked body just in front of him.

Markham saw the opening and squeezed the trigger.

The force of the bullet sent Lucas's weapon spiraling away from him but the ricochet caromed off of the metal barrel and slammed into Lucas's chest. Markham and Rahn were through the opening in the floor and at Lucas's side in seconds.

Lucas's mouth was filling with blood. Markham knelt down and stared at him with a horrified look as Lucas managed a small smile. "Hey Doug," he wheezed through the blood bubbling in his throat. Tears began to well up in Markham's eyes.

"Phil… I was only trying to hit your gun… I didn't mean to…"

Lucas coughed, spraying blood all over the front of his uniform, and then he shook his head slightly. It's all right, Doug. You helped me," he said quietly. When Markham looked confused, he went on. "I didn't kill myself … *you* killed me, so I didn't commit a mortal sin. Thank you, Doug … I passed God's test …"

As Markham watched Lucas' eyes close, he began to cry.

Denninger put his hand on Markham's arm and roughly began to pull at him. "Corporal Markham, we don't have time."

Markham wiped his eyes and quickly stood up. Denninger was already halfway down the nave and headed for the door by the time Markham got to his feet. Just as he reached a standing position, Markham looked around. "Where's Rahn?" he called out to Denninger.

The archeologist stopped just before he went through the door. Spinning around he saw that Rahn was nowhere in sight. Markham whipped around and saw Rahn starting to go through the entrance to the crypt.

Rahn wasn't about to leave without the codex. When he'd seen that it wasn't on the altar, he shone the flashlight back down through the entrance to the crypt. That's when he saw it peeking out of the shadow by the bottom stair. He had started down the steps to retrieve the codex, when he heard Markham's voice calling out to him.

"Hey! We gotta get outta here," the soldier yelled.

Rahn looked up at Markham and gave him his Cheshire Cat grin. "Not without the codex, I'm afraid," he said. His head then disappeared from view.

Markham watched him in disbelief. Fuck this! he thought. He's crazy.

Markham ran down the nave towards the door. He saw Denninger standing a few feet away and called out as he whipped passed him.

"Move your ass, Doc!"

Denninger didn't have to be told twice.

They were about two hundred feet away when the church exploded. The force of the blast sent the two men flying through the air. Markham remembered later that he felt the explosion before he heard it — the last thing he recalled was an extremely hot sensation behind him and his feet leaving the ground. When he woke up, he saw that he had been blown out of his boots and was about forty feet from where the church had been.

Denninger too, had little recollection of the explosion other than everything going suddenly quiet after the initial bang. His jacket and part of his shirt had been burned away, and his leg was fractured.

Markham saw Denninger lying on his stomach beside a tree that was on fire. Flaming branches were dropping on and around him. Markham crawled over to the prone archeologist. He brushed the branches away and shook him gently. "Doc," he said hoarsely. "Hey, Doc!"

Denninger finally stirred and slowly rolled over. He opened his eyes and saw Markham's red face staring back down at him. He was at once aware that he was surrounded in silence.

The explosion had deafened him.

"I cannot hear you, Corporal," he said weakly.

Markham nodded. He figured that the doctor might have a concussion as well. He helped Denninger up to a sitting position, and then sat down beside him. Denninger rubbed his head softly and then ran his hand down his leg. He winced then turned to Markham.

"Broken?" asked Markham, exaggerating the word for the hearing-impaired archeologist. Denninger nodded and then asked, "Otto?" Markham shook his head. Denninger looked down and sighed.

The smoke was finally clearing in front of them, and although they both knew there would be nothing left of the church, they were still shocked at the degree of destruction. There was a giant, blackened, open pit surrounded by shattered bricks and burning wood where the church ruin once stood.

No one could have lived through that. Denninger then realized to his horror that he had left his pack in the church. The scroll and Rivière's diary. He lowered his head in despair.

Markham surveyed the damage and ruminated over the events of the last few days. He thought about Johnson and Rourke, and then he considered Lucas and how he might have possibly changed the outcome, but he realized that he couldn't have. They had all chosen this course. They had all wanted to find the treasure.

And now it was gone. He knew, however, that the sadness that enveloped him had nothing to do with the loss of what could have been the score of a lifetime. He didn't care about that. Not any more.

He stood up and slowly put two fingers to his forehead. "Goodbye fellas," he said as he finished the salute.

He looked back down at Denninger who was staring off in the distance. Markham bent down to get his attention. Denninger took the corporal's arm and pulled himself up, grimacing in pain as his leg fracture throbbed. He put his arm around Markham's uninjured shoulder, balancing on his good leg. Markham hoped they could find the truck.

Just before they hobbled away, Denninger gave one last look at the smoldering hole. He thought about the Cathars at Montségur, seven hundred years ago walking into the fires to protect their treasure, and was immediately struck by the fact that once again, fires had protected their secret. It seemed somehow apropos.

"Ashes to ashes, dust to dust," he said softly as they headed for the road.

Egypt
September 13, 1947

DENNINGER WIPED HIS BROW and then took a large swig of water from his canteen. The cool liquid felt good against his parched throat. He then readjusted his hat and went back to work on the dig. This area of Egypt, a sleepy area known as Nag Hammadi, was just coming to the attention of archeologists as word filtered out that a couple of years back a number of ancient manuscripts had been discovered in a large, sealed jar by a local farmer. Although the find was still publicly unknown, a few scholars and dealers in antiquities had been the source of rumors which had made their way to Denninger. Through a colleague, Denninger had even had a chance to view firsthand one of the magnificent finds. The codices, which would eventually become known as the Gnostic Gospels, were written in Coptic on papyrus and bound in leather, sadly reminding Denninger of the Judas codex and how close he had come three years ago.

After a few minutes he had to rest again. He reached into his pocket to get a handkerchief and as he pulled it out, something small and hard fell to the ground. Denninger bent over and saw the colors dancing in the sun. He smiled. It was the beautiful stone he had discovered in the ossuary. He had kept the stone as a lucky charm of sorts, a bittersweet reminder of just how close he had come. He picked it up and put it back in his pocket, then wiped his brow with his handkerchief.

The searing heat of the Egyptian sun reminded Denninger of that day three years previous in southern France, when he had almost been blown to bits. Now *that* was hot, he thought to himself.

—■—

They had found the truck where Ambroise had hidden it. Markham struggled with the horses and cart while Denninger drove the truck back to Ste. Marie de la Mer to see to Etienne. When they got to the church, they found that he had awakened a half hour before and was bitterly complaining of a headache. When Markham was helping Denninger out of the truck and into the rectory, it was almost comical as the corporal tried to explain to the French-speaking Etienne what was wrong with Denninger who was deaf, and the only one who could translate. Eventually, Markham managed to get Denninger comfortable. He figured Etienne could keep an eye on him and get him the help he needed.

There was much he wanted to say to the older man but of course it was impossible. Denninger smiled at Markham and did the talking for both of them. "It has been quite an adventure, Corporal, and I am sorry it did not turn out the way we had hoped. We lost much more than we gained, I am afraid," he said sadly.

Markham nodded and put out his hand. Denninger smiled and took it, shaking it robustly, then added, "Perhaps it is best things turned out this way. I don't think that Christians would be able to handle the idea that Christianity was the result of subterfuge. As you are an atheist, what you saw and heard may not have an effect on you, but for tens of millions of Christians, it would have been disastrous. It is a shame really. Christ's message is a beautiful one and it should not matter whether he was the Son of God or not. For an archeologist like me though, losing that codex and the bones ... ah, well, it breaks my heart."

Markham then grinned. He reached inside his uniform and pulled out what looked at first like a smooth white branch. He held it out to Denninger.

The archeologist's mouth fell open. It was the bone which Markham had been holding when they were standing in the crypt. When they had been shut in, he had shoved it inside his jacket without thinking. He know handed it to Denninger. A tibia damaged at the ankle.

Judas's ankle.

Denninger took it tenderly, unable to speak for a moment. When he found his voice he said, "Of course, without the codex, we cannot prove anything," he told Markham.

Markham shrugged.

"At least we know the truth," he said slowly so that Denninger could read his lips.

Markham turned and headed for the door. He gave a small wave and that was the last Denninger saw or heard from the American soldier. He always hoped that he had somehow made it through the war alive. When he did manage to track him down after it was over, he was tremendously saddened to hear that he had been killed at the Battle of the Bulge.

Denninger was squinting at the disappearing sun when he heard his name being called. The deafness he had suffered after the explosion was only temporary, and although his hearing never came back to the way it had been before, he was thankful nonetheless.

"Dr. Denninger!" cried out the voice again.

Denninger looked up and saw that it was his assistant, Behdeti al-Ashmawy was waving at him. Denninger could see the little man was very excited. He didn't think much of it, however, as the Egyptian was a very highly strung young man.

"Dr. Denninger, the hotel called! The hotel called!"

"All right, Behdeti, the hotel called — so?"

Behdeti suddenly looked confused. "I ... I do not know why ..." He instantly looked embarrassed. "I did not ask. I am sorry."

Denninger did a slow burn. "Behdeti, I have told you before. You have to get more information from people when they talk to you," he patiently explained. "We have been over this many, many times."

"Yes, of course. Again, I am sorry."

Denninger immediately regretted scolding the young man. He really liked the personable fellow, but he was just so scattered. "It is all right, Behdeti. We are done here for the day. It is time to go back to the hotel anyway. They're probably calling to let me know that my guest has arrived."

Denninger had done well over the past few years. He had found a number of clay jars from the third century, some examples of early metalwork, and, most interesting for Denninger (and the reason for the arrival of his guest, Lorenz de Penta), a fragment that appeared to the archeologist to be a document about early Christian society. Although his Coptic wasn't great, he thought that it might be from an early Coptic Christian sect known as the Encratites, an early Gnostic group that refrained from taking alcohol, eating animal flesh, and having sex. De Penta was a Swiss diplomatics expert who was among the top in the field. Paleography was his specialty and his ability at authenticating ancient documents was peerless. Denninger was excited and honored that de Penta was willing to come to Egypt to verify what he had discovered.

Denninger and Behdeti arrived at the hotel in fifteen minutes. The young Egyptian grabbed Denninger's things from out of the trunk of the taxi while Denninger slowly walked into the hotel lobby. His leg, although healed from the explosion, still caused him some discomfort every now and then. To strengthen it, he often eschewed elevators for stairs.

Denninger climbed to the second floor and headed down the long hallway to his room. As he was about to put his key into the lock, he was disturbed to see that his door was slightly ajar. He always hated this hotel. The cleaning staff was sloppy and the security was extremely lax. It wasn't the first time his door had been left unlocked.

He entered his room with more than just a little annoyance, and his demeanor quickly darkened when he perceived someone standing in front of his window. The light from the sunset left the stranger in a backlit silhouette, so Denninger couldn't make out his features. Just as Denninger was about to demand to know who he was, the stranger suddenly pulled out a cigarette with a flourish. In the glow from the lighter, Denninger could now see who it was.

"What the hell?" Denninger said with astonishment. The figure exhaled a smoke ring that filled the room with a familiar yet horrible stench.

"I have more lives than a cat, eh Gerhard?"

Otto Rahn smiled and sat down in a chair by the table. Denninger was overcome with emotion. This was twice now that Otto had returned from the dead, only this time Denninger found he was more angry than happy. Otto could sense that Denninger was upset. "I get the distinct feeling that you are not too happy to see me, Gerhard," he remarked innocently. His voice sounded rougher than usual.

Denninger stood in the doorway, refusing to move closer. "What do you want me to say, Otto? You keep dying and showing up — how exactly is one supposed to react to that sort of thing?"

Rahn took a drag from the cigarette and coughed. Denninger turned on the light to get a closer look at Rahn and was shocked at what he saw. He looked terrible. Otto's face was jaundiced and withered and he looked emaciated. His fingers were bony and his eyes were rimmed with fluid.

"Otto ... what is wrong with you?" he asked.

Rahn coughed again, only this time it lasted for some time. It was a phlegmy and deep, bone-rattling cough — the kind that signaled that someone was in the last stages of a deadly disease. When he finally stopped, Denninger saw that in spite of everything, he still had his Cheshire Cat grin.

"I think that you can guess that I am dying. Cancer. They tell me I have only weeks left. Weeks? It feels more like days." He laughed feebly at the joke.

"What are you doing here Otto?" Denninger asked. "I mean, how are you even here at all? I thought you were killed in the explosion."

Rahn shrugged. "I almost was. Because of my damn leg, I couldn't leave the way you did. The only chance I had was to go through the broken window by Ambroise's body. I was able to pull myself up and through but when I landed, I fucked up my leg again. I was about seventy yards away when the building blew. I was thrown through the air and landed in a thicket. I was lucky, Gerhard. I landed on a moss-covered, rotted tree trunk which collapsed inward and cushioned my fall. I woke up hours later. Oddly enough, you would think with an explosion like that, somebody would have come around but no one did. Perhaps they thought it was shelling."

Denninger sat, stunned, in a chair opposite Rahn.

"I am sorry, Gerhard. I did not mean to get you so excited. I only came here to say goodbye."

"Goodbye? Otto, I thought you were dead already. Why come here now just to tell me you are alive and that you are going to die? It's ludicrous! It's absurd! It's ..." His voice trailed off and suddenly he wasn't upset anymore.

It was so like Rahn. Of course he would do this. Who else would?

Rahn began to cough again. "I just needed to see you before ... you know."

As Rahn continued to cough, Denninger stood up and heaved a weighty sigh. Rahn looked up at his friend then he slowly stood up as well. Denninger held out his arms and stepped closer to his dying friend. As he put his arms around Otto he was saddened to feel the bones sharply poking through his clothes. After a few moments, they stepped back and Denninger saw that Rahn was weeping.

Denninger also felt himself fighting back tears. He knew that this would be, for certain, the last time he would see Otto Rahn; he would not be coming back this time.

Rahn sniffed and wiped his eyes. He ran his hand through his thinning hair, and for a brief moment, he looked just like the crazed researcher who had burst into Denninger's office eight years ago. The memory made him smile.

Rahn put his hat on and pulled out another cigarette. As he placed it in his mouth, he saw Denninger looking at him with concern. Rahn grinned and took it out. "I was thinking of quitting anyway," he told Denninger. "I hear they are bad for your health."

He glanced at the table and saw a large book, just under a newspaper. Casting a sideways glance at Denninger who just grinned, Rahn reached over and raised the book to see the title.

Lucifer's Court.

"Hmmm," murmured Rahn. "I see you still have impeccable taste in reading material, Gerhard."

Denninger shrugged. "My old copy was destroyed in the explosion. That is a new one."

Rahn nodded and placed the book back on the table. He limped toward the door with Denninger just behind him. When he got to the doorway, he turned to the archeologist. "We were so *close,* weren't we, Gerhard? We had it all figured out. We can at least take solace in that, can't we?"

Denninger's eyes twinkled. "Oh, that and more, I think."

He went over to his suitcase and opened it up. He reached inside and pulled out the tibia that Markham had given him. He handed it to a visibly amazed Rahn.

"Unbelievable," uttered Rahn as he took the bone. He ran his hand along the smooth surface and grinned. "You were always full of surprises, Gerhard," he smiled as he handed it back to Denninger. "I can't believe that you carry it around with you."

Denninger shrugged. "After losing the codex, I don't ever let it out of my sight." Together they stepped out into the hall.

"*Auf Wiedersehen,* my friend. Perhaps I will see you on the other side."

"Oh, Otto, I have no doubt that I will run into you again. It seems to be a pattern."

Denninger watched as Rahn shuffled slowly down the hallway towards the elevator. The doors clanged shut and the gears meshed together as the car took Rahn away and out of Denninger's life for the last time. Denninger wept silently as he went back into his room and he decided he needed a shower and a stiff drink.

Denninger had just stepped out of the shower when he heard his telephone ringing. He hurried to pick it up, dripping water all over the floor in the process.

"Hello? Oh, fine, fine — I will be down in a few minutes." He hung up the phone and quickly began to get dressed. Lorenz de Penta had just arrived.

Denninger descended the stairs as quickly as he could and saw only one person in the lobby, sitting in a big wingback chair. As he headed over to greet the man, he heard the desk clerk call his name.

"Dr. Denninger, this package was left for you," the desk clerk told him. Denninger ignored him as he went to greet the paleographer.

"Mr. de Penta? I am sorry to keep you waiting. I am Gerhard Denninger. If you would like to come upstairs, I have something that I think you will find very interesting."

De Penta gave Denninger a bored look. "I am sure you do, otherwise I would not have made this god-awful trip," he said in a flat voice.

As they made their way to the stairs, the desk clerk called out to Denninger again.

"Dr. Denninger?"

Denninger made a face and hurried over to the front desk. "What is it?" he demanded. The desk clerk, miffed at Denninger's attitude, wordlessly handed a package to the archeologist. Denninger grabbed it and rushed back to de Penta. Together they climbed the stairs and went to Denninger's room. Inside, Denninger offered the diplomatics specialist a drink.

"No thank you," he said while looking at his fingernails. "I am in a bit of a hurry. I would just like to see your discovery, if you please."

Denninger went to get the document and tossed the package on the table, causing the brown paper wrapping to tear and come loose. De Penta glanced over and something caught his eye.

"Eh? What is this?" he asked as he lifted the covering.

Denninger returned with the Coptic papyrus and when he saw what was on the table, he felt his heart leap into his mouth.

He could see what looked like brown leather under the torn paper. Swiftly pouncing on the package, he ripped the rest of the paper away and found himself once again holding the Judas codex.

"Now *that* looks interesting," said de Penta, brightening. Denninger clutched the codex to his chest. Rahn, that cagey bastard. He must have retrieved it before the church blew up after all, he thought.

"May I see that?" asked de Penta. At first, Denninger was reluctant to give it to de Penta. He did not want to part with it again, but he eventually handed the leather-clad papyrus to the document expert. As de Penta took the codex, Denninger saw something on the inside of the parcel paper. It looked like a note written in Otto's shaky scrawl.

Gerhard:

I am so sorry. I know I should have told you about the codex, but, after searching all these years for my "Holy Grail," it was, as you can imagine, quite difficult to give up. It was mine and no one else could have it. Of course, I know that was foolish. I see that now.

I entrust you with the Cathar treasure. Perhaps you will have the fortitude that I did not have, to present it to the world. It should be revealed no matter what the cost. However, I caution you to be careful. I know you will.

Once again, I am sorry. Forgive me.

Otto.

As Denninger was reading what Otto had written, de Penta studied the codex. After looking at the text contained within, he looked up at Denninger.

"What exactly *is* this?" he asked.

Denninger was taken aback by the question. "Aren't you in a hurry?" he asked.

De Penta settled back onto the bed. "Believe me, I will make time for this."

Denninger related to de Penta the outline of the story including the events of the past hour. When he finished the tale de Penta was stunned. He looked at the codex in Denninger's hands and whistled. "I must take this back with me to Geneva, Doctor. It must be authenticated as soon as possible."

"Of course. I assume you will be leaving immediately?"

"Yes — it is essential that I get this looked at right away."

"Very well. Let me get something for it. We don't want it damaged."

He took the codex into the bedroom and he returned in a short time carrying a small strongbox.

"This should do the trick," he said, grinning.

De Penta put the box under his arm and was already on his way out the door. "I am heading for the airport right now. You will hear from me in a few days. You will be at this hotel, I presume?" Denninger nodded. De Penta smiled and started down the hallway with his precious cargo under his arm.

"I will be speaking with you in a few days," he repeated as he stepped into the elevator.

The man who called himself Lorenz de Penta was actually a small time historical document forger and thief named Giorgio Ferrara. He had assumed de Penta's identity when he'd murdered him the week before in London. Before Ferrara had killed him, however, de Penta had been kind enough to let him know about his meeting with Denninger. Ferrara knew of Denninger's reputation, and had banked on the archeologist not knowing what de Penta actually looked like when he showed up.

It worked beautifully. What Ferrara hadn't dreamed of was something as earth-shattering as the Judas codex. He'd originally planned on stealing whatever Denninger had found and selling it to the highest bidder, but this was obviously something extraordinary. And it had fallen right into his lap.

Maybe there was a God, after all.

He also knew a buyer who would be perfect for this particular prize. He had, in the past, provided documents to this man — and the more religiously provocative, the better, it seemed. Some of the manuscripts Ferrara supplied were real, and quite a number of them were not so real, but this buyer was always in the market. Ferrara really didn't care why, as long as the customer took them off his hands. And Ferrara was positive his buyer would take this one. There was no way he would not.

Ferrara hailed a cab and ordered the driver to take him to the airport. When the cab arrived, he ran into the terminal and up to the ticket counter where he asked to use the telephone. It was a long distance call, but when the clerk started to deny his request, Ferrara reached into his pocket and pulled out a fistful of cash. Once he had the operator on the line he gave him the number and then smiled at the ticket vendor while he waited for the call to go through.

"Hello? Giorgio here ... yes, it *is* important ... I have a document here that ... oh, I think you *will* want to see this ... well, let's see ... it starts at Montségur and ends with the true story of the crucifixion and Saint Paul ... that's right ... Saunière's document ... I thought you would ... yes, I will be flying out immediately. Thank you for your time. Goodbye."

Cardinal Giuseppe Di Pietro of the Vatican's Secret Archives hung up the phone and then picked it up again. He dialed a number that he had dialed many times in the past when it came to sensitive information like this.

"This is Cardinal Di Pietro," he said authoritatively. "I need you to pick up someone for me at the airport. His name is Giorgio Ferrara. He will be here in a couple of hours ... from Egypt ... he will be carrying an important package with him ... yes, it is imperative that you get the package here safely ... yes, the package is extremely important ... *more* important than Signor Ferrara ... ”

Ferrara was standing just outside the terminal in Rome when he was greeted by two men in dark suits who introduced themselves as associates of Cardinal Di Pietro. They directed him over to a blue sedan idling in a loading zone. One of them told him to get in the front seat beside the driver. The sedan then pulled out and was soon on its way to the Vatican.

The Cardinal was waiting outside for them when the car pulled up. When he looked in the window he noticed that Ferrara was not in the vehicle. One of the men smiled humorlessly and shrugged, then handed Ferrara’s package to the Cardinal who took it without a word. Di Pietro nodded and as the sedan pulled away, he opened the box and looked at the leather-bound codex.

The Judas Apocalypse. He was actually holding it in his hands.

But not for long.

This document would soon be joining the Secret Gospel of Mark, the Q Gospel, the Third Secret of Fatima, and other documents too sensitive for those outside the Church to see.

“It is better this way,” Di Pietro said to himself as he headed down the long hallway to the archives. Once inside, he made sure that the door was locked and that he was alone. His feet echoed in the vast archive hall as he made his way to a large table in the back. He pulled out a chair, sat down and removed the codex from the box.

He stared at the leather cover for a minute and noticed that his hands were shaking. Taking a big breath, he tentatively took the corner of the cover gently between his thumb and forefinger and opened the codex to at last see the words written by the apostle whom Jesus loved best.

—▪—

As soon as Ferarra had left Denninger's room, the archeologist was on the phone with Behdeti al-Ashmawy, informing him that he was checking out. He also told Behdeti that he was now in charge of the dig. The young Egyptian was beside himself with glee. It was quite an honor for someone not yet thirty.

"I need you to get over here as soon as possible," ordered Denninger. Behdeti assured the archeologist he could be there in twenty minutes. Denninger hung up the phone and immediately began to pack. He left the smaller finds as well as the Coptic papyrus on the table for Behdeti, and went into the bedroom to get the rest of his things, including his notes, his wallet, and his passport, which he threw into his bag along with his copy of *Lucifer's Court* he had retrieved from the other room. Denninger called the front desk and asked for a bellboy to come upstairs to get his luggage in five minutes. He then made two calls. The first was to the airport in Luxor. As soon as he made his reservation, he then hung up and dialed another number, this one in the United States. When he heard a female voice answer at the other end, he asked to speak to Frank Wetmore.

Once he hung up the phone, he finished his packing. The bellboy arrived within minutes and Denninger directed him to his luggage. He then hurried down the stairway to the lobby. He had checked out and was hailing a cab when Behdeti arrived. Denninger explained in a hasty manner that he had to leave immediately. "You are in charge, Behdeti. Don't let me down, now. I will be back as soon as I have conducted my business." He shook hands with Behdeti and was about to get into the cab when something occurred to him. He turned to Behdeti and put a hand on his shoulder.

"There may be some people who will come looking for me. This trip I am taking is strictly confidential. It is imperative that no one know where I have gone. Can you keep this secret for me?"

Behdeti realized that Denninger had entrusted him with an important job. The archeologist had shown much faith in the young Egyptian and Bedheti would not let him down.

"Do not worry, Doctor. No one will know where you are. I give you my word."

The Vatican hallway was filled with the frenzied sound of Cardinal Di Pietro's shoes clattering on the marble floor as he rushed to his office. He loosely carried the codex under his arm as he ran quickly down the hall. He heard a voice behind him calling out his name.

"Cardinal Di Pietro — you dropped your newspaper!"

Di Pietro kept up his pace as he shouted abruptly over his shoulder. "Keep it!"

The owner of the voice became confused as he took a closer look and noticed that the newspaper was in Arabic.

Di Pietro angrily slammed the door of his office and then tossed the codex on his desk, causing the newspapers with which Denninger had replaced the papyrus to spill out all over the floor. The Cardinal grabbed the telephone and dialed the number of the same men who had picked up Ferrara at the airport. As he waited for someone to pick up he raged. "No one plays games with the Church."

The bus ride to Luxor had taken a little longer than he thought, but Denninger was on the airplane and in his seat within minutes of his arrival at the airport. The short flight to Cairo, where he would catch his connecting flight to London was leaving in fifteen minutes.

He put his head back against the seat of the airplane and tried to get his breathing under control. He wondered if Lorenz de Penta, or whoever he was, would ever discover the switch that he had made with the codex. He supposed that the imposter probably wouldn't. Denninger had realized immediately that "de Penta" was not who he said he was when the the man didn't recognize the Aramaic language of the codex. It was a dead giveaway. Lorenz de Penta was supposed to be an expert in paleography after all.

When he thought about just how close he'd come to losing the codex again, his heart started to beat a little more quickly. He felt as apprehensive as he had on Mueller's U-boat when he'd studied the scroll for the first time, or when he'd first viewed the codex in the church ruin with Otto.

He stared at his hands and closed them slowly, feeling the dampness in his palms. "Relax," he told himself. "Everything is under control."

At last he began to calm down. He smiled when he thought about how shocked his old aquaintance, Frank Wetmore, the current secretary of the Smithsonian Institute, had been to get his call. Wetmore had met Denninger in 1922, when the American was traveling through Germany. Both shared an interest in the Cathars and they had promised each other to keep in touch. After the rise of Adolf Hitler, however, relationships spanning the ocean became more difficult to maintain, so when Denninger had called him after so many years it had been a welcome surprise.

When he had asked why Denninger was calling after all this time, Denninger responded cryptically, "'And ye shall know the truth, and the truth shall make you free.'"

"How's that?" Wetmore asked.

Denninger chuckled. "I am sorry Frank. I am leaving for London within the hour. Once I get there I will be going to Southampton and from there I am booking passage on an ocean liner to the United States. I should be in Washington by Friday. Will you have someone meet me when I arrive?"

"Of course, Gerhard, but can you tell me what this is all about?"

"All in good time," he remarked.

As he settled in for the flight, he rested his satchel on his knees, looked inside, and saw Rahn's book. He was pulling the volume out when an attractive woman in her late twenties sat down in the seat beside him. She had shoulder-length dark hair, expressive brown eyes, and a beautiful, exotic air about her. Her complexion suggested to Denninger that she might be of Egyptian descent, and there was something about her that reminded him of a woman he used to date when he was younger. Much younger. She smiled in a friendly way and Denninger nodded politely. As he started to turn away, he noticed that she held a large book in her hands and was mildly surprised that it was a book about the history of the Roman Empire.

The woman, observing that he was looking at her reading material, shrugged slightly and gave him a little grin. "Odd choice for a girl, right?" she said. Denninger was struck by the melodious timbre of her voice. He suddenly wished he was twenty years younger. Or maybe twenty-five.

"On the contrary," he responded. "I think it is marvelous to see someone reading something of educational value rather than the latest ... oh, what is the word for it?"

"Potboiler?" she offered. Denninger smiled and nodded. "How is it someone so young is interested in such ancient things?"

The woman shrugged again. "Oh, I've always been interested in the past. It's certainly much less upsetting than the present I find, although ...," she paused and looked down at the book on her lap, " … not much has really changed over the last two thousand years, has it?"

Denninger glanced at the satchel on his knees. "Not really," he replied.

The woman opened her book and began flipping through the pages. At one point she stopped and put her finger on one of the pages. "Look at this," she said. Denninger craned his neck to see what she was pointing at. He saw that it was a drawing of slaves in a Roman galley. "What a terrible way to live," she said with a touch of sadness. "Imagine, spending your life chained to an oar in a Roman warship. It must have been a torturous existence."

"No doubt," agreed Denninger. "However, there was something that I believe was infinitely worse." He reached for the book. "May I?"

"Of course," she responded, and handed the book over to him. He scanned the table of contents and then quickly flipped through the pages. Once he found what he was looking for, he handed it back to her. She took it and read the heading of the page he had turned to. It said *Third Servile War 73 BC to 71 BC* and underneath it was a depiction of the gladiator-slave Spartacus and six thousand of his followers crucified along the Appian Way.

"Nailed to a cross. It must have been a horrible way to die," she murmured.

"Oh it was," responded Denninger grimly. "It took many days, sometimes weeks to expire. The idea was to make it last as long as possible … and then when the Romans felt that you had suffered enough, well … they would then break your legs."

The woman gave a small gasp. "Why would they do that?"

Denninger narrowed his eyes. "When you are hanging on a cross, your body weight is constantly pulling you down, you see, making it extremely difficult to breathe.

Your natural inclination would be to push up with your legs to alleviate the pressure, though by doing so one prolongs the torture. When they would break the legs you couldn't push upwards any longer — you would eventually be unable to breathe and then it would soon be over."

"How barbaric," the woman said with disgust.

Denninger nodded in agreement. "Barbaric yes, but it *did* end the torment. Why, according to the Gospel accounts, when Jesus Christ was crucified, his followers went to the Romans to ask them to break his legs, to end his suffering. By the time they went to him however, he was already dead. It was unnecessary to break ..." His voice suddenly trailed off and he blinked twice. The woman watched him curiously for a moment and then asked, "Is something wrong?"

Denninger didn't hear her. "Break his legs ... I am such a *fool*," he whispered. In his mind's eye it was suddenly three years before and he was back in the crypt, staring down at the bones laid out in front of the ossuaries. He was looking at the shattered wrist and ankle bones and wondered why he didn't think of it at the time. How could he have missed it?

Denninger clutched his satchel and rapidly stood up. "Would you please excuse me for a moment?" he asked excitedly. "I need to ... use the lavatory."

The surprised woman stood up and stepped into the aisle, allowing Denninger to head to the back of the aircraft. Once inside the small cubicle, he shut the door and sat on the edge of the toilet bowl, placing the bag on the floor between his feet and opening it. Lying just beside Rahn's book and the codex was the bone that Markham had given him. Aside from the spike-damaged end, the bone was smooth and whole.

It hadn't been broken.

"Oh my God," Denninger said in a soft voice.

When the Roman soldiers went to the man on the cross, and they believed that he was already dead, it would have been unnecessary to break his legs. When they removed him from the cross, the leg bones would have remained intact. Exactly like the tibia that Denninger was holding in his hand.

As the airplane taxied down the runway, he held on to the satchel securely. Glancing over at the young woman, he noticed that she was gripping the armrests so tightly that her knuckles were white. He looked at her face and saw that her eyes were firmly shut as she whispered quietly. He realized that she was praying, praying for God to protect her on this flight.

Faith really is a remarkable thing, thought Denninger at that moment. He looked down at the satchel on his lap and thought about the contents and the story they told. Christianity was about to change in a very profound way and Denninger wondered how the Christian world was going to take it. It was certainly going to be shaken to its very roots. Yet the Christian faith had always survived attacks against it. The question was, would it survive this? *Could* it survive this?

He took another look at the woman sitting beside him. As she prayed, she had a serene look on her face. She was afraid, yet she believed that God was going to protect her. She had no proof that He would, but she had faith that He would. Faith, in the end, he decided, did not depend on facts or logic. It is what you *believe* to be the truth.

Perhaps, Denninger thought, that Pilate was on to something. "What is truth?" he had asked at Christ's trial.

The answer is faith. Christianity would survive, he concluded. It would have to. For the faithful.

Denninger smiled, laid his head back against the seat again, and closed his eyes. He put his hand inside his jacket pocket and his fingers closed over the stone from the ossuary.

His lucky charm.

He rubbed his thumb over the dulled edges and felt somehow comforted.

It was going to be a very long journey.

Acknowledgments

WRITING THIS BOOK WAS the hardest thing that I have ever attempted, but at the same time the most rewarding, and I owe a large debt of gratitude to a number of people for standing by me while I undertook this project. I send out a big thank you to Ron Barr for insisting that I write it in the first place, and for his constructive comments throughout the whole process; a huge thank you and a hug to Ziyada Callender, easily my number one fan and the best person anyone could ever have in his corner, for her thoroughly inspiring enthusiasm; many thanks to Taz Boga, for taking the time to read the finished product, and whose reaction to it was wholly unexpected and immensely gratifying, which made me start believing for the first time that the book was perhaps better than I thought.

Lots of gratitude to Lena Robinson for her help, guidance and suggestions once the manuscript was finished. Thanks to my brother, Kevin, and my father, Joe (who can't seem to tell enough people about what I have done), for their encouragement. A big thanks to Steve Casey (www.designit.ca) for doing a fantastic job designing my website (and for being a great song-writing partner all these years); a very large thank you to Michelle Noël and Linda Noel, for thinking the story was good enough to publish and for taking the time with me to make it even better. Special thank yous go out to my daughter Richelle for her constant support and my daughter Tess, who thinks the whole thing is pretty darn cool; much thanks to Melissa Rose, who was sure that it was a winner and was always convinced (and told me often) that it would be published; thanks to everyone who read it and offered suggestions, big and small, and especially to Sonya Singh, I reserve the biggest thank you for her undying faith in the book, and in me, and making the whole experience worth the sweat and the tears.

Dan McNeil was born in Toronto, Ontario, and grew up surrounded by books and music, ensuring a fondness for both. Currently, he works for a local television station and plays music with a number of local bands. He also had some success as a songwriter and composer. His passion for things both literary and historical, coupled with a strong foundation in storytelling from working in television news, ultimately prompted him to pen his first novel, *The Judas Apocalypse*. He lives in Ottawa, Ontario, where he is at work on his second novel, a heist story set in New York City during the height of Beatlemania.